A CRIMSON DAWN

Janet MacLeod Trotter

A CRIMSON DAWN

headline

First published in 2005
by HEADLINE BOOK PUBLISHING

1

Cataloguing in Publication Data is available from the British Library

ISBN 0 7553 0850 6

Typeset in Bembo by Avon DataSet Ltd,
Bidford on Avon, Warwickshire

Printed and bound in Great Britain by
Mackays of Chatham plc, Chatham, Kent

Headline's policy is to use papers that are natural, renewable and
recyclable products and made from wood grown in sustainable forests.
The logging and manufacturing processes are expected to conform
to the environmental regulations of the country of origin.

HEADLINE BOOK PUBLISHING
A division of Hodder Headline
338 Euston Road
London NW1 3BH
www.headline.co.uk
www.hodderheadline.com

To Donald, Torquil, Rory and Angus – the very best of brothers
– with all my love and hopes for peace

CHAPTER 1

1902

Emmie lay on the straw mattress in the tiny back room struggling for breath. She felt as if iron weights pressed down on her chest. She had used up all her strength sitting up for the doctor – the tall lady with the shock of red hair, who had come to see her and was now talking to her mother just beyond the half-open door.

'She won't improve as long as she stays here, Mrs Kelso. The river air is damp – this place is terribly damp – making her chest worse.'

Emmie marvelled at the woman's strong voice. She had breezed into their home, unjamming rags from windows and throwing them open. Emmie had no idea women could be doctors, but Dr Jameson carried a brown leather bag just like the doctor who had visited their neighbours when they had lived up the hill in Gateshead. Long ago, when her father had been alive, they had lived in a proper house with an outside closet and a parlour, and Emmie had had her own bed. Sometimes she wondered if she really remembered it or whether it was her older sister, Nell's, constant harking back to better times. To Emmie, home was two rooms in a tenement among a warren of old cottages and workshops under the dripping staithes, by the oily River Tyne.

Emmie heard her mother mumble something then sniff as if she had a cold. The doctor's voice came clearly again.

'I do understand, Mrs Kelso. It's not your fault you have to live in this sl— have to live here. Widows have a very raw deal. You shouldn't have to be scrimping like this, making brooms and dusters for a pittance. It makes my blood boil to see it. But the atmosphere – the dust from the cloth – it's only making things worse for Emmie. What she could really do with is a few months in the country – clean air and exercise. Do you have any relations she could go to?'

Emmie, suddenly alert to the urgency in the doctor's voice, strained to hear her mother's reply.

'Do you think I'd be living like this if I had family to go to?' her mother said despairingly.

'I'm sorry. Perhaps I could find a family to take her for a while . . . It's just, I can't see her lasting another winter here. Her health is very delicate.'

Emmie lay feeling light-headed. Was the doctor saying she was going to die? She wished she had the energy to get up and ask, but she could not even lift her head off the scratchy bedding. She watched a large black beetle scuttle across the stone floor and disappear under a bale of cloth that awaited her mother's cutting and stitching. Perhaps in heaven she would meet her bearded father, who stared down at them from the photograph on the kitchen mantelpiece. She would like to see him, but she would also like to live beyond her tenth birthday and stay in Miss Dillon's class, where they read poetry and never got the strap. It was the smiling Miss Dillon who had sent the doctor round to check up on Emmie.

Through the crack in the door, Emmie thought she could see Dr Jameson with an arm around her mother's hunched shoulders as if she was helping her stay on her feet. Nobody ever touched her mother like that, least of all an important person like a doctor; but then nobody came to their house except the rentman, and the salesman who collected the brooms and dusters. They could never bring friends in, because their mother fretted that she could not feed them and there was nowhere to play.

'The MacRaes,' Mary Kelso said suddenly, 'they live up Crawdene way. But I couldn't ask them – they're not family.'

'Tell me about them,' Dr Jameson urged.

'Jonas MacRae and my late husband were old friends – came from Glasgow together to find work.'

Emmie tried to quieten her laboured breathing to hear.

'My John ended up on the keel boats – Jonas moved around the area helping to sink pits. Both strong men – good men, with a bit of learning. The few times they got together they'd be putting the world to rights.'

'And does he have a wife?'

Mary nodded. 'Helen MacRae – pitman's daughter. Don't know her well, but she came with Jonas to John's funeral and sent money for the girls. But I couldn't ask her. She's got her own lads to feed – and she's not family; it wouldn't be right.'

'For Emmie's sake you could. It's a wonder they haven't tried to help you more,' the doctor exclaimed.

'They don't know where I live,' Mary confessed. 'I was that ashamed at having to move to a place like this. But I'll not have folks pitying me and telling my business to all the world. Besides, they might not be in Crawdene any more. John's been dead over five years and Jonas could've moved on again.'

'Let me try and find them,' the doctor suggested. 'I'll do the asking.' She patted Mary on the shoulder. 'In the meantime, keep rubbing the ointment on Emmie's chest and back, and try to get her to sit outside. Please don't let her help you with the dusters.'

Dr Jameson explained her idea to Emmie and gave her a reassuring smile. Just as the doctor was leaving, Emmie heard Nell humming a tune as she crossed the courtyard. The humming stopped abruptly as their mother explained the presence of the stranger.

'Afternoon, Doctor,' Nell said, putting on a posh voice.

'Hello, Nell. I've heard about you from my friend Miss Dillon too. Says you're very good at arithmetic.'

'Thank you,' Nell preened. 'Is our Emmie all right?'

Emmie's heart pounded as she heard the doctor explain to Nell how fragile was her sister's condition and how Nell would have to help her mother more. Nell would only take it out on her. She blamed Emmie for keeping her awake at night with her wheezing; blamed her for their poverty because any spare pennies went on ointments and unctions for her chest; blamed her for shirking the heavy jobs of fetching water, clothes washing and emptying the chamber pots into the stinking communal midden.

'You're just putting it on to get Mam's attention,' Nell would hiss behind their mother's back, and pinch Emmie hard in resentment.

'Course I'll help, Doctor,' Nell was saying sweetly.

'Good girl,' Dr Jameson replied.

Nell watched the doctor walk briskly away across the shared courtyard, side-stepping a dog and a baby playing in the dirt. A gaggle of curious children followed her as she stooped under the archway into the narrow alley that led back to the main street, where women were patiently queuing to fill pails at a standpipe.

As soon as she was gone, Nell brushed past her wary-looking mother and barged into the back room.

'Doctor's little pet, eh? How come you get to stay off school? It's not fair! And why's the window open? I'm not ganin' to lie in a draught and catch me death. You're just doing it so you don't have to help Mam with the dusters. Well, I'm not ganin' to either. There's a fair setting up by the Burn, and me and Dolly are ganin'. Might run off with a gypsy lad and then you'll be the one Mam picks on to do all the chores. See how you like that.'

Emmie lay as quietly as she could, knowing it was best to say nothing even if she had the breath to answer back. Nell would rant until she ran out of complaints and insults, and then turn her resentment on her mother. It had not always been like this. Emmie had faded memories of her strong-armed sister carrying her around like a doll and pushing her in a large pram beside some park railings, singing to her and giving her kisses. But that was in another life, before the wheezing and breathlessness had turned Emmie into a pale, skinny invalid.

Now Nell's fair face was screwed into a permanent scowl and her maturing body at odds with the threadbare childish dresses she was forced to wear. At thirteen, Nell only seemed happy when she was with her friend Dolly, the two of them wandering the riverbank arm in arm, giggling over some shared confidence.

There was no use in telling Nell that she longed to be back at school in the high-ceilinged classroom, reading and writing, or sitting with Miss Dillon reading storybooks when she could not join in games in the yard.

Emmie listened to Nell arguing with her mother, then slam the door as she stormed out. She thought she heard her mother crying softly, then blow her nose and start work at the kitchen table. Cut and snip. A while later, she came in with a cup of water and a piece of bread smeared with dripping.

'The doctor'll sort some'at out for you,' her mother said wearily. 'Be like a holiday – going to the country. The last time you were just a babe. Your da carried the pair of you all the way

up the fell for a picnic – you in his arms and Nell on his back . . .'
Her voice faltered.

'Don't . . . remember,' Emmie panted.

'No,' her mother said, her face twisted in sorrow, 'and it's just
as well. Makes it easier to bear this place. That's why our Nell
takes it so bad – she's got memories.'

Emmie did not like to say she had memories too, like snatches
of music that came to her when she was half awake: a smiling,
bearded face, Nell's wet kisses, her mother tucking her into a
proper bed . . .

The idea of going to the country frightened her. Who were
these mysterious MacRaes her mother had never mentioned
before? And what would Nell say if she found out what the good
Dr Jameson was plotting? Fear of her sister fought with the dread
of being sent away to strangers. She lay in the fetid room, her eyes
tightly closed, trying to conjure up in her mind a world of park
railings and sunlight flickering through a canopy of leaves.

CHAPTER 2

That evening, Flora Jameson hurried to the Gateshead Settlement to find Charles Oliphant, one of the idealistic young clergymen who helped run the Settlement Movement. The building was busy with evening classes and clubs for the working classes, and she knew Charles might not have a minute to spare. Mousy, the caretaker since an accident at the docks made him disabled, greeted her warmly.

'If you're lookin' for Mr Oliphant, he's in the meetin'. They'll be finished in twenty minutes. Come in the kitchen and Mrs Mousy'll fetch you some'at. Bet you haven't stopped to eat all day, eh?'

Flora laughed. 'Some of Sarah's cooking would be a treat, thank you.'

Mousy hobbled beside her, chatting about changes since she had last visited.

'There's two more residents come – one a medical student, the other a trainee vicar like Mr Oliphant. Think they'll be here till Christmas. Dockers' Union are holding their meetin's here now, an' all. Oh, and there's a concert on Friday night – some Scotch singers – so you'll want to come to that, eh?'

'I'll insist on a front-row seat,' Flora smiled.

Mousy liked to tease her about being Scottish, though she seldom went back to Edinburgh since her parents had died. As an only child, she had nursed them both through illness and then used their legacy to put herself through medical school, one of Sophia Jex-Blake's pioneering women doctors. She had given up

6

much to do so – a leisured life on a private income or a suitable marriage. Now, at thirty-two, she was safely past marriageable age. Gateshead was her home and hard work her lot. She would not change it for anything.

Sarah scolded her into a seat with a bowl of broth and ordered Mousy back to the entrance with a sharp, 'Don't think you're ganin' to sit here suppin' tea.'

Sarah's list of grumbles about untidy residents, noisy youth club and unwashed dockers was interrupted by the welcome appearance of Charles. He sauntered in with a big grin, hands in pockets, fair wiry hair untamed. He had the ruddy, full face of a country squire rather than the academic he was, a cherubic look that belied his twenty-six years. Flora's heart skipped a beat as she smiled back.

'Ham broth, my favourite! Just what the doctor ordered. Flora, I hope you haven't eaten it all? Sarah, sit back down – I can help myself.'

Sarah tutted in disapproval and rushed to serve him. She had refused to flout convention and call him Charles, as he had suggested, or allow him to help in the kitchen. He might like to pretend he was one of them, living among Gateshead's poor, but they all knew he was gentry, one of the Oliphants of Blackton. And hadn't Mousy said he was heir to Major James, and due to inherit a huge estate and half a dozen pits on the fell? He should be ashamed of himself, playing at being kitchen boy, was her opinion.

'I thought you'd met a surgeon and run off to London,' Charles teased Flora between slurps of soup. 'You've been neglecting us, Doctor.'

Flora snorted. 'You're not the only one saving the world – others are busy too.'

He reached out and squeezed her hand. 'I know. You're a wonderful woman.'

Flora blushed under Sarah's critical gaze and withdrew her hand quickly.

'I want your help, Charles, to track down a mining family. I think they might live in one of your father's villages.'

Charles rolled his eyes. 'Do you hear that, Sarah? She's only interested in my connections, not in my good looks or personality.'

'Be serious for a minute,' Flora said, losing patience.

He bolted the rest of his soup and stood up. 'Thank you, Sarah, delicious. I must go and say prayers at the youth club and hope they haven't tied the new student teacher to the flagpole. Would you like to come, Doctor?'

Flora nodded, wondering if she had annoyed him with mention of Major James. Charles was easily irritated by reference to his coal-owning father, as if he was embarrassed by his vast wealth. But she wanted nothing from him financially, and if it would help Emmie Kelso then she would keep on asking.

As they walked out of the kitchen and across the quad, she hurriedly told him about the sickly girl.

'She's such a bright little thing and the mother doesn't like keeping her off school, but she's in a bad way. That terrible place! Raw sewage spilling out of a communal midden and no ventilation in those hovels. Can you believe people are still having to live like that in this day and age?'

Charles shook his head. 'We've conquered half the globe and helped ourselves to its riches, yet the common man sees none of it.'

'And the common man's wife sees even less,' Flora retorted.

'Can't you alert the sanitary officer?' Charles suggested.

'Oh, he's been,' Flora grew more indignant, 'but his orders fall on deaf ears. The magistrates won't enforce improvements because they are also the rate payers who don't want the expense. Those slums were condemned over twenty years ago, but they're as overcrowded as ever.'

The summer evening light retreated behind the tall brick buildings; the chapel bell began to toll. Flora stopped in the doorway to the hall. This place was incongruous, like a university college dropped in the middle of Gateshead's teeming back-to-backs, an oasis of learning and pleasure amid the relentless poverty. It was a brave, madcap idea to bridge the social chasm – young, idealistic students living among the poor to bring about social change. Flora had heard from Charles how the Settlement Movement had begun with Oxford students going to live in London's East End to teach, and research into poverty. It had been a revelation to both social classes and the idea had soon spread to other industrial cities, often instigated by universities or theological colleges. Like the fountain that splashed in the centre of the courtyard, the place revived her flagging spirits.

Charles sensed her mood and took her gently by the arm.

'I'm sorry I was flippant before. Any mention of my father . . . I don't want to go through life expecting privileges just because I was born an Oliphant – or for people to expect favours.'

Flora held his look in the twilight. 'I'm asking for Emmie's sake, not mine.'

'Of course. I'm sorry. I'll do what I can to help.'

He looked so boyishly unsure that Flora's heart squeezed in sympathy. She told him about the MacRaes of Crawdene.

Charles gave a mirthless laugh.

'You've heard of them?' she queried.

He nodded. 'Jonas MacRae is notorious in Crawdene – he started a socialist Sunday school in opposition to the Chapel. Imagine that! In a village that's ninety per cent Methodist. The last I heard he was trying to set up a branch of the Independent Labour Party.'

'Well, I applaud him for that – they support women's emancipation,' Flora said.

'Yes, but miners round here are almost solidly Liberal. Men like MacRae are too radical for most. He's what my father would call a troublemaker and Mousy would call a "worky ticket".'

Flora looked dashed. 'So you think I'm wrong to interfere and go looking for these MacRaes? Mrs Kelso talked of Jonas as a good, hard-working man.'

'I'm sure he is,' Charles said quickly. 'And you're right to try on the girl's behalf. You can't let her die; it's unthinkable.'

'But sending Emmie into a household of atheists?'

'Why not?' Charles laughed. 'Better to be atheist than dead.'

'That's a strange notion for a future vicar,' Flora remarked.

'God can use atheists to build a better world too,' he smiled. 'I'll make enquiries and find out where they live, though I don't think you'll have any difficulty finding them.' He hesitated. 'I'd offer to come with you, but I really don't think it would help to have the boss's son pleading your cause. From what I hear of Jonas MacRae, he'd say no on principle to an Oliphant.'

Briefly, she touched the hand that still rested on her arm. 'Thank you, Charles. I just needed to hear I was doing the right thing.'

'Come on,' he said brightly, 'let's go and sort out the little anarchists in here.'

Together, they mounted the steps towards the shouts and shrieks beyond the hall door.

It was the following Saturday afternoon before Flora had a spare moment to make the journey to Crawdene on her bicycle. Armed with an address from Charles, she left the sprawl of Gateshead and the smaller riverside towns behind. Doubts soon set in. She had no idea what these people were really like or whether her request would be a huge burden. Only the thought of Emmie lying panting in that squalid room, and Charles's encouragement, kept her peddling forward.

The climb grew steeper. She dismounted and pushed her bicycle up the last slope, into a westerly wind. Finally, Crawdene hove into view over the lip of the hill: a long line of terraced cottages with shorter streets running off into surrounding fields fringed by woods. Dominating the skyline, a short walk further uphill from the village, was the Liddon pit, named after Charles's dead older brother. The pithead was flanked by sheds and a massive spoil heap. She passed a solidly built brick Methodist chapel and a more modest hall with a tin roof. As they drew closer, Flora noticed the cottages were back-to-backs, the lanes in front mere rutted tracks. In winter they would be rivers of mud. On the breeze came a pungent smell of cesspools. Her heart sank. Emmie would be exchanging one dismal, unsanitary home for another. She stopped, debating whether to turn and leave before she was noticed.

Suddenly she was hit by a fresh blast of wind. It smelled of honey and hay. A cock crowed. She was reminded of childhood holidays in the countryside of East Lothian. Flora looked around more closely and noticed how some of the pitmen had carved out allotment gardens on steep ground across the dusty lanes. Sheds, made of old fencing and corrugated iron, clung on precariously amid chicken coops, rows of onions, climbing runner beans and sweet peas. It was the mix of colourful flowers grown among the practical vegetables that made Flora press on. This was ten times better than any riverside slum.

She stopped at the co-operative store, crammed with tins, sacks, jars and cooking utensils. Shoppers stood aside for the tall, red-headed stranger in her outlandish cycling breeches and listened to her ask directions to the MacRae house.

'Aye, they're here all right,' the head shopkeeper laughed. 'Old Jonas still trying to turn Crawdene into Utopia.'

A woman snorted. 'Well, he's got a job on his hands.'

'Not in any bother, are they?' another asked suspiciously. 'That Rab's a wild one – and young Samuel's not much better. Turning their mam grey.'

'No,' Flora said quickly, 'there's nothing wrong. I'm just visiting on behalf of a friend.'

A third woman took her to the door and pointed up the hill and off to the right.

'Don't listen to them – the lads are canny,' she said in a hushed voice. 'Bit hot-headed like their da and some take offence at them not ganin' to the chapel, but they'd give you the shirts off their backs if you asked them. Up there. China Street – number eighteen – left-hand side.'

'Thank you,' Flora smiled. 'It's an unusual address, isn't it?'

The woman chuckled. 'Reckon pit owner stuck pins in an atlas when he named the streets. We've got the whole world in Crawdene from Italy to Siam.'

Flora had to stop herself telling the woman she was right. Except it had been twelve-year-old Charles and his four-year-old sister, Sophie, who had prodded their father's atlas to choose the street names. Charles had told her the story with that mixture of shame and amusement he displayed when talking about his family.

Leaving the bicycle at the store, being looked after by two eager boys, Flora picked her way between the ruts and open drains to China Street. Groups of children stopped their games to stare, but there were few men, just two elderly neighbours sitting out on stools and a glimpse of a man bent over a spade in his allotment.

A dark-haired woman with lively eyes answered her knocking, wiping her hands on her apron. 'Aye, I'm Helen MacRae. If it's Jonas you're after, he's down at the hall, getting it ready for tonight's speaker.'

'Oh . . .' Flora paused, wondering if there was any point speaking to Helen without her husband.

Helen took charge of the situation. 'Looks like you need a sit-down. Come away in. I'm putting on a broth for the lads.'

Flora followed the pitman's wife into the low-ceilinged cottage. 'We're expecting a good turn-out for the meetin', but Jonas shouldn't be too long – unless he's already arguing with the speaker,' she laughed.

'What's the occasion?' Flora asked, intrigued.

'Independent Labour Party – monthly meetin'. Jonas started a local branch after he heard Keir Hardie down Gateshead. There's a debate tonight on universal suffrage.'

'How interesting.' Flora was impressed, despite her disquiet about the MacRaes' reputation.

'But you haven't come to hear me prattle on about politics. Please sit down. You'll have a cup of tea, Miss . . . ?'

'Dr Jameson. And thank you, that would be very welcome.' Flora sat on the horsehair sofa and glanced around the kitchen-parlour. The furniture was solid: a well-scrubbed table with five chairs, a chiffonier that probably pulled out as a bed, and a big chest of drawers. The range was arrayed with pans and a large blackened kettle. The hearth was sooty and the fender dull, but the boots beside it were well polished, and a warm smell of baking made her mouth water.

There were pictures of landscapes on the wall and a large family photograph: Helen in an old-fashioned bonnet beside a stout man with a thick moustache and side whiskers and, in front of them, a row of three solemn, handsome boys. Beside it hung a large framed text proclaiming the Socialist Ten Commandments. Flora had a pang of misgiving. She did not want Emmie to be left with troublemakers. But when Helen thrust a warm scone and a cup of tea at her, Flora dismissed her doubts. Any arrangement over Emmie would only be for a few months – a year at the most.

With plate balanced on her lap, Flora launched into her story about the Kelsos. Helen's round face creased in concern.

'Poor Mary! We thought she'd remarried. Jonas's letters got returned saying she'd gone away – we just assumed – with her not keepin' in' touch, like. And they were such bonny bairns. Nelly, wasn't it? What a live spark. And wee Emmie, bright as a button and full of chatter for one so young. Like she'd been here before.'

'She's hardly able to speak now, her breathing's so bad,' Flora told her. She took a deep breath and came out with her request that the MacRaes take her in for a while.

'I know it's asking a lot and I won't think any the worse of you for saying no – and of course you'll have to consult your husband – but could we just see if the change in air helps? And it goes without saying that you'll be reimbursed for the cost of food and clothing. Mr Ol— er – friends of mine at the Settlement in Gateshead and I will help. A good diet would make such a difference to the girl; she's quite malnourished. You don't have to let me know now – but after you've had a chance to talk to Mr MacRae . . .'

Helen fixed her with a curious look. 'Why are you doing all this for the lass?'

Flora hesitated. She had kept asking herself the same question. It was anger at the poverty she saw daily, the appeal from her friend Maria Dillon to intervene on behalf of her brightest pupil, the wish to do something for the helpless widow, Mary Kelso. But there were a score of Mary Kelsos in her area. It was Emmie herself – her lively, intelligent eyes – the potential Flora sensed in her, that goaded her to act. She reminded Flora of herself at such an age – a girl with a thirst for life. Why should Emmie be denied a future because of poverty and ill health? Flora's generation were going to change the world for all women – working-class women as much as any. In the meantime, if she could act to save one of her patients from dire poverty, she would.

Flora simply answered, 'Her teacher asked me to help.'

Helen nodded. 'Of course we'll take the lass. My Jonas and her da were like brothers. They may not have seen much of each other over the years, but they'd each do owt for the other. John would've done the same for one of our lads.'

Flora hid her surprise at the woman's forthrightness; she had expected a pitman's wife to defer to her husband's wishes in all things, especially on such an important matter. She felt a wave of gratitude towards the kind-hearted woman. 'Thank you so much.'

'And I won't hear of taking money off you.' Helen brushed aside her thanks. 'What about the other lass?'

'Nell? She's much more robust. Must be nearing leaving school. I had it in mind to offer her cleaning work at the surgery.'

Just then, the back door banged open to a clatter of boots and loud voices. Flora turned to see two youths in filthy jackets and caps stamp into the kitchen. Their faces were so smeared in coal dust, it was impossible to tell their ages.

'Boots off, lads, before you take another step,' Helen ordered.

They stopped and stared at the well-dressed visitor. The slighter one pulled off his cap to reveal a thatch of dirty fair hair. He blushed and bent to untie his boots. The taller one with the curling dark hair gave Flora a keen gaze.

'Are you the speaker for the night, miss?'

'I'm afraid not,' Flora smiled, 'though it sounds interesting. I belong to the Women's Suffrage Society in Gateshead, as it happens.'

'Fancy that!' Helen exclaimed. 'These are my sons, Rab and Samuel.'

Flora introduced herself, gingerly taking the grimy hand that the elder boy thrust at her.

'Boots off, Rab.'

But he carried on staring. 'Would you like to gan to the meetin'? You could put in your penny's worth. There's plenty'll argue against you.'

'Rab, leave her be,' Helen warned.

'I'd like nothing better,' Flora said, 'but I have calls to do this evening.'

Rab nodded. 'You could come and speak another time. We like to hear what's ganin' on in the towns. If Oliphant had his way, there'd be no newspapers or books in Crawdene, save the Bible to read.'

'Really?' Flora felt uncomfortable. Should she mention her connection with the coal-owner's family?

'Aye, he's the ogre that owns everything round here—'

'Rab!' his mother said sharply. 'You'll get us all into trouble with that tongue of yours.'

Rab grinned as he pulled off his boots.

Helen looked apologetic. 'Major Oliphant's the landlord – owns the Liddon pit and several others round here. You'll not repeat my son's words, will you? He's just having a joke.'

'Of course I won't,' Flora assured her as she rose to go. Now would not be the time to confess a friendship with Charles. 'I can see you have much to do. I'll leave my address and you can send word when it's convenient for Emmie to come and stay once you've had a chance to talk it over with Mr MacRae.' It still seemed possible to Flora that the patriarch Jonas might say no.

'Who's Emmie?' Rab asked.

Helen raised a hand to silence him. 'I'll explain after.'

'I'm very grateful,' Flora said, taking the woman's hand. 'I can see you are good people.'

Rab laughed. 'That's not what they say about us down the chapel.'

His mother glared at him. 'Take no notice,' she sighed at the doctor.

Flora turned at the door with a smile for the mischievous Rab and his bashful brother. They grinned back. As she left, a small skinny boy appeared at the loft hatch overhead and peered down at them.

'That's our pet ferret,' Rab joked, as the boy dodged out of sight.

'Our Peter, he means,' Helen said with a roll of her eyes. 'He's a bit shy – not like some.'

On the way home, free-wheeling down the bank from Crawdene, Flora had pangs of doubt again. Was the house too small? Where would Emmie sleep with all those boys? And that Rab – so quick to speak his mind, like a moth flying at a flame. And she had not met the infamous Jonas, who was no doubt ten times more outspoken.

Then she shook off her worries. Helen MacRae was warm-hearted and caring. She would welcome Emmie with open arms and that's all that mattered. She could not wait to tell Charles all about her visit. The thought made her pick up speed and race back to town.

CHAPTER 3

In early August, Flora returned to the Kelsos with news that the MacRaes were willing to take Emmie. Emmie was asleep when she came, but was woken later by Nell shouting at her mother about the unfairness of it all.

'Do you want your sister to die?' Mary finally snapped.

'No!'

'Then stop your complaining. The doctor's offering you work at the surgery once you're fourteen.'

'Aye, scrubbing floors,' Nell said indignantly.

'Least it's work,' Mary sighed. 'If you keep in, she might give you a bit book-keeping or clerking.'

'I'm ganin' to swing on the trapezes,' Nell declared.

Mary closed her eyes in despair. 'If you're offered a job you'll take it and be grateful – then maybe we can leave this terrible place and find somewhere better for Emmie.'

'Emmie! Always Emmie,' Nell railed and stamped out of the room.

After letters to and fro about travel arrangements, it was decided that her mother would take Emmie as far as Swalwell on the train. The MacRaes would fetch her from there.

Emmie began to dread the moment when she would have to say goodbye to her mother. Nell made it worse with her stories of gloom.

'Pit folk aren't like us. They live under the ground – and eat coal. Never get to see daylight. More like animals than humans, Dolly says. You'll be tret like a slave – like Cinderella.' She came at

Emmie, making scary noises, laughing when her sister screamed.

The more their mother told Nell to stop her nonsense, the more she persisted. But on the last night, when Emmie could not sleep, Nell cuddled up close and stroked her hair.

'Won't be for ever,' she whispered. 'You'll get well again, then come back to me and Mam. Course, by then I'll be working for the doctor, so it'll be better than this.'

Emmie burrowed into Nell's hold. So often her sister was a monster by day, yet kind when they lay in bed together, their mother working late to catch the dying summer light. Tomorrow night there would be no one to cuddle.

'Tell me the story of when we were bairns,' Emmie whispered. 'About the house and the park.'

She was lulled to sleep by her sister's hushed words of a beautiful home with soft beds and a park nearby with grand railings and trees as tall as houses.

The next day, Nell carried Emmie's jute bag with her much-mended spare clothes, to the station. Even this short walk left her exhausted. Emmie hung on to her big sister and cried. She had been told there were only boys in the MacRae household. Tonight there would be no Nell. Even an angry, contrary Nell was better than no Nell at all.

'Didn't mean it about pitmen being animals,' Nell muttered, kissing her on the head. 'They'll be canny and kind and spoil you rotten. You'll not want to come back.'

'I will,' Emmie sobbed, as Nell pulled away.

Emmie stared out of the carriage window for a last sight of her sister before she disappeared in the steam of the locomotive. She clung to her mother's clammy, calloused hand and wondered when she would ever see Nell again.

Her mother kept repeating, 'They're good people. You'll be grand. We'll come and visit. It's not for ever.'

Emmie was too anxious to say a word.

At Swalwell station they stood waiting, Mary gazing round nervously for someone she recognised. Moments later, a broad-shouldered youth who had been eyeing them from the entrance, sauntered forward whistling. His upper arms strained at the seams of his too-tight jacket. His blue eyes stared out from rings of coal dust that much scrubbing had failed to erase. To Emmie he looked terrifying.

'Mrs Kelso? I'm Rab MacRae – come to fetch Emmie.'

His deep booming voice sent the girl scurrying behind her mother, burying her face in her skirt.

'Rab!' Mary said in amazement. 'You're all grown up. Haven't seen you since you were Emmie's age. Must be sixteen by now?'

'Seventeen,' he grinned. 'Is that Emmie hiding in your dress? I don't bite, lass. Well, only when I haven't been fed.'

Mary tried to prise her daughter from behind her, but the girl clung on, whimpering.

'Has your mam not come?' Mary asked anxiously. 'I expected her to be here. Emmie's not used to lads.'

'Mam's getting dinner ready and I can walk twice as quick.' Rab got down on his haunches. 'Haway, lass. Do you like liquorice?'

Emmie shook her head.

'She's not used to the taste.'

'By heck, you've a treat in store,' Rab chuckled, and produced a long string of the sticky sweet. He waved it at the frightened girl. 'You bite one end and I'll bite the other.'

Her mother coaxed her out, encouraged by the boy's friendliness. He reminded her of a young Jonas.

Emmie peered up into Rab's intense blue-eyed gaze. Was he trying to trick her like Nell did, by offering something he would then snatch away? Swiftly, she grabbed the end of the dangling liquorice and bit into it.

Rab roared with laughter and let go his end. 'You can eat the rest on the way to Crawdene.' He took the jute bag from Mary Kelso. 'Haway, lass, it's mince and dumplings for dinner.'

Mary hugged her daughter briefly then pushed her forward. 'Go with Rab now and be good for Mrs MacRae.'

Emmie walked a few steps, then the enormity of the moment overwhelmed her. She turned and gave her mother a beseeching look. But Mary waved her on. Emmie's vision blurred in tears and she swallowed hard, trying to be brave. Her mother would come for her soon. She gripped the black liquorice stick and turned to follow Rab.

Out of the station, she struggled to keep up with his big strides, and by the time they were at the edge of the village she was gasping for breath and crying for her mother. Rab, who had been chatting to her all the while about his family and the

18

chickens they kept and the girls in the street she could play with, stopped and bent down.

'Jump on me back, lass,' he ordered, 'or we'll have grown beards by the time we get home.'

Emmie scrambled on to his back and clung on tight. Wayward curls of hair from under his cap tickled her cheek, but she liked the soapy smell of his neck. He strode up the hill, away from the river, as if she were weightless, talking to her between snatches of song. Emmie did not answer, but relaxed against his warm back, lulled by the rhythm of his walk, gazing at the swaying corn. She dozed off and woke to the sound of Rab's boots crunching on a cinder track.

'This is the short cut through Oliphant's Wood,' he told her. 'Me and Samuel catch rabbits in here, but you're not to tell anyone.'

Emmie gasped as the light filtered through the branches overhead.

'You all right, lass?' Rab felt her tense. 'We'll be out in a minute.'

'I like it,' she whispered close to his ear, 'the sun peeping through the leaves.'

She felt his grip tighten round her legs. 'That's grand.'

He began to speak in a rhythmic voice, almost to himself.

> 'Does the road wind up-hill all the way?
> Yes, to the very end.
> Will the day's journey take the whole long day?
> From morn to night, my friend.'

Emmie recognised the poem: 'Up-hill' by Christina Rossetti; one of her favourites, which Miss Dillon had read to them often. Timidly, she joined in the final verse.

> 'Shall I find comfort, travel-sore and weak?
> Of labour you shall find the sum.
> Will there be beds for me and all who seek?
> Yea, beds for all who come.'

They laughed in delight that each should know it. Emmie soon clammed up again as they emerged from the sheltered woods.

Before her stretched narrow lanes strewn with washing and rows of brick houses puffing smoke. She felt dizzy at the vast sky overhead and the steepness of the hill dropping away below them. Children called to Rab as he ducked under a line of flapping shirts, curious to know who the girl was. Abruptly they turned in through an open door, Rab almost bending double, and a moment later he was tipping Emmie on to a high-backed sofa.

'Delivered – one Emmie Kelso,' he panted. 'Doesn't say much, but she can spout poetry.'

Helen bustled across the room. 'Let's take a look at you. By, look at those bonny brown eyes – big as spoons – just like your da's!' She gave Emmie a kiss on the forehead. 'Are you hungry? Looks like you could do with a bit fattening. How's your mam?'

Emmie's lip quivered at the mention of her mother. Helen gave her a swift hug. She smelled of baking and raw onions. 'Don't you worry, pet. Auntie Helen'll look after you till you're strong enough to gan back. Your mam and sister won't know you once we've put a bit flesh on your bones. How about a cup of milky tea, eh? Do you drink tea?'

Emmie nodded. She watched the plump-faced woman dart around the room, talking all the while and issuing orders.

'Will you wake Samuel – and don't let him turn over again.' As Rab disappeared up a ladder into the loft, Helen went to the door and called for her youngest son. 'Peter, time for dinner!'

A thin-faced boy with a watchful gaze appeared silently in the doorway and gave Emmie a quizzical smile. He did not look much older than she.

'Are you a lass?' he asked. 'You look like a lass.'

'Yes, she is. Now wash your hands and set the table,' his mother ordered. 'An extra place for Emmie, remember. Save your questions for later.'

Emmie looked on warily as one by one the boys gathered around the table. Samuel had fair hair that stuck out like straw. He yawned and winked at her. Peter continued to stare at her and ask again if she was a girl. Helen doled out plates of steaming mince and onion with a solid dumpling perched on top.

'If you cannot eat the dumpling, Emmie,' Samuel teased, 'we can play bowls with it later.'

'Take no notice,' Helen snorted. 'Eat what you can, pet; the lads'll finish what you can't.'

Emmie took small mouthfuls, her stomach too knotted to eat the tasty-smelling food. She kept glancing up at Rab, who was sitting beside her. When he cleared his plate and got up to go, she clutched at his jacket. He gave her a look of surprise.

'I have to gan to work now, lass. Me and Samuel. But Peter can keep you company.'

Her eyes brimmed with tears and he quickly dug out another stick of liquorice. With a brisk ruffle of her hair, he jammed on his cap and led his brother out.

'You look worn out,' Helen said in concern. 'You have a lie down till your Uncle Jonas gets in. Peter, fetch a blanket from the dresser.'

Emmie tried to stay awake, but the heat of the room and the exhaustion she felt soon overwhelmed her.

When she woke, the sun had left the doorstep and a burly man with bushy grey moustache and side whiskers was sitting by the hearth reading a newspaper. For a moment she lay still, staring at him. He must have sensed it, for he suddenly looked up and frowned.

'John's bairn,' he said in a booming voice that made her jump. 'I can tell right enough. Helen, she's awake!'

To Emmie's relief, the woman came rushing in with an armful of washing. 'Don't go scaring her with your big voice,' she chided. 'Emmie, this is your Uncle Jonas – he was a great friend of your father's and he wouldn't harm a fly. But he's a bit deaf from working at the pit forge, so he doesn't know he's shouting.'

Emmie sat up and gazed at the man who had been like a brother to her own father. He could tell her stories about the man she could hardly remember, just like Nell told her stories about their past life in a long-ago world.

She swung her weak legs over the side of the sofa and cautiously walked towards him. She had never seen such a hairy man. Grey hair sprouted from his ears, his cheeks, his upper lip and sprang from his head in an unkempt mane. Wiry eyebrows framed bold blue eyes like thatch. He reminded her of a picture on Miss Dillon's wall of Moses parting the Red Sea.

'Uncle Jonas,' she asked, 'will you tell me a story?'

He looked at her fiercely. 'Story, did you say?'

She nodded.

Helen laughed. 'He's not got much patience for tales and story-telling, pet. Rab's the one with a head for stories.'

Emmie's face fell.

'What kind of story do you want, lassie?' Jonas barked.

Emmie swallowed the tears welling in her throat. 'About me da,' she murmured.

He looked quizzically at Helen and she explained what the girl had said.

Suddenly, his severe face broke into a warm smile. 'Oh, I can tell you stories about your father till the cows come home.'

With that, he dropped the newspaper and drew her under his strong arm.

CHAPTER 4

1903

By the following May, Emmie found it difficult to remember a time when she had not lived in the noisy, vibrant household in China Street. The MacRaes were loving, boisterous and argumentative. Samuel and Rab fought and laughed in equal measure, while strange Peter talked to himself or retreated into the loft to play his penny whistle.

Mealtimes would be punctuated by hot debate over politics and religion, a local quoits match or British treatment of the Boers. Neighbours would call in to share a bowl of tobacco and good conversation. Jonas declared all war waged by governments as imperialist and Emmie puzzled that they had not celebrated victory in the Boer War with bonfires and fireworks as they had in Gateshead.

Rab and his father would argue over the housing given to pitmen by Oliphant.

'He hasn't spent a farthing on the cottages since they were built,' Rab declared. 'We don't even have proper sewers. We'd all be better off with a rent allowance and find somewhere fit to live in.'

'Where?' his father scoffed.

'County Council can build houses. But they won't as long as folk prefer to crowd into Oliphant's hovels.'

'At least it's a roof over our heads when trade is slack,' Jonas pointed out.

'Aye, and you're at the beck and call of Oliphant. If you complain about the middens, he threatens to hoy you out.'

It amazed Emmie how the father and son could be shouting at each other one minute and laughing over a remark made against them the next.

Even her Aunt Helen waded into these verbal battles. One evening after tea, she got up from the table and put on her coat and bonnet.

'Where do you think you're going?' Jonas growled.

'To me Guild meeting,' she announced. 'Medical officer's giving a talk.'

'But you haven't cleared the table—'

'No, you and the lads can do that for once. Like it says in that paper of yours, if lasses are to play their part in the class struggle, the men have to help out more so we can gan to our meetings.'

'What paper?' Jonas demanded.

'The one Rab was reading me.'

They all gawped at her.

'And don't you dare leave it all to Emmie – she's got her spellings to practise.' With that, Helen hurried away to the Co-operative Women's Guild, leaving Rab and Samuel hooting with laughter at their astonished father.

Emmie grew to love her adoptive aunt and uncle, who had mollycoddled her through the winter and encouraged her at her lessons. She had a proper coat and boots to go to school in and a warm truckle bed next to theirs to snuggle into at night when the wind howled in the chimney. Week by week she had grown stronger, shaking off the lethargy and breathlessness that had confined her to bed at home. Only one severe bout of wheezing and cold had kept her confined to the house most of January. Helen had plied her with hot infusions, steam baths and rubbed her chest with grease, while Rab had kept boredom at bay by reading to her. He had walked to Blackton, a larger neighbouring colliery, and borrowed novels from the penny library in the Miners' Institute. He read her history books and poetry, despite Helen's chiding not to give the girl a headache. Samuel, when he sat still for more than a minute, played cards with her and taught her how to whistle.

All of them had lusty singing voices and were the mainstay of the socialist Clarion Club in the village. They shared a tin-roofed hall with the Co-operative Guild. Here, they put on short plays and concerts, and ran a socialist Sunday school to rival the religious ones at the Methodist chapel and Blackton's parish church. Emmie loved to hear the MacRae boys sing and was thrilled to be given the job of announcing the acts at their spring concert.

Most of all, Emmie was revelling in being back at school. The teacher, Miss Downs, was stricter than Miss Dillon, but the hours at school flew by. For the first time in ages, she was able to join in skipping games in the school yard and play with the other children. She had been taken under the wing of a talkative girl, Louise Curran. Louise was athletic and prone to be bossy, but she stuck up for the new girl when others tried to pick on her.

'If you want to fight Emmie, I'll get me big brother on you,' Louise declared, facing down a couple of the older girls. Louise's older brother, Tom, had a reputation as a fighter and the threat seemed to work. Emmie marvelled at the way Louise befriended her and was happy to follow in her wake. The MacRae boys teased her.

'Our Emmie's gettin' in with the Bible thumpers,' Samuel crowed.

'Aye, Currans will give you a ticket into heaven,' Rab winked.

'What d'you mean?' Emmie asked, bewildered by their mirth.

'Take no notice,' Helen answered. 'It's just 'cos the Currans are good chapelgoers.'

'Aye, and Liberals,' Rab grunted.

'And think they own the lodge,' Jonas joined in.

'And live in Denmark Street,' Samuel said in a posh voice.

Emmie put her hands on her hips and answered back. 'Well, Louise is me friend and she's canny and what's wrong with ganin' to chapel, any road?'

The boys clapped and burst into laughter.

'Good on you, Emmie,' Rab cried, ruffling her hair, 'sticking up for your marra.'

Much of what the MacRaes said baffled her, but she loved them all the same. Sometimes, Emmie felt guilty at not missing her mother and sister more. For the first few weeks, she would dissolve into tears at the mere thought of her mother. She missed her gentle way of speaking, the times she would let her sit on her

25

lap while she worked, her sad smile. Emmie hugged a pair of mittens at night because they smelled of her mother. When the smell faded, she wore them to remind her of her mother's hands cutting and sewing.

On Boxing Day, Dr Jameson had brought Mary and Nell up to Crawdene in a borrowed horse-drawn trap, and the MacRaes had made a fuss of their visitors and fed them well. The boys had entertained them with songs and Peter's whistle, and Nell had joined in, her slim face flushed and excited at all the attention. She had turned fourteen and grown, her brown hair pinned up like an adult's, and Emmie was bashful with her suddenly mature sister.

'I'm thinking of going on the stage,' Nell announced to the consternation of her mother.

'I'll come and watch you any day,' Samuel grinned, making Nell giggle.

But as far as Emmie knew, her sister was cleaning Dr Jameson's surgery and running messages. A card had come on her tenth birthday, but she had heard nothing for over a month. An Easter visit had been called off because of a freak snowfall on the fell. Instead, Emmie had gone to chapel with the Currans and the planned picnic had ended in a snowball fight, with Tom Curran shoving an icy snowball down her back. High-spirited Tom was belted by his father for making Emmie cry. Full of remorse for getting him into trouble, Emmie had given him her paste egg.

Emmie was at the Currans' now, helping Louise's mother make egg sandwiches for the Sunday school outing to Oliphant's Wood. The houses in Denmark Street for colliery officials were bigger than most, with proper stairs up to two bedrooms, which had fireplaces and casement windows instead of skylights. No Curran needed to sleep in the kitchen, which Mrs Curran kept spotlessly clean and tidy. No matter that her husband was an important deputy at the pit, he was not allowed beyond the scullery door with his filthy pit clothes and boots. Tom had to change in the wash house and hop across the yard in his underdrawers, to Emmie's blushing amusement.

Today Tom was getting his own back. As the youngsters set off up the cinder track to the woods, he pulled the ribbons out of Emmie's hair and ran off laughing.

Furious, Emmie dropped her parcel of sandwiches and ran after him.

'Come back. I hate you!'

She was lithe and fast, but no match for brawny Tom, who pushed tub loads of coal for miles underground and could sprint like a hare.

'If you want them, come and get them!' Tom taunted, and disappeared into a mass of bluebells among the trees.

Emmie thrashed around, trying to find him, growing crosser and crosser as her wavy dark hair fell in front of her eyes.

Suddenly, Tom reared from behind a tree with a deafening roar. Emmie screamed, making him hoot with laughter. He dangled the ribbons at her. She lunged.

'Give 'em over, Tom!'

'Give me a kiss first,' he challenged.

Emmie looked at him in disgust. 'I don't kiss lads.'

'No ribbons then.'

Emmie turned her back and stalked off. Tom ploughed after her, trampling bluebells.

'A secret then,' he bargained.

Emmie stopped and faced him. 'What d'you mean?'

'You tell me a secret and I'll give you yer ribbons.'

'Don't have any,' she said impatiently.

Tom stood over her, tall and grinning, his hazel eyes teasing. For the first time it occurred to Emmie he would be considered handsome.

'Who's your favourite lad – out of them MacRaes?'

Emmie was nonplussed. 'I don't have one. They're all canny.'

Suddenly, Tom caught her by the arm. 'If there was an accident at the pit and only one of them was saved – which one would it be?'

Emmie swallowed. Tom was not smiling any more.

'You have to say or you won't get your ribbons back ever.' His grip tightened on her arm. Fear flickered in her stomach.

'Rab,' she whispered.

Instantly, Tom loosened his hold and was smiling again.

'Here you are,' he said, offering the green ribbons. Before she knew it, he was planting a sloppy kiss on her cheek.

'Ugh!' Emmie cried, wiping it off, which only made him laugh.

He watched her tie back her hair into lop-sided bunches.

'Funny,' he mused, 'I thought you would've chosen Sam.'

She gave him a sharp look. 'I didn't mean what I said. Wouldn't want any of 'em to die. You were just being daft.'

He laughed and lunged at her ribbons again, but she darted out of the way and ran for the path, half-laughing, half-screaming. Louise was waiting with the battered sandwiches.

'Haway, you two, stop carrying on. We'll be late for the races.'

Back on the wide path, arm in arm with Louise, Emmie felt safe again. Tom hadn't meant any harm, it was mere devilment away from his parents. Emmie liked the Currans and their ordered way of doing things. They were kind to her in a reserved way. Mrs Curran fussed over her when she came round for tea and Mr Curran read her stories from the Bible in a mesmerising, singsong voice. But she couldn't help noticing how different they were with Tom.

His mother was always telling him to mind his manners, while his father ordered Tom to stand up like a man and take his punishment, even though he was only fourteen and just out of short breeks. The only thing she grew to hate in the polished and shining kitchen was the worn leather strap that hung on a nail beside the soup ladle and toasting fork, in readiness for Tom's frequent punishments.

The friends enjoyed the Saturday afternoon of games, races and picnic tea with Reverend Mr Attwater refereeing a football match in which his spaniel was attempting to take part. Sam and Peter appeared and the minister invited them to join in. Tom and Sam captained opposing teams with a triumphant Tom scoring the winning goal.

He tossed his prize of cinder toffee to Emmie. 'Sorry about the ribbons,' he panted, then ran off to wrestle with Sam.

When it came to the final hymn and prayer to round off the afternoon, the older boys had disappeared into the trees. Reverend Mr Attwater pretended not to notice.

'Do you want to stay at my house the night?' Louise asked, as they dawdled back to the village.

Emmie hesitated. There would be Louise's soft bed with sheets smelling of starch, rousing hymn singing at the chapel in the morning and a huge roast for Sunday dinner. But then there would be the long, slow afternoon of keeping to the house while the adults slept, with nothing to read but the Bible. Emmie had not minded in the winter when she had squatted by the fire with Louise, gossiping about neighbours and school. But now the days were longer and the MacRaes would be spending their free hours out of doors, walking the fell or paddling in the burn above Blackton Heights, the Oliphants' pillared mansion.

'Gan on,' Louise insisted, 'you're stopping with me.' She threaded her arm through Emmie's and pulled her up the street towards her home.

'I'll have to tell me auntie first,' Emmie said, pulling the other way.

'Tell her later,' Louise said crossly. 'If you don't come now, you're not me friend.'

Emmie quickly relented. There was no harm in staying out a bit longer. The girls soon became absorbed in a game of tig around Denmark Street and Chile Vale. Only when the shadows lengthened and air grew cold did Emmie realise they must have been playing there for hours.

'Eeh, I'll have to gan home, Louise. Auntie Helen might be worried.'

'Just one more game,' Louise pleaded.

At that moment, the girls spotted a dark figure striding up the lane towards them. Emmie recognised Rab at once and knew she was in trouble. Louise immediately came to her defence.

'She's staying at my house the night,' she called out. 'Emmie was just ganin' home to tell your mam.'

'Not the night,' Rab's deep voice answered in the gloom.

He sounded cross. Emmie said a hasty goodbye to her friend. Louise looked disappointed.

'Will I see you at chapel?' she asked.

'Maybes,' Emmie answered, running down towards the waiting Rab. His look was brooding under the large cap. 'Sorry – I forgot the time – have you been lookin' for me long? I wouldn't just have stayed without askin'. I was ganin' to come back—'

'It's all right, lass,' Rab interrupted, 'you're not in any bother.'

He reached out and took her hand, giving it a friendly squeeze. Emmie felt relief flood through her. She loved the feel of Rab's large warm hand wrapped around hers. Yet she puzzled why he said so little as they walked down the bank. Perhaps there had been a row at home? Or maybe Rab had courting trouble? He was nearly eighteen and she had noticed how older girls gave him looks and some bold ones called out to him as he passed in the street.

She contented herself with walking beside him and glancing up now and again to see him smile back in reassurance. When they reached the back lane of China Street, it seemed unusually quiet for a May evening. No children played out late. Their neighbours' back doors were closed. At the back gate, Rab hesitated. He looked down at her.

'Emmie – I don't know – I should tell you . . .'

Emmie gazed up at him with a quizzical smile. He sighed and laid a gentle hand on her head.

'You're a grand lass,' he said softly. 'I'm sorry.'

She was baffled by his words. But before she could ask anything, he was steering her forward through the back door.

Helen and Jonas were standing in the middle of the room, waiting. They looked at Rab, who shook his head. Helen rushed over and put her arms around Emmie, drawing her into her soft bosom.

'Emmie, oh, Emmie. Come here and sit down, pet. We've something to tell you.'

Emmie's heart lurched at the alarm on their faces. Helen pulled her on to her knee.

'Dr Jameson's sent a message. There's been fever in the town. Would've come herself but she's rushed off her feet – and she's Nell to see to.'

'Nell?' Emmie gasped. 'What's happened to Nell?'

'Oh, no, pet, I'm saying it all wrong,' Helen said in agitation. 'Nell's grand.' She looked on the verge of tears.

Jonas came forward and crouched on his hunkers beside them.

'Lassie, your mother caught the fever. She died two days ago. We're very sorry.'

He laid a hand on her head, just like Rab had done, his hairy face creased in sorrow.

'Mam?' she gasped in bewilderment.

Jonas nodded. Helen's arms clutched her tighter. But it was her mother's arms she wanted right then, her mother's crooning and soft words.

Emmie felt a huge sob rise up inside like a wave. She turned and buried her head in Helen's lap and wept.

CHAPTER 5

The funeral was a week later. Jonas and Rab went, but no one suggested that Emmie go too.

'I want to see Nelly,' Emmie whimpered, clinging to Helen. 'I want Nelly.'

'Dr Jameson will bring her up to see you soon,' Helen promised, trying to calm the girl. She had hardly spoken a word for days, but would not let Helen out of her sight. At night she cried in her sleep and wet the bed.

The men walked into town on the Saturday afternoon and attended the dismal parish funeral. A handful of people were present, but Jonas recognised no one but Dr Jameson. She stood with a young fair-faced man in a dark coat, who nodded at them in a friendly fashion but disappeared quickly at the end.

Afterwards, they stood around the unmarked grave.

A drawn-faced Flora said, 'There's nothing to give Emmie. Everything had to be burned. By the time I got there it had all gone. I know there was a picture . . . I'm sorry.'

Jonas shook his head. 'You've done enough.'

'Half Mary's neighbours died in the epidemic,' Flora said bitterly. 'And now they're going to knock the tenements down when they should have years ago. I was hoping to get Mary a job at the Settlement.'

Jonas sighed. 'She wouldn't let us help. Said we were doing more than enough for Emmie.'

Flora touched his arm. 'You have. How is the poor girl?'

'Lost her tongue,' Jonas said sadly. 'And she wants to see her sister.'

'Of course,' Flora nodded. 'Nell is missing Emmie too. The sooner their futures are settled the better.'

They turned towards the cemetery gates. Jonas scratched his beard.

'What will become of Nell?' he asked.

Flora turned to him in surprise. 'She'll continue to live with me, of course. She's been doing so since Christmas, thank God, or she might not be alive today. Nell's a bright girl, if a bit wilful, but she gets along well enough with my housekeeper, Mrs Raine. As my ward, she will learn book-keeping and clerking, so one day she can support herself.'

'Not ganin' on the stage then?' Rab said wryly.

Flora snorted. 'I'll make sure she keeps her feet on the ground.'

At the gates, she turned to shake their hands. 'You're good people. Thank you for what you've done for Emmie. Once she comes to live with me and Nell, I'll see she gets the best schooling and plenty of exercise. Perhaps we can come and visit from time to time?'

Jonas and Rab gawped at her. 'Live with you?' Jonas queried. 'Is that what Mary wanted?'

Flora nodded. 'In a way. She wanted her daughters to stay together – that's what she wanted above everything. And Nell wants her sister back too.'

Jonas said gruffly, 'It's just we've grown very fond of the wee lass.'

'I know,' Flora sympathised. 'But no one expected you to take her on for ever. You've your own family to think about. I have no family – there's room for the two girls at my house and I can provide for them.'

She looked at the two men, surprised at their looks of dismay. 'You did say Emmie wanted to be with Nell again, didn't you?'

'Aye,' Jonas conceded.

'We'll come and fetch her next Saturday. It'll be easier once Emmie and Nell see each other again,' Flora encouraged.

The men trudged home, subdued.

'What gives the doctor the right to decide Emmie's future?' Rab was indignant. 'Boasting about her housekeeper and a bigger wage.'

'She's right,' Jonas answered sadly. 'The lassies should stay together.'

'Emmie should have a say in where she lives,' Rab protested. 'She's not a possession to pass around.'

'We knew she wouldn't be with us for ever,' Jonas warned. 'Don't you go stirring things up and making it harder for her to leave.'

The MacRaes did not tell Emmie that night that she would be leaving Crawdene for good. Somehow they could not bring themselves to say it. She brightened at the news that Dr Jameson and Nell would be visiting the following Saturday. On Monday, she went back to school, her large sad eyes like deep pools in her pale face.

At tea time she seemed brighter, chattering to Helen as she helped set the table.

'Miss Downs says I can join in the races at Whit, now I've got me strength back. Will you come and watch, Auntie Helen?'

Helen turned from the stove with a heavy heart.

'Sit down a minute, pet,' she said quietly. Only Peter was in the house. She knew it had been left up to her to break the news. She pulled Emmie on to the horsehair sofa, explaining how the doctor and Nell wished for her to go and live with them.

'You'll live in a grand house again — just like your mam and dad did when you were little. It's what your mam would've wanted. And you'll be with Nell — and the kind doctor. She'll make sure you gan to a good school and learn your lessons.'

Emmie's eyes welled with tears.

'But I like it here, Auntie Helen,' she said in bewilderment. 'Why can't Nell come and live here with us?'

Helen sighed. 'Nell wouldn't want to live in our little cottage, pet. The doctor can offer much more — for both of you.' She stroked her hair. 'You can come and visit as often as you like. Now let's get the tea on before Uncle Jonas gets in.'

She steeled herself against Emmie's hurt look and quickly busied herself at the stove so the girl would not see her own tears.

When Rab and Sam returned from the pit, Emmie looked at them mutely with accusing eyes. All week, the family tried to spoil her with treats, stories and trips to the store or woods, but

Emmie did not respond. Her silence was worse than tears and angry words.

'Shall I gan over to Blackton library and fetch you a book?' Rab offered.

'Would you like to have Louise round for tea on Friday?' Helen asked.

Emmie shook her head to both requests. She showed no interest, as if in her own mind she had already left them. She only spoke to ask questions about her new life, which the MacRaes could not answer.

'What's the doctor's house like? Will I sleep with Nell? Can I gan to school with Miss Dillon again?'

At night, Helen cried at the thought of her going, but Emmie slept peacefully.

'See, the lassie's got more sense than the pair of us,' Jonas grunted as they lay sleepless, listening to her even breathing. 'She knows what's best for her.'

Emmie watched Helen pack her clean laundry into her jute bag on Saturday morning without protest. She sat staring at Rab and Sam as they ate plates of egg and fried bread before going off to their shift below ground.

Rab forced the food down, only too aware of the dark-eyed gaze fixing him across the table.

'Walk with us to the end of the lane, eh?' he suggested. The girl said nothing.

'Haway, Emmie,' Sam cajoled, 'Rab'll tell you a story.'

Helen watched her two eldest sons marching down the back street with Emmie between them, hand in hand. She marvelled at how gentle they had always been towards the girl, when they were used to rough ways with each other. At the end of the street, she saw them drop hands, ruffling Emmie's dark curls and giving her bashful kisses on her head.

Helen swallowed her tears. Emmie stood watching them stride up the hill until they were out of sight. How was it that this young girl had stolen into their hearts so completely in less than a year?

Jonas paced around the kitchen, until Helen sent him off to the allotment.

'Peter'll fetch you when they come,' she said briskly. 'I can't have you under me feet when I'm baking.'

Emmie sat on the step with Peter, looking out for her sister. Peter chattered about the chickens and a retired pit pony he liked to feed in Lawson's Paddock, seemingly unaware of the sadness of the occasion. The day was unusually airless and still, heat bouncing off the brick walls, dazzling the eyes.

Emmie sensed the arrival of their visitors before she caught sight of the horse and trap. She stood up, shading her eyes to look. Helen came to the door in dread, sending Peter to summon his father.

When Emmie set eyes on her sister, the numbness that had been holding her feelings in check dissolved. She ran up the street, arms flung wide, to greet Nell. The older girl met her in a big hug. They clung to each other and cried openly in the street.

'There, there, girls,' Flora said soothingly, steering them forward. 'Best to go indoors.'

Nervously, Helen bustled around the kitchen, fetching cups of tea and girdle scones. Jonas tramped in from the allotment and Peter scampered outside again with a brief nod at the guests. As Jonas had no trivial conversation, he launched straight into local politics with the doctor.

The two sisters huddled close on the sofa while Nell gabbled in excitement about their new life together, overheard only by Helen.

'You'll have your very own bedroom and I've chosen the eider-down and curtains — blue and pink flowers. Just think of that — a place all to yourself! And Mrs Raine's a canny cook. She won't stand for any mess, mind. You'll have to keep your room tidy and she's a bit bossy, but I can get round her. And we'll gan shoppin' together — we live walking distance from the shops,' Nell enthused.

'Is there a park?' Emmie asked.

'Park? Aye, there's one not far away. Sometimes gan there for a stroll around on a Sunday with Dolly — eye up the lads,' Nell giggled. 'And there's a boating lake, but that costs money. Mind you, you'll be doing some of my jobs around the house, so Mrs Raine'll probably give you some pocket money of your own. I'll be stoppin' cleanin' at the surgery soon,' Nell preened, "cos I'm ganin' to learn book-keepin' and get a job in an office. Aye, and Mam always thought you were the clever one.'

At the mention of her mother, Emmie's eyes welled with fresh tears.

'I miss her, Nelly,' she whispered. 'I never got to see her again.'

'Aye, well,' Nell glanced resentfully at Helen, 'you should've come home as soon as you were better.' She dropped her voice low. 'Don't know how you've stuck it here so long. Crawdene's a dirty dump.'

Helen intervened. 'Emmie, why don't you gan up to Louise's and say goodbye? You could take Nell with you. Get a bit fresh air – it's too hot to stay indoors.'

Emmie nodded and stood up quickly. But Nell smoothed out her skirt and sat back.

'No, ta, I'll wait here. Wouldn't mind another of your tasty scones, Mrs MacRae,' she smiled prettily.

An hour passed and Jonas offered to show Flora around his allotment. Again Nell declined to move. Helen was irritated by the girl but tried not to show it. She got on with making the tea, with no offer of help from Nell.

Eventually Nell asked, 'Where are the older lads?'

'Still at the pit,' Helen told her. 'Be back in a couple of hours.'

Nell's face fell. She grew impatient to be gone.

'Where's Emmie? How long does it take to say ta-ra to someone? I want to gan home.'

'Louise has been a good friend to your sister,' Helen pointed out. 'It's not easy for the lass to leave.'

'She's only been here a few months.' Nell was dismissive. 'Me and Emmie's been friends all our lives. She doesn't need this Louise – she's got me.'

Helen bit back a retort about the world not revolving around Nell Kelso. But the girl had just lost her mother; she mustn't judge her too harshly. Still, she could not help feeling that Nell just wanted Emmie there as company in a house of adults, someone to boss around and do her bidding. Perhaps she was wrong.

'Let's go up to Denmark Street and fetch her, eh?' Helen suggested.

Nell looked at her sulkily, then with a big sigh got to her feet. They walked up the hill in the sunshine, Helen trying to draw Nell out of her moodiness.

'Don't suppose you see much of Dr Jameson, with her being that busy?'

Nell shrugged. 'I work at the surgery, so I see her plenty.'

'And in the evenings?' Helen asked.

'Aye, we eat together. Or sometimes I have to meet her at the Settlement if she's got a meetin' or lecture.'

Helen nodded. 'Jonas heard Keir Hardie speak there once.'

Nell looked at her blankly. 'I hate ganin' there,' she said with distaste. 'It's in a dirty, smelly part of town down by the docks. The people who gan there smell an' all. I can't see what posh people like Mr Oliphant want to live there for.'

'Mr Oliphant?' Helen said in surprise.

'Aye, Charles Oliphant,' Nell said importantly. 'They say he's stinkin' rich, but wants to live with the poor. I think the doctor's taken a fancy to him.'

Helen hushed her. 'Eeh, lass, you mustn't gossip about your guardian like that.'

Nell was amused. 'But it's true. She goes all soppy-voiced when she speaks to him. And he goes red as a beetroot when he speaks to her.'

They arrived at the Currans' before Helen could question her further.

Tom came to the door. He stared at Nell and stammered, 'Sh-she's not here. We're having our tea.'

Nell gave him a generous smile. 'We don't want to disturb you. But do you know where me sister went?'

Tom blushed. 'I'll fetch our Louise.'

It was Mr Curran who came to the door and nodded curtly. 'Emmie hasn't been here today. Louise hasn't seen her since school yesterday. We thought she'd already gone.'

Helen was nonplussed. 'But she came to say goodbye.'

Mr Curran gave her a pitying look. 'The lasses had a falling-out at school. Emmie was boasting about going to live in a posh house in the town. Our Louise took it to mean that we weren't good enough for her any more. It's a shame she didn't learn a bit more humility in your care, Mrs MacRae.'

Helen wanted to give him a mouthful. How dare he lecture her about humility, the pompous oaf! She did not believe Emmie had been boastful. It was far more likely that the domineering Louise had taken affront at the girl's departure and caused the rift.

She clenched her fists. 'If you should happen to see Emmie, please send her straight home, Mr Curran.'

Tom, who was hovering behind his father, eyeing Nell, piped up, 'We could gan out after tea and look for her.'

Without a glance, his father barked, 'Get back inside, son. No one asked for your opinion.'

'Thank you, Tom,' Helen called, before the door was firmly shut in their faces.

Helen hurried to the allotments, Nell running to keep up.

'Emmie's gone missing,' she panted.

At once, Helen and Jonas began knocking on neighbouring doors, asking if anyone had seen the girl. Peter was dispatched to the shops to look for her there and to call on Emmie's teacher, Miss Downs. Flora waited anxiously at the house in case she returned, Nell fretting that they would not get back before nightfall.

She instantly lost her sullen look when Rab and Sam traipsed in. They stopped in surprise as Flora explained. Without taking off their filthy clothes, they went straight back out to help in the search. There was no sign of her around the village.

'You take Peter and gan to Oliphant's Wood,' Rab told Sam. 'I'll gan out the top road.'

Wheeling his father's old bicycle up the dirt road, past the pit, he mounted it and set off across the fell towards Blackton Heights. He had an inkling that if Emmie was looking for escape, she would have headed up to her favourite waterfall above Oliphant's place. It was on private land and Rab should never have encouraged her to go there, but Emmie had thrilled in the secrecy.

An evening breeze was stirring as he emerged on to the moorland that stretched in a great arc of heather and bracken above the village. He cycled along an old drover's track that in winter was a stream, dismounting to carry the bicycle across a series of gullies. At the old quarry he abandoned it and continued on foot. There was no one about, the only sound that of a lone skylark. Rab almost turned back. She would never have come on her own to such a desolate place.

Still, he pressed on round the ridge and climbed the last steep ascent to Lonely Stones, a ring of weathered stones marking an ancient Iron Age hillfort. Down below, sheltered in a copse of beech and pines, sprawled Blackton Heights, the Palladian mansion of the MacRaes' employer. Rab scrambled down the steep outcrop of rock and edged towards the waterfall hidden in the plantation of pines.

He could hear its roar muffled by the trees. It lay beyond, on Oliphant's private estate, though when his mother had been a girl, it had been a popular picnic spot for local families. Rab had kept up the tradition in defiance of the notices threatening to shoot trespassers. Climbing the fence, he hoped the gamekeeper was at home for the evening.

It was gloomy in the trees and the air smelled damp. He did not believe in ghosts, but he could almost feel the presence of long-dead pagan Britons, peering at him from behind the trees. Surely Emmie would not have lingered here?

He rounded a large rock. Huddled in a moth-eaten blanket that Helen used on the wash-house floor, crouched a familiar slim figure.

'Emmie! Rab cried.

She stood up, letting out a loud sob. In an instant he had her in his strong arms, hugging her tight. She was shaking with cold and distress.

'We've been lookin' all over. What you run off for?'

Emmie buried her head into his grimy jacket and wept, unable to speak. He stroked her head, calming her down.

'It's all right. Nobody's ganin' to be angry. You're safe and that's all that matters.'

He felt her shaking lessen, the sobs growing quieter.

'I don't want . . .' she tried to speak, '. . . don't want t-to . . .'

'Don't want what, Emmie?'

She looked up at him with huge sad eyes. 'I don't want to leave here – l–leave you and Auntie Helen.'

Rab felt his insides twist. 'But Nell? You want to be with your sister, don't you?'

She shook her head. 'Not if it means leaving Crawdene.' Suddenly her sorrow came tumbling out. 'I hate the town; I don't want to live there. And Nell's working now; she'll soon get tired of having me around. I just annoy her and I don't even know why. And I don't want a room of me own. I like sleepin' with the fire and Uncle Jonas snoring. It makes me feel cosy. And I want Louise to be me friend again like before. She's angry at me for ganin' away and says she won't be me friend, 'cos I like me sister more than her.' Her chin trembled again as she searched his face. 'And you tell the best stories ever – and you and Sam make me laugh. I've never been as happy – even with Mam. And now I haven't got Mam, but I've got Auntie Helen and I don't want to gan away, even if the doctor is kind.'

Tears spilled down her cheeks again and she rubbed them on Rab's chest, smearing her face with coaldust.

After a long moment, he said, 'You don't have to. I'll not let them take you away, if that's what you want.'

She gazed at him in awe. 'Can you stop them?'

Rab looked at her stubbornly. 'MacRaes can stop owt they want, once they put their mind to it.' He gave her a quick smile. 'Haway, little 'un. Let's get you home.'

He picked her up and carried her in his arms, hauling her over the fence and back down the hillside to the quarry. She perched on the back of the bicycle and they bumped their way down to the village, now engulfed in shadow.

There was consternation at her reappearance. Helen threw a warm blanket around her, cuddling her tight, while Jonas mixed her a hot toddy. Flora looked on in disapproval at the shot of whisky he poured for Emmie, then the one for himself. But the MacRaes' relief was so palpable, she said nothing. The other boys returned and fussed over Emmie too.

'Now we can go home at last,' Nell snapped, resentful of the attention her sister was getting. 'Come on, Emmie. I'll carry your bag if you like.'

Emmie eyed her sister nervously, but did not move. Flora caught the looks passing between the MacRaes. She also noticed Emmie's exhausted state.

'It's getting late. Emmie looks tired out. Perhaps we should leave it a day or two? Rab could bring her into town during the week. Less fuss,' she murmured.

Helen nodded with relief. But Rab stepped over to Emmie and laid a protective hand on her head.

'Why don't you ask Emmie what she wants?' he challenged. They all stared at him. 'She wants to stay here. She wants a mam – her Auntie Helen's the nearest she's got to one now. She's settled in here and made it her home. What you want to take her away to a strange new place for? Don't mean to be disrespectful, Dr Jameson, but she'll get just as much learnin' with us as she would with you. And Emmie's like family to me mam and dad – to all of us.'

Flora flushed at his directness. But looking at the anxious faces in the room, she knew that what the outspoken Rab said was true. One look at Emmie's adoring expression for the handsome miner told her that she could never replace these kindly people in Emmie's affections. Her idea of playing mother to these girls and moulding them for a great new world of equality was a fantasy. At least for Emmie, that job was Helen MacRae's.

'Is this true, Emmie?' she asked quietly.

Emmie nodded.

Helen said at once, 'We're more than happy to keep the lass, aren't we, Jonas?'

Jonas grunted in agreement, still dumbfounded by his son's brazen defiance of the doctor.

Nell erupted. 'But I'm Emmie's family, not you! You can't take her away from me! Tell them, Dr Flora, tell them they can't.'

'Nell, we can't force Emmie against her will. It wouldn't be right. She'd only run away again,' Flora reasoned.

Nell turned on Emmie in fury. 'You always want to spoil everything! Don't you want to be with me?'

Emmie said in distress, 'Aye, I do – but I want to stop here. You could live here too, Nelly.'

'In this pigsty?' Nell was contemptuous. 'Not if it was the last place on earth.'

'That's enough, Nell,' Flora warned. 'Don't say anything you'll regret later.'

'Oh, I'll not regret it,' Nell said savagely. 'She's the one'll regret it. Turning her back on a good home and the only real family she's got.' She glanced around her in contempt. 'You're not her real family – never will be. You're just common pitmen. Me and Emmie have proper breedin'. Our mother was a proper lady, she was.'

Flora took hold of Nell and steered her to the door. 'Come on, Nell, we're going.' Pushing her into the street, she turned to the MacRaes. 'I'm sorry, she's upset. We all are. Please don't take offence.'

'No, course not,' Helen said quickly. The men were speechless at Nell's outburst.

Flora gave a strained smile. 'Goodbye, Emmie. I will keep in touch. If there's anything you ever want . . . You can come and visit Nell whenever you feel like it.'

'Thank you, Doctor,' Helen answered. 'Jonas will see you down the hill.'

Jonas was galvanised by his wife's words and followed the doctor outside. The others listened to their footsteps growing more distant, Nell's indignant voice fading.

Emmie peered out of her blanket, wondering what she had done. The boys stared at her, then at each other.

'By heck,' Sam exclaimed, 'who would've thought a lass your size could cause as much bother?'

'Aye,' agreed Rab. 'Should make you lodge official.'

'You're one to talk,' snorted his mother.

They laughed in relief. Helen looked at Emmie huddled in her blanket like a defiant imp.

'Eeh, little pet,' she cried, 'give me a hug.'

Emmie's skinny arms threw off the blanket and opened wide for Helen's plump embrace. They squeezed each other tight.

Emmie mumbled into her warm, floury hold, 'I love you, Auntie Helen.'

Helen could not stop the tears that flooded her eyes.

'I love you an' all, you little troublemaker,' she laughed. 'Love you like me own daughter.'

Later that night, when Emmie was asleep on her truckle bed and Helen lay contented in her husband's arms, she asked, 'What's the name of Major Oliphant's son?'

'Charles,' Jonas yawned. 'Why?'

'Strange,' Helen mused, 'there's a Charles Oliphant works at the Gateshead Settlement. Nell says Dr Jameson's in love with him.'

Jonas snorted. 'Can't be the same one. The major's son went into the army, as far as I know. No doubt he's abroad somewhere, shooting natives.'

'No, that was Liddon, the one who died.'

'Liddon – Charles – what's the difference?'

'They're not all as bad as the old man,' Helen reproved. 'Miss Sophie came along to one of our Guild meetin's on women's suffrage.'

'Spying, no doubt,' Jonas teased.

43

Helen dug him in the ribs, then snuggled into his hold. Jonas chuckled.

'Quiet, or you'll wake our lass,' Helen whispered.

They fell silent, listening to Emmie's soft breathing. Helen felt the luckiest woman in the world.

CHAPTER 6

1909

Emmie was late leaving school that chilly spring afternoon. She had stayed on to help Miss Downs prepare lessons for the following day. She loved sharing the teaching, though she knew she was now too old to stay on as a pupil teacher. In a week she would be sixteen. The MacRaes had indulged her long enough; she would have to find a job. She felt a familiar restlessness as she crossed the school yard.

Louise, already seventeen, was courting twenty-year-old Sam MacRae. They had paired off at the Christmas dance at the Co-operative Hall and now Sam called round at the Currans' more often than Emmie did.

'It won't last,' Jonas predicted. 'Old man Curran won't want a heathen for a son-in-law.'

But Emmie thought he underestimated both Louise's determination to have Sam, and Sam's ability to charm the dour Currans. Besides, Sam and Tom had been friends since school and Tom welcomed an ally in the house. Mr Curran was not above using his belt on his twenty-year-old son, but Louise said he never beat Tom when Sam was present.

The cottage at China Street had never been quieter. Peter had been found a delivery job with a patient grocer in Blackton and was away long hours. And Rab had gone. Even now, two long years after Rab's disappearance from Crawdene, Emmie's insides clenched in familiar distress. She flinched at the memory of the monumental row Rab had had with Jonas. It started when Rab had led an unofficial strike in protest at a friend nearly drowning in a flooded pit gallery. Oliphant's manager had threatened to evict all the MacRaes.

'What use is a pit house now?' Rab had accused his father. 'You'll always be a boss's man as long as your job depends on living in his poxy cottage!'

'Don't you call me a boss's man.' Jonas had leaped at his son in fury. Helen and Emmie had tried to break up the fight, but only when Emmie received an elbow in the eye did the men stop, appalled at what they had done. Rab blamed himself. He could not bear to look at Emmie's bruised face. Two days later he disappeared and the threat of eviction was dropped.

Emmie had cried night after night, worried that he had nowhere to go. She felt somehow responsible for his disappearance and refused to be comforted by the others. Helen and Jonas did not speak for days. Only Sam joked about it.

'The bugger will be starting a revolution wherever he is – and writing songs about it.'

A month later, a letter came from Glasgow. Rab was labouring at the docks and taking night classes in literature and philosophy. He was lodging with three Gaelic-speaking merchant seamen, a boiler-maker's apprentice and an anarchist.

A card came at Christmas from a different address, but no longed-for return to his family. Two years on and only a handful of postcards, none of them replying to Emmie's chatty letters, she had to admit that Rab was not coming back.

Rab. Her heart ached a little when she allowed herself to think of him. Vital, talkative Rab, with his curling dark hair and lively eyes, filling the house with singing and laughter, teasing and debate. She knew Helen missed him as much as she did, but Jonas grew short-tempered if they talked about him too much.

'Your Uncle Jonas can't forgive himself for raising his fists to his own son,' Helen once confided, her plump face scored with sorrow.

As Emmie made her way downhill, she thought she might look for work outside Crawdene. The bank was slippy from a week of heavy rain and she stepped cautiously, clutching her poetry books from Blackton library. Dr Jameson would help her if she asked. Nell was, by all accounts, a proficient book-keeper for the doctor. Yet, Emmie was reticent in asking for help. Nell still accused her of betrayal for not going to live with them after their mother died. They saw each other only when Emmie made the effort to travel into Gateshead. The last time had been to see Nell perform in a musical evening at the Settlement.

Emmie had never seen her sister look so happy, nor realised what a beautiful singing voice she had. The MacRaes had made it a big outing and fussed over Nell, to lessen the strained atmosphere between the two sisters.

'Next time,' Emmie had enthused to Louise, 'you and Tom must come too.'

'If we tell me father it's hymn singing,' Louise had laughed with a roll of her eyes.

Louise would always be more like a sister to her than Nell ever would, Emmie had to admit. They could tell each other anything. Except now there was Sam vying for Louise's attention. Things were changing.

Emmie was so deep in thought and concentrating on avoiding puddles, that she did not see the demonstration until she was upon it. Outside the co-operative store, a group of women was standing on a flat cart bedecked in red, white and green bunting, exhorting the crowd.

'Don't vote for Hauxley, the Liberal! His party pretend to stand for freedom, when all the time they are denying women the right to vote. What equality do we have under the Liberal Government? None! We pay taxes yet have no say in how our taxes are spent.'

'Why aren't you at home looking after yer bairns?' a man heckled.

'Sir,' a fresh-faced young woman on the cart rounded on him, 'you men expect your wives to do the best for their children and families, don't you? Yet they are not consulted over laws that affect those children and families. Is that fair? No, it is not!'

There were murmurs of agreement as Emmie joined the crowd of onlookers.

'Men!' The older speaker took over again. 'You have it in your power to send a message to the Government in this by-election. No taxation without representation. Vote for fairness for your wives and daughters. Women! It is your duty to persuade your husbands and fathers to vote against the Liberal. Don't vote for Hauxley next week!'

A few people clapped, others shook their heads. Canvassers

began to mingle with the crowd, handing out leaflets before people hurried out of the biting wind. Emmie glanced around to see if Helen was there, but could not see her. She took a leaflet from the smiling young woman in a large-brimmed hat who had dealt with the heckler. Emmie turned for home, so engrossed in reading the leaflet that she quite forgot about going to the store to buy a new exercise book. Halfway up China Street, she remembered.

The sky looked heavy with more rain. The first spatters arrived as she retraced her steps. When she emerged on to the main street again, she heard shouting further up the hill and the thud of feet in mud. A gang of men and young boys were bearing down on her, cursing and screaming.

Emmie stood in stunned confusion. Had something terrible happened at the pit? Then a stone whistled past her head and smacked into the mud just beyond. They were on the attack. Whirling about, Emmie suddenly saw their target. The canvassers had halted halfway up the road, unsure of what to do. Their cart was in the middle of the street, the horse stamping fretfully at the noise of the mob.

'Run!' Emmie yelled, as a volley of stones and coal rained down the hill.

The women scattered with screams of alarm. The horse reared up and bolted with the cart. Leaflets flew about on the wind and were trampled underfoot by the pursuing miners.

'Get back in the kitchen, yer harridans!' a man bellowed, barging past Emmie and knocking her books from her hold. 'We don't want yer here upsettin' ower lasses.'

Emmie was furious as she bent to retrieve her library books. Most of the attackers were young boys, but she was shocked to see some members of the lodge among them, goading them on. She watched horrified as they drove the canvassers down the hill and out of the village. One woman slipped and fell in the mud a few feet away. Emmie recognised the large hat. She dashed forward and yanked her to her feet. A group of youths saw her and doubled back. The woman protestor was cornered.

'Quick, come with me,' Emmie urged, pulling her into China Street.

They ran up the lane, chased by the boys. Emmie thought she

might outrun them, but the young woman was gasping for breath, her mud-drenched skirts weighing her down.

Screwing up her courage, Emmie rounded on her pursuers.

'Stop right there!' she ordered, shielding the woman. 'Any one of you touches this lass – you'll have the MacRaes at your door.'

They were crowding about, laughing at her threats.

'Give her over – we're not after you,' one of them jeered. 'She needs teaching a lesson.'

Emmie gripped the woman tighter, hearing her whimper.

'You should be ashamed of yourselves,' she answered. 'Big, strong lads picking a fight with one lass. Maybes you should listen to what she has to say before you kick her down the street like a dog. Would you tret your mams like that – or your sisters?'

The faces in front of her seemed less certain. Abruptly, a voice from the back of the gang called out, 'Haway, lads, that's enough. Leave the lasses be.'

Emmie felt her insides jolt. She knew the voice.

'Tom Curran?' she cried, as Tom pushed his way through. She stared into his slim good-looking face. 'I never thought you'd be part of this shameful business.'

Tom came close and whispered, 'Get her inside.' Immediately, he turned and began cajoling the others to leave.

'You've seen them off, that's all you were asked to do. Beatin' up lasses isn't part of it. Haway, scarper.'

As Tom herded the boys away, Emmie gripped the woman tight and helped her along to number eighteen. They stumbled in at the door, Emmie calling for Helen to help. Within minutes they had the woman out of her sodden dress and wrapped in blankets by the fire, sipping piping hot tea. Fair, bedraggled hair hung down over her flushed pretty face. Her dark blue eyes looked around her, wide and curious. When she spoke, it was with an upper-class drawl that Emmie had only heard on the hustings or from visiting preachers.

'It's so kind of you to help me.' She smiled for the first time. 'Those awful boys – I thought—'

'They're more bark than bite,' Helen reassured.

'They were hoying stones,' Emmie pointed out. 'And that Tom Curran was one of them. If his da only knew.'

'His da probably organised it,' Helen retorted. 'He's a strong Liberal. He'll hate the idea of lasses telling him how to vote.' She leaned forward and patted the woman's shoulder. 'Good on you, pet. At least your da doesn't stop you speaking your mind.'

She gave them a sheepish smile. 'Actually, he doesn't know I'm here.'

They all laughed.

'What do they call you, miss?' Helen asked.

She hesitated. 'Sophie.'

Helen gave her a quizzical look. 'I could swear I've seen your face somewhere. Ever been in Crawdene before?'

She shook her head, then said, 'Well, yes. I've been to the Guild.'

Emmie saw Helen's eyes widen as recognition dawned.

'Eeh, it's never you, Miss Sophie!'

The young woman went puce and nodded. 'But please don't tell my father; he'd only worry.'

Helen spluttered with laughter. 'I've no more chance of talkin' to Major Oliphant than growing wings.'

'Major Oliphant?' Emmie cried in disbelief.

Sophie covered her face in embarrassment. 'Everyone looks at me differently once they know. You see why I like to go incognito?'

Helen said, 'There's nowt to be ashamed of – you should use your connections to help women get the vote. Men like your father have influence in the world.'

Sophie grimaced. 'Yes, but it's the wrong kind. His political friends don't think women should trouble themselves with anything more taxing than menus and guest lists.'

The women laughed ruefully. They drank more tea.

'You know about my family then?' Sophie asked.

Helen shrugged. 'You keep yourselves to yourselves, as far as I can see. Of course, we knew about your father's heir dying in the first Boer War – there's that big memorial to him in Blackton.'

'My brother Liddon,' Sophie sighed. 'Mama never got over it – she took to her bed and now she's an invalid. And Papa . . . We younger two are a bit of a disappointment to my father,' Sophie confided.

Emmie caught Helen's embarrassed look. She didn't want the role of confidante to Oliphant's daughter. But Sophie seemed oblivious to their discomfort.

'My brother Charles is trained as a vicar but refuses to take a good living in a decent parish. He's running a mission in Gateshead. That's where I help out too. There's a printing press we use for the suffrage campaign.'

'The Settlement?' Helen queried.

'Yes, you've heard of it?'

Emmie nodded. 'We know it well. Dr Jameson is a friend of ours – and my sister Nell sings in their choir.'

Sophie clapped her hands. 'Flora Jameson is a dear friend of mine! She's known Charles for years. It's Flora who got me interested in women's suffrage. You meet such interesting people at the Settlement – women from all over Europe on lecture tours and conferences. It's so much more interesting than stuffy old Blackton Heights. Course, Papa thinks I'm in town shopping or going to the theatre. He's so terribly possessive since Liddon died – and because Mama takes no interest.' She stopped, clapping a hand over her mouth. 'I've said too much as usual. And I don't even know you. It's just you've made me feel so welcome.'

Suddenly Emmie asked, 'This printing press – do you need any help? I'm looking for work. I could do anything – sweep up, make the tea.'

'Hold your horses,' Helen protested. 'You're too bright to be sweepin' floors.'

'Please, Auntie Helen, it's time I was bringing in a wage. I want to be like Nell – able to stand on me own feet – not like Louise, just waiting to get wed.'

Sophie looked between them. When Helen did not protest, she said to Emmie, 'It's run by a couple called Runcie. They're Quakers. I just help out now and again – folding leaflets, that sort of thing. I'm not paid. You should call in some time and see.'

Emmie looked appealingly at Helen. 'Please can I go?'

'I could put a word in for you,' Sophie encouraged. 'It's the least I could do after you rescued me.'

'But it's such a distance,' Helen fretted.

'I'll go on the bike,' Emmie enthused.

Helen sighed. 'We'll ask your Uncle Jonas,' she conceded.

They were startled by a knock on the back door. Emmie opened it to find Tom standing in the rain. He pulled off his cap.

'What do you want?' Emmie said curtly.

'Came to see if the lass was all right.'

'Aye, she is.'

51

He flushed. 'I'm sorry, Emmie – the lads got a bit lively.'

'Fancy tretting defenceless lasses like that,' she reproved.

'Aye, but it's not the way lasses should carry on, is it? Ganin' around shoutin' their gobs off like fishwives and telling men what to do.'

'Well, men could do with listening to lasses a bit more often, in my opinion,' Emmie sparked back.

'You don't agree with them, do you?' Tom was incredulous.

'Aye, I do,' she declared. 'In fact I've made up me mind to join them!'

He gawped at her.

'And if you want to make yoursel' useful, instead of standing there with your mouth open, you can walk the lady safely out the village to find her friends.' She challenged him with her look.

Tom's expression was stubborn.

Emmie dropped her voice. 'Unless you want Major Oliphant hearing about what you nearly did to his daughter?' She saw his eyes widen in disbelief. 'Aye,' she hissed, 'that's Miss Sophie Oliphant sittin' in our kitchen!'

'Never!' Tom exclaimed.

Emmie put her finger to his lips. 'Not a word, Tom Curran. She doesn't want folk to know. Now will you help me or not?'

To Emmie's amazement, Tom nodded without any more protest.

Tom was left in the scullery while Sophie got dressed again. She tried to press money on them, but Helen refused. Having learned Emmie's name, though, Sophie promised to mention her to the Runcies. Together, Emmie and Tom walked Sophie down the lane, Tom completely tongue-tied in the presence of the older woman. The rain had driven everyone indoors and the light was fading fast. By the time they found the electioneering cart outside the inn at the Blackton crossroads, all three were soaked through. Sophie thanked them profusely and hurried inside to join the others. Tom and Emmie trudged back up the hill to Crawdene.

By the time they neared China Street, Tom saw it all as a huge joke.

'Fancy old man MacRae havin' the boss's daughter to tea,' he laughed. 'Mixing with the aristocracy, eh?'

'Tom, you're not to say a word,' Emmie warned. But the more she protested, the more he teased her about it.

'The socialists defending the bosses,' he crowed. 'Wish Rab MacRae was here to see it.'

Emmie gave him a shove. 'Wait till your da hears you've been attacking Oliphant's daughter.'

Tom swung an arm about her. 'I won't tell if you won't tell.'

She wriggled out of his hold. But he followed her along China Street.

'I must see the lady safely home,' he mocked.

'Don't bother,' she said, hurrying ahead.

'I want to.' Tom kept pace. At her back door, he caught her hand. 'You're not like them lasses, Emmie. You're one of us. One day you'll make a canny pitman's wife.'

She looked at him, startled. Before she could answer, he planted a kiss on her lips.

'Ta-ra, Emmie,' he grinned.

She turned in confusion and fled inside. Jonas was home and demanding to know where she had been in such foul weather. Her attempts to keep secret their important visitor were to no avail. By the following day, the whole village was talking about Emmie saving Oliphant's daughter from a lynch mob and harbouring her at the MacRaes'.

Jonas had to endure a week of jibes as the tale grew in length and exaggeration. Emmie was a suffragette. Jonas had no control over his militant women. They'd be chaining themselves to railings next. Emmie supposed it was Tom who had spread the news, or maybe Miss Sophie had been recognised by others in the village.

Tom filled her with a mixture of annoyance and something else she couldn't quite name. She often found herself thinking about his fresh-faced good looks, the way he looked at her with his hazel eyes as if he found her pretty, his quick smile, the feel of his lips on her cheek. She was unsettled by it, flattered even. Tom might look younger than his twenty years, but he was a man now and his teasing no longer felt like childish horseplay.

On her sixteenth birthday, Tom came round with a bunch of daffodils and a bottle of lavender water. He endured Sam's ribald teasing with good humour but bolted when Helen suggested he stay for tea.

'I'll see you at chapel, Emmie?' he asked in hope, grinning when she nodded in assent.

'Breaking hearts already,' Jonas chuckled as they tucked into the birthday tea. 'Pity it's a Curran.'

'He was brave to come,' Helen defended Tom, 'seeing as his da won't allow either bairn over our doorstep.'

'You might poison them, Mam,' Sam said, clutching his throat and gasping.

'You wouldn't poison Tom, would you?' Peter asked in alarm.

'No, pet, Sam's being daft,' Helen reassured. 'Still, I think it's a shame. We'd never stop any of you ganin' round there, just because we don't see eye to eye with the Currans. You can be friends with who you like.'

'Aye,' Sam said, winking at Emmie, 'even the gentry.'

Jonas gave him a thunderous look.

Emmie said quickly, 'No arguments on me birthday!'

The Easter holidays came and Emmie left Miss Downs for the last time. The next day, she rode all the way into Gateshead on Jonas's rickety bicycle to visit the Settlement. She had written to the Runcies about seeking work and they had invited her down for an interview.

The elderly couple welcomed her into the cramped untidy room they used as an office behind the dining hall. Every inch of floor, table, chairs and filing cabinet was covered in mounds of paper. There was nowhere to sit, so Emmie perched on a chair arm while they talked to her about their work. She warmed to them and their courteous manner at once. Philip Runcie was small, wiry and full of vigour, with an engaging smile. Mabel Runcie resembled the late Queen Victoria, though with a calm, otherworldly air.

'We produce a weekly news-sheet, the *Gateshead News*,' Philip Runcie explained, scratching his nose with inky fingers. 'You could help by finding new advertisers. And we print pamphlets for church groups and societies, such as the Women's Suffrage Society. But you know that from Miss Oliphant.'

Emmie nodded.

Mabel Runcie gave a regal wave of her hand. 'And you could start by finding a home for all this paper,' she sighed. 'We're not the tidiest of people – and with my arthritic knees and hands I'm finding it harder to manage.'

The Runcies looked at Emmie expectantly.

'Now?' she queried. 'You mean I've got the job? Don't you want to ask me any questions?'

They looked at her in surprise. 'No, dear, we know all about you from Dr Jameson and Sophie,' Mabel smiled.

'We can't offer you much of a wage –' Philip looked apologetic – 'a lot of our work is voluntary – but you can take a percentage of the advertising revenue.'

'And eat as much as you like in the refectory,' Mabel added eagerly. 'Mrs Mousy is an excellent cook.'

Emmie beamed. 'That's grand. I'll start right away.'

It was dark by the time Emmie wheeled the bike back into the village. Helen was watching out anxiously, convinced she had had an accident. Flopping in exhaustion into a chair by the fire, Emmie gabbled about her first day at work.

Helen looked at her wistfully. 'You're not ganin' to live down there, are you? You're not unhappy here?'

'Course not!' Emmie exclaimed. 'This is me home. But there aren't the jobs here for lasses. And I want to work at the Settlement. It's grand what they're doing – helpin' the working class. We're ganin' to make a difference.'

Jonas and Helen exchanged glances. Jonas laid a hand on Emmie's head and nodded.

'Oh, lassie, I'm proud of you.'

CHAPTER 7

Flora made umpteen excuses not to go to Blackton Heights with Charles. She could not leave her practice. She could not leave Nell for two days after the last time, when she had drunk a bottle of sherry and been sick and ruined her only valuable Persian carpet.

'You don't need me there,' Flora said in panic.

'I want you there,' Charles laughed. 'Sophie wants you.'

'Your father detests me,' Flora retorted. 'He blames me for Sophie's pleurisy yet won't let me near her, as if I'm not a proper doctor. And I had no idea she was going campaigning round the mining villages.'

'He doesn't blame you,' Charles insisted. 'Anyway, he'll be in a good mood because Hauxley got in.'

Flora looked at him and sighed. When he smiled at her like that it felt churlish to refuse. He worked so hard for others, day and night, that she did not want to spoil his brief respite in the country. She knew that, despite his complaints about his father and his obscene wealth, Charles loved him and his old home. He always looked younger and more relaxed as soon as he was back on the fell, walking the grounds with the major's dogs. And he liked to sit in his mother's sunny bedroom, chatting quietly about life and work with his reclusive mother in a way he never could with his father.

Flora also knew that the only reason Charles asked her was to have someone else there to deflect his father's criticisms at his lack of ambition. It would be two days of relentless pressure from

Major James on Charles to give up his mission work and be groomed as heir to Blackton Heights and its business interests.

'If you won't end up a canon at Durham Cathedral,' Major James had said on one occasion, 'then the Church be damned! You'll come home and learn to be a country gentleman.'

Flora groaned at the thought of two days in the company of the blustering, bullying, hard-drinking major. Over all of them would hang the ghost of Charles's older brother, Liddon, the dashing officer killed in Africa, to whom Charles could never compare in his father's eyes. Yet she would do it for Charles. They might never be more than colleagues and confidants, but he was her closest friend and she would do anything for him.

They were met at the station by a noisy hooting. Major James was behind the wheel of his brand-new blue and green Rolls-Royce. Flora steeled herself to be civil.

'Charles, my boy!' He greeted his son with a clap on the back. He nodded at Flora but no hand was extended. She forced a smile, ignoring his rudeness.

'Jump in, jump in,' he ordered. 'Charles, you must sit in the front so I can show you the controls.'

They bumped over the rough road up to Blackton village and on towards the Heights. Flora was feeling queasy and cold by the time they reached the mansion. She was happy to be shown to her room and lie down. Sophie sought her out before tea.

'I thought you were ill in bed?' Flora said in surprise. 'I was going to come and see you.'

Sophie rolled her eyes. 'A little cold, that's all it was. Papa made such a fuss. Wanted to know everything about the escapade – even demanded the name of the kind family who took me in.'

'The MacRaes?' Flora asked in concern.

'Yes. He ranted on about them as if it had been their fault. Said they're a bunch of revolutionaries and if he could rid the village of them he would. When he starts on one of his rants, there's no reasoning with him. Mama is the only one who can soothe him. I just seem to make him crosser.'

'Have you any idea why your father has summoned Charles?' Flora asked anxiously.

Sophie shook her head. 'But he's up to something. The Hauxleys are being invited over for dinner and he knows Charles can't stand them.'

Flora groaned.

'It's all right for you!' Sophie exclaimed. 'Papa's been trying to marry me off to Captain Arthur since I was in the nursery. He and Liddon served in Africa together, so he can do no wrong.'

'Is Arthur as pompous as his father?' Flora grimaced.

'No, he's too dull to be pompous.'

Flora laughed. 'Oh, poor Charles. At least we women can escape to the drawing room when they bring out the port.'

'Promise me you won't leave me alone with the captain?' Sophie ordered.

'Promise,' Flora agreed. 'We suffragists will stick together.'

Sophie laughed and hugged her in affection.

The dining room was thick with cigar smoke. Charles felt sleepy after the gargantuan meal and wished he could join the women in the airy drawing room. His father was patting his large belly in contentment, laughing over some story of Reginald Hauxley's from the magistrates' court where he was a JP. Charles was not fooled by the man's casual air. He was a shrewd businessman who had made a fortune in shipping, bought a large estate adjoining Blackton Heights and embarked, single-mindedly, on a career in politics.

Earlier, Sophie had taken their neighbour to task about his opposition to women's emancipation, despite thunderous looks from their father. Surprisingly, Arthur had supported her and averted a full-scale row at table. Whether the quiet captain had done so out of conviction or admiration for Sophie, Charles was not sure. Still, he envied Sophie her courage in speaking her mind and not caring for the consequences. He was always one to avoid confrontations and let differing opinions go unchallenged.

Which was why he was stifling a yawn, rather than joining in the older men's banter about the feckless poor and how they should all be conscripted into the army or navy.

'Well, tell him, Reginald,' Major James ordered, refilling his port glass.

Charles was suddenly aware they were all looking at him. He roused himself. Reginald fixed him with a look.

'The parish of Blackton and Ongarfield is soon to become vacant. The vicar is retiring. As you know, the parish straddles your father's estates and mine. We are looking to call a young, enthusiastic man to fill the vacancy. Someone who knows the area and its needs.' Reginald smiled knowingly.

'It would provide a very good living,' his father enthused. 'Three pits in the parish, and a levy on every tub of coal goes to the vicar. It would tide you over well until you inherit the estate.'

Charles stared at them, his instinct telling him to say no at once.

Reginald continued persuasively, 'In such a large rural parish there would be much to do – caring for the needs of farm labourers and miners.'

'Setting them a good example,' Major James added, 'keeping them on the straight and narrow.'

'Social concerns,' Reginald murmured.

'Time you stopped this mission business. You're thirty-three,' his father said bluntly. 'It's time you were looking to your responsibilities.'

'Responsibilities?' Charles bristled.

'Yes, to your family – your position. You should be settling down and marrying. Blackton Heights needs an heir.'

Charles reddened. 'I feel called to work at the mission.'

Major James thumped the table with impatience, but Reginald cut in quickly.

'Charles, what you do is admirable. But I can see how it is taking its toll on your health. Isn't it time to leave the mission to someone else? And there is so much you could do to better the lives of the common people around Blackton.'

Arthur piped up unexpectedly, 'It would be good to have you back, Charles. You're like me – this place is in your blood.'

Charles glanced at him in surprise. Perhaps there was more to Arthur than he had thought. What he said hit a nerve. He was never more at home than striding out across the moors under a vast open sky, free as the skylarks that sang above.

'All we are asking is that you consider the vacancy,' Reginald said reasonably. 'You will need time to think it over.'

Charles nodded. He would discuss it with Flora. He trusted her judgement above all.

The following morning, Charles declined his father's invitation to go out with the guns and dogs. Major James grumbled in annoyance.

'I'm taking Flora for a walk around Ongarfield,' Charles

quickly explained, 'to have a look at the parish.' That silenced his father's protests, as he knew it would.

They climbed to the top of the fell, beyond the estate boundary, above the disused lead mine workings and gazed about. Below, smoke wafted from isolated pit villages and the vast woods of Blackton Heights sighed in the blustery April breeze. On the lip of the horizon was the village of Ongarfield, solid stone houses gathered around a picturesque Norman church and a strip of green sward. Charles explained about Hauxley's proposal.

'The vicarage is in Ongarfield – a pretty little village.' Charles pointed it out. 'And far enough away from Blackton Heights not to be bumping into my father daily,' he smiled.

'You're tempted?' Flora asked, trying to hide her dismay.

'It's a large parish – there would be much to do.' His expression was eager. Flora said nothing. 'What do you think?'

Flora faced him. 'Wouldn't you run the risk of your father – or Hauxley – interfering in anything you did? You would be Hauxley's appointee – he'd expect something in return – toeing the party line in the pulpit, perhaps.'

Charles looked hurt. 'You think I'd compromise my principles for Hauxley?'

'That's not what I said,' Flora answered. 'I'm merely pointing out that there will be great pressure on you to agree with their beliefs – their way of running things.'

'Such as?' Charles asked in irritation.

'Such as not siding with their employees – the pitmen, the field hands – in any dispute. In not championing women's right to vote,' Flora said pointedly.

Charles flushed. 'You think I'm that weak?'

Flora was frank. 'No, I think you're too nice not to be browbeaten by their bullying.'

Charles stared off into the distance, his lips pressed tight in annoyance. Flora felt a pang of sympathy.

'I'm sorry, Charles, I didn't mean to offend. But you did ask my opinion.' She put a hand on his arm. 'I know you love it up here, but that's not enough. You have to decide why you really want to come back. Is it because you feel called to do this job? Or are you, deep down, just trying to please your parents – make up for not being Liddon?'

He gave her a sharp, pained look.

'Dear Charles,' she urged, 'think about the Settlement. What you do there is worth the work of ten parishes. But if you feel you have done all you can there, and that you can do as much or more for the people of Blackton and Ongarfield, then do it. For you have many great gifts and you would be generous with them, I know. But put the people first, not any desire to please your father – because sooner or later you will clash with him. And when that time comes, you'll have to be strong enough to stand your ground.'

Charles regarded her from under a mop of tousled blond hair, his look bashful and unsure.

'Flora . . .'

She waited, convinced he was going to choose the parish over the Settlement. She could not imagine life in Gateshead without him, but if that was his choice she would do nothing more to dissuade him.

'If I took the parish . . . would you . . . could you see yourself . . . would you like . . . ?'

'What, Charles? Would I what?'

'Marry me?' he blurted out, blushing furiously.

She stared at him, in open-mouthed amazement. This was the last thing she expected to be asked. Often she had daydreamed of him proposing, but had thought it would never happen. For a moment she allowed herself to revel in the idea. Mrs Charles Oliphant, living in the large Georgian vicarage at Ongarfield, receiving the gentry of the county in her drawing room with a view over the fells. There would be visits to the sick and needy too, but it would be a life cosseted by her husband's comfortable stipend, and in time she would become lady of Blackton Heights. Endless days with Charles, with maybe a child before it was too late . . .

'Oh, dear, sweet Charles,' she smiled at him regretfully, 'you are the only man I have ever held in such affection. But I couldn't be part of all this.' She swept her hands at the surrounding fells. 'I would soon tire of presiding over the teapot – would miss my practice and my work in Gateshead. I'd become intolerable to live with and you'd very soon rue ever asking me. And I could not live in your father's shadow – he would never accept me. Look for someone younger, Charles, more acceptable as a vicar's wife.'

Charles looked away, trying to hide the hurt of her rejection. He forced a laugh.

'Well, I'm not having much luck in persuading you to my way of thinking, am I? No to the parish, no to marriage. The old Oliphant charm not working any more?'

Flora smiled, relieved he was taking it light-heartedly. Perhaps he had never really meant it seriously.

'There's nothing wrong with the Oliphant charm,' she answered, squeezing his arm. 'But the decision to come here must be yours, Charles, and yours only.'

They returned to the mansion, saying little. Charles cursed himself for having spoiled their walk with his impulsive marriage proposal. Why had he said it? He had hardly thought of marriage up till now. Perhaps he had asked her so that she would share the burden of his decision-making? If so, she had seen right through it.

Flora gazed about her as they descended down the steep moorside and into the newly budding trees. This would probably be the last time she came here, or enjoyed this quiet countryside with Charles. They had passed from the stage of being companions to that of rejected suitors. However brave a face he put on things, she had hurt his pride. She longed to tell him how much she wanted to be his wife, yet would do nothing to sway his future. No matter how deeply she cared for him, she knew she could not give up who she was, or change to please his ghastly father.

When they returned, Charles disappeared to his mother's quarters and did not appear at afternoon tea.

'He'll be discussing the details of Hauxley's offer,' the major said in satisfaction. 'Charles will want to please his mother.' He gave Flora a hard look. 'I hope you're in favour of my son taking such a worthwhile position, Miss Jameson?'

Flora swallowed her irritation at his deliberate refusal to call her 'Doctor'.

'That is entirely up to Charles, Mr Oliphant,' she replied, noticing with satisfaction how he scowled at not being called major and turned his back to speak to Sophie.

She sat tensely, under the scrutinising gaze of Liddon's portrait that hung in pride of place over the large marble fireplace. A handsome, solemn young man in uniform. If only he had lived, Flora thought sadly, then Charles would have been free of his father's frantic ambitions. But perhaps not. Charles would never be free of such a controlling man, she realised.

All at once, Flora had had enough. The major would continue to ignore her, or make petty jibes at her expense. Charles no longer needed her. She stood up.

'I wonder if I could trouble you to give me a lift to the station?'

The major and Sophie stared in surprise.

'You can't go home yet,' Sophie protested.

'I want to be back for my surgery in the morning,' Flora said quickly.

'As you wish,' the major said, waving her away. 'Thompson can take you down in the trap.'

'But, Papa—' Sophie began to protest.

'If Miss Jameson wants to go, we'll not stop her,' he said, not bothering to hide his contempt.

Flora hurried off to pack her bags, scrawling a note of apology to Charles. In twenty minutes she was jostling in the open carriage on her way to the station to catch the six o'clock train back to Gateshead.

Charles came downstairs to find Sophie sulking in the library, a rug wrapped around her knees.

'Where's Flora?'

'Gone. Have you two had a row or something?' Sophie demanded.

Charles flushed. 'What do you mean, gone?'

'Caught-the-train-home kind of gone,' Sophie said sharply. 'Pleased Papa, of course. But how dull for me with no one to talk to at dinner about anything interesting.'

'Did she say why?' Charles demanded.

'Left you this,' Sophie said, waving Flora's note. Charles took it quickly and read.

Dear Charles,

Forgive me for rushing away – I know it's cowardly. But you need time to consider things alone, or with your family. I can't be part of your decision. I have much with which to be getting on and am not good at sitting around pretending to be leisured! Whatever you decide, be assured you have my full support and good wishes.

Flora

Charles crumpled the note and threw it on the fire. He ran his hands through his wiry hair.

'Good wishes! The infuriating woman,' he cried.

His father walked in at that moment. 'Talking about Miss Jameson?' he grunted. 'My sentiments indeed. Don't worry, she's gone.'

'Papa!' Sophie remonstrated. 'She's our friend.'

'She's a bad influence,' he scoffed. 'Your mother and I worry about the ideas she puts in your head. Look where it gets you – chased by pitmen into the lions' den of troublemakers – the MacRaes.'

'Don't talk to me as if I'm still a child,' Sophie complained. 'I'm a woman of twenty-five.'

'Still young enough and silly enough to need protecting from all this radical nonsense about equal rights. Women aren't made for politics – it's a man's world – we have to make tough decisions for the good of others. Women's natures are naturally soft, more suited to domestic life.' He stood over his daughter, smiling indulgently, warming to his theme. 'That's why there are certain professions that only men should undertake, like politics, high office, business.' He glanced at Charles, who was standing mutely, staring into the fire where Flora's note had turned to hot ash. 'And doctoring,' the major added. 'Women doctors are unnatural, if you ask me. Your mother and I don't want you associating with that Jameson woman again.'

Charles turned and glared at his father. 'Mama thinks nothing of the kind. She has nothing against Flora or any women doctors.'

Major James was dismissive. 'I believe I know best what your mother thinks.'

'And how would you know that?' Charles challenged. 'You don't spend five minutes a day in her company. You never ask her opinion on anything.'

'Your mother's health is very delicate,' his father blustered. 'She doesn't want to be troubled with questions that don't concern her.'

'Dear God!' Charles expostulated. 'Flora was right. You want to control everybody. I must be mad to even contemplate taking over this parish. You'd never let me be free to run it as I see fit – you'd always be interfering.'

'How dare you?'

'And you're quite wrong about Flora. She's a wonderful doctor – the most dedicated, compassionate, hard-working woman I know.'

'What's she got to do with anything?' the major barked.

'Everything,' Charles said with passion. 'I don't want Hauxley's patronage or a comfortable parish. My place is at the Settlement – that's where I'm needed. And that's where Flora is, so that's where I want to be. I want to marry her, but if she won't have me, I'll make do with her friendship.'

'Charles, that's wonderful!' Sophie cried.

'Marry that woman?' his father thundered. 'Not while I'm alive and breathing you won't!'

'I'm sorry if you can't see what a splendid person she is,' Charles defended, 'but you can't stop me.'

'I can – I'll disinherit you!'

Charles looked at him pityingly. 'It would be a relief not to inherit all this,' he cried.

'Don't be such a pig-headed fool—'

Charles walked past him.

'You're making a huge mistake. Your older brother would never have been so stupid. I'm ashamed of you!' his father raged.

Charles turned at the door. 'I know you are, Papa,' he said, saddened by the realisation. Then with a small bow of dignity, he walked out.

Flora was woken by urgent knocking at her front door. She threw on her dressing gown to answer it before Nell or Mrs Raine were woken. It would be some anxious patient with a feverish child, no doubt.

'Charles?' she exclaimed. 'What are you doing – what's happened?'

'Let me in, Flora, please?' he said in agitation. She stood aside at once.

'Is it Sophie? Has she had a turn for the worse? I'll come immediately if she needs me.'

Charles spun round in the hallway. 'No, not Sophie. It's me . . .'

'Charles, whatever's the matter?'

Running his hands in his habitual manner through his

unkempt hair, he suddenly became aware of her undressed state. He blushed and stammered, 'I'm so sorry – I've got you out of bed. I shouldn't have come this late—'

Flora stepped towards him. 'For goodness' sake, tell me.'

He studied her bare feet. 'I've turned Hauxley down. I want to stay at the Settlement. Papa's thrown me out.'

'Oh, Charles, I'm sorry . . .'

'Don't be. It's a blessed relief.' He met her gaze. 'And I couldn't have done it without your words ringing in my head about standing up to him.'

'I didn't mean—'

He reached out and seized her hand. 'He didn't throw me out for turning down the parish – he did it because I said I was going to marry you.'

'Charles!'

'I told him how wonderful you were and that if I couldn't marry you I would settle for friendship. I know you said you didn't want to marry me, but maybe in time you might change your mind . . . ?' He looked at her, unsure.

Flora put her hands up to his face and smiled. 'I want us to marry.'

'You do? But you said—'

'It's you I want, Charles. Not Blackton Heights or a fancy vicarage. If you are really free from all that, then yes, I long for us to be married.'

Charles gave a laugh of triumph. He flung his arms about her and hugged her tight.

'What's all the noise about?' a sleepy Nell asked from the top of the stairs.

They turned guiltily, but Charles would not let her pull away.

'Flora has agreed to marry me! Isn't that the most wonderful news?'

Nell's pretty face lit up. 'About time too. I thought you were never going to ask Dr Flora.'

'Nell!' Flora reproved.

Charles laughed. 'How right you are, Nelly.'

She descended the stairs, her face eager. 'Does that mean we all get to live up at Blackton Heights? Eeh, wait till I tell our Emmie. She'll be green as a peasouper with envy!'

Charles and Flora exchanged glances.

66

'No, Nell,' Flora answered, 'it most certainly does not.'

The smile died on her face. 'But the wedding will be up there?'

Charles sighed. 'I'm afraid not.'

'We'll marry in the Settlement chapel,' Flora declared. 'There could be no better place.'

Nell's mouth curled in disgust. She whipped round and stamped back up the stairs in utter disapproval.

CHAPTER 8

Emmie stood at the back of the packed chapel, craning for a view of Dr Flora and Mr Oliphant.

'It's to be a quiet wedding,' Mabel Runcie had told her, so Emmie was pleased to be asked. But standing there, among the throng of well-wishers, she realised just how popular the couple were with local people. This was no consolation to Nell. She had railed at Emmie on several occasions that summer.

'Fancy not getting wed up at Blackton Heights! And none of the Oliphants will be there. They've cut him off without a farthing, so I've heard.'

'Miss Sophie will come,' Emmie had reassured.

'She might if the fancy takes her,' Nell was scathing. 'She'll make a grand entry and take all the attention. And it's me who's supposed to be bridesmaid – Dr Flora promised.'

'It'll be a grand day,' Emmie insisted.

'How can it, when it's at the Settlement?'

'But it's a bonny chapel. Me and Mrs Mousy are ganin' to decorate it. Uncle Jonas said I can pick all the flowers I want from the allotment.'

'Won't hide the smell of the riffraff who turn up.' Nell was dismissive.

'Nelly!'

'Well, it's true,' she pouted. 'Most of them come from the slums.'

'Just like we did, you mean?' Emmie said.

Nell's look was furious. 'Don't ever talk like that to me! I remember when we were respectable folk, living in a grand house, even if you don't.'

Emmie grew impatient. 'And you live like that now, so why are you always complaining?'

'Because that precious Mr Oliphant is going to spoil it all,' Nell snapped.

'I thought you wanted them to wed?'

'I did, until Miss Flora started talking about us moving out the house.'

Emmie was surprised. 'Won't they set up house there together?'

'No,' Nell said angrily. 'She says we should move to the Settlement, 'cos Mr Oliphant needs to be resident at the mission. Mrs Raine doesn't want to move there and neither do I.'

'But, Nelly, we'll see more of each other if you do.' Emmie was enthusiastic.

Nell gave her a hard look. 'That's all right for you to say, but you can escape back to Crawdene after work. I'd have to stay there. It's not a home, it's an institution full of strangers coming and going all day long. If she thinks I'm going to live in that filthy part of town, she's wrong. I'll not go there, Emmie. They can't make me!'

Emmie had tried to calm her sister, but she would not be comforted.

Now, straining for a view of her in her pale yellow brides-maid's dress, Emmie thought she looked happy. Given time, Nell would come round to the idea of living at the Settlement.

She hardly had time to talk to her sister after the service. There was a large tea laid on in the dining hall, and Nell was surrounded by young men from the debating club while Emmie helped pour out endless cupfuls. Nell could change her expression and mood quicker than the weather, Emmie thought in amusement. With all this attention, perhaps Nell would settle into her new home quicker than she expected.

Just before Flora and Charles left for their brief honeymoon in Scotland, Flora sought out Emmie.

'Thank you for helping, kind girl,' she smiled.

'I've enjoyed it, Doctor. The day's flown over. You looked right bonny.'

Flora laughed. 'Take a box of food back with you, for Mrs MacRae, won't you?'

'Ta, Doctor.' Emmie nodded.

'And, Emmie,' Flora paused and glanced over at the laughing crowd around Nell, 'will you keep an eye on Nell while we're away? It's not that I don't trust her – I just don't want her getting moody and bored on her own. She hates not having company. But it's just for a few days.'

'Don't worry about Nelly,' Emmie smiled. 'I'll see if she'll come and stay with us for a day or two.'

Flora looked relieved. 'That would be kind.'

After that, the couple said their goodbyes, Charles giving Sophie an especially generous hug for defying their father and attending the wedding. They were waved away in a hired cab that was taking them to the station.

'Don't they look happy?' Mrs Mousy beamed, unusually emotional.

'Aye,' Emmie agreed.

The cook nudged her. 'It'll be you before long – or more likely your sister over there.'

Nell was still holding forth in the middle of a group of young people, some of whom Emmie recognised from the amateur productions in which her sister had acted.

Once Emmie had helped the Mousys clear and wash up, she looked for Nell, eventually finding her in the music room with some of the guests. They were gathered around the piano singing, Nell's strong voice soaring above them all. Emmie beckoned her over for a word and finally Nell came.

'Do you want to gan back to Crawdene with me? You can stay a few days while the doctor's away. She said she'd like you to.'

'Did she?' Nell snorted. 'And what about the MacRaes?'

'Aunt Helen wouldn't mind a bit – and I'd like you to come, Nelly.'

Nell considered. 'Is Sam still courting that friend of yours?'

'Louise? Aye.'

Nell glanced back at the others, who were calling her over for more singing. 'Maybes in a day or two,' she agreed swiftly. 'Aye, I'll come up to Crawdene – Tuesday or Wednesday.'

'Grand,' Emmie smiled. 'I'll call round for you after work.'

'No, don't do that – I'll make me own way up,' Nell answered.

She gave Emmie a quick kiss on the cheek and pushed her towards the door. 'Look after yourself.'

Cycling home, a box of food tied to the front basket, Emmie wondered about Nell's words. She was not convinced her sister would come; she had sounded half-hearted. She seemed much more interested in the singsong round the piano. Emmie did not mind, as long as she was happy. It had made her nervous when Nell had asked about Sam. The last thing she wanted was her flirtatious sister causing trouble between Sam and Louise, just for a bit of sport.

It was a calm summer's evening, lacking the usual wind off the fell. As she drew nearer the village and home, Emmie felt contented at the sight of men digging in their gardens, back doors thrown open to catch the soft breeze, and the sound of children calling down the back lanes.

She pondered Mrs Mousy's teasing words. *It'll be you before long . . .*

Emmie smiled to herself. If she could be half as happy with a man as Dr Flora appeared to be, then maybe she would marry.

Tom had been increasingly attentive these past months, since the incident over Miss Sophie. He was kind and brought her presents, hung around waiting at the end of China Street so he could walk her to the shops. Sometimes she caught him watching her during Sunday services; he would wink and make her blush.

'Come and watch me play footy in Lawson's Paddock,' he encouraged.

'I'd rather read a book,' she always replied with a laugh, dodging out of the way before he could kiss her.

Tom was playful and uncomplicated, sometimes funny, occasionally bad-tempered. She enjoyed his company more often than not. Emmie looked out for Tom now, half hoping to see his lean, loping figure saunter out of the shadows, hands in pockets, watching out for her. But tonight there was no sign of him. Probably, with the long summer evenings, he was kicking a football around with his friends. She felt a momentary pang of disappointment.

Humming, Emmie pushed the bicycle up the back lane and into the yard. Laughter reverberated out of the open door. Beyond the scullery, the kitchen sounded full. She squeezed her way past a couple of neighbours, friends of Jonas's.

'Here's our Emmie!' they cried.

Emmie smelled whisky on their breath as they made way for her. Jonas had a bottle out on the table he kept for special occasions. He was beaming. But it was the sight of Helen, her face red and puffy as if she had been crying, that made her stomach lurch.

'What's ganin' on?' she asked breathlessly.

'Oh, pet!' Helen threw out her arms. 'What a day this has been! Haway in and see for yourself.'

There was laughter as they pushed her forward. A bearded, dark-haired man rose from a stool by the hearth. There was something familiar in his brawny stance and the keen, blue-eyed look. Her heart thumped.

'Little Emmie?' He stared at her, equally disbelieving.

'Rab?' she gasped.

'Aye, it's the prodigal returned,' Jonas boomed.

Rab held open his arms and grinned. Emmie flew at him with a squeal of delight.

'I cannot believe . . . ! Why didn't you say . . . ?'

They hugged tight and suddenly Emmie was overcome. A huge sob rose up inside and she burst into tears.

'Emmie,' Rab laughed and cuddled her, 'it's more of a shock for me. I turn me back for a minute and you've gone and grown up into a beautiful lass.'

'A minute? Years, more like,' Emmie half laughed, half cried. 'What's the beard for? Do all revolutionaries have to wear them?'

'Aye, of course,' he chuckled. 'I see you haven't lost any of your cheek.'

He loosened his hold. Emmie quickly wiped away her tears, trying to compose herself.

Helen fussed around, pushing Emmie into a seat at the table and pressing food on her, while gabbling out the story of Rab turning up on the doorstep at midday. The house had been a circus ever since, she complained, but the look of adoration she gave Rab told how happy she was.

'I've a parcel of food on the bike,' Emmie remembered, pushing the plate of baking away. 'I've had a big tea, thanks, Auntie Helen.'

'Aye, tell us all about this society wedding you've been to,' Rab teased. 'I hear I'm the only MacRae who isn't a personal friend of the Oliphants these days.'

Jonas let go an oath and Helen gave him a sharp look. Rab laughed.

'It was a canny weddin',' Emmie smiled. 'They're good people, so don't you mock. Some folk just talk of social change — others get on and do it.'

Sam guffawed. 'That's one-nil to our Emmie, Rab!'

Rab pulled on his beard ruefully. 'And apart from the debating society, what do they do at the Settlement to change the world?' he needled.

'They give lectures in every kind of subject, and run music clubs — drama, art. Some of the unions hold their meetings there and they have campaigns to press for better conditions — sanitation and that. And there's the chapel—'

'Ah,' Rab cried, as if he had caught her out, 'religion — the opium of the people. It's just a bourgeois trick to keep the people passive.'

'One-all,' Sam chimed in.

'Don't talk daft,' Emmie said hotly. 'You can be socialist and Christian at the same time.'

'Course you can, pet,' Helen agreed. 'Don't rise to the bait.'

But Emmie was stirred. 'And there's the printing press. We print all sorts for the ILP and suffrage societies.'

'Aye,' Jonas joined in, 'our Emmie's a suffragette these days.'

'Middle-class ladies chaining themselves to railings in between tea parties,' Rab goaded. 'But what do they do for working-class lasses, eh? It's universal suffrage we need, not just for bourgeois women.'

'Ding-ding! Two-one to Rab, Emmie,' Sam chortled.

'Oh, shut up, the pair of you,' Emmie cried. 'There's nowt bourgeois about the Runcies' printing press — come and see for yourself if you don't believe me. And you're wrong about the vote. Plenty men already have it, but not one lass does. We'll fight the lot of you to have our say in how the country's run — no matter what class we're from. We don't care about that — we lasses stick together!'

'Knock out punch from Miss Emmie Kelso,' Sam shouted. 'I declare her the winner.'

Laughter rang around the crowded kitchen. Rab uncrossed his

arms and gave Emmie's hair a playful rub. She pushed him off and straightened it down.

'Oh, lass, how I've missed all this. It's grand to be back,' he grinned fondly.

'Aye,' she relented with a laugh, 'I've missed you an' all.'

CHAPTER 9

Emmie was so overjoyed at having Rab back that it was a couple of days before she thought about Nell's promise to come up to Crawdene. She was hardly surprised when her sister did not appear on the Tuesday or Wednesday; she was probably happy ordering Mrs Raine about in the doctor's absence, and inviting friends round to the house.

So it was a shock when Flora came rushing into the printing works, the day they returned from honeymoon.

'Have you seen your sister?' she demanded, quite flustered. 'Is she at the MacRaes'?'

'No, Doctor. She never came.'

'But Mrs Raine says she left on Monday, telling her she was going to stay with you. She was expected back two days ago.'

Emmie grew alarmed. 'She talked about it, but didn't. I haven't seen her all week. Oh, miss, what do you think's happened? Shall we call the police?'

Flora looked aghast. 'No, not the police.'

'Maybe's she's gone to Dolly's.'

'No, they had a falling-out – Nell thought Dolly too common.'

'Her acting friends then?' Emmie suggested. 'She was singing with those lads from the debating society the last time I saw her – the afternoon of the weddin'. Maybe she's gone to stay with a friend till you got back – you know she doesn't like to be on her own.'

'Did she say anything to you?' Flora asked urgently. 'Can you remember if she spoke of going away somewhere?'

'No, nothing,' Emmie said, feeling guilty. 'I meant to go round and see her. But you see, Rab came back – and the house has been full of visitors since.'

'Rab!' Flora softened. 'Oh, Emmie, that's good news. I'm so glad. I didn't mean to snap at you – it's just I'm worried about Nell.' She sank on to a chair.

'Doctor,' Emmie said tentatively, 'there is one thing.'

Flora looked at her in hope.

'Nell wasn't happy about having to move – to come and live here. Maybe she's taken off somewhere . . .'

Flora covered her face with her hands and groaned. Emmie went to her and put an arm around her shoulders in comfort. Flora looked up at her with eyes welling with tears.

'She's run away, hasn't she? She's planned this and it's all my fault.'

'We don't know—' Emmie began.

'Yes, I'm sure of it.' Flora cut her short. 'I insisted that we would move into the Settlement to be with Charles and his work. Nell made a fuss, but I thought she'd come round to the idea.'

'Aye, so did I,' Emmie admitted.

'So that's why she's gone. I've driven her away.' Her look was harrowed. 'I know your sister can be difficult, but she livens up my home – my life. I love her like a daughter.'

'She'll be back,' Emmie said kindly. 'She's never been as happy as with you, Dr Flora. I think she was a bit jealous of Mr Charles taking you away. This is her way of gettin' a bit attention. Anyways, she'll not last long on her own without money and that.'

Tears spilled down Flora's cheeks. 'She's taken money from the surgery – and jewellery from my dressing table.'

'Never!' Emmie was shocked. 'Nell's not a thief.'

'The money's not important. What hurts is that she has so little regard for me – that she couldn't talk to me first.' Flora's look was full of pain. 'Why, Emmie? Why would she do that after all I've done for her?'

Emmie was speechless, too stunned that Nell could have stolen from the kind doctor and then disappeared without even a word to her own sister!

Flora shook her head. 'I thought I knew Nell; now I'm not sure I know her at all.'

Word soon went round the Settlement and the community beyond that Dr Jameson's foster daughter had run away. No one had seen her since the wedding weekend or taken her in. But she had been spotted leaving Saltwell Park on the Sunday with a man who helped out at the drama club. Jackman was a drifter, a one-time music-hall artist, a good talker. He had left Gateshead too. Flora grew angry that Nell could have been so reckless, but as Charles pointed out, she was a grown woman who had just turned twenty-one and they could not stop her making her own mistakes.

The rumour about the stolen money and jewels spread too, probably by a disaffected Mrs Raine, who did not want to housekeep at the Settlement. Too often, Flora had to intervene in arguments between her housekeeper and the Mousys.

Weeks went by and no news came of Nell. Emmie experienced again the feeling of vulnerability and loss of someone close to her disappearing. She worried for her sister, yet felt bursts of anger that she had gone without thinking of the consequences. Rab seemed to sense her mixed feelings the most.

'She probably felt guilty the minute she was gone,' he told her, 'after the relief of getting away.'

'Then why doesn't she write?' Emmie pointed out. 'Even you sent a postcard so we knew you were alive.'

'Maybe she thinks no one will be bothered that she's gone.'

'She's just selfish, that's what.'

Rab said gently, 'Nell may want to come home but thinks she won't be welcome after what she's done. It was different for me – I knew I'd be welcome.'

'How?'

'Because of those canny long letters you sent – made me feel like I was right there in Crawdene.' Rab smiled at her. 'You've no idea how much they meant to me, Emmie.'

Rab's return compensated greatly for the worry and guilt over Nell's disappearance. Emmie thought life at China Street would return to how it was before Rab went away. But it could not. Nearly three years had passed and Rab had changed. He was still fun and full of conversation, able to infuriate and make his family laugh in equal measure. But at times he would fall silent, introspective, as if he was far away in a place where none of them could reach him.

'Tell me what Glasgow was like,' Emmie would urge. He would describe tall tenements and noisy shipyards, large families packed into one or two rooms.

'What about the shops, the theatres?'

Rab would shrug. 'Where the rich folk gan, you mean? We took our entertainment where we could find it – in the bars or the cheap concert halls.'

He often talked affectionately about the characters in his boarding house, or those at his night classes.

'And the lasses – what were Scottish lasses like?'

He would give her a strange look. 'No different from anywhere else.' But after such questions he would go quiet, brooding almost. Someone had taught him to play the piano and he would disappear to the tin-roofed hall to play slow airs and melancholy tunes.

Emmie and Helen speculated on what had happened.

'He doesn't like being asked about lasses,' Emmie said. 'Even Sam can't get out of him whether he's been courtin'.'

'I think he's had his heart broken,' Helen sighed, 'and that's why he's come home. Not that he'll ever tell us.'

After a month of sleeping on the truckle bed in the kitchen, Rab moved out of the cottage. Now that Emmie had half the attic curtained off as her bedroom, there was no room upstairs, and they all knew he would have to go sooner or later. He rented a downstairs room in India Street from Mannie, a retired saddler and friend from the Clarion Club, and went back to work at the Liddon pit.

That autumn he began teaching classes in politics and literature at the Miners' Institute in Blackton, so that Emmie saw even less of him.

One day, early in 1910, he sought her out.

'Will you take me to see this printing press at the Settlement?' he asked, almost shyly.

'You mean, that bourgeois printing press?' she smirked.

'Aye, that one,' he smiled.

'Why the sudden interest?'

'I'm thinking of starting a news-sheet – a political one – let people air their opinions.' He eyed her, as if seeking approval. 'I want to see how much it would cost.'

Emmie nodded. 'Come down next Saturday while I'm at work and talk to the Runcies.'

By the time Saturday afternoon came, she was full of excitement and kept rushing to the door of the printworks whenever she heard footsteps cross the icy quad. Miss Sophie breezed in to discuss a fund-raising leaflet and found Emmie telling her employers all about Rab, right from the time he had fetched her as a frightened, sickly child from the station in Swalwell.

'He doesn't sound like the two-headed radical monster my father thinks he is,' Sophie joked. 'But maybe he should publish his news-sheet under a different name from MacRae.'

Just at that moment, Rab came stamping in out of the cold.

'And why would I want to do that?' Rab asked with a quizzical smile, pulling off his cap.

Emmie rushed over and drew him into the warmth, proudly introducing him all round. He seemed unusually tongue-tied, but the kind Runcies soon put him at his ease, pressing a mug of hot tea into his frozen hands and asking him about the news-sheet.

'I'll have to charge for it – maybe a penny or tuppence,' Rab suggested.

'Weekly or fortnightly?' Mr Runcie asked.

'Haven't thought . . .'

'You could try and get advertisers,' Emmie suggested.

Rab laughed. 'Get the capitalists to pay towards their extinction, eh?'

'Donations,' Sophie suddenly announced. 'That's how we pay for newsletters. You need a fund-raiser for your cause.'

Rab stared at her. 'My readers are not going to be the type with money to throw around like you suffragettes.'

'Suffragists, if you don't mind,' Sophie corrected him with a cool smile. 'And you don't know yet who your readers will be. Presumably you want to attract as wide an audience as possible – not just preach to the converted?'

'Miss Sophie's right,' Emmie agreed.

Rab seemed lost for words.

'Do you have any examples of articles or editorial?' Philip Runcie prompted.

Rab dug into an inner pocket and pulled out some crumpled pieces of exercise paper. Philip skimmed over them and passed them around. Rab sat tensely while they read. Emmie gave him a reassuring smile.

'Perhaps a monthly issue to start with?' Mabel suggested. 'Test the water?'

'You say you are going for a variety of opinions, Mr MacRae?' Sophie's look was challenging.

'Aye,' he answered stifly. 'There's little enough free opinion allowed around Crawdene and Blackton.'

'Do you mean by my father – or the union officials who intimidate women suffrage campaigners?' she answered sharply. Rab's protest was cut short. 'I suggest you offer your pages to guest writers, covering the themes of the day. They might not be the editor's opinion, but will provoke debate on the issues.'

'Such as women's suffrage?' Rab grunted.

'Precisely,' Sophie nodded.

'And you, no doubt, would like to write the first article, Miss Oliphant?' he asked, his tone sardonic.

Sophie gave a broad smile. 'If that's a commission, I'd be happy to accept. Though I think I should write under a *nom de plume*, to avoid giving my father a seizure.'

After that, the afternoon passed in lively talk and planning of the first issue. They argued over content, layout and what to call it, agreeing finally on the *Blackton Messenger*, to be sold fortnightly for a penny-ha'penny.

Sophie gave Emmie and Rab a lift in her brougham as far as Blackton crossroads. As Rab pulled up his collar against the frost, she quipped, 'Don't worry, it's too dark to have been spotted riding with an Oliphant.'

He glanced up at her. 'Or for one of your father's spies to have seen you giving succour to a MacRae.'

They heard her laugh as she drove off into the gloom. Emmie slipped an arm through Rab's as they walked up the hill to Crawdene.

'It went well this afternoon, didn't it?' she asked. 'I told you they were canny people.'

'Aye, you were right,' Rab agreed. 'Maybe I'll get the Runcies to write a piece about the Quakers – how they opposed the Boer War.'

'Ooh, a religious article,' Emmie teased. 'This news-sheet is sounding dangerously bourgeois.'

Rab squeezed her arm. 'You're right again. See what happens when I spend half a day in the company of the middle class!'

They walked on in companionable silence.

'You liked her, didn't you?' Emmie suddenly asked.

'Who?'

'You know who – Miss Sophie,' Emmie laughed. 'Don't think I didn't notice the sly looks you were giving each other.'

'Don't be daft,' he blustered.

'Well, she took a liking to you.'

'Emmie,' he said impatiently, 'you've been reading too many penny romances while I've been away.'

Emmie laughed. 'So you haven't taken a fancy to her?'

'No!'

'Not even a tiny bit?'

'Give over, Emmie!'

As they reached the village outskirts, Emmie stopped to draw breath.

'Rab, have you ever been in love?'

'Why the sudden interest in love, Emmie?' he asked, amusement in his voice. 'Is it because you've fallen for a lad? It is, isn't it? I can see you blushing even in the dark!'

'Stop it.' She pulled away, embarrassed.

'It's not that Tom Curran?' He chuckled.

'What's wrong with Tom?' Emmie was stung.

'Nowt – for a good chapel boy,' Rab crowed. 'Bet the most exciting thing he's ever done is beat Ongarfield in the amateur league.'

'Just 'cos you've seen a bit of the world, doesn't mean you're any better than the likes of Tom,' Emmie reproved.

'No, course not. I'm sorry.' Rab threw an arm around her shoulders. 'I'm just being protective of me favourite lass. Tom's a canny enough lad.'

Mollified, she said, 'You never answered my question about being in love.' They began to walk on.

'Maybes I have been,' Rab admitted.

'How do you know?' Emmie questioned. 'How can you tell?'

'You want to be with that person all the time, I suppose. And it hurts when you're not.'

Emmie's heart twisted at his words. She suddenly envied whoever it was who had made Rab feel so strongly.

'Did you – love her enough to want to marry her?' Emmie whispered.

'Marry?' Rab's tone hardened. 'Don't confuse marriage with love.'

'But—'

'Marriage is a capitalist trick – it's all about money and property and amassing more of it. There's no freedom in marriage, Emmie – specially for lasses. Steer clear of it as long as possible, lass.'

Emmie was dashed by his words. They walked the rest of the way in silence. As they approached China Street, they saw a figure smoking under the gaslamp and stamping his feet to keep warm.

'It's Tom,' Emmie said, feeling awkward.

Tom ground out his cigarette, hurried forward and gave Emmie a bold kiss. He exchanged nods with Rab.

'Where've you been? I've been waiting ages.'

She began to tell him about the afternoon at the print shop, but he was not listening.

'If we hurry, there's a lantern slide show at the chapel the night. You can have your tea at ours.'

Emmie stood, feeling torn. She was annoyed with Rab for his dismissive remarks about Tom and marriage, yet she wanted to have an evening in his company, sitting around the MacRae kitchen table in lively conversation.

'Louise and Sam are ganin' too,' Tom said eagerly.

'I'll tell Mam you've gone to the Currans',' Rab offered swiftly.

'Right you are then,' Tom said, taking Emmie by the arm. 'Ta, Rab.'

Emmie glanced back at Rab and saw the amusement in his look. Her annoyance quickened. He could scoff all he wanted, but she was happy with Tom's attention and an evening of entertainment at the chapel. What did he know of love? He was too wedded to his pamphlets and politics to care. She would take love where she could find it, and right now she could feel it in the warmth of Tom's possessive arm round her waist and the admiring look in his hazel eyes.

She turned from Rab and slipped her arm through Tom's.

'Haway, tell me about the lantern show, then.'

CHAPTER 10

1911

That June, Emmie attended a huge suffrage rally, walking into Newcastle in the pouring rain behind one of the hundreds of banners. The Settlement was full of visitors, some of them from the Continent. Frau Bauer from Germany and Dr Korsky from Hungary fascinated her with their thick accents and their talk of international gatherings. They smoked and laughed a lot. In the evening, they sang in the suffrage choir together, wearing the green sash of the Women's Internationale. Everyone was optimistic. The Government was revising the Conciliation Bill to allow women the vote, and the suffragettes had responded with a truce and a halt to window breaking.

At eighteen, Emmie was enjoying life. She loved her work at the Settlement, with its constant activity and variety of people. She often worked late for the Runcies and on Fridays joined in the choir practice. Sometimes, she managed to persuade Rab to sing with the Settlement choir.

'It's not a church choir – we sing all sorts,' she cajoled, 'and we're short of bass singers.'

Through the summer there were trips to surrounding villages and towns to perform at open-air concerts or church halls. Tom, Louise and Sam would turn up to watch.

Emmie was flattered by Tom's interest and the way he came and stood possessively by her when refreshments were being served, so everyone knew they were courting. She had grown fond of Tom. He worked hard, saved carefully, did not drink, was reliable and loyal. When they went out together with Louise and

Sam, he was good company. He teased her in a kind way, held her hand and, at the end of the evening, pulled her into the shadows and kissed her on the mouth, making her heart hammer.

When Sam proposed to Louise, with Mr Curran's permission, and she accepted, everyone looked to Tom and Emmie. But every time she thought Tom was about to bring up the subject of marriage, Emmie changed the conversation.

One time, Tom lost patience. 'You know what I want, Emmie. I want us to be wed, like Sam and Louise. I love you, Emmie. Don't you love me?'

Emmie squirmed with embarrassment. 'Aye, but . . .'

'But what?' Tom cried, baffled.

'I'm only eighteen; we've plenty time,' she countered.

'I've saved up enough, Emmie. We can afford our own place. There's two rooms ganin' for rent in Berlin Terrace. Just think of it? Our own home. No one telling us what to do, plenty space. You can do it up however you like. How grand would that be, eh?'

Emmie felt a surge of excitement at his talk. He wanted her that much. The thought of having their own place also thrilled her. No more sharing a stuffy attic with the noisy MacRae boys, or tripping over each other in the cramped kitchen. And Berlin Terrace was not far from China Street so she could call in whenever she wanted and go round for Saturday tea.

'Give me time to think about it,' Emmie answered, giving him an encouraging peck on the cheek.

She put off making a decision all summer. Only to herself could Emmie admit the real reason for her indecision: Rab. For the truth was, Emmie had always adored him. From the very first time she had clung to his back and nestled her face in his curly hair, on the way up to Crawdene, she had loved Rab MacRae. When Rab had said that love was always wanting to be with the same person, Emmie had known for sure. She felt a dull ache when he was not there and lived in anticipation of the next meeting. Ridiculous to think he might ever marry her; he had made his contempt for marriage plain and never once had he given her reason to hope. He did not love her in that way and would be astonished if he knew just how much she cared for him.

Even though Emmie knew it was fruitless to go on hoping, a

small part of her believed that if she waited long enough, waited until she was older and wiser, Rab would grow to love her. All at once, he would see her as an equal, a grown woman, and not just little Emmie. This was why she put Tom off every time he pushed for them to get wed.

Rab came to the printing press whenever he had a spare moment. His news-sheet was popular but struggled to finance itself. Emmie knew that Miss Sophie kept it afloat with anonymous donations, but she was sworn to secrecy. Rab assumed his patron was some prosperous freethinker, a Quaker or a union leader.

Emmie was well aware that Miss Sophie always happened to call in at the press on evenings when Rab would be busy preparing the *Messenger*. It was obvious to all of them, apart from Rab himself, that Oliphant's daughter was in love with him. Emmie tried to quell her feelings of jealousy.

Finally, Mabel Runcie let slip her concern. 'It worries me where it might lead. Sophie is so used to getting her own way. Even Charles has cautioned her about being foolish over Rab. Philip spoke to him about it – and we've tried to dissuade her from coming in quite so often.'

Emmie was startled. 'But she can't possibly think of marrying Rab!'

'She's quite capable of thinking such a thing, even though it's out of the question,' Mabel fretted. 'It would be just like her to defy her father and make Rab elope with her. Social differences mean nothing to her – and she is brave enough and foolhardy enough to do just about anything.'

'Rab would never do such a thing,' Emmie was adamant. 'He is very aware of social differences, however much he detests them.'

'Yes, my dear, that may be true. But Miss Sophie is very much in love with him – she's told her brother as much. Rab might find the attention flattering, might even be tempted to enter into a liaison to defy Oliphant. Sophie can act impulsively and regret her rashness later. She has a rich father to run back to – but what of Rab? He could lose his job.'

Suddenly, it struck Emmie that what Mabel said was true. Rab could be impulsive too. He had run off to Glasgow without a thought to the future; he could do it again.

Mabel looked at her pleadingly. 'Perhaps you could have a word with him – warn him to give her no encouragement?'

When Emmie plucked up the courage to tackle Rab about Miss Sophie's infatuation, he laughed it off as ridiculous. They were crossing the quad towards the printworks, having been to a Saturday lunchtime lecture. Emmie noticed the Oliphant brougham through the far archway and her heart sank.

'It's not just me. Mrs Runcie's worried too,' she said.

'Women's gossip.' Rab was derisive.

'You're the only one who doesn't see it,' Emmie said, stopping him with a hand on his arm.

He looked at her with amusement. 'And why are you so concerned for my moral welfare? I was a lost cause years ago.'

She blushed furiously under his blue-eyed gaze.

'Listen, what if she says something indiscreet to Major Oliphant – implying there is something between you? He could have you sacked – or the family evicted like he's threatened before. Have you thought of that?'

Rab shook his head in disbelief. 'But there's nothing between us. I only see her when I come to the Settlement – if she happens to be around.'

'She plans it, Rab. Sometimes she waits around all day in the hopes you'll come in.'

'Don't be daft.'

'It's true. Why else do you think she helps out on the *Messenger*? She doesn't believe in socialism or the anarchist movement. She just wants it to be a success for you. Look,' Emmie pointed to the carriage, 'she's here again.'

Rab pulled on his beard, growing uneasy.

'But she has other things to do here. She doesn't help me that much—'

'Doesn't help?' Emmie threw up her hands in frustration. 'She keeps it ganin' with her money. There wouldn't be a *Messenger* without her.'

Rab stared. 'What do you mean?'

'Those monthly donations –' Emmie said pityingly – 'who do you think's got the money to pay for them?'

Rab looked dumbstruck. 'Miss Sophie?'

Emmie nodded.

Rab gave a mirthless laugh. 'Oliphant's money. What a daft fool I've been.' He pushed past her.

'Rab, wait,' Emmie said, alarmed by his thunderous look. 'What are you ganin' to do?'

'Have it out with her.'

Emmie rushed behind, pleading with him not to say anything rash. Sophie turned, startled by the door banging open. Her smile of greeting turned to confusion at Rab's sharp words.

'The money for the *Messenger*,' he demanded, 'is it Oliphant's?'

Sophie flushed. 'It's my money – not that you were supposed to know.' She threw an accusing look at Emmie.

'No! You didn't want me to know that all the work I'd done was built on Oliphant charity. Blood money squeezed out the pitmen – that's what's been keeping the *Messenger* going!'

'There's no need to be so dramatic,' Sophie defended. 'What does it matter where the money comes from? I did it because it means so much to you.'

'I'm not one of your little causes,' Rab cried. 'I thought you believed in what we were doing.'

'I totally disagree with most of it.' Sophie was blunt. 'But I agree with your right to print it – as long as it doesn't incite bloody revolution.'

Rab cried out with impatience. The Runcies withdrew quickly, beckoning Emmie to follow.

'I did it for you, Rab,' Sophie tried to explain. 'I care for you greatly.'

He stared at her, disbelieving. 'Don't talk daft.'

Sophie went to him and grabbed his hand. 'I'm not. I've fallen in love with you – and I know you have feelings for me too, don't you?'

Emmie glanced back from the doorway. Rab was shaking his head. She hurried out, but could still hear them.

'How could I? You're an Oliphant—'

'You don't care for social differences and neither do I,' Sophie declared. 'I'll find a way for us to be together – just tell me you care for me too.'

'I can't deny I like your company,' Rab admitted, his anger deflating. 'But it would be impossible—'

'Nothing's impossible,' Sophie said eagerly. 'We could run away to Glasgow together – live in that commune you told me about.' She pressed his hand to her lips.

Rab pulled away gently. 'And when you've tired of free love and me, what then? You go back to Oliphant and your life of privileges – I'm out of work.'

'I'm not some silly child playing games,' Sophie reproached. 'I want to be with you.'

'You don't know me,' Rab answered. 'If you did, you would know that I'd never give up me work here to follow you.'

'That job at the pit?' Sophie was scathing. 'You can do better than that.'

'That's just to put bread in me mouth,' Rab said. 'My real work is teaching – and the *Messenger* – doing my bit to bring about socialist revolution. So that men like me father are not beholden to men like yours. Or me to you.'

'I don't want you beholden to me either.' Sophie was impatient. 'I want us to be equal in marriage.'

'Marriage?' Rab said in derision.

'Yes, marry me, Rab!' she urged. 'Now do you see how serious I am about you?'

Rab was amazed. 'You'd really give up everything you've got to marry me?'

'Why would I have to give it up?' Sophie asked. 'We could live on my private income – and you could teach or do your newsletter anywhere you choose.'

Rab gave a short laugh. 'I can't say I'm not tempted.'

'Then let's do it,' Sophie cried.

'No!' Rab was suddenly serious. 'How could I live off capitalist money and preach socialism at the same time? We can never be together – not as long as the class system exists.' He gave a wry smile. 'Come back and ask me after the revolution.'

'Don't be flippant; I'm being serious.'

'And so am I,' Rab said.

She looked at him in frustration. 'There's someone else, isn't there? You're promised to someone else. You can't accept me, out of loyalty to another woman.'

'No . . .'

'Is it Emmie?' Sophie demanded.

'Emmie? Course not – she's just a young lass.'

'Then who?'

'Nobody,' Rab said in frustration. 'I've no intention of getting wed to any lass – not even you. I don't love you, Sophie, and I don't want to take your money either.'

She glared at him, scarlet with indignation. 'So you throw my love and my help back in my face! What a fool you make me feel.'

'I didn't mean to,' Rab answered.

'No,' she said, turning away. 'Nevertheless, I feel very foolish. Foolish to have so misjudged your feelings for me.' She grabbed her hat and gloves from the table. 'I'll not trouble you again, Mr MacRae. You'll no longer have to endure my presence at the *Messenger*.'

'Sophie, please—'

'Don't call me that!' she cried. 'We are no longer friends on equal terms. You have made it quite clear that is not what you want.'

She pushed past him and stormed from the room, nearly knocking Emmie out of the way in the entrance as she rushed for her carriage.

'There was no need to tell him about the money,' Sophie accused, looking on the verge of tears.

'It just came out,' Emmie said, embarrassed.

'I'm not taken in by that,' Sophie answered bitterly. 'You're all against me – you, the Runcies, my brother. Why don't you want me to be happy with Rab? What is so frightening about that?'

'Your father would never accept it,' Emmie answered back.

'My father has nothing to do with this—'

'Aye, he does,' Emmie persisted. 'He has power over all of us – our jobs, our houses, even you, Miss Sophie, no matter how much you gan on about being equal with men.'

For a moment, Sophie stared at her with a mix of anger and sorrow.

'Don't be so impertinent!' she cried, then swept past without another word. In minutes, the brougham was clattering away from the Settlement.

Emmie went into the printing room, glancing warily at Rab. She had overheard everything, including his dismissive comment about herself. He was standing by the window, deep in thought. Emmie went back to her work, setting blocks on the printing press. He looked so shattered, as if realising too late he had made the wrong choice. She felt sick with guilt that the row between Rab and Miss Sophie was all her fault. She should have kept out of it, let the friendship take its own course.

As she bent her head to her task, Emmie faced up to the bleak truth. Rab did not love her in a romantic way. He had made it clear he was not the marrying kind. She should put behind her any silly thoughts of ever being Rab's wife.

Emmie heard him cross the room. She looked up to find him watching her, his face grim.

'How long have you known about the money?' Rab demanded.

'Several months,' Emmie admitted. 'What does it matter where the money came from? It was being put to a good use.'

'The principle matters!' Rab cried. 'I wouldn't take Oliphant's blood money if I was starving.'

'Then you're daft!'

'Maybes,' he glared, 'but that's the way I am.'

He marched from the room without another word.

Within a month, Rab had been sacked at the pit for arguing with the overman.

'They've been itching for an excuse to get rid of him,' Jonas protested to Helen. 'Ever since he's agitated over unfair rent allowances.'

Emmie wondered whether Sophie could have had any influence in the matter. Had she told her father about his talk of revolution? There was no way of knowing. Sophie no longer came to the printing works.

Soon, Rab's appearances at the Settlement almost stopped. The struggling *Messenger* was cut to a quarterly issue, the lack of funds made worse by gossip of an affair between Rab and Sophie Oliphant that scandalised the chapel readership. Further rumours that Rab was funded by the coal-owner caused derision among radicals, and sales almost dried up.

Rab took to knife-grinding among the pit villages and towns along the Tyne. He cycled for miles across County Durham, sharpening tools by day and teaching adult classes by night.

Emmie was impatient for independence and life as a grown woman. She was tired of being seen as young Emmie whom all the MacRaes felt they had to fuss over and protect, and she had given up on Rab completely. Finally, she agreed to marry Tom. He was cock-a-hoop. Immediately, he secured the two rooms in Berlin Terrace and set about decorating them with wallpaper chosen by Emmie from the co-operative store. His excitement was infectious and Emmie convinced herself that she would be happy with Tom. She threw herself into the wedding plans, overseen by Louise, her self-appointed expert on dress material, flowers and wedding teas.

Louise, alarmed that her brother and friend might marry before her, declared that she and Sam would be married on the third Saturday in September, and Tom and Emmie the following one. The month was taken up with comings and goings between the Currans and MacRaes, arguing over the details. The Currans planned a chapel wedding and a temperance tea for Louise and Sam; the MacRaes wanted a party at the Clarion Club with a dance and a barrel of beer for Emmie and Tom. The Currans threatened not to attend.

To stop the warring, Emmie announced that she intended getting wed in the Settlement chapel with tea and dancing in the dining hall afterwards. Tom was dubious, but Emmie talked him round.

'It means my friends at the Settlement can attend – and there won't be any drink, so your folks won't be offended. And Charles Oliphant has agreed to marry us.'

'Oliphant, eh?' Tom chuckled, taken by the idea.

Occasionally, Rab would turn up at China Street, looking leaner and longer-haired, to goad Sam about marriage to a Curran.

'Marrying the deputy's daughter,' he scoffed. 'We know you're just after Curran's bigger house.'

'Aye, that's right,' Sam retaliated, 'anything but have to share with you again.'

'You've turned into a right bourgeois bugger,' Rab snorted.

'Aye, well, when I'm gone to Curran's palace, you can have me bed in the attic. You'll need it now you're just a knife sharpener.'

'And a teacher, you cheeky—'

'Ooh, teacher,' Sam mocked. 'Bit middle class, isn't it?'

Emmie intervened. 'I hope you two aren't ganin' to argue like this at me weddin'?'

'If I was you,' Sam winked, 'I wouldn't invite him. He'll

probably stand up halfway through the service and start singing "The Red Flag".'

'Well, at least I still remember the words,' Rab laughed. 'Not like some class traitors.'

Bafflingly, Rab never made any comment on her own planned marriage. Until one day, when she went round to India Street with a box of eggs from Jonas. In the yard a rickety table piled with exercise books was abandoned in the mellow sunshine. The sound of classical music being hesitantly played on a piano was drifting out of the open door. Entranced, Emmie stopped and sat down on a stool by the door to listen.

When it was over, Rab came out, startled to find her there. Still, moved by the notes, Emmie blurted out, 'Who taught you to play like that?'

His face was reflective. 'A music teacher in Glasgow — she lived in the same boarding house.'

'Was she the one . . . you know, when we talked of being in love . . . ?'

Rab nodded. Emmie's insides twisted.

'What happened to her?' she asked quietly.

He gazed at the table with the pile of books unmarked and Emmie thought he would not answer.

'She had TB,' Rab said abruptly. 'She's dead.'

'I'm sorry,' Emmie murmured. She stood up and put the eggs on the table.

'Don't go,' Rab said suddenly. 'I'll fetch another stool.'

He brought out two mugs of lime cordial and they sat in the warm yard enjoying the moment. They talked of the Settlement and his teaching; they reminisced about the past. Emmie had not had such a long conversation with Rab in months. It was relaxed and affectionate. But there was an underlying awkwardness. Perhaps it was because Emmie had conjured up his dead lover or because each knew that their relationship was about to change. In less than two weeks, Emmie would be married. As Mrs Tom Curran, she would have a new set of priorities and obligations. One of them was not likely to be sitting in the sun chatting to him about literature and politics.

Suddenly, the light-hearted tone of the conversation died.

'Why are you getting wed, Emmie?' Rab asked abruptly, searching her face.

Emmie's heart jumped. "Cos – I want to."

'It won't be the same. You'll have to give up your work, be at Curran's beck and call.'

Emmie flushed. 'It won't be like that. I'll be carrying on at the Settlement.'

'Have you discussed it with Tom?' he asked.

'Not exactly. But I'll work until – well, till we have – if we have – bairns . . .'

His look made her cheeks burn hotter.

'What's it to you, any road?' Emmie exclaimed.

Rab leaned close and took her hands in his. 'Look at me, Emmie. You're a free spirit, like me. Just when you're growing up – beginning to see a bit of life – you turn your back on it all. For what? A bit more space to call your own and the title of missus. You're making a big mistake. Marriage to Tom won't suit you. It'll tie you down, lass. You're too young to be enslaving yourself to Curran.'

Emmie snatched her hands away. 'Enslaving? That's rubbish! I'm marrying 'cos I love Tom. It's nowt to do with two rooms in Berlin Terrace. Just 'cos you think marriage is a waste of time, doesn't mean everyone else does. You're still mad at me interferin' with you and Miss Sophie. That's it, isn't it? Well, I'm sorry about that. But it doesn't give you the right to tell me who I shouldn't marry!'

She sprang up. He stood and reached out to stop her going.

'Emmie, I'm sorry. I didn't mean to offend you. I didn't realise you felt that strongly for the lad.'

'Well, I do,' Emmie said, so flustered she just wanted to escape. Shaking off his hold, she rushed from the yard, leaving him staring after her.

The next time she saw him was at Sam's wedding, but they hardly spoke. Rab kept in the background. Sam had asked Tom to be his best man. Emmie saw Rab slip away before the end of the tea party.

A week later, it was her turn and any thoughts of Rab were pushed from her mind in the preparation and excitement of the day. Jonas hired a charabanc to take the wedding party down to Gateshead. Emmie was touched to see how Flora and Mrs Mousy had decorated the chapel and hall with ribbon and greenery and small sprays of flowers.

The afternoon passed in a blur of images: Charles Oliphant leading them through their vows, Tom's beaming face, serious words of congratulation from Barnabas Curran and jokes from Jonas. She remembered the fiddlers striking up a dance tune and Tom taking her in his arms and pulling her around the floor in a polka, more enthusiastic than nimble. Then her next memory was of a sea of faces, friends waving them away as a hired trap took the married couple back up the hill to Crawdene. When she thought about it later, she could not remember seeing Rab among the waving well-wishers.

She sat in her new kitchen while Tom coaxed the reluctant stove into life. It belched smoke at them.

'Let's just gan to bed,' Emmie yawned. But Tom was determined to get it going.

Emmie made ready for bed in the adjoining room. As she sat on the edge of their bed in her nightgown, wondering how long lighting a fire could take, she guessed that Tom was feeling as nervous as she was.

Finally, she heard him clearing up the hearth and going to wash in the scullery. When he joined her in the bedroom, he undressed with his back to her, pulling on a nightshirt that had been neatly starched and pressed by his mother. They climbed between the chilly sheets and shyly rubbed each other to warm up.

'Right then, lass,' Tom whispered, 'let's gan to it.'

He kissed her warmly on the mouth, stroking her dark hair away from her face. His hands fumbled with her clothing and Emmie tensed for what would come next. Helen had told her to think of something pleasurable, like a trip to the seaside or a concert, to help her relax.

'It'll make it gan over quicker,' Helen had said with a laugh.

Unbidden, the memory of sitting in a sheltered yard, listening to classical music, came to Emmie. She forced the image away. She thought of sitting by the fireside in China Street while Jonas read out the newspaper, of racing Sam and Rab up to Lonely Stones above Blackton Heights, of snowballing with the MacRae boys, of Helen singing her to sleep as a child . . .

Tom moved over her, kissing and squeezing, exploring her with nervous fingers. She must concentrate on pleasant thoughts of her new husband; Tom grinning at her from the audience in a choir concert, waiting for her at the street corner, slipping her kisses in the shadows. She was lucky to have him; he was one of the best-looking lads in the village, with a steady job and prospects at the pit. As Tom's wife she would have security and standing in the community. Today, she had shed her old identity as the Kelso lass from the slums taken in by the radical MacRaes. More than that, she was distancing herself from their colourful notoriety – the family who eschewed chapel for the socialist Sunday school, who hung out a red flag on Empire Day, whose mother was too busy going to meetings to keep her doorstep whitened or windows cleaned, whose eldest was nicknamed Radical Rab and peddled anarchy and social revolution in his news-sheets.

As Tom made love to her for the first time, Emmie realised how strong her desire had been to escape their shadow and forge a life of her own. She clung to Tom, the man who was offering her this new life. Although she would always be grateful to the kind family for taking her in and treating her like one of their own, it was exciting and frightening to have cut herself loose from the apron strings of the MacRaes.

Afterwards, she lay in Tom's hold, relieved it was over without too much pain and exultant that she was properly Mrs Curran. A fierce thought seized her: she would make a success of her marriage. She and Tom would make each other happy. She would prove Rab wrong.

CHAPTER 11

By the end of October, Emmie had given up work at the Settlement and singing for the choir. It was not that Tom had forbidden her to go, just that it did not fit in with his shifts. She cut down to half-days, then twice a week, then nothing. Tom needed a good hot meal in the late morning, before going on the back shift, and his bait made ready. Emmie did the shopping while he slept and left the noisy jobs of sweeping, banging mats, possing the washing and wielding the iron to the afternoon.

Tom slept lightly and complained if he did not get enough sleep. In the evening, when he returned from the hard labours of loading tubs of coal below ground, he expected a hot bath in front of the fire and a nourishing meal.

One evening, she came back from the weekly meeting at the Co-operative Guild to find him sitting at the table in his filthy clothes, bad-tempered and unfed.

'Where've you been?' he demanded.

'The Guild,' Emmie said in surprise, pulling off her jacket and hat. 'You haven't even washed—'

'There's nee hot water,' he grumbled.

'It's in the pot – what's that smell?' Emmie rushed to the stove to find the source of the burning. What remained of the broth was stuck to the bottom of a blackened pan. 'Why did you let this burn?'

'I didn't burn it, you did,' Tom accused.

'You could've taken it off the stove,' she said in exasperation, 'or helped yourself.'

'And you could've been here to serve it out. I slog me guts out all day long, don't I deserve a little attention at the end of the day?'

Emmie bit back a retort. He looked exhausted. There was no point in falling out over a pan of soup. She set to, filling the tin bath with hot water and putting together a hasty meal of egg and fried potatoes.

'Scrub me back, Emmie lass,' Tom smiled in forgiveness. He whistled as she did so, splashing her with water.

'Give over, Tom!' She tried to duck out of the way, but he grabbed her and gave her a wet hug and kiss.

'I just want to have you here with me,' Tom told her. 'It's what keeps me ganin' all the day – thinking of you back here waiting for me. I'm the luckiest lad in Crawdene.'

Emmie felt a flood of affection for him. She should be more content staying at home – a home that she had helped furnish and decorate. It still thrilled her to think it was hers and Tom's alone. Few lasses her age in the village had so much.

The following week, Emmie did not go to the Guild. Helen came round the following day to see if she was sick. Her calling out at the back door woke Tom. He stalked around the kitchen, scowling at the women, and Helen soon took the hint.

'Call in on your way back from the shops,' she told Emmie. 'I've a turnip and leeks from the garden.'

'Best not to come round on a morning,' Emmie whispered at the back door, as Helen left.

Tom grew to resent the occasions when Emmie rushed round to China Street for a recipe or advice on housekeeping.

'Why did you bother gettin' wed when you spend all your time round at their house?'

'I don't,' Emmie protested. 'I just gan when Uncle Jonas has some'at from the allotment for us – or for one of Auntie Helen's recipes.'

'Well, these leeks have got nee flavour. Any road, me mam makes a better leek puddin',' he declared. 'You should ask her.'

As Emmie's visits to the MacRaes dwindled, the number of times her mother-in-law visited increased. Mrs Curran would call in with a cake or steak and kidney pie, an invitation to Sunday dinner or a piece of advice.

'I don't wish to interfere,' she would always begin, 'but this is the way Tom likes his . . .' and she would launch into instructions on how best to bake pastry, or darn socks or fold an ironed shirt.

Emmie tried to concentrate and remember these household tips, feeling like the worst of apprentices. She realised how much Helen had done for her and how little she had enquired into domestic details. Or perhaps the Currans were just more fastidious than most about cleanliness and order.

To forestall these lectures and to get out of the house, Emmie took to visiting the Currans instead. She looked forward to an hour of chatter and companionship with Louise, when they would sit and sew or work on a hooky mat together.

'You're lucky having your own place,' Louise told Emmie. 'It'll be grand when me and Sam can do the same. Sam's not as good at saving as our Tom.'

Yet when Emmie and Tom went round for Saturday tea or Sunday dinner, Emmie could see how happy Louise and Sam were, even though living under the strictures of Barnabas Curran's rule. Sam laughed off any carping by his father-in-law and flattered his mother-in-law over her cooking. He ignored the snide remarks about Helen's lack of domestic skills. He even agreed to go to chapel.

'You shouldn't let them talk like that about your mam,' Emmie reproved, when they were walking back from chapel one wintry Sunday.

'I don't see you rushing to defend her either,' Sam pointed out.

'Aye, but she's your mam,' Emmie hissed, glancing round to make sure no one overheard, 'and it's not right.'

'Mam wouldn't give two hoots for what the Currans say about her,' Sam said in amusement, 'so neither will I.'

Emmie let it go, not wanting to argue. She enjoyed Sam's company, all the more because she was seeing less and less of the other MacRaes. Once a week, Peter would deliver groceries to the Reverend Mr Attwater's manse at the end of Berlin Terrace. Emmie would listen out for the horse-drawn van, and waylay Peter on his return.

'I've made a custard tart for you,' she would call, beckoning him in. He would sit on the same chair, methodically cutting up the tart into quarters and eating them in a clockwise direction, while Emmie plied him with questions.

'How's Mam? Shall I get your da some baccy for Christmas?

Are they workin' you hard? Is Rab still at the knife-grinding?'

Sometimes Peter would reply and sometimes not. His mam was knitting socks for orphans in Manchuria, or was it Manchester? Mr Attwater had ordered a goose for Christmas. Rab was doing a job in Gateshead, but Peter didn't think it had anything to do with knives. Emmie always sent him away with a sugar lump for the horse and kiss on the cheek. He always thanked her for the sugar and wiped off the kiss.

Just before Christmas, Emmie had a tearful argument with Tom.

'But I hardly ever see them. Why can't we gan round to China Street on Christmas Day? Auntie Helen asked us before your mam.'

'They don't even believe in Christmas,' Tom scoffed. 'No, we'll gan to chapel, then dinner at Mam's. They're expectin' us.'

'Then can we gan to China Street for our tea?' Emmie pressed him.

'You can if you want,' Tom said grudgingly.

Emmie thought of the humiliation of turning up at the MacRaes' without her husband, on her first Christmas as a married woman. She burst into tears. Tom hurried to console her.

'What you cryin' for?' He hugged her to him. 'We'll have a grand first Christmas. Think of it – waking up in our own home, just the two of us. Then the best dinner you're ever likely to eat and maybe a bit singsong with Sam and our Louise.' He kissed her. 'And if it means that much to you, we can call in on the MacRaes on our way home, eh?'

Emmie hugged him in gratitude.

'Aye, that'd be canny,' she sniffed and smiled.

By Christmas Day, Emmie was feeling unusually tired and unwell. She could not face half the food on her plate at dinner and Tom's mother insisted she lie down for the afternoon. It was dark and icy underfoot by the time they walked home.

'Better give the MacRaes a miss, eh?' Tom suggested.

'But I've got their presents,' Emmie said. 'We'll just stay a few minutes.'

'I can take them round the morra—'

'No, Tom, please,' Emmie insisted, though she wanted nothing more than to lie down and stop feeling sick.

They found the family in the middle of a raucous card game. Jonas and Rab were slamming down cards, Helen sweeping them off the table with shrieks of excitement while Peter held up the game with questions.

'Put out your seven of spades!' Jonas bellowed, as Emmie and Tom walked in.

Helen sprang up and rushed to embrace her.

'I knew you'd come! Didn't I tell you, Rab, she'd come?'

The game was abandoned as they made room for the visitors by the fire. Emmie rejected tea or anything to eat.

'Just a cup of water would be grand,' she smiled.

'She's not well,' Tom said stiffly, 'we won't be stoppin' long.'

'By, you look pale as milk,' Helen fretted, putting a hand to Emmie's forehead.

'That's what comes of being locked away by young Tom,' Rab teased. 'Pair of love birds.'

'Currans not feeding you well?' Jonas joined in. 'You should have more meals round here, Emmie.'

'It's nowt to do with me mam's food,' Tom said hotly. 'And I don't keep her locked up.'

Helen glared at the MacRae men. 'Don't listen to them, Tom, they're only teasing.'

'Tom, give out the presents,' Emmie said swiftly. There was soap for Helen, tobacco for Jonas, a tin of humbugs for Peter and a handkerchief for Rab, embroidered with his initials.

'It's not much but . . .' Emmie almost let slip that Tom had given her no money for presents. She had saved on the housekeeping to buy them gifts.

'They're grand, pet,' Helen assured.

'I'll think of you every time I blow me nose,' Rab grinned. 'I've something for you, Emmie.'

He rose and went to his canvas bag, pulling out a parcel wrapped in newspaper.

'That looks classy,' Tom sneered.

Rab laughed good-naturedly and handed it to Emmie. She unwrapped it to find a slim book of poems, a well-thumbed collection of nineteenth-century Romantics. Rab scratched his close-shaven beard while watching her.

'Thank you,' she said, with a quick glance at Tom, 'I'll look at it later.'

Tom was smirking at the worthless present. He had given her a large leather shopping bag, a bottle of lavender water and a soft woollen bed jacket. Emmie quelled her curiosity at the book and wrapped it up again.

Tom stood up. 'Haway, Emmie, it's time I got you home.'

Helen's face fell. 'But you haven't had your tea – stay a bit longer.'

Emmie avoided a row and followed Tom. 'I couldn't eat a thing. I'll call round soon,' she promised.

Helen held her at arm's length and looked her over. Then she nodded and let her go. Emmie hurried out after Tom, glad of the frosty air after the stuffy kitchen full of cooking and tobacco smells that made her nauseous. She slipped her arm through Tom's.

'I can't wait to get home,' she sighed.

He patted her arm and smiled in satisfaction. 'Aye, just the two of us.'

Helen turned from waving them away, her look thoughtful.

'What's bothering you, lassie?' Jonas demanded. 'They're young and want to get back to their own fireside.'

'Aye,' Helen agreed. 'And if I'm not mistaken, there'll be another one at their fireside, this time next year.'

'What's that?' Jonas asked. 'Speak up. What did you say?'

'I think our Emmie's expectin', that's what.'

CHAPTER 12

1912

Emmie stood in the shade of the back door, trying to catch some breeze. She could not get comfortable. The kitchen was too hot; the hard chairs made her back ache. The baby kicked within her, restless. It was difficult now to walk all the way to the shops and back without having to sit down, especially in the sudden hot spell of late June.

But she revelled in being pregnant. The Currans treated her like a queen, not letting her lift a finger. Even Louise, who had been miffed at Emmie becoming pregnant first, was now full of excitement at the impending birth and knitting endless hats and booties.

'Auntie Louise, eh? We can take the bairn out every day, once you're out of confinement.'

Helen called in when she knew Tom was at work and helped Emmie with the heavier chores of washing and blackening the grate. From her aunt, she heard news of the family and the wider world. Rab was working part time for the ILP, helping put out its weekly newspaper, so he had little time for knife-grinding.

'Getting a name for himself teaching night classes too,' Helen said proudly. 'They want him to start giving lectures at the Settlement come the autumn.'

'That's grand,' Emmie said with a small pang of envy. She had lost touch with her friends in Gateshead. She had not heard from Dr Flora since Christmas, and the occasional letter from Mabel's arthritic hand was hard to decipher. Yet she blamed herself for not keeping in touch. After writing with news of her forthcoming baby, Emmie had nothing to tell. Life was humdrum, one day much like the last.

Once she had started to feel less ill, Emmie had filled the days with preparing for the baby, sewing small sheets and knitting an elaborate shawl. Keeping house for her and Tom was now routine, and often on wet wintry days time had hung heavily while she waited for her husband's return. Talk of the Settlement made her restless. She did not tell Helen how much she missed her old job at times, as well as the modest wages. Now she had no money to call her own. For over two years she had earned ten shillings a week, five shillings to spend how she wanted after giving the rest in housekeeping to Helen.

Tom gave her twelve shillings' housekeeping every Friday night, before they went out to the chapel social. She had to account for every penny and pay the shortfall in rent not covered by the meagre allowance from Oliphant's coal company. Now she appreciated why Rab had protested so loudly at the unfairness. Tom paid into an insurance scheme, a burial fund, chapel collection and football subs. He treated himself to five Woodbines a week and kept their spare cash hidden in the linen drawer. Emmie did not dare help herself to any of it as Tom knew exactly how much was there. At least now that he had changed to the early shift, they were able to have a weekly evening out at the chapel, at little or no cost.

Helen came with other news too. That spring, she had fulminated at the defeat of the Conciliation Bill in Parliament. It sparked off a spate of window smashing and militancy.

'They're saying Miss Sophie got arrested,' she said, wide-eyed.

'Never! What for?' Emmie gasped.

'For chucking a brick through a town hall window in Gateshead,' Helen answered with glee. 'She's joined the suffragettes.'

'Is she in gaol?'

'No – magistrates let her off with a caution. They say one of them was that MP, Hauxley. Well, he's thick with Oliphant, isn't he?'

'Still, it was a brave thing to do,' Emmie said in admiration.

For the umpteenth time, she wondered what would have become of Miss Sophie and Rab if she had not interfered that day. Once, she would have been able to talk to Rab about such things; now she rarely saw him and had no idea what he thought any more. Only the volume of poems given her at Christmas provided a tantalising clue. Why the sonnets of Keats and Shelley? Was it saying that he hoped she would stay happily in love with Tom, or was it one of his jokes, mocking the very idea of love? The radical Shelley, who despised marriage, royalty and religion, was one of Rab's favourite poets.

'There's a march in Newcastle planned for July,' Helen told her on the most recent visit, 'a pageant – Great Women from History. The Guild can't decide whether to go as Florence Nightingale and her nurses or Boadicea and her spear carriers. Jonas says we should gan just as we are – pitmen's wives.'

'Where's the fun in that? You want to dress up,' Emmie laughed. 'I wish I could come.'

Helen looked her over. 'Not this year, pet. You look fit to burst. In a week or two you'll have a bonny bairn to nurse.'

Emmie nodded. Neither of them admitted that Tom would never allow her to go, even if she was not carrying his child. He disapproved of her involvement in anything outside the home, especially if it had to do with the Women's Guild or suffragism. Before, when they were courting, Tom had tolerated her meetings and marches. But now, as his wife, she was made to feel disloyal for supporting anything with which he did not agree.

Once he had said, 'Emmie, what do you need to gan to the Guild for? Aren't you happy here with me?'

'Course I am, but—'

'You'd rather spend an evening gossiping with a bunch of wives than with yer husband.'

'It's not gossiping,' Emmie replied, 'we have talks and debates – we learn things.'

'Mam never saw the need to join,' Tom reproved. 'She says leave the talkin' to the men. There's more than enough to do in the home – and those who spend too much time at meetings divn't look after their homes properly.'

Stubbornly, Emmie continued to go to the Guild on Wednesdays until April, when she found it too tiring. Secretly, it was a relief not to come home to an offended Tom who would not speak to her or touch her in bed. It was easier to go along with his likes and dislikes. Then she was rewarded with Tom in a good mood, being funny and affectionate.

He was overjoyed at the pregnancy and fussed over her protectively, even doing jobs around the house. He filled the coal hod and dadded his work clothes against the yard wall to shake out the coal dust. He lifted heavy pans and went to the standpipe for water. He talked with impatience of the day he would become a father and she loved him for it. Once the baby arrived, they would be a proper family. She longed for the time when she would be too busy looking after her child to miss her old life.

Standing in her back doorway that hot June afternoon, she pushed away the dark tresses that clung to her damp brow, listening out for Tom's footstep. But it was a breathless Louise who appeared first, waving a handbill.

'Emmie! You'll never guess what?' she called in excitement.

Emmie smiled quizzically. 'We've won the vote?'

'Don't be daft,' Louise said impatiently. 'Look at this. They're coming to Blackton tomorra night.'

'Who are?' Emmie tried to look at the piece of paper her friend was jiggling in front of her.

'The Yorkshire Players – a touring variety act. But look at the names. There – the soprano singer – Nell Kelso. Isn't that your sister?'

Emmie felt winded. She clutched her stomach in shock. 'Nelly?'

'Eeh, Emmie, get inside and sit down,' Louise ordered.

She steered her to a kitchen stool and smoothed out the paper on the table. Emmie stared at the list of performers, her sister's name in bold black ink as a star turn. Louise thrust a cup of water into her shaking hands.

'Could it really be our Nelly?' Emmie whispered.

'Course it could.' Louise was adamant. 'She ran off with a music-hall lad, didn't she? And Nell was a canny singer. Didn't you say she was always threatening to run off with the circus or music-hall acts when you were bairns?'

Emmie nodded. She looked at Louise, hardly daring to hope. 'But what if it's not her?'

Louise shrugged. 'There's only one way to find out.'

Emmie's heart quickened. 'I want to gan and see her. Will you come with me, Lou?'

'Better ask Tom first,' Louise cautioned. 'He might not want you gallivantin' around so near to your time.'

Emmie reached out and squeezed her hand. 'Back me up, won't you?'

When Tom trudged in, he gave his sister a suspicious look.

'What you two plottin'?'

Louise showed him the advertisement.

'Will you take me?' Emmie asked. 'Please, Tom.'

He shook his head. 'You're in no state to be ganin' to a variety show.'

'You could get a lift over in Mr Attwater's trap,' Louise suggested. 'I'm sure he'd help if he knew the reason.'

'I divn't want you gettin' in a state – think of the bairn,' Tom fretted. 'What if it's a wild-goose chase?'

'I won't get in a state,' Emmie said, her look pleading. 'It might be me only chance of findin' out what really happened to Nelly.'

His look was dubious. 'I thought she was a bad 'un? If she gets you all upset—'

Louise intervened. 'Look at her, Tom. She'll do herself more harm staying here and not knowing.'

Tom bent and kissed Emmie on her head.

'All right, lass. If that's what you want, then I'll take you,' he conceded.

Emmie clutched his hand in gratitude. 'Thanks, Tom.'

The young Methodist minister was happy to take them across to Blackton, declaring he liked a bit of theatre now and again. He was more liberal in this than Barnabas Curran, who believed all theatre was the work of the Devil. Louise, who had instigated the trip, was not prepared to provoke her father's wrath by going with them. So Emmie was grateful for the minister's support, and especially for Tom being prepared to defy his father for her sake. She had noticed how much more Tom stood up to the senior Curran since their marriage. The leather belt of chastisement had gone from its hook by the fireside the day Tom left home.

By the time the curtain went up in the Miners' Hall at Blackton, Emmie was nearly sick with anticipation. When Nell Kelso walked on stage in a sequined dress, arms spread out in long black gloves that came up past her elbows, Emmie had a moment of doubt. Her hair was the colour of corn and her body pencil-thin. But the broad mouth and dark eyes, made more alluring by make-up, were instantly recognisable.

106

She clutched Tom's hand. 'That's her – that's Nelly!'

Tom gave her an answering squeeze. They sat holding hands as Nell's vibrant voice filled the hall and she glided around the stage in her glittering gown, captivating the audience with her songs and ready smile. When she sang in the finale, Nell was given a standing ovation and even Mr Attwater stood up and shouted, '*Brava!*'

Afterwards, they waited for the hall to empty and then sent a message backstage to ask for Nell. She appeared some minutes later in a slim-fitting dress of pink chiffon, her hair, released from its tight pins, framing her elfin face.

She came towards Emmie grinning, with hands outstretched. As Emmie stood up to greet her sister, Nell caught sight of her pregnant state and froze.

'Emmie, you're expecting!'

Emmie smiled and went to hug her. They embraced awkwardly over Emmie's bulge.

'I married Tom,' Emmie said proudly, turning to nod at her husband. He was looking handsome in his best suit and stiff collar, grinning bashfully as Nell came forward to shake his hand.

'Congratulations. Our Emmie's a lucky girl.'

'I am,' Emmie agreed. 'Eeh, it's grand to see you, Nelly! Why did you run off like that? You had everyone that worried. And not even a card—'

'Don't nag,' Nell said, rolling her eyes. 'I bet the fuss was over in days. I told you I couldn't go and live in that mission place.'

Emmie stopped herself asking about the money. 'Dr Flora missed you a lot. Will you gan and see her while you're in the area?'

Nell shrugged. 'We're near the end of the tour – I might do.'

'I've so much to tell you. Sam got married to Louise and we got wed at the Settlement and—'

Tom interrupted. 'Emmie, the minister's waiting outside to take us home.'

Emmie looked at him in dismay. 'Can Nell come back with us? I just want a bit time with her.'

Tom looked unsure.

'Can you come, Nelly?' she urged. 'Stay the night at ours and catch up with the others the morra. That's all right, isn't it, Tom?'

Tom hesitated then nodded. Nell looked between them. 'I

suppose I could – I mean, I'd like to. Give me a few minutes to fetch my bags.'

They went outside to explain to the minister. He laughed and said he might get her to lead the singing in chapel on Sunday.

'Oh, she'll not be stoppin' that long,' Emmie said hastily, imagining the consternation Nell's brash appearance would cause in their spartan chapel.

Tom helped Emmie up into the carriage and stood around whistling while they waited.

'She talks posh, doesn't she?' he mused. 'Not like you, Emmie.'

Emmie flushed. 'That's just an act – some'at she's learned for the stage.'

'Still,' Tom said, 'it's canny to listen to.'

That evening, they sat up late, listening to Nell's amazing tales of travel through England with different theatre troupes. She had parted company with Jackman soon after leaving Tyneside. Nell was vague about how she had managed to break into music hall.

'I made a name for myself singing in various establishments around Leeds,' she said grandly. 'Jackman got me introductions, but he wanted me to stay put. I told him I wouldn't end up in the West End of London by hanging round Leeds beer halls all my life.'

'Beer halls?' Tom said, wide-eyed.

'Concert halls,' Nell smiled.

Emmie found it hard to keep her eyes open or stop yawning. While Nell carried on chatting to Tom, she made up a bed for her sister on the horsehair sofa, a wedding present from the Currans.

'Tom needs to be up for the early shift,' Emmie told Nell.

'Get yourself to bed,' Tom told her. 'I'll come when I'm ready.'

Emmie lay in the stuffy bedroom, unable to get comfortable, listening to the drone of conversation and laughter. It struck her that she and Tom did not laugh together like that any more. When had it stopped? After their courting days or the first few weeks of marriage, when it had all been new and exciting? The boundaries of her world had gradually shrunk. Life had become dull; she had become dull. Perhaps Tom found her so, compared to the vivacious Nell. He had never met anyone of Nell's type before.

Emmie tried to be optimistic. It was just because she was

pregnant and not able to do as much. Once the baby was here, there would be plenty to laugh about together.

Emmie turned over again, a sharp pain gripping her, as if an invisible hand squeezed her womb. She stifled a cry. It eased off, but as soon as she closed her eyes, it came again. The pain came and went for half an hour or more. She longed for Tom to come to bed, but did not want to make a fuss. Was this normal, or was something terrible happening to the baby?

When Tom finally crept to bed at two o'clock, the pain had worn off. He leaned over and kissed her. There was a sour smell to his breath.

'You've been drinking,' she whispered in astonishment. 'You never drink.'

Tom sniggered. 'That sister of yours had a drop of brandy. Said it helps her sleep after performin'. Seemed bad manners not to join her.'

Emmie was surprised, but did not really mind. Jonas and the boys had a drop of whisky on holidays without coming to harm. And this was a special occasion, being reunited with the wandering Nell. She decided to say nothing about the pains. She would ask Helen in the morning.

But rising early to make Tom breakfast before he left for work, she felt ill. And when she went to the outside water closet, a rush of colourless liquid poured between her legs. She leaned against the wall, shaking. Returning to the kitchen, she felt faint.

'Tom, I don't feel well . . .'

He eyed her groggily over a cup of tea. Behind him, Nell slept deeply.

'I think the baby . . .'

At once he was alert. 'The baby?'

'I had pains in the night,' she confessed, 'and just now – I – wet mesel'.'

Tom sprang up. 'Why didn't you say owt?' he cried. 'I'll fetch Mam.'

Emmie wanted to stop him, tell him to go and call on Helen for help. The house was not clean enough for her mother-in-law and she would disapprove of Nell.

'What about me sister?' Emmie whispered.

Tom hesitated, glancing at the sleeping Nell, her arms thrown

109

out, mouth open, golden hair loose across the pillow. Emmie noticed the flush that came to his cheeks.

'Why don't you call on Auntie Helen? Let's not bother your mam yet,' Emmie said quickly.

To her surprise, Tom nodded. He jammed on his cap and made for the door.

'You gan back to bed and stay there,' he ordered. Then he dodged back and gave her a quick kiss of encouragement.

She climbed under the covers and closed her eyes. Dull twinges of pain came and went. Within twenty minutes, Helen was knocking on the door and bustling in.

'My poor lamb! Have your waters broken? Let's get you comfy. Are you feeling any twinges yet?'

Emmie nodded, gulping back tears at her aunt's kind fussing. Helen changed her into a clean nightgown and lined the bed with brown paper that she had brought with her.

'It may be ages yet,' she reassured, 'but best be prepared.' She sat on the edge of the bed, taking Emmie's hand. 'And who's Sleepin' Beauty in the kitchen?'

Emmie smiled. 'That's Nelly.'

Helen gaped in disbelief. 'Never in the world!'

Emmie explained what had happened the previous day. As she finished, a tousled-haired, yawning Nell padded into the room. Helen greeted her warmly.

'Can you stay and help your sister?' Helen asked. 'The baby's on its way.'

Nell played with her hair as she considered. 'I could stay a day or two, I expect.'

'But aren't you performing tonight?' Emmie asked.

'A couple more pit villages,' Nell shrugged dismissively, 'then the tour is over. I was thinking of looking for work in Newcastle anyway.' She gave a generous smile. 'They can do without me. I'd rather stay and be of use to my little sister.'

Emmie eyed her warily. It was the same sarcastic tone Nell had used when they were young, a prelude to being pinched or having her hair pulled. But Helen was pleased.

'That's grand, isn't it, Emmie?'

'Aye.' Emmie mustered a smile, then closed her eyes as a new sharper pain gripped her.

The room grew hot and fetid as the day wore on. Helen

opened the small window, but it brought little relief. She organised Nell into sitting by her sister, wiping her face and arms with a damp cloth. Nell did it distractedly, while chattering about her itinerant life.

By tea time, word had spread to the Currans. Louise and her mother came hurrying round.

'Fancy taking Emmie over to Blackton in her state – and calling out the minister,' Tom's mother scolded her son. Tom was hovering in the doorway, anxious yet embarrassed by the sight of Emmie in bed surrounded by helpers. 'And to a variety show,' Mrs Curran said with such distaste that Emmie wanted to laugh.

'It was very sweet of Tom to do so,' Nell defended him. 'Otherwise I would never have been reunited with my dear sister. You should be proud of your son, Mrs Curran, for his mission of mercy.'

Mrs Curran flashed her a look of disapproval, unsure if she was being made fun of. Emmie glanced at Nell, knowing full well her sister was mocking Tom's upright mother. She lay back, letting them spar with each other, too hot and uncomfortable to care. The contractions continued, weak but robbing her of rest. Helen left to see to her own family and the Curran women to their husbands.

'Fetch Mrs Haile from upstairs if the pains get stronger,' Mrs Curran commanded her son.

Nell declared she would make them all cheesy potato pie, commandeering Tom to peel the potatoes. Amazingly, Tom did not protest. Emmie listened to them clattering about in the kitchen, joking and chatting over the task. She heard Nell offer Tom a brandy in a loud stage whisper.

'A nip for the cooks,' she laughed conspiratorially.

Emmie longed to get up and join them, but she was pinned to the bed with nagging pain and fatigue. She lay awake through the long night. Tom came to bed late, lying on top of the covers as if she was somehow contaminated. For the second night running, she smelled alcohol on his breath and felt a stab of annoyance at Nell for encouraging it.

In the early morning, she shook Tom awake. 'Can you get your own breakfast?' she asked, as he sleepily pulled on his work clothes. He grunted an agreement.

'Mam'll be down shortly,' he told her, with a peck on her forehead as he left.

Twenty minutes after he left for the pit, Emmie was seized by a wave of acute pain.

'Nelly? Nell!' she cried out. When her sister did not stir, she screamed her name louder.

Nell came stumbling in, dishevelled and bleary-eyed.

'Emmie, what's happened?'

Emmie shouted in pain, 'Gan and fetch Auntie Helen – quickly – please, Nell!'

Nell looked aghast. 'I'll have to get dressed, Emmie. Can you hang on?'

'Just hurry,' Emmie groaned, and clutched the bedclothes.

Nell fled. Emmie could hear her pulling on clothes and brushing out her hair. Beyond the door, she could see Nell in front of the mirror, pinning up her dyed hair. Emmie felt a sudden pushing sensation between her legs. She shuddered and gasped at the acuteness of the pain.

'Nelly, don't go!' she called out. She flung back the covers, her body drenched from the heat of the wool blankets. She screamed again for her sister.

Nell appeared in the doorway. 'Emmie, you're not . . . ?'

'Aye, I am. You'll have to stay—'

'I don't know what to do,' Nell protested.

'Well, neither do I!'

Nell inched round the bed, nose wrinkling at the stench of labour.

'Help me sit up,' Emmie panted. Nell took hold of her arm and hauled her upright. Emmie pulled up her sodden nightgown and let her legs fall open.

Nell screamed in disgust. 'My God, Emmie! It's coming.'

She would have fled if Emmie had not been clinging on to her like a limpet. She stared in fascinated horror at the birth unfolding before her reluctant gaze. One moment, Emmie was roaring at the agony, the next a bloodied, slippery creature was lying on the crumpled brown paper between her shaking legs.

'Is – it – all right?' Emmie gasped, breathless.

Nell stared at the ugly specimen covered in mucus and blood. She snatched a towel from the rail at the end of the bed and threw it over the baby, dabbing at the blood and trying not to retch. This provoked a querulous howl from the infant. Emmie reached forward and pulled the bundle into her arms. She pressed her lips to its tiny crinkled face.

There was a call at the back door, and the neighbour from upstairs came in.

'I heard the noise and thought you might— By heck, it's here already!' Mrs Haile exclaimed.

Emmie beamed, exhausted but triumphant. 'Me sister helped me, Mrs Haile.'

Nell swiftly recovered her composure and smiled. 'It came so quick – I couldn't have left Emmie to fetch anyone.'

Mrs Haile nodded. 'You look a bit green round the gills. You put the kettle on, lass, and I'll see to the clearing-up.'

Nell sped from the room, grabbed one of Tom's rationed Woodbines and rushed into the back yard. She lit up the cigarette, coughed as it burned the back of her throat and breathed in the aromatic smoke, trying to rid her nostrils of the sweet stench of blood. She swore to herself, then and there, that she would never make her sister's stupid mistake of getting pregnant.

Yet, when she returned to the bedroom later and saw the cleaned-up baby nestling beside Emmie, swaddled in a white sheet, she felt a surge of envy. Emmie lay dozing, her smile tired but happy, her wavy black hair streaming across the pillow. Nell was struck by how beautiful her sister looked, a grown woman. She had never noticed before. Jealousy twisted inside. Why was Emmie always the lucky one, the one everyone fussed over and took to their hearts – their mother, the MacRaes, even Dr Flora? And now she had handsome Tom and this baby to love her. Life was so unfair.

'He's a little laddie,' Mrs Haile told her.

Emmie smiled. 'You've got a nephew, Nelly. Tom said if we had a boy, he wants to call him Barnabas after his father.'

'Well, if Tom wants it, Tom must have it,' Nell said breezily.

Mrs Haile threw her a cautious look. 'Will you be all right looking after them?'

'Of course,' Nell beamed. 'I'll make us some tea and toast. How about that, Emmie?'

Soon afterwards, Helen arrived to help, as did the Curran women. Nell took up the role of hostess in the kitchen, presiding over the teapot and regaling visitors with the drama of the birth and the crucial part she had played in it all. By the time Tom returned, Nell was the hero of the hour, and even Mrs Curran was giving her reluctant approval to Emmie's brash sister.

Tom was overjoyed with his new son, at first hardly daring to touch him for fear of harming him. Then, encouraged by Emmie, he boldly held him in his arms and paced back and forth, talking and whistling to him in delight. That night, Emmie fell into an exhausted sleep to the sound of Tom and Nell clinking cups of brandy and toasting young Barny. She woke in the night to a strange noise she could not locate, then realised it was the baby crying for milk. Tom hardly stirred as she reached across and put Barny to her breast, the way Mrs Haile had instructed.

At dawn, she was roused from a deep sleep by Tom shaking her awake.

'You've let me sleep in, lass. I never heard the caller,' he said in annoyance. 'Why didn't you wake me?'

Emmie blinked at him in confusion. 'Sorry, Tom, but the baby kept me awake half the night . . .'

Tom peered over at the sleeping infant and smiled. 'Divn't worry. You'll soon get used to it. Is he feedin' canny?'

Emmie nodded. The baby seemed to know exactly what to do.

'It's grand having your sister around to help, isn't it?' Tom grinned. 'Nell says she'll stop as long as you want.'

Emmie looked at him in dismay. 'I thought she was ganin' to Newcastle to find work?'

Tom glanced away. 'She will – once you're up and about.'

'Tom,' she stopped him, 'don't you think Nell should stop at the MacRaes' of a night? It's a bit awkward having her sleep in the kitchen.'

Tom shrugged. 'Doesn't bother me. You sort it out if you want.'

But Nell was so reproachful at the suggestion, Emmie quickly backed down.

'Haven't seen you for ages, then you want me out,' she chided. 'Suppose you think you don't need me now the baby's here.'

'Course I don't want you out,' Emmie said hastily. 'Just thought you'd be more comfortable at Auntie Helen's with your own bed.'

Nell soon tired of helping with Barny, disgusted by the mess and smell of changing and washing nappies. So, while Emmie was confined to the house with the baby, Nell came and went as she pleased. She would leave in the morning to do any shopping and not return for hours. Emmie could not imagine how she filled in the time, but from Helen she heard how her sister paraded around the village in her green high-heeled shoes, chatting to anyone who had the time of day. Soon she was being invited into people's houses to drink tea and eat scones, she went to support Tom in a football friendly against Blackton and she sang for Mr Attwater at the chapel social. The chapel summer picnic came and Tom took Nell. Louise called round afterwards and told Emmie that Nell had larked around like a giddy foal and pushed Tom in the river.

'Me da wasn't best pleased, but Tom's a married man now and he can't tell him what to do.' Louise was forthright. 'I wouldn't let my husband carry on like that.'

Emmie blushed. 'How can I stop him when I'm stuck in here?'

'You should tell her to go.' Louise was blunt. 'She's making a play for our Tom, that's what I think.'

But Emmie could not believe Nell would be so heartless.

'She's just enjoying a bit attention – and not having to kip in a different place every night, that's all.'

Yet Emmie's doubts about her sister were growing. She yearned to take her baby out in the July sunshine, but until she was 'churched' she could not leave the house. Left alone for long hours by Nell, sore from breast-feeding and short-tempered from lack of sleep, Emmie began to resent her sister's presence. Most of all, her anger was growing over Nell's monopolising of Tom.

In the evenings, he would rush in and pick up Barny for a few minutes. While he hardly spoke to Emmie, he was quick to agree to walk Nell round to someone's house, or go with her to the shops for something she had forgotten, or sit at the back door as the sun set, drinking tea laced with brandy. This was not how she had imagined their family life to be. Louise was right: whether Nell meant to or not, she was undermining her marriage.

The Sunday came when Emmie and the baby could come out of confinement and the Currans laid on a special meal after the long service. Still, Nell showed no sign of leaving. When Nell and Tom pushed Barny out in his pram one summer evening, leaving her to wash up the dishes, Emmie could take no more.

'Don't you think it's time you paid a visit to Dr Flora?' Emmie suggested the next morning after Tom had gone to work.

'There's plenty of time.' Nell was offhand.

'Did you really steal money and jewellery from her?' Emmie blurted out in frustration.

'Is that what she said?' Nell sniffed. 'Well, I might have taken the odd fiver – but she had plenty to spare – owed it to me really – I worked hard for her.'

'And the jewellery?'

'I only took the worthless paste necklace and earrings – needed them to make me look respectable when I was looking for work. It wasn't asking much. I could have taken far more by rights.'

Emmie was amazed at her sister's lack of contrition. 'And when are you ganin' to look for work now?' she demanded.

Nell's look was hard. 'When I'm good and ready. I like it here, I'm in no hurry to leave.'

Emmie lost patience. 'Well, we can't keep you for ever – not now there's the bairn to pay for – and you spend the housekeeping quicker than water. I want you to go, Nelly.'

Nell surveyed her. 'You've turned into a right little nag. I wonder Tom puts up with it.' She picked up her green felt hat, arranged it neatly on her well-groomed hair. Emmie caught her by the arm.

'You leave my Tom alone. He's a good lad, but he's easily taken in by fancy clothes and a posh accent. He might not see you're leadin' him on, but I do.'

Nell was dismissive. 'Don't know what you're talking about. Tom just likes a bit of a laugh. You bore him, Emmie; he told me so.' With that she walked out.

Emmie stood there shaking with anger and disbelief. Had Tom said such a thing or was Nell being malicious? Why did her sister hate her so? She had the world at her feet, free to go where she pleased, yet never seemed satisfied. Nell was never going to change. She would always be resentful towards Emmie for some reason and desire whatever she had. Well, Tom would have to choose.

Emmie stormed back into the bedroom and got dressed. Wrapping Barny in his new shawl, she pulled on her coat over her too-tight skirt and blouse, bundled some spare clothes into

116

the pram and went out. She would not stay a minute longer while her sister swanned around the village making a fool of her and her marriage.

Still weak from confinement, she was nearly finished by the walk to China Street. She arrived breathless and shaking at Helen's door. Her aunt took her in at once.

'I'm stoppin' here till she gans,' Emmie declared. 'If Tom wants me and the bairn then he'll have to come and ask.'

That evening, Tom came banging on the MacRaes' door, demanding to know if they were hiding his wife and son. Emmie confronted him.

'Nobody's hidin'. It's a wonder you noticed me gone, Tom.'

'Where's Barny?' he demanded, puce-faced.

'Sleepin', so don't you gan waking him with all your shoutin'.'

'What do you think you're playing at?' he hissed. 'All the neighbours are talkin' – makin' a laughing stock of me.'

'You're doing that yourself – carrying on with me sister.'

'There's no carry-on and don't blame me,' he said angrily. 'You're the one wanted her here in the first place.'

Jonas came to the door. 'Come inside – I'll not have you shouting at Emmie on my doorstep, laddie.'

Tom glowered. 'I'll speak to me wife how I want.' He grabbed Emmie's arm. 'Haway, fetch the bairn, you're comin' home with me now.'

Emmie shook him off. 'Not till you've told Nell to leave.'

Tom struggled with her. 'You're me wife and you'll do as I say.'

Jonas stepped between them and shoved Tom off the step. 'Away you go. She's told you what she wants. Look to your marriage, Tom, and tell that besom to go.'

Tom's look was livid, but Jonas was more than a match for him and Emmie knew he would not risk a fist fight in the street. He stalked away, glaring at the neighbours watching from their open doors. Emmie retreated inside, avoiding Helen's anxious look.

Peter gave her a puzzled frown. 'Should I not call tomorra for me custard pie, Emmie?'

Emmie said gently, 'Not this week, Peter. I'm sorry. But we'll be back to normal soon.' She glanced at the others. 'Once Nell's gone, things'll be canny again.'

By the next day, word of Emmie's leaving Tom had spread

around the village. Barnabas confronted his son outside the pit bank at the end of his shift.

'What sort of husband are you?' he said angrily. 'Running about with this common actress instead of looking after your wife and child. You're bringing disgrace on the name of Curran!'

'It's Emmie's fault,' Tom snapped. 'I just did it to please her.'

Barnabas' look was withering. 'You're weak. You can't control your wife and you let her sister lead you a merry dance. Your duty is to provide for your family, not neglect them. What sort of father is that?'

Tom was stung. 'How can I be a father when the MacRaes have kidnapped me son?'

Barnabas was blunt. 'Fetch them home – or become the laughing stock of the village. And get rid of that Kelso woman. Your mother doesn't want to see you till you do.'

Tom marched home in a fury. Emmie and her sister had made a fool of him. He had done nothing wrong. He had indulged Emmie's wish to have her sister to stay and then been blamed when she had stayed on too long. To be humiliated in front of his workmates by his overbearing father was the final straw. It hurt him deeply to think that his mother had been turned against him too. Fuelled by anger, he screwed up his courage to confront Nell.

She was not there. She would be out at the shops, spending his money, he thought in irritation. There was no tea cooking on the stove, no hot water in the hanging pot. Tom looked around more closely. Nell's bags had gone from under the sofa, her hairbrush and eau-de-Cologne from the mantelpiece. Quickly he checked his secret store of money in the linen drawer. It was gone, all twelve pounds of it, money he was saving for Emmie and the baby. Stunned, he sat down on a stool.

There was a noise at the back door, a baby's grizzling. Tom sprang up. Emmie stepped into the kitchen, carrying Barny. They hesitated, eyeing each other.

'How did you know she'd gone?' Tom demanded.

'Louise came and told me,' Emmie said, rocking the fretful Barny. 'Your sister told her to get out – the way you should've done, Tom.'

'I was ganin' to,' he said hotly.

'Louise gave her a bit money to find lodgings in Newcastle.'

'Gave her money?' Tom cried. 'She's run off with all our savings, the thieving bitch!'

Emmie gasped, 'Oh, Tom . . .'

'Don't blame me. If you'd stopped at home like you should, you could've kept an eye on her. I've been too soft on the pair of you,' he fulminated.

'Well, she's gone now, so there's an end to it.' Emmie kept her temper. 'I'll not let her come between us again.'

'And what about my hard-earned money?' Tom demanded.

Emmie sighed. 'We can save up again. All that matters to me is that we're back together – you, me and the bairn.' She looked at him squarely. 'Is that what you want, Tom?'

He felt full of anger and resentment, yet as he looked at Emmie and Barny, he knew that all he ever wanted was them. Nell had flattered and made him feel important, desirable even. But she was dangerous, destructive. Suddenly he felt a wave of relief that Nell was gone, vanished like a bad dream.

'Aye, that's what I want, an' all,' he admitted. He held out his arms.

Emmie rushed forward. Tom wrapped his arms around her and Barny.

'Oh, Tom, I'm sorry about Nell and the money . . .'

He kissed her. 'I'm sorry too – for givin' your sister too much attention and that. You know it's you I care for, no one else, don't you, lass?'

Emmie nodded.

'Here, give me that bairn,' Tom said, taking Barny in his arms and jiggling him. The baby's whimpering grew louder.

'He needs a feed,' Emmie said.

Tom smiled bashfully and handed him back. 'I'll put the kettle on for a pot of tea, eh?'

Emmie smiled, encouraged. She knew it would be all right as soon as the meddling Nell was gone. As she fed Barny, she watched Tom brew the tea, then fry up some potatoes and onions for their meal.

She blurted out, 'I love you, Tom Curran.'

He looked round in surprise and grinned with pleasure.

Later, as they lay in bed listening to the sounds of Barny's soft breathing, Tom said, 'I didn't like the way you ran off to the MacRaes, Emmie. Why did you do that?'

'They're me family,' Emmie said, feeling awkward. 'I didn't know where else to turn.'

'You should've turned to me.' Tom was adamant. 'I'm your family now. I don't want other folks poking their nose in our business – not the MacRaes, not even me da. I'll not have him bawlin' at me in front of me marras again. Do you hear?'

Emmie was dismayed at Tom's bringing up the subject again, but she agreed. 'Aye, Tom, if that's what you want.'

'It is. I love you, lass, and I'll always tret you well. But I'm yer husband and you must do as I say from now on.'

Emmie almost laughed, imagining how Helen would greet such pompous words from Jonas with a pithy denial.

But Tom continued, 'And don't you ever take Barny away from me again. 'Cos if you do, I'll take me belt to you, good and proper.'

Emmie was speechless. She peered at Tom in the half-dark, but his expression was serious. He sounded chillingly like his father. She realised then how much the Nell episode had humiliated him. She wanted to reply that if he ever took his belt to her, she would leave him good and proper. But her first instinct was always to back away from confrontation, to be conciliatory. So she said nothing.

Tom rolled on to his side and fell asleep, while Emmie lay awake, plagued with thoughts of Nell's mischief and Tom's threats. Finally, she convinced herself that Tom would give her no cause ever to take Barny away. They had both been overwrought these past few days. Together, they would make a happy home for their beloved son.

CHAPTER 13

Nell was never mentioned again by the Currans and Emmie settled contentedly into motherhood, delighting in baby Barny and all he did. Tom was a besotted father, playing with his son and proudly showing him off when they went for walks or round to his parents. Only Emmie appeared to notice how this sometimes irritated Louise and Sam. She knew they longed for a baby too, but two years after marrying they were still childless.

A down-turn in trade meant a period of short time at the pit and Sam never managed to have enough put by to rent their own place. Emmie and Tom managed on less and lived frugally, Tom giving up smoking and Emmie her books from the penny library in Blackton.

'You don't have time to read anyways,' Tom pointed out. 'We've got the Bible — you don't need to fill yer head with owt else.'

Sometimes Emmie would pull out her book of sonnets and read them aloud to Barny. He would babble at her, laugh and clap his hands as if it was a great joke.

'It's just a secret between you and me,' she said, tickling him. 'Your da's forgotten I've got it.' Barny would roll over and giggle. But when the small boy began to stagger about on his feet and say the occasional word, Emmie had to hide the book from his inquisitive reach.

Everyone adored Barny. He had Tom's hazel eyes and Emmie's mop of dark curls. He was quick to smile and slow to throw tantrums. 'A little chatterbox,' Mrs Curran called him affectionately. 'Where do all those words come from in someone so small?'

Emmie did not say that she talked to Barny all the time, filled the routine drudgery of household chores by chatting to her son. She taught him nursery rhymes, sang songs from her choir days, talked to him about everything from the cleaning power of vinegar to votes for women. It did not matter that he did not understand most of what she said; it passed the time before Tom came home.

That was the best part of the day, when she and Barny helped wash the grime of the pit from Tom's aching body. Then they fed together and played with Barny before putting him to bed. At times of such contentment, Emmie pushed any mutinous thoughts about the boredom of Crawdene firmly from her mind.

For outside news she could always rely on Helen. She kept her visits to the MacRaes to once a week for fear of upsetting Tom, but she looked forward to them greatly. Tom had taken to going with Sam on a Friday evening to a new temperance club where they played backgammon and listened to visiting speakers, pianists and brass bands. When Tom went out to the club, Emmie bundled Barny into his pram and went round to China Street.

Barny loved to listen to Peter on his tin whistle, be fed currant buns by Helen, and swung in the air and boomed at by Jonas. Very occasionally, Rab would be there. He would get down on all fours and give Barny rides on his back. He was still teaching at the Settlement and in recent months had revived the moribund *Blackton Messenger*.

Whenever Rab was there, Emmie asked eagerly for news of the Runcies, Dr Flora and the Reverend Charles.

In the early summer of 1914, he told her proudly, 'Runcies say I can have one of their presses. They're not taking on as much work these days.'

'Where will you put it?' Emmie asked, astonished.

'Old Mannie says I can store it in his workshop.'

Jonas snorted. 'He means outhouse.'

'Doesn't matter what you call it,' Rab laughed, 'as long as the roof doesn't leak.'

'And what news of Dr Flora?' Emmie asked.

'You'll like this,' he smiled. 'She's to speak at the Miners' Gala this year about women's suffrage. The women are getting one of the platforms to themselves – miners' leaders are backing them.'

'At last!' Helen cried. 'That's grand.'

'I can't wait,' Emmie said in delight.

'So you'll be going this year then?' Rab asked.

Emmie blushed. 'Tom thought Barny was too young last year – what with all the crowds and such a long day. But now he's nearly two, he can ride on his daddy's shoulders.' She cuddled her son.

At the MacRaes' for a couple of hours a week, she could catch up on outside events and talk over the rumours of unrest in Europe without the censure of her husband. Tom refused to talk politics with her, whereas Jonas and Rab could not sit in the same room for five minutes without discussing it.

'It'll never come to war,' Jonas declared. 'The rulers are all related.'

'Aye, but Germany wants colonies like the rest of them – and they fear despotic Russia,' Rab pointed out.

'But it's nowt to do with us,' Emmie said.

Rab snorted. 'Where land is at stake, all the imperialists club together. If one goes to war we'll all be dragged into it.'

Jonas was optimistic. 'There's no appetite for war here. The working man sees more in common with his comrades in Germany than our own rulers.'

'And the women,' Helen joined in. 'There's a suffragist from Germany coming to speak at the Guild next week – Frau Bauer.'

'Frau Bauer!' Emmie exclaimed. 'I met her at the rally three years ago. I wish I could come.'

'Why don't you?' Helen suggested. 'Then you can have a word. It's on Wednesday at two o'clock. Day shift's not over till four.'

Emmie hesitated, aware of Rab's scrutiny. She knew Helen was telling her that the meeting would be over before Tom got back from work; he need never know.

'But what would I do with Barny?'

'I'll look after him for an hour or so,' Rab volunteered.

Emmie stared at him. 'I couldn't ask you . . .'

'Why not?' he smiled. 'Wednesdays I work on the *Messenger* at home. Mannie won't mind having the little 'un around.'

'There you are,' Helen cried. 'Barny'll be fine with our Rab, won't you, pet?' She tickled the boy under his chin.

Giggling, Barny pointed a finger and said, 'Wab.'

Emmie was emboldened by their encouragement. 'Aye, that'd be grand,' she smiled.

By the following Wednesday, Emmie was almost sick with nerves and excitement. As she waved Tom away that morning, she felt a surge of guilt as if she was doing something illegal. But all she was doing was attending a harmless meeting, she told herself firmly; something she had done week in, week out before she was married.

The May afternoon was blustery with sudden gusts of rain when she wheeled Barny round to India Street. Her heart hammered the nearer she drew to Mannie's house, with its untidy outhouses covered in briars on the edge of Oliphant's Wood. What would Tom have to say if she knew Rab – anarchist, atheist, MacRae – was looking after his son?

As they arrived, a sudden squall sent them racing across the yard into Rab's lodgings. Barny threw out his arms in excitement, squealing to be freed from the pram. Rab unclipped his harness and swung him out. Emmie noticed Rab had erected a fireguard of chicken wire around the hearth. The furniture was threadbare and the clippy mats on the floor were cast-offs of Helen's – ones that Emmie had worked on long ago.

But the paintings on the wall, books on top of Mannie's old piano, periodicals strewn across the floor, and the reading lamp gave it a cosy feel. Half the kitchen table was covered in papers smelling of ink, the other in chipped teacups and a huge teapot. The room reminded her of the Runcies' printing works and she had a stab of nostalgia for those busy days.

'Pour yourself one before you go,' Rab nodded. 'It's freshly made.'

She glanced at the clock on the mantelpiece. She had got there early. 'Just while he settles,' she murmured.

As she poured out tea for them both, she watched Rab carrying Barny around the room, pointing out the pictures. 'And that one's of the Campsie Hills – I used to gan walking there when I lived in Glasgow. See the cows – or coos as they say up there.'

'Coos!' Barny repeated, enjoying the sound.

Emmie perched on the edge of a stool, feeling ridiculously tongue-tied and trying not to stare at the narrow bed in the corner covered in a tartan blanket. The room was so intimate, a glimpse into Rab's personal life that felt like trespassing. Abandoning her half-drunk tea, she stood up. Barny sensed she was leaving and twisted in Rab's hold.

'Mammy,' he cried, struggling to be put down, his face beginning to crumple.

She came to him and gave him a quick kiss.

'Mammy's ganin' to a meetin'. I'll be back soon. You stay and play with Uncle Rab.'

'Mammy!' he began to wail as she retreated to the door. She hesitated.

'Perhaps I shouldn't . . .'

'Off you go,' Rab encouraged. 'He'll be all right once you've gone.'

Rab spun Barny round to the piano. 'Look at this!' he cried, striking the keys with his free hand. Emmie slipped out and stood beyond the door, listening to Rab playing and singing 'My Grandfather's Clock'. Barny's crying stopped in abrupt amazement. She could imagine him wide-eyed, his head cocked to listen. Then she heard him giggle and wondered if Rab was making faces as he sang along. She hurried away, warmed by a sudden tenderness.

To her delight, Dr Flora was at the meeting in the Co-operative Hall, having brought Frau Bauer from the Settlement, where she was staying. After the lively discussion, the choir got up to sing and Frau Bauer pulled Emmie to her feet.

'We will sing together like old times, *ja*?' she beamed.

Emmie stood beside her and belted out the song of the 'Women's March', exultant to be one of them again.

Over a cup of tea, Emmie was warmly greeted by Flora.

'Emmie, you are looking so well.' The doctor kissed her on the cheek. 'Motherhood suits you. And where is the wee one? I'd love to meet him.'

'I'll bring him down to see you,' Emmie promised, carried away with excitement at seeing her friends again. Now was not the time to ask her about Nell. She would speak of her sister when she visited properly.

Helen was going around with cards to sign up new recruits as Friends of Women's Suffrage.

'You'll want a Friend's card, Emmie?' she almost ordered. 'This is for ordinary lasses to have their say, not just the Pankhursts and Oliphants of this world.'

Emmie registered and tucked her card into her coat pocket. The meeting over, she hurried round to India Street, picking her way round the muddy puddles, bursting to tell Rab all about it. She found him and her baby squatting on the floor, drawing on brown paper with a piece of charcoal. Barny's face, smeared in charcoal, lit up at the sight of her. He scrambled to his feet, abandoning his scribbles, and threw himself at her legs.

Hugging him tight, Emmie cried, 'You look like a pit lad.'

Rab grinned, going to fetch a cloth. 'I knew we'd be in trouble. But at least I stopped him eating it.'

As they cleaned up Barny, Emmie gabbled about the meeting and the reunion with Flora, still elated.

'And I've signed a Friend's card, an' all,' she said proudly, showing him her membership card.

'That's grand,' he smiled. 'So you're going to get involved again?'

Emmie hesitated. 'Aye . . . when I can.'

Rab nodded. 'I'm happy to have Barny, if it helps.'

Emmie gave him a quizzical smile. 'Fancy you helping the women's cause, eh?'

He grunted. 'Even the Labour Party's supporting women's emancipation these days. You won me over long ago.'

Emmie blushed at the look he gave her. Turning away, she said, 'Ta for the offer.'

Quickly she buttoned Barny into his jacket and lifted him protesting into the pram.

'Stay Wab's,' he cried.

Rab laughed and ruffled his hair. Emmie's heart squeezed at the memory of how he used to do that to her when she was little. She hurried away, forcing herself not to glance back at the tall figure leaning in the doorway watching them go.

Tom was baffled by her restlessness that evening.

'Can you not sit down for two minutes?' he asked.

'Let's gan for a walk,' Emmie suggested. 'It's a canny evening – not one to be stuck inside.'

'I see from the mud on the pram you've already been out today,' Tom commented.

Emmie's heart skipped a beat. Now would be the time to tell

him about the meeting; say she had gone just to see Dr Flora. But her courage failed.

'Aye, I went down the village.'

'That's good,' he nodded. 'Give the bairn some fresh air now the weather's better.'

He agreed on a walk. While they were out, Emmie said as casually as possible, 'I'd like to take Barny down to see Dr Flora and Reverend Charles sometime.'

'Why d'you want to do that?' Tom was dismissive. 'That mission's in the slums – don't want Barny catching fever.'

'The Settlement's clean as can be,' Emmie reassured, 'and it wouldn't be for long. Please, Tom, they've been good to me – and the Reverend married us, remember? It's only right that I take Barny to see them.'

Tom was grudging. 'Well, I can't take you Saturday, not with the final against Tow Law coming up.'

'I'll gan during the week,' Emmie said hastily, 'then we can watch you in the final.'

The following week, Emmie dusted down her old bicycle and wheeled it round to India Street with Barny staggering along beside her.

'Can Mannie fix a seat for the bairn on the front?' she asked Rab.

Between the two men they cobbled together a seat made of old saddle leather and half a basket, and lashed it to the handlebars. The old saddler coughed and spat in satisfaction as Emmie and Barny gave it a trial run down the lane. Barny screamed with delight and shouted, ''Gain, a–gain!'

'Who made this?' Tom asked suspiciously that evening.

'Mannie, the saddler in India Street – the one Rab lodges with,' Emmie admitted boldly.

'Did it cost owt?'

'No, he just made it out of scraps from his workshop.'

To Emmie's amazement, that was all Tom asked. He seemed pleased to have something for nothing.

Two days later, Emmie rode down to Gateshead with Barny. Wheeling in under the arch to the Settlement quad, she felt a lifting of her spirits at the familiar brick buildings and the chapel bell tolling midday. Mousy hobbled to greet her, calling for his wife to come and see. The cook bustled to the door of the kitchen and clamped the visitors in a floury hug. Barny was immediately led away to be fed. In the dining room, Emmie found her old friends gathered for lunch. She was shocked to see how Mabel had aged and could only walk with the aid of two sticks. But they were overjoyed to see her again.

Afterwards, Flora and Charles took Emmie to their flat. It smelled of Frau Bauer's Turkish cigarettes. In the privacy of their sitting room, Emmie told them about Nell's reappearance two years before. Flora looked harrowed.

'No, she never came to see us. I'm thankful she's still alive, but saddened that . . .' her voice trailed off. 'I'm sorry if she made trouble between you and Tom. Everything's all right now, I trust?'

Emmie nodded. 'He doesn't know about me carrying a Friend's card, mind. He wouldn't approve. He doesn't see why lasses want a say in things.'

'He's not the only one by far,' Flora sighed.

'And it's not just men of his class,' Charles said ruefully. 'My father is as stubborn an opponent as you'll ever find.'

'How is Miss Sophie?' Emmie asked.

'Still defying my father,' he smiled.

'And refusing to marry Hauxley's son until women get the vote,' Flora added with a laugh.

Emmie plucked up courage to ask, 'Do you think Rab lost his job because of Miss Sophie? Did she tell Major Oliphant about him?'

Charles and Flora exchanged uncomfortable glances. 'I'm afraid she might have said too much in anger,' Flora conceded.

Charles sighed. 'It was more to silence my father's pleas for her to marry Captain Hauxley. She said something rash about being in love with an anarchist and how they were going to run off together. Father, being the man he is, soon got out of her who the supposed lover was. It didn't matter how much she then denied there had ever been a liaison, Rab was black-marked. He'll never be employed by the company again, I fear.'

'That's why Charles offered him work here,' Flora explained, 'he felt so responsible.'

'And because he's such a good teacher,' Charles added swiftly.

Emmie nodded. 'He's much happier here, I know that. I don't think he'd gan back to work for your father if they offered him twice as much.'

'No, you're right,' Flora agreed. 'Money's of little interest to Rab.'

As Charles played bagatelle with Barny, Flora, Emmie and Frau Bauer chatted about the likelihood of women gaining the vote at the next election.

'We're pushing at an open door now,' Flora was convinced. 'Think of recent successes at by-elections.'

'This time next year, maybe you have ze vote, *ja*?' Frau Bauer nodded.

'And now I'm twenty-one I'll be of voting age!' Emmie cried.

Flora asked her, 'Can you help out at the Durham gala this year, Emmie? We need plenty of help with leaflets and selling *Common Cause*.'

Emmie hesitated. Tom would be against it. 'I'll have to see . . . I'd like to . . . but with Barny . . .'

Flora gave her a long look. 'I know it's difficult for many women with families – and husbands who don't want them getting involved. But even just for half an hour while our speakers are on would be a great help. Try if you can.'

Emmie left, promising to meet up with them in Durham if she could.

June came and Emmie took Barny out as often as possible. They explored the woods and brought back sticks and cones and jam jars of caterpillars for Tom to admire. On Saturday afternoons the three of them would take a picnic tea and climb above Blackton Heights, Barny on Tom's shoulders. Not once did they speak of the rumours of war that Emmie picked up from the MacRaes, nor did she pluck up the courage to ask his permission to leaflet in Durham for the Friends of Women's Suffrage. They talked of Barny's ability to kick a ball, what Mrs Curran would be serving up for Sunday dinner, Tom's hopes of becoming a hewer on more pay by next year.

Emmie kept to herself the times she and Barny dropped by Mannie's on the way back from the woods, to sit drinking tea with Rab and discuss what was going in the *Messenger* that week. While Barny played in the yard with a hobbyhorse made out of bits and pieces from the workshop, she listened to Rab's passionate views, occasionally voicing her own.

'If you feel that strongly about lasses like you signing up with the Friends, why don't you write a piece for the *Messenger*?' Rab challenged. 'I'll give you a free advertisement.'

Emmie exclaimed, 'Aye, and the Currans would have a blue fit if they found out.'

'I remember a time when you didn't give two hoots what people thought – not even the Currans.' Rab scrutinised her. 'Where's the lass that went on rallies and printed leaflets for the suffragettes?'

Emmie held his look. 'She got wed and had a bairn.'

'Doesn't mean you can't have opinions of your own,' he answered.

'No,' Emmie sighed, 'but it's easier not to.'

Rab leaned close and covered her hand with his. 'I warned you marriage was bondage for a lass, didn't I?'

Emmie snatched away her hand. 'Maybes it is for my generation – but not the next. Once lasses get a say in how things are run, we'll change all that.'

'Change it now,' Rab urged. 'Stand up to Tom and his father. Don't leave it to women like Sophie Oliphant – they're just seeking power for their own kind, not ordinary women like you and Mam. A new world order, that's what we need! Turn the world on its head – the workers in charge, not ground down and old at forty.'

' "Workers of the world unite – you have nothing to lose but your chains",' Emmie quoted drily.

'Exactly,' Rab said, jumping up and striding to the piano. He lifted the lid. 'Listen to this.'

He began to play the same slow, haunting tune he had played before her marriage. As the music filled the room, Emmie felt her eyes prickle.

'Schubert,' Rab said, his blue eyes ablaze. 'They should be playing it in the streets for all to hear – not just in the posh concert halls. When we change the world, Emmie, it'll not just be for better pay and working conditions – we'll have music and books and learning – so lads like Barny will have what Oliphant and Hauxley take for granted.'

Emmie's heart hammered at his words. In Rab's company she could believe in such a Utopia. Unable to speak, she hurried into the yard to fetch Barny, blinking away tears.

On the point of leaving, she turned to Rab and said, 'I'll write some'at for the newspaper. Long as you print it under a made-up name.'

He grinned at her in approval. 'That's my lass.'

No one knew who Artemis was who wrote in the *Blackton Messenger*, advocating women's suffrage and urging pitmen's wives to pledge themselves to the cause. The pieces were written in plain language and some said the author must be Radical Rab's mother, known for her outspoken support. But Helen laughed it off, flattered but baffled at the suggestion.

'It's someone better with words than me,' she declared.

Then, one week in early July, she called on her son to find Emmie writing at his kitchen table. A flustered Emmie swore her to secrecy.

'I'm amazed you've kept it secret this long,' Helen laughed. 'Folk cough one end of Crawdene and the other end catches cold.'

'We come through the woods,' Emmie blushed. 'Barny gets to play with the hobbyhorse. It'll have to stop once he's talkin' more.'

'That won't be long,' Helen observed. 'You can write at my house and I'll bring it round if you want.'

Emmie nodded, not wanting to admit that these regular visits to Rab's were the highlight of her week. She would miss them badly if Tom ever found out and put a stop to them.

With the writing of her column, Emmie found her confidence increase. One evening, while she and Tom were chatting about going to Durham Gala on the special train, she faced up to him.

'We'll follow the band with Barny,' Tom said, 'get a good spot on the racecourse for the speeches. You can help Mam and Louise in the temperance tent this year – I'll keep an eye on the bairn if you like.'

'I'm ganin' to help Dr Flora for a bit,' Emmie blurted out.

'What d'you mean?' Tom asked.

'She's speaking on Women's Suffrage – needs leaflets handin' out and pledge cards.'

Tom gawped at her. 'You're not doing that!'

'I said I would. What's the harm in it?' Emmie replied.

'Harm in it?' Tom spluttered. 'It's lasses gettin' above themselves.'

'Most people don't think like that any more,' Emmie argued.

'Labour and the pitmen's leaders are backing us now. Plenty Liberals do too. It's only the Government—'

'Currans have always voted Liberal,' Tom snapped, 'and the party's against such nonsense. God made Adam in charge of Eve. It's just human nature.'

'And it's human nature to want the best for your family, for your bairns. Lasses should have a say in such things. We're fightin' for all working people,' Emmie insisted.

'You sound like a MacRae,' Tom scoffed. 'I'll not have you makin' a fool of yourself at the Big Meetin'.'

'And you sound like one of the bosses,' Emmie said in frustration.

Tom leaped up and grabbed her arm. 'Don't you go against me, or I'll take me belt to yer.'

'Ow, Tom, you're hurtin' me.' She tried to shake him off.

Barny looked up in alarm. 'Mammy!'

Tom quickly let go. 'Do you want to spoil Barny's first Big Meetin'?' he accused.

'I just want to hand out a few pledge cards for half an hour.' Emmie spoke as calmly as possible.

His eyes narrowed in suspicion. 'Have you got one of these cards?'

She coloured. 'Aye, I have.'

'Give it here,' he demanded. When she hesitated, he marched to the pegs by the door and started searching her coat pockets, throwing bits of string, handkerchiefs, scraps of paper, pencil stubs on the floor. Any minute he might discover some scribbled notes to do with the *Messenger*. Emmie sprang after him.

'It's in the kitchen drawer,' she said, pulling it open and scrabbling for it under matches and candles. She held it out to him. He snatched it and stared at her carefully written name, Emmeline Curran.

'How dare you use the name of Curran on such a thing?' he shouted. Maddened, he tore it into tiny pieces and threw them on the fire.

Emmie watched in anger and dismay. She bit back the retort that it made no difference what he did; she had signed and her name was counted. He could stop her campaigning, she thought bitterly, but he could not stop the momentum that hundreds of thousands of women had begun. Without another word, Emmie picked up Barny and marched into the bedroom to dress him for bed. Burrowing her face into his warm, soft neck, she kissed him fiercely.

'I won't let you become like the other Curran men,' she whispered. 'I swear to it!'

They went on the early train, Emmie banishing the ugly argument from her mind and resigned to a day of doing as she was told. Soon the excitement of being in the grand medieval city, of following the thousands of pit folk with their hundreds of bands and banners, took hold. It was a day when working people took over the narrow streets of the town (the shops boarded up in fear at their coming), and marched to the riverside to listen to their leaders speak. Emmie felt a surge of pride to be part of the sea of people who poured down the narrow streets behind the massed brass bands, the colourful banners flapping like huge sails above them. Jonas held one of the banner ropes, the longest serving official of the Crawdene lodge.

Arriving at the racecourse, where the bandsmen laid down their instruments and families picnicked, Emmie helped her mother-in-law spread out their tongue sandwiches and slabs of pork pie. Not far away, the MacRaes sat with others from the Clarion Club. She could not see Rab; he was probably among the crowds, selling copies of the *Messenger*.

Guiltily she craned for a sight of the women's platform. It was on the far side of the field, bedecked in the red, white and green bunting of the North East Society of Women's Suffrage.

Suddenly, Sam stood up and stretched. 'Haway, Tom, we'll miss the speeches.' He turned to Louise and winked. 'Why don't you and Emmie take Barny for a swing on the shuggy boats?'

The men went off to listen to the miners' leaders.

'We'll meet you in the temperance tent, Mam,' Louise said, taking Barny by the hand.

Swinging the little boy between Louise and herself, Emmie could hardly believe that slipping away from Tom had been so easy. They made towards the far side of the field and the rows of amusement stalls, coconut shies and fortune-tellers. As they queued to go on the shuggy boats, Emmie strained to hear what they were saying on the women's platform.

Louise nudged her. 'Gan and have a listen. I know that's what you want.'

Emmie gave her a startled look.

Louise laughed. 'Sam's in favour, even if my family isn't. He told me to get you over here while he kept an eye on Tom and Father.'

Emmie grinned and squeezed her friend's arm. 'Ta, Lou. You're a canny friend.'

She slipped off to listen to Dr Flora and Frau Bauer, and a visiting speaker, Catherine Marshall, who spoke with passion of their successes.

'It may be the militants prepared to go to prison who grab the headlines,' she cried, 'but it is the dedication of the ordinary thousands who will turn the tide. Year after year, we have marched, petitioned and walked from the provinces to London. We have argued our case on the hustings, in hundreds of town halls and out on the streets. And we are being listened to! The new dawn is coming, the tide is on the turn!'

Emmie came away with a new optimism, scribbling down what she could remember on a scrap of paper before she forgot Marshall's words.

'What's that you're writing?' Louise asked in curiosity.

Emmie stuffed it in a pocket. 'Nowt important.'

Louise gave her a knowing look. 'Nowt to do with writing for the *Messenger*, then?'

Emmie looked at her friend in alarm. 'The *Messenger*?'

Louise smiled in triumph. 'I'm right, aren't I? Sam let it out that he knew who Artemis was. I put two and two together. MacRaes aren't very good at keepin' secrets.'

'You'll not tell—' Emmie gasped.

'Course I won't,' Louise promised. 'Good on you, I say. Anything that'll make things better for lasses. I'm sick of being at Father's beck and call and not allowed to speak me mind on owt – just like Mam. You don't know what it's like, Emmie.'

'I do.' Emmie pulled a face. 'Tom's gettin' more like his da by the day.'

Louise laid a sympathetic hand on her shoulder. 'Still, you've got your own place. I sometimes think me and Sam will never get away. It's the only thing we argue about – enough money to have a couple of rooms to ourselves. Sam thinks Father should help us out, but I know he never will, he's that tight with money. And Sam's beginning to argue back more than he used to. I tell him to work harder like Tom and get a hewer's job, then maybe we can get out and start a family . . .'

Emmie looked at her friend. 'I didn't realise it was so difficult. I'm really sorry, Lou.'

The next week, Artemis's column gave a full account of the women's speeches at the Gala. Emmie bought a copy, intending to send it to Dr Flora. Tom found it in the kitchen.

'Where's this come from?' he demanded.

Emmie looked up from rolling pastry. 'I bought it.'

'What d'you do that for?' he asked, horrified. 'It's anarchist rubbish — dangerous, me father says.'

'Have you ever read it?' Emmie asked.

'No, but I don't have to,' Tom blustered. 'It's ungodly. Everyone knows Radical Rab wants to start a revolution — kill all the bosses in their beds — and not just the bosses, but respectable types like us and the minister.'

'He wants nothing of the sort,' Emmie said, trying not to laugh. 'Revolution yes, but social not bloody. Read it, Tom. There's all sorts of different opinions in it.'

He eyed her suspiciously. 'How do you know so much about it? Have you read this before?'

'Aye, I have.'

'Well, you're not spending my wages on this filth,' Tom declared. 'It's ganin' on the fire.'

She watched him tear it up and feed it to the fire, her words about Marshall turning to black ash. Emmie bent her head and continued thumping with the rolling pin, venting her frustration on the pastry. Tom was so narrow-minded he would not even consider reading the newspaper, just because his father had censored it. Well, she would not be censored! Emmie determined she would carry on writing for the *Messenger* for as long as it took to win the vote. She quelled any fears about what Tom might do if he ever discovered she wrote for it.

CHAPTER 14

The talk of war came suddenly in late July, like the hot summer weather. Only those handful who had followed events in Europe were not taken unawares. Nobody could really believe it possible.

'Why should we fight the Germans?' Tom asked his father in bafflement. 'We've nowt to do with the carry-on in the Balkans.'

'The Liberal Government won't allow it.' Barnabas was adamant. 'Grey will do his best to pour oil on troubled waters.'

Emmie itched to point out that the Foreign Secretary had bound them up in alliances with France and Russia that would drag them into war if their allies were attacked. This she knew from Rab. But she was not allowed to hold her own opinions, especially ones that differed from the Currans'.

When she visited the MacRaes, they talked excitedly of plans for a peace rally in Blackton the following Sunday. Rab was to be one of the speakers. They thought Charles Oliphant was to address the rally too.

'All over the country, there'll be marches and church services against war,' Jonas told her. 'Nobody wants this.'

'Aye,' Helen agreed, 'the Guild are marching with the suffrage societies. Will you come with us, pet?'

'I'll try,' Emmie said.

At chapel, Mr Attwater announced the peace march.

'We must send a message to our Government that we do not want war. We must urge restraint. Remember the commandment, Thou shall not kill. All those wishing to join the march should assemble outside the Co-operative Hall after morning service. I can offer transport for those unable to walk all the way to Blackton.'

Emmie was greatly encouraged by the minister's support. If the leaders of the Church were behind them, then the politicians might listen.

It was discussed around the Currans' table at Sunday dinner.

'The lodge are sending a delegation,' Barnabas confirmed. 'But I'll not march on the Sabbath.'

Tom looked torn. Emmie knew he liked the idea of a trip out, somewhere they could take Barny rather than be cooped up indoors on a summer's afternoon.

It was Sam who suggested they go.

'If the union supports the rally then some of us should gan,' he argued. 'We can take a picnic – a canny afternoon for the bairn.'

Emmie yearned to say she agreed, but knew this might provoke the Currans to say no. The words had to come from Tom. She gave him a look of appeal.

'Aye,' Tom nodded, 'and the minister's in favour.'

Barnabas grunted. 'That young man has some strange notions about what's proper and what isn't.'

They all knew he was referring to when Mr Attwater had encouraged Nell to sing in the chapel.

'Please, Father,' Louise pleaded.

Finally Barnabas nodded in assent. 'As long as you conduct yourselves respectably.'

That week's *Messenger* carried a message from Artemis urging all women to take their families on the peace rally.

'It is women who take the brunt of any war. Do we go through the pain of birth and spend years nurturing our sons just to see them sent off to war as cannon fodder? Support the peace march. We have no say in Parliament, but we can vote with our feet next Sunday.'

The day arrived fine and blustery. Emmie was overjoyed at the sight of so many villagers gathering in the main street behind an array of banners, many home-made. The Guild was there, the lodge, the Clarion Club and Jehovah's Witnesses. The socialist Sunday school had a banner alongside the Methodists, and the Suffrage Society rubbed shoulders with the Crawdene brass band.

Emmie waved at Helen as they moved off, Barny riding high

on Tom's shoulders. She felt the same stirrings of solidarity as she had a month ago at the gala. If this was being replicated across the land – across the Continent – then their rulers could not make war.

The nearer they drew to Blackton, the bigger the crowds grew. People had tramped for miles around, from smaller pit villages to converge on the larger one. They congregated in the Board School playing field where a makeshift platform had been hastily erected. Barny ran around with the other children as the adults rested and ate their picnics.

Tom was in good humour and bantering with Sam. Louise lay back, sunning herself in the grass. Barny was attempting to play a big drum and laughing in delight at the sound. It was all so light-hearted, Emmie could not imagine they could be on the brink of war with people just across the North Sea.

The speakers began to assemble on stage and people drew nearer to hear.

Charles Oliphant began, his fair tangle of hair whipping across his ruddy face, still boyish-looking in his late thirties. His words wafted into the wind.

'. . . the Christian way is the way of peace . . . there is no just war . . . pull back from the brink . . . our German brothers in Christ not our enemy . . . we are all God's people in the eyes of the Lord . . .'

He was given polite handclaps, many curious to see the son of the mighty coal-owner dressed in faded tweeds like a down-at-heel gamekeeper.

'Bet the major's not turned up to hear him,' Tom scoffed. 'Looks a right state.'

'Na,' Sam chuckled. 'Boss probably hopes there'll be a war so he gets conscripted!'

'Sam!' Emmie chided. 'He's a canny man – married me and Tom, don't you forget.'

Louise sat up, her face anxious. 'There won't be conscription, will there?' They all exchanged glances.

'Course not,' Sam assured. 'They only do that in countries with despots.' He swung an arm around his wife and kissed her boldly. Emmie's heart twisted. Tom had not shown her such open affection in a long time.

Flora followed her husband on the platform, speaking for the women's movement and their international friends. She introduced Frau Bauer.

'There are many like her who are working for peaceful change. We women do not want war between our men. It will undo all our efforts over the last few years to gain justice and equality. We have no quarrel with Gemany – she is a natural friend of England. Our government should be fostering friendship with Germany, not war.'

Two other speakers followed, their voices too faint in the strong breeze to be heard. The crowd was growing restless, drifting away. Then Emmie heard Rab's strong voice boom out and felt the back of her neck prickle.

'Haway,' Sam said, 'let's get nearer to hear.'

Rab strode up and down the stage, no notes to prompt his passionate denouncement of war.

'This is not our fight! This is a scrap between the imperialists, the money-grabbing, land-grabbing capitalist class. They are the ones who start wars for their own ends, but we are the ones they use to do their fighting! The working classes on both sides fighting the bosses' battles, while they sit back and count all the money they make out of war. Do you want to be dragged into war just because our government has made a pact with a despotic tsar? Course you don't!'

Some of the crowd shouted out in agreement. He had caught their attention.

He shook his fist in the air, his bearded face full of urgency, exhorting them like a prophet.

'But they cannot fight their wars if we refuse to fight – if our comrades in Germany refuse to fight, if our Russian brothers refuse to fight. Give them the lead and they will have the courage to follow. Stop the war!'

There was a burst of applause. Suddenly, Emmie caught sight of Barny. Somehow he had clambered on to the stage and was throwing his arms around Rab's legs.

'Wab! Wab!' he giggled.

Rab swung him up and tickled him. Tom looked dumb-struck.

'What the hell's he doing with Barny?'

Before Emmie could stop him, Tom was shoving his way through the crowd to the stage. He held up his arms.

'Give him o'er,' he ordered.

Rab smiled and handed the boy down. Tom returned, his face thunderous.

'What's he sayin' about Rab and grandfather clocks?'

Emmie went puce. 'Must be some'at he sings to him.'

'Sings to him?' Tom was indignant. 'When does he sing to him?'

'When I gan round to China Street on Friday evenings.' Emmie tried to make light of it. 'Barny's that quick at pickin' things up.'

'Didn't know Rab was there. You've never said,' Tom accused.

'He isn't often,' Emmie said, aware that people were beginning to stare.

'I'll not have him fillin' the bairn's head with his rubbish.' Tom was shouting now. 'You're not to take him round there if that anarchist's gan to be there, you hear me?'

Sam and Louise arrived beside them, their glances embarrassed. Emmie knew they would say nothing about the *Messenger*, but it worried her that a slipped word might land her deeper in trouble.

'Haway, Tom,' Sam cajoled, 'don't be hard on the lass. All Rab did was pick the bairn up. Let's gan back, eh?'

'Aye, it's getting chilly,' Louise agreed, hastily packing up the picnic.

They tramped back to Crawdene, a more subdued band than had set out a few hours earlier.

As she lay in bed that night, wrestling with whether she should give up writing for the *Messenger*, Tom reached for her hand.

'Emmie,' he said awkwardly, 'I'm sorry for shoutin' at you earlier – about the bairn.'

She shifted to look at him in the half-dark, his expression contrite.

'It's this talk of war – puts me on edge,' he continued. 'Then the sight of that man holding our Barny in his arms – and the bairn lookin' all happy – it made me jealous, like.'

Emmie puzzled. 'Barny's your son – he could never love anyone like his daddy. Why should you be jealous of Rab?'

Tom gazed at her for a long time before answering. ''Cos of the regard you have for him – have always had. Remember that time you told me in the woods how Rab was your favourite

MacRae? I've never forgotten that, Emmie.'

Emmie went hot with embarrassment. 'I was just a bairn – and the question wasn't fair. I just said owt to get me ribbon back!'

Tom drew her hand up to his lips and kissed it. 'Me sister tells me I'm too hard on you – too possessive. But it's 'cos I love you. Can't bear the thought of you being with any other lad – even if it's just for a bit crack. It's just the way I am, lass.' He squeezed her hand. 'Tell me I'm being daft and that there's nowt ganin' on between you and Radical Rab.'

Emmie's heartbeat was drumming in her ears. She thought guiltily of the times she had spent at Mannie's place working, chatting, laughing and arguing with Rab. But even if she had wanted more from Rab, he would not have given it. To him, she was the same young Emmie he had grown up with; teased, played with, protected and ignored. He had up and left Crawdene and her for over two years. There had been a music teacher in Glasgow for whom he still grieved, she was sure of that.

Emmie tried to keep the tremor out of her voice. 'If you mean, is there more than childhood friendship between me and Rab, then no, there's nowt ganin' on – never will be.'

Tom let out a sigh and pulled her towards him. He kissed her on the lips.

'You make me that happy, lass, you and Barny,' he smiled. 'I never want to lose you. Don't know what I'd do if—'

'Don't talk daft.' Emmie silenced him with a kiss back. She felt differently towards him when he was tender and loving like this, like the old Tom of their courting days. She knew that the other Tom, who bossed her around in front of others, was all about impressing his father and his marras that he was a firm husband and a true Curran.

Through the night, she held on to the Tom that she loved. This was the man she had chosen and the one she had to make her life with, whatever happened in the future.

It was two days later that the news reached the village. Britain was at war with Germany and her allies.

CHAPTER 15

Flora worried about Charles. He worked tirelessly, a lone voice preaching against the war in a town that was filling up with men in uniform and Union flags. So many had flocked to the recruiting stations, hastily set up in halls and hotels, that they were issued with armbands to show they had volunteered until enough uniforms could be provided. During those first feverish days of patriotism, mobs of young men smashed the windows of German pork butchers and grocers, baying for them to come out while their families cowered in upstairs rooms.

Alerted by one of the dockers, Charles rushed round late at night to the Werners in Olive Street to find their delicatessen a sea of glass and their stock raided. Mrs Werner, a Durham woman, was calming her children while her bewildered husband stood among the debris.

'But they are my customers,' he said, throwing his arms wide with incomprehension, 'my neighbours. Why do they do this?'

Charles could offer no reason to the grocer who sang in the Settlement choir every Sunday. His children came to the Sunday school. Every year, the Werners donated the ingredients for the Christmas pudding and sweets for the poorest families. All Charles could do was help them clear up the mess and offer a bed for the night in case the mob returned.

Flora organised bedding and gave Mrs Werner a sedative to help her sleep, but the tearful children kept them all awake. After a couple of days in hiding, the Werners returned to their home, but few people dared to be seen going into the German's shop and business rapidly dwindled. A week later, Mr Werner was detained as an enemy alien. His frightened wife boarded up the shop and fled with her family to cousins in Durham.

While student helpers at the Settlement enlisted and left, Charles drove himself to work ever harder. The docks teemed with shipping and their soup kitchen was overrun with an influx of merchant seamen and migrant workers. As well as her medical work, Flora was preoccupied with helping families left to cope without money by their wage earners abruptly joining up.

Amid all the dislocation, Flora received a despairing letter from Frau Bauer. She rushed to find Charles.

'Maria's been arrested in London!' she gasped, waving the letter at him. 'They're threatening to deport her or keep her in prison.'

Charles took the letter and read it, his face grim. 'Dear God . . .'

'Can't they tell the difference between a spy and a respected academic?' Flora blazed. 'She's an Anglophile, for goodness' sake! Spends as much time here as in Germany. Maria has nothing to do with this ridiculous escapade – quite the opposite. Can't they use their common sense?'

Charles sighed. 'Common sense was the first casualty of this war, as far as I can see.'

'We must do something.' Flora grew more agitated. 'They can't just throw her out of the country. There's no guarantee she'd get safely back to Munich – she could be blown up at sea or attacked on the road—'

'We'll send a telegram right away,' Charles reassured, rushing to hold his wife. She hugged him, wishing they could awaken from the deepening nightmare.

They wrote letters to officials, trying to find out more about Maria Bauer's case, and sent a friend from Toynbee House, a settlement in London's East End, to visit Maria and take her food and clothing.

Then an unexpected summons came to Charles from Blackton Heights.

'My father wishes to see me,' he told Flora, tugging nervously at his wavy hair.

Flora was impatient. 'To tell you off for speaking at the Blackton rally, no doubt. Don't go.'

Charles shook his head. 'No, it's about Sophie.'

'Is anything wrong?' Flora asked quickly. Charles shrugged. Flora said at once, 'I'll come with you.'

They made hasty arrangements to visit the Heights the following day, borrowing the Runcies' pony and trap. Flora felt guilty that they had seen nothing of Charles's sister for months, only reading about her suffragette protests and letters in the daily newspapers. Perhaps her health was suffering from overwork.

But when they arrived at Blackton Heights, Sophie came bounding out to meet them, flushed with excitement.

'It's so good to see you!' she cried, almost pulling Charles from the carriage.

He beamed in relief. 'We thought something awful had happened—'

'No, silly,' Sophie laughed. 'Didn't Papa tell you? Oh, come on. We're all on the terrace – even Mama – the weather's so glorious.' She kissed Flora warmly. 'I'm glad you both came.'

Charles and Flora exchanged encouraging glances as they handed over the trap to the footman and followed Sophie round the side of the ivy-covered mansion. Flora's heart sank to see the Hauxleys seated around the tea table. The MP and his son had already organised local recruitment drives with military bands around the area, and she part-blamed their jingoistic appeals for the ugly attacks in Gateshead. Arthur Hauxley was sitting in his captain's uniform. He rose to greet Charles.

Charles kissed his mother and shook hands with his father and neighbours.

'Well, tell him,' the major ordered, before the pleasantries were over.

Sophie smiled and went to stand by Arthur. To Flora's surprise, she slipped an arm through his and announced, 'We're engaged to be married. Arthur proposed the day after war was declared – and I accepted.'

Charles and Flora stared at them in astonishment. Charles managed to stutter, 'That's wonderful. Congratulations.' He shook Arthur's hand again.

Arthur beamed. 'Never thought she'd say yes.'

'We want to marry straight away,' Sophie declared, 'before Arthur has to leave.'

'September,' Arthur added.

'Just a small do for family,' Sophie insisted.

'Small do be damned,' the major laughed. 'My only daughter finally sees sense and marries an officer of my old regiment – we'll invite the whole county!'

'No, we won't, Papa.' Sophie was firm. 'I'll not have us squandering the harvest in such a time of national need. Arthur and I want a service in Ongarfield and a small luncheon here.'

'With a guard of honour,' Arthur added.

The major eyed his son. 'So if you can drag yourself away from that mission for a few hours, your sister and mother will be very happy.'

'Of course,' Charles agreed.

'And, Charles,' Arthur looked bashful, 'I'd like you to be my best man. Would you consider . . .'

'I'd be delighted,' he said at once.

His father grunted. 'Course, Liddon would've done the job if he'd lived.'

There was a moment of awkwardness around the table, then Reginald Hauxley spoke. 'That's all settled. Charles, come and tell me what's happening at the Settlement. Are you winding it up for the duration of the war?'

Charles gave him a startled look. 'Good heavens, no. There's more need than ever.'

'Charles is rushed off his feet,' Flora explained supportively, 'especially as many of the volunteers have left to join up.'

'Good for them,' Sophie enthused. 'I think it's marvellous the way everyone's rallying round to defend our country.'

Flora looked at her in dismay, but Charles replied, 'If that's what their conscience tells them to do, I certainly wouldn't stop them.'

'And what about joining them?' his father asked.

Sophie cried, 'Yes, Charles, you could go as a padre – you and Arthur together in this great crusade. Wouldn't that be a noble thing to do?'

Charles's mother cut in quietly, 'Your brother can be just as effective offering up prayers at home.'

'Nonsense.' The major was dismissive. 'Sophie's right. Actions are more effective than words when it comes to war.'

Flora could keep silent no longer. 'But words can be more effective in bringing peace and restoring sanity. I'm astonished,

Sophie, that you can want your brother rushing off to war, knowing his pacifist views.'

'It's all very well preaching peace and harmony when there's no threat,' Sophie bristled, 'but when our nation is under attack from evil hordes, then the only honourable course is to fight.'

'Well said!' the major crowed.

'And the women?' Flora questioned. 'What are we to do in your great crusade?'

'We must support our men to the hilt,' Sophie declared. 'I wish I could go and fight but I can't, so I'll do my best to encourage others to go – and for women to volunteer to do the jobs left by the men. We can serve in other ways.'

Flora held on to her temper. 'So women are to be subordinate once more? We are to accept this war that the diplomats have led us into – that women have had no say in – without a murmur?'

'Yes,' Sophie snapped. 'If we give ourselves wholly to the nation in this time of peril, we'll win the right to political freedom!'

'We don't need a war to prove that right!' Flora cried in exasperation.

The major thumped the table. 'That's enough,' he bellowed. 'I'll not have you spoiling my daughter's betrothal tea party. I'm proud to be welcoming a son-in-law who will be defending his country in a few short weeks. I hope, Charles,' he said with a frown, 'that the least you can do is preach for national unity at such a time – and for victory.'

Charles looked at his wife's scarlet face under her red hair, her blue eyes furious.

'I shall pray for Arthur and his comrades – and for Sophie and the other families left behind. And I shall preach for victory as I do every Sunday,' he said quietly, 'victory for the Prince of Peace.'

The tea party was strained and the Hauxleys left soon afterwards. The major retired to his study in a foul mood, and Charles helped his mother upstairs. Flora tried to make amends with Sophie, taking her by the arm and suggesting a stroll around the grounds before they left.

'I'm sorry for arguing,' she said contritely. 'I didn't mean to spoil things. All this has come as a bit of a shock – the engagement, your conversion to a warrior,' she teased gently.

Sophie was defensive. 'Suffragettes have always been warriors.

The Pankhursts were the first to call a truce with the Government and tell us to get behind the war effort.'

Flora pointed out, 'We don't all have to do what Mrs Pankhurst says. There are many women who are speaking out against the war – as mothers, as socialists, as pacifists.'

Sophie pulled away from her, but they walked on in silence. Flora tried again.

'You are a brave and intelligent woman, and you have every right to hold the opinions that you do. But so does Charles. It's bad enough that his father ridicules him so openly – he relies on the support of his dear sister. Can't you at least do that?'

Sophie stopped and fixed her with a direct look. 'I've always stuck up for Charles. But I reserve the right to tell him if I think he's making the wrong decision.'

Flora held her look. 'And you, Sophie, have you made the right decision?'

'About what?'

'Marrying Arthur,' Flora said softly. 'You've always resisted parental pressure before.'

Sophie coloured. 'This is no one's choice but mine.'

'Do you love him?' Flora asked.

Sophie looked away. 'I'm fond of him, and we'll make a success of it.'

'You're not just feeling sorry for him because he's been called up?' Flora persisted. 'Because that wouldn't be fair to Arthur in the long run.'

Sophie gave her a sharp look. 'Don't tell me what's fair! You all made sure I didn't have the man I fell in love with. Well, at least as Arthur's wife I'll have a position in society – as a Hauxley I'll have power. People will listen to me more than they ever will to Charles in his backwater mission. I'll be the best recruiting sergeant the army's ever had. And one day I'll be a Member of Parliament just like Arthur's father.' Her look was passionate, her eyes hostile. 'Maybe I do feel sorry for Arthur – but I respect him too. I'm proud to be marrying a captain in the British Army, just as I was proud of my brother Liddon. Charles may be loveable and well-meaning, but he will never match up to either of them.'

Flora watched her march off without trying to follow or make up. She stood shaking at Sophie's angry words, wondering how they had grown so far apart so quickly. Would it ever be possible for them to stand on the same platform again and demand equality, when their views were so opposing? With that bleak thought, she went to find Charles. They travelled back in the trap, sitting close together, comforted by their proximity, wondering if they would be invited to the wedding after all.

CHAPTER 16

The consensus in Crawdene opposing war evaporated like the morning dew. Within days the patriotic frenzy of London was being reported in the newspapers and spreading around the country. Recruiting offices were swiftly set up to cope with the numbers volunteering to fight. Posters went up and the national press was filled with vitriol about the terrible Hun.

Peter came back from a trip to Gateshead with the grocer, worried about broken glass in the street outside a pork butcher's shop.

'The butcher's a German spy,' Peter reported, wide-eyed, 'that's what Mr Speed said.'

'Daft nonsense,' Jonas cried in disbelief.

'Mr Speed says he deserved it,' Peter frowned. 'He was trying to poison us. Won't buy his sausages any more.'

When Jonas swore, Helen put out a restraining hand.

'Don't shout at the lad; he's just repeatin' the lies he's been told.'

The next day, Jonas came back from an acrimonious lodge meeting. The village was split over the war.

'Nothing's changed since last week,' Jonas protested. 'The reasons against the war are still the same. Let the imperialists send their own sons to be butchered if that's what they want – but not our sons.'

'Of course things have changed.' Barnabas Curran squared up to him. 'We're under attack from foreigners. This is a holy war against unholy heathen hordes. It's our duty to support the lads being sent to France – and to work hard at the coal face.'

Jonas was scathing. 'And I suppose that means working whatever hours Oliphant says and for any wages? The bosses will use this as an excuse to cut back our working conditions.'

'And what would you rather have? England overrun by Germans?' Barnabas shouted.

'Resist the war.' Jonas thumped the table. 'Tell the recruiting officers and the armchair patriots to go to the devil!'

Apart from a vociferous core of socialists and radical non-conformists, the MacRaes were increasingly in the minority. Even Mr Attwater had changed his tune.

'We do not seek harm to our brethren in Germany, only that they rise up against the evil Kaiser who oppresses them and leads them astray. This is a just war against evil forces. We must support our troops . . .'

Talk around the Curran dinner table was bullish, as a British Expeditionary Force was hastily assembled for France.

'We'll have them whipped in a few months,' Barnabas pronounced. 'Best soldiers in the world, us British.'

'Aye,' Tom agreed, 'we rule the world; a few Hun aren't ganin' to be any bother.'

Emmie sat mutely waiting for Sam to temper their jingoism. But he said nothing and avoided her look. She swallowed her dissenting words, dismayed by the family's sudden thirst for war. Like her, Louise kept quiet, though she acted as if it had little to do with them.

When Emmie tried to talk about it, Louise merely grumbled that she would see less of her husband. 'Sam'll have to work longer hours down the pit. Give him another excuse to stop away.'

Emmie was at a loss as to what to do. She felt cut adrift. The campaign for the vote had collapsed, the leaders of the major women's groups calling for a truce with the Government and national unity while the country was at war. The Pankhursts had gone further, exhorting all women to rally behind the war effort. Emmie avoided going round to see Rab and had not contributed to the *Messenger* for over a month, not knowing what to write. Women were divided by the war and her own feelings were mixed.

Then Emmie heard that the MacRaes had had their windows smashed for opposing the war and went hurrying round. They seemed unconcerned.

'Was just a couple of bairns throwing stones at the kitchen window,' Helen said, dismissing the incident.

Jonas blamed the pomp of the recruiting banners and bands marching through the village every Saturday.

'It's that Captain Hauxley filling the lads' heads with tales of glory,' he growled. 'You would think they were going on a picnic – no word about the bloody business of killing.'

Helen shook her head in concern. 'The Guild are in two minds. There's worry over lads joining up. At least we can make sure their families are properly provided for.' She put a hand on Emmie's arm. 'Have you heard the news about Miss Sophie?'

Emmie shook her head.

'She's marrying Captain Hauxley. The banns were read out in Blackton last Sunday, Mannie told our Rab.'

'Tell her about the message,' Jonas grunted.

Helen gave an indignant nod. 'Aye, she sent a message to the Guild. Told us it was our duty to stop any agitation against the war and report anything unpatriotic to the authorities. Said we should be proud if our men volunteered and that women should support them in any way they can.'

Emmie stared in open-mouthed astonishment. 'She never did?'

Helen snorted. 'Said if we showed how strong women could be, holding the fort at home, we'd get the vote all the quicker. That Hauxley's turned her head with his fancy uniform, if you ask me.'

'It's to be expected,' Jonas said angrily, 'the ruling class closing ranks. For all her talk of equality, she knows where her interests lie. The Oliphants and Hauxleys of this world will do anything to protect those interests – including sending their workers off to fight and die for them.'

'How's our Sam?' Helen asked suddenly.

Emmie caught her worried look. 'Canny,' she answered non-committally. 'Why do you ask?'

Helen flushed. 'He hasn't been round to see us in weeks.'

Emmie was surprised. Louise complained that Sam never stopped in the house any more. Emmie assumed he had been spending time round at his parents'.

'Are the Currans giving him a hard time about the war?' Helen questioned.

Emmie felt awkward. 'No, not really. Sam doesn't say much about it; keeps his opinions to himself.'

Jonas grunted. 'Best way, with old man Curran. He harangues the lodge like a recruiting sergeant these days.'

'As long as he's not avoiding us for any reason,' Helen said, scrutinising Emmie.

'Course not,' she reassured. 'Probably making the most of the summer weather – ganin' for long walks.'

'At least you and Barny are still visitin',' Helen smiled, giving the boy a quick cuddle. 'Don't know what I'd do if you stopped comin'.'

'Course we won't,' Emmie insisted.

Jonas eyed her over his pipe. 'But you've stopped writing for the *Messenger*, Rab tells us.'

Emmie went hot. 'He shouldn't have said—'

Helen was quick to reassure her. 'It won't go beyond these four walls that you wrote as Artemis. And he doesn't blame you for changing your mind, specially living with a Curran.'

Emmie was indignant. 'Tom doesn't tell me what to think. And who says I've changed me mind?'

Jonas was blunt. 'Well, you're not writing for the paper any more, lassie.'

'I've been busy,' Emmie floundered, holding out her arms for Barny.

Helen handed him back with a wistful look. 'Course you have.'

Emmie felt awkward in their company and suddenly wanted to be gone. She wished she could be as convinced as they were in their opinions, but could not. Perhaps Sophie Oliphant had a point, and they were being unpatriotic. Should they not all be burying their class differences for the greater good while their country was under threat? She could think of nothing more terrifying than being overrun and conquered by barbarians who the newspapers claimed had murdered fleeing women and children in Belgium and butchered babies.

But she knew the MacRaes were good people and not dangerous agitators, as the Currans would have them. The look of disappointment on their faces when she left them haunted Emmie and she could not settle back into her mundane life. The news of Miss Sophie's forthcoming marriage to an officer unsettled her too. What did Rab think of it? What of Sophie's brother, Charles, and Dr Flora who had been so outspoken against the war before it began?

The desire to visit the Settlement fuelled Emmie's restlessness. She longed to speak with her old friends and discover what they felt.

One mellow sunny day in September, Emmie hitched a ride on Peter's delivery cart as far as Swalwell and took Barny into Gateshead. The town looked unchanged apart from the sprouting of recruitment posters on walls.

The Mousys greeted her warmly and took Barny off for a drink of milk.

'You go and see Mrs Oliphant,' Mousy said with a wink, 'cheer her up. We'll look after the bairn.' When Emmie asked what the matter was, the old man shook his head and would say nothing more.

Emmie found the doctor writing letters in Charles's study. She leaped up at sight of Emmie.

'My dear!' she cried, rushing forward to embrace her. They hugged and Emmie felt the numbness that had gripped her for weeks melt at Flora's torrent of warm words and questions about the family and village. She swept her into the kitchen and made a pot of tea.

Emmie asked about the wedding. Flora gave her a stricken look.

'We weren't invited. Oh, this wicked war,' she railed, 'dividing families and friends. Charles's father won't speak to him because he preaches pacifism. That was to be expected. But for Sophie to cut him off too . . . it's hurt him deeply.'

Emmie was surprised at the doctor confiding in her, but was encouraged.

'Perhaps she feels torn between her brother and husband,' Emmie suggested.

'Not torn at all,' Flora answered angrily. 'She has sided completely with her father and the Hauxleys. She sees it as some new crusade she can throw herself into – going around on the arm of the dashing captain at recruitment rallies and challenging the men to enlist. I think she's enjoying it all.'

'Surely not.' Emmie was shocked.

Flora laughed mirthlessly. 'Oh, yes. Sophie never cared for Arthur Hauxley until war broke out. I think she married him because she felt sorry for him – he's already left for France.' She stopped and glanced at Emmie, perhaps regretting her frankness. 'Oh, don't mind me. I just find the whole thing too depressing. To think we have lifted ourselves so little above the barbaric that we can contemplate going to war with our neighbours.'

Emmie had a sudden thought. 'Frau Bauer? Where is she?'

Flora hung her head. Quietly she said, 'She was arrested a month ago. We did what we could to have her released but it made no difference; she's been deported. Dr Korsky too. They're somewhere in the chaos on the Continent. I've written but heard nothing. Perhaps my letters never get through . . .'

When she looked up, her eyes were brimming with tears. Emmie went to her and touched her shoulder. She was suddenly filled with anger at the injustice meted out to their suffrage friends. They had been fighters for greater freedom for all, yet cast out as enemies. Kind, funny, talkative Frau Bauer was not her enemy. Neither were millions more women on the opposing side whose fathers, sons and husbands would soon be fighting their own.

'This is madness,' Emmie said in bewilderment.

Abruptly, Flora wiped her eyes and turned away. Leaving the tea half made, she marched over to the kitchen table and pulled out a chair.

'Sit here and read this,' she ordered, pushing a pile of newspapers towards her. She picked a pamphlet off the top. 'The Runcies passed it on to me. It's written by a missionary's wife – head of the local suffragists in India.'

Emmie sat down and began to read.

. . . women get no benefit from war. Whatever is of glory, it is for men. The fascination of war, its pomp and pride of uniforms, gold lace, medals and pensions are for men . . . The Church colludes in war, yet two-thirds of its members are women. We must appeal to the Church to work hand in hand with the mothers of mankind in this crusade against the war. Christianity demands of women this crusade of peace! Mothers, wives, daughters, sisters! Go forward – God wills it.

Flora brought her tea while she read on, poring over copies of other suffragist newspapers that called for women to organise for peace. One advocated a Women's Peace Expeditionary Force to go to the front and place themselves between the two armies, unarmed and carrying white banners with doves. Emmie's heart quickened.

'I thought the suffrage movement was backing the war,' she questioned.

'Not all, by any means,' Flora encouraged. 'There are many like us on both sides who want negotiation and peace before this escalates.'

'I've been so confused about it all,' Emmie admitted. 'Frightened of speaking up – there's such a hunger for winning at all costs in the village.'

Flora reached across the table and squeezed her hand. 'I know how difficult it must be for you, but you are not alone, surely? The MacRaes and their friends are not afraid to speak out, I bet.'

Emmie met Flora's encouraging look. 'Can I take some of these articles?' she asked.

'Of course,' Flora smiled, 'as many as you want.'

Emmie smuggled the pamphlets home in the lining of her coat, not quite knowing what to do with them. She hid them under the mattress.

That Saturday afternoon, Tom insisted they went to watch the parade of Northumberland Fusiliers through Blackton.

'Be a canny sight for Barny,' he said, 'and you like the bands. Louise and Sam are ganin' too.'

Emmie was encouraged that Sam would be coming with them; he was so subdued of late.

A platform had been erected outside the mine offices, and jugs of beer were provided from the public house opposite. Red, white and blue bunting was strung across the street and there was a festive air about the large crowd that had gathered to listen to the band and hear the speeches. As they approached, Emmie strained to catch the speaker's words. With a jolt she realised it was Miss Sophie under the huge-brimmed hat.

'. . . and my husband sends encouraging news from France – they have stopped the German advance in its tracks. Morale is very high. But we need more men now. How glorious it will be for those brave men who are there to bring us victory – what tales they will have to tell. I ask you to join the finest regiment in the land and serve under my dear courageous husband. Wives and mothers, I appeal to you. Don't be selfish – let your men go. Onwards to victory!'

There was a burst of applause and the band struck up 'The British Grenadiers'. A queue began to form at the open-air recruitment table.

'Haway,' Sam nudged Tom, 'let's have a glass of Oliphant's free beer.'

Tom hesitated then shook his head. 'You gan. Barny wants to see the carthorses up the lane.'

Sam ignored Louise's disapproving look and sauntered off. The others wandered up the lane, Tom and Emmie swinging Barny between them. Louise looked on enviously as Barny chattered about the horses and they watched the field hands bending over rows of cabbages.

Suddenly, she announced, 'I'm ganin' home,' and stalked off.

Emmie said quickly to Tom, 'I'll gan after her.'

Louise brushed aside Emmie's concern and hurriedly looked for Sam. But he had found friends among the drinkers and refused to leave.

'We'll be late for tea,' Louise said tersely.

'You gan on.' Sam waved her away.

'Don't think you can come home stinking of beer,' his wife scolded. 'Me father will have some'at to say if you do.'

'The old bugger's always got some'at to say,' Sam snorted, setting his friends laughing.

Louise reddened. 'Please, Sam, come home.'

But one of his workmates said, 'Leave the lad alone – it's not every day we get owt for free out of Oliphant.'

Louise grew angry. 'Well you can stop at your mam's the night if you drink any more.'

Sam's mates nudged him and made ribald comments.

Louise turned abruptly and marched off, Emmie hurrying after her.

'He'll not stay long,' Emmie tried to reassure. 'Just having a bit crack at Oliphant's expense.'

'He can stay as long as he wants,' Louise said crossly. 'I'll not stop him making a fool of himself with the drink.'

'Is everything all right between you?' Emmie asked, slipping an arm through her friend's.

Louise was suddenly tearful and shook her head. 'He hardly speaks these days. Takes hisself off whenever he's not at work. Don't know where – or who he's with. Might have a fancy woman, for all I know.'

'Not Sam!' Emmie protested.

'He's sick of living at Father's,' Louise sniffed, 'but won't do owt about finding our own place. If only he had a better job at the pit like our Tom.'

'It'll come in time,' Emmie encouraged.

'No it won't.' Louise refused to be comforted. 'He'll find another lass – someone who can give him bairns – then he'll leave me.'

Emmie threw her arms about her friend. 'Sam's not like that.'

'I thought he was different,' Louise sobbed, 'but he's just like the other MacRaes underneath – a bucketful o' trouble.'

Halfway home, Tom caught them up with Barny on his shoulders. Louise said quickly, 'Don't tell our Tom what I've said.'

Emmie threw Tom a warning look. 'Sam's coming on later.'

'Aye,' Tom grunted, 'saw him drinking for England.'

Darkness had fallen by the time Sam came home, singing at the top of his voice and supported by two workmates. Emmie and Tom were still at the house in Denmark Street, waiting tensely for Sam's return.

Barnabas went to the door, his look thunderous.

'Get in here quick,' he ordered. Tom hurried to help his brother-in-law over the step. Once inside Barnabas berated him.

'You're a disgrace,' he said contemptuously, 'smelling like a brewery.'

Sam laughed and swayed in front of him.

'I've a good mind to put you out the house until you see the error of your ways,' his father-in-law lectured. 'MacRae might accept such behaviour but I won't.'

This made Sam laugh hysterically. Tom steered him into a seat while Emmie rocked a fretful Barny, the boy alarmed by the raised voices. Louise would not look at her husband.

Barnabas continued, 'If I catch you drinking again, you're out.'

Sam pushed Tom away and struggled to his feet again.

'Can't tell me what to do any more, you old bastard,' Sam sneered.

'Sam!' Louise gasped.

He faced her. 'I'm leavin'. Had enough of your da ganin' on 'bout the bloody army. Joined up. That should please yer all.'

They stared at him in shock. No one said a word. Then Louise covered her face with her hands and burst into tears.

CHAPTER 17

Emmie thought Sam would change his mind once he'd sobered up, but he did not. The outrage of the MacRaes only seemed to harden his resolve.

'Bloody class traitor!' Rab accused, almost coming to blows.

'Stuff your class war,' Sam sneered. 'I'm doing me bit for me country.'

'You're running away from the Currans, more like,' Rab scoffed.

'You callin' me a coward?' Sam came at his brother menacingly.

'No, just a capitalist puppet,' Rab answered, squaring up to him. 'Sawdust for brains.'

Helen barged her way between them. 'Stop it, the pair of you. What's come over you lads?' She appealed to her second son. 'Have you thought what you're doing, Sam, really thought on it?'

'Aye, I have,' Sam answered stubbornly.

Rab glared. 'Just remember when you're sticking your bayonet in some poor German conscript – he's probably a socialist comrade.'

'The only comrades I care about are me marras – and the lads I'm joining up with,' Sam shouted as he stormed out.

To Helen's distress, Sam did not visit again before he left. Jonas pretended not to care. His son was a grown man and was free to make his own mistakes. Peter drove them to distraction with descriptions of the battlefield, repeating what Mr Speed read to him daily from his patriotic newspaper. Peter was full of excitement at his brother going off to war and perplexed by his father's stormy refusal to talk about it.

Helen pressed a small package on Emmie and asked her to take it round to Sam.

'It's only a piece of tiffin – his favourite – and an extra pair of socks,' she said. 'Tell him to take care of hissel'.'

The atmosphere at the Currans' was strained. Outwardly, Barnabas boasted about his brave son-in-law, but at home the bitterness over Sam's drunken words sullied the days before departure. As Tom was at work, Louise asked Emmie to go with her to see Sam off at the station. An open wagon was bedecked in bunting to take the four new recruits down to Newcastle with their families. The young men were all members of the Chapel; Mr Attwater sent them off with a blessing on a blustery October morning and the colliery band led them through the village, neighbours turning out to wave them away. The atmosphere was so jolly that Emmie had to remind herself the men were going off to war, not the gala.

As they passed the end of China Street Sam glanced round. Emmie had hoped the parcel might have prompted him to go to see his mother, but it had not. If he regretted that now, his expression gave nothing away. Then, as they trundled past the Co-operative Hall, there were Helen and Peter, standing among a small band of Guild women. They had bunches of chrysanthemums and roses. Peter stood waving a red flag in excitement and shouting his brother's name.

Someone laughed, 'Look, the communists have come out to see you, MacRae.'

Sam stared in astonishment as the wagon drew closer and the women threw flowers to the men and their loved ones.

'Peter! Mam!' Sam cried, standing up in the open carriage.

His mother rushed forward, thrusting a white rose at him. 'Don't do anything daft. Come back safe, me bonny lad!'

Sam seized the rose as they passed. 'Me dad'll gan light when he finds his best roses chopped,' he shouted.

'Not for you he won't,' Helen cried, a hand stretched up in farewell.

Sam grinned and waved back. 'Tell him ta-ra from me – and to that bugger Rab!'

Peter ran behind the wagon all the way down the main street, shouting goodbyes, his flag snapping in the wind. Sam laughed and impulsively threw his cap to his brother.

'Wear it for me, Peter lad. I'll not need it now.'

Peter stopped to pick it up and put it on over his own. The wagon pulled away and plunged down the hill out of sight.

Barny clung to the side and babbled happily about horses as others made frantic conversation. Emmie saw Sam reach for Louise's hand. He sat holding it as they jostled down the rutted road. Emmie saw tears start in her friend's eyes and looked away, her throat constricting. When they reached the bridge over the River Tyne, she was distracted by Barny's squeals of interest and the gasps of excitement from the travellers, some of whom had never been to Newcastle before.

Central Station was cavernous and echoing. The platforms were a noisy confusion of soldiers embarking with kitbags, and new recruits in their Sunday best, clutching homespun packages in brown paper. Emmie held tight to Barny as they searched for the right train, the small boy round-eyed at his surroundings.

'Write and tell me what camp's like,' Louise urged, as they congregated by the barrier.

'Aye,' Sam promised. 'We'll not be off to France till they teach us a trick or two. Be dull as ditch water.'

Emmie hugged him briefly. 'Take care, won't you?'

He nodded and winked, swinging Barny up into his arms and tickling him. He handed him over.

'Tell Mam I'm wearing the socks – and sorry I didn't come round,' he said bashfully.

Emmie nodded, smiled and stepped back to allow Louise the final minutes alone with him. Her friend clung to Sam.

'I wish you weren't ganin',' Louise said, her face crumpling.

'If I don't, it'll all be over and I'll miss me chance to be a hero,' Sam joked.

'Heroes can dig coal, an' all. Working canny hard at the pit would be helping win the war just as much. You know nowt about soldiering,' Louise despaired.

Sam gave her a wistful smile. 'I'm doing this 'cos I want you to be proud of me, Lou. I don't want to be second best to your da any more.'

Louise looked at him in exasperation. 'Oh, Sam!'

She flung her arms around his neck and they hugged each

other tight. Too soon, the men were being ordered aboard and Sam had to pull away from his sobbing wife. He looked beseechingly at Emmie. Clutching Barny in the press of people, Emmie pushed to Louise's side and took her arm.

'Let him gan, Lou,' she said gently.

She stood supporting Louise as the train shunted forward and the waving men were enveloped in a waft of steam. Moments later they were gone and the crowds of well-wishers ebbed back. The return journey was subdued; one or two cried quietly, a baby wailed, Barny was fretful. Louise sat, pale and rigid, not saying a word.

The following weeks were quiet ones, Louise's initial anxiety lessening with news from Sam that camp was cold but the food plentiful. There was no word of his being sent to France and there was little news of any action at the front. The worst losses were at sea, among merchant ships carrying supplies to Britain.

When Emmie visited the MacRaes, they put on a brave face about Sam's going. But Helen confided nearer Christmas, 'It's like the lamps are dimmer without him. And Rab doesn't laugh as much.'

Emmie had seen nothing of Rab for months. She had made herself keep away from Mannie's after Tom's jealousy over Barny and his suspicions about her. She had never even been to explain why she had given up writing her column. She had just stopped visiting.

'How's Rab managing?' Emmie asked tentatively.

'Has to be careful with the *Messenger*,' Helen replied. 'Police gave him a friendly warning that he can't write anything that'll put folk off enlistin'. But it's still sellin' and he's doing his teaching. Keeps full of busy.'

Lists of casualties from the front began to grow. The son of a deputy, two doors from the Currans, was killed in action. A cousin of Mr Speed, the grocer, died of dysentery in Egypt.

Just before Christmas, Emmie went to visit the Settlement and found Flora and Mabel full of talk about the newly formed No Conscription Fellowship.

'One day soon the war machine will run out of willing volunteers,' Flora predicted. 'That's when they'll force men to join up.'

Emmie was alarmed. 'But they can't do that.'

'They can do anything, my dear,' Mabel sniffled, full of cold. 'They have given themselves great emergency powers.'

'We have to nip any such ideas in the bud,' Flora said, 'get the matter raised in Parliament.'

Emmie thought such work beyond her, but she wanted to help in some way. The Settlement was full daily with needy families, whose men were seeking work or gone to war. The children especially needed winter clothes. Emmie went to Helen and the Guild for help. Over the winter, they knitted, sewed, patched old clothes and cut them down to size. Once a week, Emmie got a lift with Peter on the grocery cart and took them down to the Settlement.

Tom tolerated these trips, boasting to his friends that she was doing something patriotic. She knew he missed Sam's companionship and their trips to the club on Friday nights. But Tom had grown affectionate and attentive again, and she enjoyed their evenings together with Barny by their own fireside.

'What would you do if they brought in conscription?' Emmie asked him once.

Tom shrugged. 'I'd have to gan, I suppose. But it won't happen for pitmen – job's too important.'

'Good,' Emmie said. 'Barny needs his dad. I'm glad you're more home-loving than Sam.'

Tom bristled. 'It's not that I'm scared of fightin'. Us lads are graftin' harder than Sam in his cushy camp. He's on a bloody holiday by the sounds of it.'

Emmie let him have the last word and never mentioned conscription again.

Spring came with the dark news of heavy fighting at the front. For the first time they began to read about deadly gas attacks, of massive casualties and numbers of missing. On a visit to the Settlement, Emmie found Flora preparing to travel. Women across Europe were forming an international league for peace and were planning to meet in The Hague in late April. The national press were up in arms, denouncing them as traitors and Hun-lovers. The Government had refused them travel permits.

'I've just heard that a handful of us are to be allowed to go,' Flora said excitedly. 'There's rumour of a ship ready to take us from Tilbury docks.'

'Won't it be dangerous?' Emmie asked in alarm.

'There are scores of women from all over the Continent making far riskier journeys – and dozens sailing from America.' Flora was buoyant. 'We won't be stopped.'

Not for the first time Emmie admired the older woman's stubborn courage and optimism. After the huge losses at Ypres, the planned congress was deeply unpopular with the general public, yet there was local support that stopped the Settlement being a target for window-smashing. Flora was convinced there were large, silent numbers who were sympathetic to the women's peace campaign but dared not speak out.

Emmie kept from Tom that the doctor was so deeply involved in the conference. He would see it as women interfering where they should not. His father would call them ungodly and treacherous. But the next time she visited Gateshead, Flora had returned frustrated. The Government had abruptly closed all the North Sea ports, preventing the women from travelling.

'The conference is still going ahead,' she said defiantly. 'We'll just have to wait and see what comes of it.'

There were no reports in the daily newspapers, and Emmie would not have heard about the plans to send women envoys to lobby for peace if it had not been for her friends at the Settlement. Flora went off to attend a meeting in London in mid-May to hear all about the conference. Emmie was filled with a new restlessness at the thought of what the women might achieve – a swift end to the fighting and rising death toll. If only she could be a part of it. Already, there were rumours of conscription being introduced, just as Flora had feared. Sam's last postcard to Louise said they were due to be shipped to France within the month. Anxiety among the Currans and MacRaes grew.

June came and with it the news that Sophie Hauxley had given birth to a son, Arthur Liddon. The miners were given a half-day holiday in celebration and an extra shilling each in their pay by a proud Major James. He had his longed-for heir.

Tom and Emmie took Barny for a picnic on the fell on the half-day off, revelling in the warm sunshine and seeing their son tripping about happily in the heather. They both hoped for another child, but Emmie had failed to fall pregnant again.

'You can almost forget there's a war on, up here,' Emmie mused, pulling at the coarse grass and scattering seeds.

'Aye,' Tom agreed sleepily, lying back in the heather.

'I wish Lou had come with us,' Emmie said.

'Too busy knittin' for our Sam,' Tom grunted. 'He'll have more socks than the rest of the regiment put together.'

'Keeps her busy, poor Lou.'

Tom reached across and pulled her towards him. 'Stop thinkin' about me sister for once and give us a kiss.'

Barny came rushing across and jumped on his father. 'Me too!' he giggled.

Emmie laughed and hugged the pair of them.

Tom had just gone off to work the next morning when a neighbour of the Currans came banging on the back door.

'Come quick, missus,' he panted, 'Mrs Curran sent me to fetch you.'

Emmie's heart thumped in alarm. 'What's happened?'

'Wouldn't say,' the youth mumbled, and dashed off.

Emmie knocked on Mrs Haile's door and asked her to take care of Barny. Ten minutes later, she was catching her breath at the Currans' back door. Even before she went in, she could hear wailing and her insides clenched.

Louise caught sight of her and ran over in hysterics.

'Sam,' she screamed, 'my Sam! Says he's dead.' Her eyes were wild, her face swollen and red from crying.

Emmie clung on to her, looking with incomprehension at Louise's frightened mother.

'Telegram came half an hour ago,' she explained in agitation. 'I've sent for Mr Curran.'

'But how?' Emmie asked in bewilderment. 'He hasn't even gone to France.'

Louise clutched at her. 'Aye, that's right. Didn't I say that, Mam? They must've made a mistake – not my Sam – he's still in England.'

'But the telegram says—' Mrs Curran said weakly.

Louise wailed, 'I don't care what it says – it's lies!' She buried her head into Emmie's shoulder and wept uncontrollably. All Emmie could do was hold on to her shaking body and stroke her hair, trying not to dissolve into tears herself. She thought of Helen and her knees almost buckled.

Barnabas arrived and his presence calmed his daughter.

'You must accept it, lass,' he told her, patting her shoulder in a rare show of affection. 'It's not for us to question. What will be, will be. God be merciful on his soul.'

Louise was helped to bed and lay under the cover, hunched into a ball, her face buried in the pillow Sam used. Emmie stayed with her for a while, but her friend refused all comfort and would not speak.

In the Currans' parlour, Emmie asked, 'Sam's parents . . . ?'

Barnabas nodded grimly. 'I'll go up to the forge – tell Jonas face to face. He can let his family know.'

Emmie said quietly, 'No, I'll go and tell Aunt Helen.'

The walk down to China Street seemed endless, her heart banging in dread, throat dry, legs shaking. But when she reached number eighteen, Emmie was filled with a sudden calm. She walked into the familiar kitchen with the sun pouring in through the low doorway and called out a greeting as she had on countless occasions. Helen turned from rolling pastry, wiped her hands on her apron and beamed in surprise.

'Pet lamb!' she cried. It was the old babyish expression that shattered Emmie's brave front.

'Oh, Auntie Helen,' she gasped, holding out her arms.

Helen froze. 'What's happened? Is it Barny?' she whispered.

Emmie shook her head, tears streaming down her face, 'Louise got a telegram this morning . . .'

'Not Sam!'

Emmie nodded. She squeezed her eyes shut at the sight of Helen's stricken face. Moments later, she felt her aunt's arms wrap around her.

'Oh, my bonny, bonny bairn!' Helen sobbed.

For the first time, Emmie heard Helen weep aloud and the sound tore through her heart.

CHAPTER 18

A few days later, a letter came from Sam's commanding officer with more details. Four days after landing in France, they were moving up to the front when Sam had been run over. He had gone to help pull a supply wagon out of a ditch; the horse had bolted. The officer praised Sam's good humour and bravery in the line of duty. He was a good soldier, one who kept up the spirits of his fellow men. He was given a Christian burial.

Jonas railed at the news. 'Good soldier! He hadn't even got to the front. He was a good pitman, that's what. The waste of it all – the stupid, wicked waste! Oh, my laddie,' he broke off, kicking the fender.

A bouquet of flowers and a card of condolence came to Louise from Mrs Sophie Hauxley. Louise was pathetically grateful. For the first time in a week, she gave a wan smile and set about arranging the flowers. This, more than anything, angered Emmie. Sam's death had been futile, not heroic. All the condolences in the world would not bring him back, or make up for sending him off to fight a senseless war. She blamed Miss Sophie's red-blooded jingoism that day back in September for filling Sam's head full of ideas of glory. Bunches of flowers were to silence dissent, encourage yet more young men to rush off and die for the cause.

Emmie looked at the sombre Currans dressed in black and began to resent their piety. They had turned Sam away from his family. He had closed his ears to the MacRaes' arguments for a socialist future, without war or poverty. Sam had been tricked, just as the Currans were under the spell of militarism. It would always be like this, as long as too few of them stood up against the tide of hatred and bloodshed.

Emmie swallowed her bitter words against the Hauxley bouquet and set off home in the rain. It came on harder and she suddenly diverted down India Street. The rain drummed on the uneven bricks as she crossed Mannie's yard, but above the din she heard music playing loudly. Pushing at the half-open door, she peered into the gloom of Rab's room. The melancholy piano music swelled around her, the fire hissed and smoked.

Rab's hair was longer, beard untrimmed, sleeves rolled up over brawny arms like a navvy as he played. Emmie said his name, but he did not respond, so totally absorbed was he in the music. As her eyes grew accustomed to the shadows, she saw the untidy heaps of paper and unwashed crockery, the unmade bed.

Suddenly, he broke off playing, his shoulders heaved and he let out a groan or a laugh. Rab's thick-set body shook and the strange gulping noise grew louder. In shock, Emmie realised he was crying. Embarrassed, she had stepped back towards the door when he turned and saw her.

Tears were streaming down his face. He made no attempt to hide his weeping. They stared at each other.

'I'm sorry,' Emmie whispered. 'I didn't mean . . .'

She backed away, rushed out the door and fled across the slippery yard. She ran home, haunted by the sight of Rab's open grief. Of all of them, he knew Sam the best. As boys they had been inseparable; as youths they had worked, sung and played together. Only since Sam had married had they grown distant. The war had split them asunder. Helen had told of the brothers' bitter parting. Now Rab would never be able to make amends. What a terrible burden! Emmie's heart ached for him. She had gone hoping to find comfort, yet had run away instead of comforting Rab. It would be doubly difficult to go back now. Rab was a proud man and she had caught him in a rare moment of weakness.

Over the next few days, Emmie tried to forget she had ever been. She took comfort in her three-year-old son, his cheerful chatter and generous hugs. She tried to talk to Tom about Sam, but he nursed his grief privately and resented her harking back to old times.

Louise obeyed the call from Sophie Hauxley to sign up at the labour exchange as a patriotic duty, and got a job in the local hardware store. Sam's became a hallowed name in the Curran household, a saintly soldier who had never done any wrong. Emmie did not recognise the virtuous teetotal chapelgoer who was eulogised by Mr Attwater at a memorial service for her brother-in-law. To Emmie, they were robbing her of her true memories of the happy-go-lucky Sam. She found it a trial to be at the Currans' and preferred to slip out to see the MacRaes. They talked about their son all the time, and Peter repeated old jokes of Sam's, proud to wear his brother's cap.

The summer brought no relief from the grim news of numbers dead and maimed at the front. One time, visiting the Settlement, Emmie listened with horror to a wounded soldier tell of the carnage to a packed meeting of the No Conscription Fellowship. But by the autumn there was open talk of conscription. A first step was for young men to come forward to attest that they were willing to be called up if necessary. Tom came home talking bullishly that he and some of his marras were going to register.

Emmie was dismayed. 'Don't be daft! You'll join up over my dead body.'

Tom gave her a sharp look. 'Don't tell me what to do. We all have to stand up and be counted.'

'And be shot down twice as quick,' Emmie retorted. 'It's not a game of footy over there.'

'How would you know?' Tom said irritably.

'I've heard lads tell what it's like – at the Settlement. And it's working-class lads are having the worst of it – and not just from the enemy. One Durham Light Infantry lad was shot by his comrades for fallin' asleep at his post – made to do it, they were.'

'I don't like you ganin' there,' Tom snapped. 'They're fillin' your head full of dangerous nonsense.'

'Not like the nonsense they're filling your head with in the papers and at chapel, you mean?' Emmie challenged. 'How many more lads have to die before both sides see the only way to end this war is to sit down and negotiate?'

Tom sprang at her, shaking her by the arms. 'Don't talk like that in my house! That's bloody treason.'

Emmie was scared by his look of fury. 'And what about me and Barny if you get called up?' she gasped.

At mention of their son, Tom let go his grip. 'I'll always provide for the pair of you.'

'Not if you're dead,' she said, shaking.

He turned from her, his expression hard to read.

'It's just a name on a piece of paper – to show I'm no coward. Married pitmen won't get called up.'

'Please, Tom,' Emmie pleaded, 'don't do it.'

But he would not listen to her and went with his friends to register under Lord Derby's scheme. He was issued with an armband to show he had attested and wore it proudly around the village. One time, at the MacRaes', Emmie found Peter upset at having been forced to take a white feather in Gateshead for not wearing an armband.

'Poor lad thinks he's done some'at wrong,' Helen said angrily. 'Jonas told him to wear the feather in his cap with pride, but he doesn't understand.'

Emmie had not been down to the Settlement in many weeks, but the Guild decided to provide warm clothing again through the coming winter. When she took a sackful of clothes one November day, she found her friends in an agitated state.

'The police raided the printing press two days ago,' Flora told her, showing Emmie around the workshop. The filing cabinet drawers were still gaping open, their contents spilling. 'They confiscated all copies of this week's paper. Philip was taken in for questioning.'

'Why?' Emmie asked, appalled.

'They were running an article on the number of casualties – accusing the Government of withholding the true figures.'

'Are the Runcies all right?' Emmie asked quickly.

Flora nodded, her face strained. 'Philip was released, but only after a lot of questions about the Fellowship – they wanted names and addresses. He refused to give them. Thinks it's a matter of time before they come back. Next time they might close down the printing press. Mabel's in a terrible state – very shaken.'

Emmie glanced at the wreckage around her and thought of the kind Runcies being treated like criminals. She followed Flora to the Runcies' small flat, shocked to see how frail and gaunt-faced Mabel looked. She could hardly stand to greet her, and wheezed as she spoke. She was cheered to see Emmie but grew exhausted quickly and they did not stay long.

Standing in the dank quad, Emmie asked angrily, 'What can I do to help?'

Flora looked hard at her. 'I won't involve you in any of this unless you are quite sure you know what you're getting into. It could land you in a lot of trouble.'

Emmie gulped. 'I've stood back and watched for too long,' she said stoutly. 'I want to do something to stop this war.'

Flora smiled and took her by the arm. 'Come inside.'

Later that day, Emmie left, the precious envelope of papers entrusted to her tucked into the lining of her coat.

'Give these to Rab,' Flora had instructed. 'Tell him to hide them. They're duplicate lists of NCF members and details – just in case we are arrested.'

Emmie had nodded, amazed at her calmness.

'Tell him not to come to the printing press this week – he must manage without our help for the time being. The Runcies don't want him implicated in anything here. They know they are being watched now.'

The next day, Emmie screwed up her courage to go and see Rab. She had hardly seen him to speak to all year; a nod in the street, passing on the doorstep at his mother's, that awkward encounter after Sam had died. She decided to take Barny with her to make it seem like a casual visit. The day was dark, the clouds lowering and burdened with coming rain.

Barny ran ahead, hopping across the mossy yard as if he knew where he was going. Rab's door was ajar. He banged it open and ran in.

'Rab!' the boy shouted.

'Hello, bonny lad,' Rab laughed in surprise.

Emmie walked in to find Barny wrapped around Rab's legs, Rab ruffling his dark hair. She was amazed her son remembered him after all these months. Rab looked at her with vivid blue eyes through thin-wired spectacles.

'Didn't know you wore readin' glasses,' Emmie blurted out.

He took them off, self-conscious and reddening. 'Mannie gave me a lend.'

'Look like a real revolutionary,' she teased. 'They suit you.'

They stared at each other, suddenly tongue-tied. Barny tugged at Rab's hand.

' "Grandfather Clock", singing,' he urged, pulling Rab towards the piano.

' "Grandfather Clock"?' he grinned. 'Why not!'

It made Emmie think of the last time when music had been pouring out of the room, drowning Rab's grieving.

She said, 'No, you're workin'. We'll not stay.'

Rab's look was sardonic. 'You stay away over a year and turn up for half a minute. I think we can both spare the time for a cup of tea.'

He played Barny his favourite song twice through. Then Rab made a pot of tea and cleared a space on his paper-strewn kitchen table, chatting all the time to Barny. Only when he had poured tea did he sit down and eye Emmie.

'I hear about you from Mam. You look grand, Emmie.'

She blushed and quickly pulled out the package from Flora, explaining why she had come. Rab was full of concern to hear about the raid.

'You're taking a risk coming here,' he said quietly. 'What would Tom say?'

'I think you know what he'd say,' she answered, glancing away.

'Is that why you stopped coming?' Rab asked. 'Stopped writing for the *Messenger*?'

Emmie shrugged. 'That day Barny ran up to you at the rally . . . Tom gets jealous easily. Didn't want him gettin' the wrong idea.' She glanced at him. 'And the *Messenger* – didn't know what to write any more – what to think.'

'And what about now?' Rab pressed.

She looked at him directly. 'I think the war is wrong – for all the reasons you said and people wouldn't listen to. I want to do something, because of what's happened to the Runcies, to all of us, to Sam . . .' she faltered. Tears stung her eyes.

Quickly, he put out a hand and covered hers. His grip was warm, strong, encouraging. She saw his jaw clench. He could not speak of his brother yet, but she saw the compassion in his eyes.

Emmie whispered, 'Give me a job to do and I'll do it – leafleting, anything.'

Rab smiled. 'You can start by writing something for this

week's *Messenger*. I'm running out of paper, but I'll put it out on brown if I have to.'

Emmie sat at the table and wrote her first column as Artemis in sixteen months. She exhorted ordinary women to work for peace, to stop their husbands and sons being used as cannon fodder, to resist conscription. Rab read it and grinned.

'We'll both end up in gaol at this rate.' He looked at Barny, building a house with dominoes by the hearth. 'I'll take out the bit about conscription – can't have his mam being arrested.'

Emmie fixed him with a look. 'Leave it in – I stand by every word. What would happen if every woman hid behind her bairns? Nowt would change. I don't want Barny to grow up and be in the next war. I'm doing this for him.'

He gazed at her for a long moment. 'By, lass, I've missed your company.'

Emmie reddened. Softly she asked, 'Then why did you stop coming round to your mam's on a Friday when you knew I'd be there?'

Rab answered in a low voice. 'I thought it better if I stayed away. I'd grown to care too much.'

Emmie stared at him, her heart thumping. What did he mean? She wanted to ask him but dared not. Suddenly she longed to fling her arms around his neck and kiss him so that he would know how much she cared for him. But such actions would be madness, a betrayal of Tom. She held herself in check, even as her heartbeat drummed in her ears.

She thanked him for the tea and called to Barny it was time for home. Rab thanked her for bringing the documents from Flora and Charles. The charged atmosphere of moments before dissolved into an awkward formality between them and Emmie swiftly left. Even so, she knew that by going there that day she had stepped over some invisible barrier from safety into danger and the unknown.

CHAPTER 19

1916

The revolt against conscription brought new allies to the peace movement: trade unionists, chapelgoers and socialists who had hitherto supported the war. In January, as a Military Conscription Bill was being passed in the Commons, the Miners' Union and the Labour Party voted heavily against any conscription. Britain had always relied on a volunteer army; conscription was the mark of despots. Even the Reverend Mr Attwater preached concern at such a development.

'Far better for young men of strength and courage to go forward and fight for the nation's salvation,' he exhorted, 'than to be forced against their will.' But he added a severe caution against the unpatriotic. 'Those who choose to belittle the sacrifice of our brave soldiers and sailors, or incite them to mutiny, are to be despised. The words of Artemis in the ungodly *Blackton Messenger* are unbefitting for a woman, if indeed they are written by one. I urge you, brothers and sisters, do not buy or read such vile treason.'

Emmie was unnerved by such condemnation and hardly dared glance about, thinking her flushed face would give her away. Louise gave her a suspicious look but said nothing. She knew Emmie had stopped writing her column after war broke out and probably doubted she would dare write it now. Tom never suspected her. As renewed speculation as to Artemis's identity grew, Emmie continued to write impassioned articles for the *Messenger*. The publication was reduced to a couple of pages fortnightly because of paper restrictions, but people were still buying it. Rab told her it would be safer to give her column to Helen to pass on to him, rather than be caught visiting Mannie's. On two occasions, Rab's room and workshop were raided by the police, but both times the small hand-press had been removed in time; once to the MacRaes' outhouse and once to a friend of Mannie's. Rab was tipped off by a young constable, Johnny Collier, who had attended Jonas's socialist Sunday school, and all the police found to take away were a handful of pamphlets and unmarked essays.

But after a spring assault on the Western Front by Germany, the mood turned belligerent again. Asquith denounced those who tried to start a peace debate, and striking leaders on the Clyde were arrested for halting armaments production.

'I worked with some of those lads,' Rab told Emmie when they managed to meet at China Street. They briefly discussed what should go in the next issue and Emmie brought news from the Runcies. The new Military Service Act was imminent.

'The Quakers are talking of setting up a network to help those resisting conscription,' she whispered, not wanting Helen to overhear and be implicated. 'Safe houses – maybe get lads out the country to Canada or America.'

Rab nodded. Emmie eyed him. 'You'll be one of the first to be called up, won't you? As an unmarried man and no protected job.'

'I'll appeal for conscientious objection,' Rab declared.

'But you're not religious,' Emmie snorted.

'Political conscience.' Rab gave a wry smile.

Emmie shook her head. 'Reverend Charles is worried his father or Hauxley will sit on the tribunal and decide who goes. You wouldn't stand a chance in front of them.'

'Not on my own,' Rab said with passion, 'but I'll not be the only one. If enough of us refuse to go, we can turn the tide.'

Emmie was encouraged by his optimism.

Two days later, Helen came rushing round to Emmie's more agitated than she had ever seen her.

'They set on him!' she cried. 'In Blackton – beat him up proper.'

'Who?' Emmie demanded, steering her into a chair.

'Our Rab,' Helen replied. 'He went to hand out leaflets with two other lads.'

'Is he all right?' Emmie asked in fear.

Helen nodded, gaining her breath back. 'Lads brought him to ours. Told him to rest but he's all in a state about you.'

Emmie coloured. 'Why me?'

'Thinks the police might gan round to his and search. He's worried they'll find papers about you and the *Messenger*.'

Emmie's stomach churned. She fetched Helen a cup of water, thinking quickly.

'You take Barny to yours and I'll gan round to Mannie's,' she instructed.

She left before Helen and dashed to India Street. Mannie was there, clay pipe clenched unlit between his teeth. He took out the pipe and gave her a gap-toothed smile.

'Had the press moved already,' he wheezed.

'I need to search his room.' Emmie blushed. 'I left some papers.'

He nodded for her to go ahead. Inside, she quickly rummaged through the piles of old newspaper and printed sheets. What she really wanted to find were the lists of names and addresses of the local NCF. She hesitated, then began to search his chest of drawers, finding nothing but well-worn clothes and sheet music. She looked among his books, under the bed, in the kitchen cupboard.

'Don't be long, lass,' Mannie warned from the door. 'Coppers could be here any minute, or that mob from Blackton.'

Where would he keep such secret papers? Emmie thought frantically. A sudden thought made her go back to the bed with its tartan rug and lift the mattress. There was the familiar brown envelope. She snatched it and stuffed it into her coat. On the spur of the moment, she seized the pile of leaflets from the table and stuffed them in a canvas bag that hung on the back of the door. She paused as she left.

'Will this get you into trouble too?'

Mannie gave a wheezy laugh. 'What can they do to an old gadgy like me, eh? Me hearin' will be twice as bad if they come asking questions,' he chortled.

'Ta, Mannie, you're a good man,' she smiled.

'Take care, lass,' he smiled back, propelling her out of the door. As she dashed across the yard, he locked Rab's door behind them and shuffled off.

Some instinct made Emmie go home first and hide the

documents. She wrapped them in a towel and put them under Barny's mattress on the low cot bed. Tom would never come across them there. Then she hurried round to China Street.

Emmie's first sight of Rab's battered face made her feel faint. He was hardly recognisable, his left eye closed and weeping, dried blood around his cut and swollen lips. He was hunched in a chair by the fire, nursing his arm and bruised ribs. Barny was sitting at his feet, staring.

'Rab talking funny,' Barny said, leaping up to greet her.

Emmie swallowed. 'Oh, Rab!' She went forward and put a tentative hand to his face. He winced and she quickly withdrew.

'Not – bad – as – looks.' He tried to smile.

'Don't try to talk,' Emmie said in concern.

'That'll be difficult,' Helen said drily, once again in charge of the situation. 'You shouldn't stay, pet. Police are bound to come – best they don't find you here.'

'I've nothing to hide,' Emmie said stoutly, 'and they'll find nowt at Mannie's of any interest.'

Rab spoke with difficulty. 'Good – man. But – wha' 'bout lists?' His look was urgent.

Emmie reassured him. 'They're safe – I found them.' She looked at him pityingly. 'Who did this to you?'

Rab shrugged. Helen spoke for him. 'Lads said they were ready for him, like it was all organised. Didn't have a chance to start handing out leaflets. I think Oliphant's stirring up trouble 'cos conscription's that unpopular.'

Rab nodded. 'Frightened – it'll spread – to – pits. Strikes . . .'

'What will they do to you?' Emmie asked in dread.

Helen answered again. 'They'll try and charge him for handing out leaflets, but they won't find any. His marras burned them before the police got there.'

There was an abrupt hammering on the door. The women looked round nervously. Helen went to answer it.

'Mrs MacRae?' said a craggy-faced police sergeant.

'Aye.'

'I'm Sergeant Graham. Is your son here? Rab MacRae. We'd like a few words.'

'He's in no fit state,' Helen said brusquely. 'The lad can hardly talk.'

The sergeant pushed past her, followed by an embarrassed Constable Collier, who nodded at Helen.

'Rab MacRae,' Sergeant Graham growled, as he spotted Rab by the fire, 'you're to come with me for questioning.'

'He's not ganin' anywhere,' Helen said in fury.

The police officer ignored her. 'You can walk, can't you?' he demanded.

Rab struggled to his feet. Johnny Collier went quickly to support him. Emmie stepped up to the sergeant.

'And what about arresting the thugs who left him like this?' she accused. 'Thought you were supposed to stop fighting, not stand by and let it happen!'

He gave her a dismissive look. 'Who are you?'

'A friend,' she glared.

'You've too big a gob for your own good, missus. I can bring you in too for obstructing an officer.'

Helen swiftly pulled Emmie back. Barny rushed to his mother and clung on to her skirt.

'Are you hiding any printing machinery?' Graham demanded. Helen shook her head, but he sent Collier to search. The young constable returned with nothing. Graham ordered him to get Rab out of the house.

'Where are you taking him?' Helen cried.

The sergeant ignored her and marched out of the cottage.

Rab put out a hand as he passed and gave a swollen smile.

Collier said in a low voice, 'I'll make sure the doctor looks him over, Mrs MacRae. Don't worry. It's just a few questions.'

Emmie watched speechless as Rab was led away down the lane to the police station.

'Don't know that man, Graham,' Helen fretted, 'he's new round here. But Johnny Collier's a good lad.'

The women stayed together until early afternoon, when a drawn-faced Mannie appeared.

'They've been and searched his room,' the old man said, 'turned it upside down. Best if the lad stays here a while.'

'They've no right!' Helen was indignant.

'Tore up his sheet music,' Mannie said, shaking his head.

Emmie was aghast. 'They never did?'

'Aye, all of it,' the old man sighed. 'But they found nowt to arrest him for. They'll have to release him.'

'He'll have to stop the *Messenger*,' Helen said in agitation. 'It's too dangerous.'

Emmie felt the anger that had knotted her stomach all day rise up and choke her. What had become of their village, that idealists like Rab could be beaten up, hounded from his home, forbidden to tell the truth about the war? All free speech was being snuffed out. Well, they might silence him, but they could not silence them all.

Emmie could bear inaction no longer. She took Barny by the hand and abruptly left. Storming back home, she pulled the bag of leaflets from their hiding place.

'Haway, Barny,' she said grimly, 'we'll tell this village what's ganin' on under their noses!'

Together they hurried down to the main street, handing out leaflets to everyone they met. They went into the co-operative store and left a pile on the counter.

'Read the truth – the Government are hiding the real number of dead,' Emmie told the startled queue of shoppers. 'They won't stop till they've bled our country dry of men. And for what? To keep their own kind in power and keep the working class in their place. Resist conscription – don't let them take away your husbands and sons. Join the No Conscription Fellowship before it's too late!'

Emmie hurried around the village in the chilly March breeze, thrusting leaflets at young and old. She stood with Barny outside her old school and told the children to take a leaflet home to their parents. The caretaker rushed out and shook his fist, telling her to get on home. Barny grew fretful, but Emmie reassured him.

'We have to tell the men to stop fighting. Just a few more minutes, pet.'

She hoisted him on to her back and laboured up the hill to the pit gates. Already men for the back shift were beginning to straggle in for work. They took her leaflets in surprise.

'Read them, please,' Emmie pleaded. 'One of your marras got beaten up by Oliphant's lackeys for trying to give these out. Rab MacRae.'

One man spat at her feet. 'He deserves owt he gets – bloody Hun-lover.'

Emmie faced him. 'Better to be friends with the working man

179

in Germany, than doing the dirty work for the ruling classes here. Divide and rule, that's their game, to stop us ever coming together to improve our lot. If more people thought about their comrades in different countries there would be no war.'

He swore at her and pushed her back. Barny clung on in fright.

'Haway, don't touch the lass,' another chided. 'You're Curran's missus, aren't you? Better scarper 'fore he hears of it.'

But Emmie carried on until the under-manager came out and shouted, 'I've called for the police. Get off home, woman, unless you want to be arrested.'

Emmie flung a leaflet at him. 'Give this to Major Oliphant,' she cried.

Many took her leaflets, only a few grinding them under their boots. Within minutes, Johnny Collier was panting up the hill.

'Emmie,' he said apologetically, 'I'm sorry, but you've got to stop.' He took her by the elbow and steered her away. 'Haway, Barny, time to go home.'

Emmie was still riled up and shook him off. 'What have you done with Rab?'

'Sergeant let him go,' Johnny said. She gave a sigh of relief, but he cautioned, 'He's being watched. Tell him to be careful. There are those who want to see him inside. And you, Emmie, this is just a warning,' he told her, 'but if we catch you leafleting again, we'll have to arrest you. Do you understand?'

She nodded, picking up Barny. Suddenly, a voice bellowed behind them. She turned to see Tom striding towards them, filthy from the pit. Her heart thumped in fright.

'What the hell are you doing?' he cried, shaking a leaflet at her. He was livid. 'You been giving these out? What the bloody hell for? What's the bairn doing here?'

Barny clutched his mother, wide-eyed at the shouting.

'Don't scare him,' Emmie said as calmly as possible.

Tom grabbed Barny from her. 'Give him here. You're not fit—'

'Steady, Tom,' Johnny said, trying to intervene.

'Bugger off, Collier,' Tom snapped. 'I'll deal with me own wife.' He pushed Emmie ahead of him, a wailing Barny pinned under his arm.

The constable stood back, unsure what to do. Emmie tried to placate Tom.

'Put the lad down, Tom,' she pleaded. 'He can walk between us.'

But Tom strode off ahead, the captive Barny kicking his legs and wailing in bewilderment. Emmie hurried after them, trying to reassure the boy, not caring about the gawping onlookers. When they got home, Tom put Barny down and turned on her.

'You've made a fool of me in front of all me marras,' he raged, shoving her backwards. He raised his arm and punched her in the face. Emmie howled in pain and shock. 'You're a disgrace to the Currans. Where d'you get them leaflets?' He seized her by the hair. 'Tell me!'

Emmie screamed, 'Let go!'

He dragged her around the room. 'Them yellow-bellies at the Settlement, eh? Or bloody MacRaes? I'll beat it out of yer!'

Emmie cried, 'Doesn't matter where − I'd do it again.' She swivelled round and bit the hand that tore her hair. 'Anything to stop this war!' she gasped.

Tom was maddened. He cursed her and threw her away from him. She fell and hit her head on the fender. Barny howled.

'Mammy, Mammy!'

Dazed, Emmie struggled to sit up, bracing herself for further attack. Barny ran to crouch beside her. She clung to him. Tom stopped, his belt half unbuckled. She looked at him in horror. Abruptly, Tom turned on his heels and stormed out, leaving the back door banging in the wind.

Emmie sat shaking, gritting her teeth against the sob in her throat. Barny cried in her arms. She tried to calm him. For a long time she huddled on the hearth, waiting for Tom's return, wondering if she should take Barny and escape to the MacRaes. But they had enough trouble on their hands; she must stand up for herself.

Wincing at the pain in her cheek, she hauled herself up and forced herself to set about preparing tea. Numbly, she heated water for Tom's bath and made a vegetable soup. She scrambled an egg and fed it to Barny, talking to him softly, ignoring the ache in her jaw. The daylight waned and still her husband did not come back. She put Barny to bed.

After dark, Tom came in at the door and hung up his cap. He

was washed and wearing old clothes of Sam's, Emmie noticed with a pang. Neither said a word. He watched her serve the dried-up soup, but did not come to the table. No doubt he had eaten at his mother's. She sat alone and forced down a mouthful, then another.

'Is it true?' he asked at last.

Emmie put down her spoon and faced him. He reddened at the sight of her swollen cheek. 'Is what true?'

'You're Artemis?' Tom demanded. 'Louise said it was you. Said it was common knowledge.'

Emmie nodded.

'We're the talk of the village, you'll be pleased to know,' he said bitterly. 'Tom Curran and his conchie wife. I'm a laughing stock. Me father says if it was his wife, he'd take a belt to you.'

'The Curran way,' Emmie said in disdain, 'and what good does that do? Never changed anything you did as a lad.'

Tom flashed her a hard look. 'You're not welcome round there till you promise to stop all the nonsense. I'm to see you do.'

'And how are you ganin' to do that, Tom?' she challenged. 'Tie me up and shoot me at dawn?'

He sprang up and came towards her, fists clenched. 'Don't mock me, yer bitch!'

Emmie rose to confront him. 'Want to black me other eye? Wake the bairn with your shouting again?'

He dropped his fists. 'I didn't mean to frighten the lad,' he muttered.

Emmie looked at him in despair. 'See what this war's doing to people, Tom? Soon there won't be a family in the land hasn't lost someone. We need lads to stand firm and refuse to gan. That's the bravest thing any man can do.'

He gave her a look of incomprehension. 'Me be a conchie? Save me own skin? Never!'

'It's not about saving your own skin — it's about saving thousands of others,' Emmie urged.

'Your mind's been poisoned by them MacRaes,' Tom said with contempt. 'You may be beyond savin', but you'll not fill Barny's head with treason. If I catch you takin' him round there, I'll take him off yer.'

Emmie gawped at him in disbelief, but the look of hatred on

his face froze her heart. He was beyond being reasoned with, so she swallowed her anger and said no more.

Tom refused to speak to her for days. He treated her with a coldness she had never experienced before. She stayed close to home as the bruise on her face yellowed, ashamed at the sidelong looks she got from her neighbours. Helen came round to check on her, but she made light of her injury, edgy in case Tom found out.

'Tripped over Barny and fell on the fender,' Emmie lied. 'Tell Rab I can't write for the *Messenger* just now.' Then she changed the subject.

Helen shook her head. 'Its days are over, pet. That's what I came to tell you. Rab's had his call-up papers.'

Emmie's heart lurched. 'When?'

'Came the day after all that bother,' Helen said, her face taut. 'He's down at the Settlement – put in for exemption. Dr Flora and the Reverend said they'd help with his case.'

All the next week, Emmie was preoccupied with thinking of Rab. On Friday morning Tom announced abruptly that they were going to his parents for tea. It was the first conversation they had had since the row.

'They want to see Barny,' Tom told her curtly.

Emmie steeled herself for a lecture from Barnabas and censure from her mother- and sister-in-law. But they were stiffly welcoming, as if tolerating a great burden. Nobody made mention of the old bruises on her face. Barny's chatter helped dispel some of the awkwardness. Then, halfway through tea, Louise startled her.

'Isn't Tom brave?' she said, eyeing Emmie.

Emmie looked quizzical.

'Joining up before he's called up,' she said with a strained smile.

'Brave indeed,' Barnabas echoed, 'and an example to us all.'

Emmie looked at them all, aghast. She spluttered at Tom, 'Is this true?'

'Didn't you know?' Louise exclaimed.

'No.' Emmie swallowed hard. 'Tom . . . ?'

'I'm off on Monday. Pit manager's lettin' me gan,' he said, avoiding her look.

'But me and Barny . . .' Emmie stuttered.

'We've told Tom we'll take care of you both until his army pay comes through,' Barnabas announced grandly. 'It's a proud day when a Curran goes to fight for his country. Barny will learn about it one day.'

Emmie found it almost impossible to sit there and listen to their jingoism. Barnabas made snide remarks about her disloyalty and Louise grew tearful over Sam. But Emmie knew that nothing she said to the Currans would change their thinking, so she sat in silence, yearning for the ordeal to end.

After tea, Tom went straight to the Temperance Club with his father, so she took Barny home on her own. She sat up waiting for Tom to return, but when he did, he went on the defensive.

'You've forced me to it,' he accused. 'It's the only way I can hold me head up round here any more, after what you've done.'

'Oh, Tom!' Emmie protested. 'Don't blame me.'

'Well, I do,' he hissed. 'I'm ashamed of yer. And don't pretend you won't be glad when I'm gone.'

'This is the last thing I want,' Emmie said, hurt by his callousness. 'Tom, talk to me about it, please.'

'What's done is done. And I don't want you and the bairn coming to see me off,' he ordered; 'don't want him upset.'

After that, he turned his back and refused to talk again about his enlisting.

All weekend the strained atmosphere continued. Emmie could not believe it was happening. On Sunday afternoon, despite the spitting rain, she cajoled her husband, 'Let's take the bairn for a walk through the woods.'

Tom was reluctant, but as they walked among the wild narcissi, the strain on his face eased. He swung Barny up on his shoulders and ran with him, pretending to be a horse. The boy laughed and gripped on with delight. Emmie watched them, storing up the memory, trying to banish the image of Tom's furious face when he had hit her.

That night she lay on her side, sleepless. In the middle of the night, she felt Tom get up. He lit a candle. She watched him cross the room and stand peering down at Barny in his small bed. He stood there for a long time. After a while, she thought she heard Barny whimpering in his sleep. She sat up, then realised it was Tom sniffing back tears.

Quietly, she said, 'I know you'll miss him more than anything.'

He looked over, startled, and blew out the candle. He came back to bed and Emmie knew she had embarrassed him by catching him weeping over his son. But suddenly, Tom whispered, 'I'll miss you an' all.'

Emmie held her breath, wondering if she had misheard him.

He continued, 'I'm sorry, Emmie – 'bout hittin' yer – and in front of the bairn. I'm that ashamed . . .'

She reached out for him quickly. Their arms went around each other in comfort.

Emmie whispered, 'I know you didn't mean it.'

'I hate mesel' for it,' he confessed. 'It's partly why I joined up – I'm not being brave like me father says. I'm a coward that hits his wife.'

'Hush,' Emmie said, hugging him to her. 'You've said all that needs saying.'

'I care for you and Barny more than anything in the world,' Tom whispered. 'Don't let him forget his da, will yer?'

'Course not,' Emmie said. 'We'll talk about you plenty.'

He kissed her with a sense of desperation, as if he could make up for the days of not speaking. They lay in each other's arms, waiting for dawn to come.

At five, Emmie got up to make his breakfast, as if he was going off on the early shift. He ate it in silence as the clock ticked away their final hour together.

'I could still come with you to the station,' Emmie offered.

Tom shook his head. 'I want to remember you just like this,' he said bashfully, 'sittin' at our table with yer hair down.'

Emmie blushed. He stood up quickly and went to kiss Barny goodbye. The little boy stirred as his father hugged him, but did not wake completely.

Briefly, Tom held Emmie to him.

'Ta-ra, Emmie,' he said hoarsely. 'Please forgive me?'

She nodded, unable to speak. This was the affectionate Tom she knew of old, the one who cared for her and loved their son with a simple delight. Why was it that he could only be like this on the point of going? Surely the censorious, bullying man of the past fortnight was a charade for others – his father, his marras? It made her bitter to think his only way of escaping their bigoted influence was to go to war.

She watched him go in the early morning light, a coat

wrapped around her nightdress. He turned to wave and she waved back.

Returning indoors, she found a sleepy Barny emerging from the bedroom and wondered how she could ever explain his father's going away. She held out her arms and he ran to her. Emmie hugged him tight, feeling the emptiness of Tom's going. Yet even as the sadness gripped her, she was aware of another, less loyal emotion struggling inside. She puzzled over it. As she kissed Barny's head, Emmie had to admit that the feeling deepest within was one of relief.

CHAPTER 20

With Tom gone, Emmie was no longer afraid to visit the MacRaes, for she did not care what her in-laws or their friends thought of her. She had lost Louise as an ally. Her old friend avoided serving her in the hardware shop.

When she met her in the street, Louise said cattily, 'Now you know what it's like to be without your husband. You don't deserve our Tom. Don't know how you can hold your head up round here, mixing with them pacifists.' She had almost spat the words at her.

Emmie was shocked, yet knew Louise still grieved deeply for Sam and she took the rebuff without a word. Despite Barnabas' promise of help, Emmie found herself without funds for a fortnight. The Co-operative Guild helped her out. She knew from the hidden lists that some had donated to the NCF and were sympathetic to her cause. It made her all the more determined to fight conscription. Even Peter had received the call-up, but his employer, Speed, had lodged his papers stating he could not run his business without a delivery man. After a medical report, showing Peter's low intelligence, he was exempted.

'What can I do to help men like Rab?' Emmie asked Helen and Jonas.

'Charles Oliphant's the man to ask,' Jonas replied. 'He's sticking his neck out, by all accounts. Helping lads at their tribunal hearings. Word is, Major James is furious.'

'Go to the Settlement,' Helen urged. 'I'll look after the bairn for a few days.'

Emmie left Barny in their care, feeling the wrench at leaving him for the first time for so long. But Helen distracted him with rolling pin and pans for drums, and Emmie left her son giggling and banging them with Peter.

She found the Settlement much changed. The printing press was closed, the lecture rooms turned into storerooms, most of the shabby buildings commandeered by the navy. All the student volunteers were long gone, Mousy was bed-bound and his wife struggled to cope with the daily soup kitchen on dwindling funds and rising prices.

Mrs Mousy greeted Emmie bad-temperedly, disappointed not to see Barny.

'Shouldn't leave the bairn without his mam,' she disapproved, making Emmie feel the more wretched.

She was rescued by a cheerful cry from Rab.

'Emmie! What are you doing here?'

'I've come to help,' she smiled.

'By, it's grand to see you, lass.' He took her hands in his and she felt herself blushing under his blue-eyed gaze. He still had a cut above his left eye. 'Where's Barny?'

Quickly she told him about the past fortnight, skimming over the trouble with the Currans.

'Peter was here last week,' Rab told her; 'said there'd been bother about you leafleting. Are you telling me everything? How has Tom let you come here?'

'He's joined up,' she said stiffly. 'I feel it's my fault.'

Rab took her by the arm. 'Don't talk daft. I'm surprised old man Curran hasn't bullied him into it long ago. It's you that's kept him at home so long.' The smile he gave her eased Emmie's guilt. He took her to join the others.

The Runcies were now sharing the cramped flat with Charles and Flora. Rab was sleeping in a store cupboard with two other men whose tribunals were pending. Somehow, the Oliphants still managed to make their dismal quarters homely and they welcomed her with enthusiasm. Flora was full of optimism about their new work with the Quakers.

'Every man who goes before the tribunal is represented by a friend – a sponsor,' she explained. 'Charles and the Runcies help the COs write their petitions and speak up for them in court if they want.'

'What can I do?' Emmie said keenly.

'Help me with the paperwork,' Flora said at once. 'I'm not very organised at that. We need to keep track of each case – the verdicts – whether we can appeal or where the men are taken.'

'Everything must be done in duplicate,' Charles said, 'so when the police raid again, we have a safe copy of all the conscientious objectors' details.'

'Again?' Emmie queried. 'You've been raided before?'

Rab laughed. 'Plenty.'

'It'll get a lot rougher,' Flora warned. 'Attitudes are hardening. Town's full of migrant factory workers.'

'There's terrible overcrowding,' Charles added. 'People look around for scapegoats – the new one is the conchie.'

'Folk have short memories,' Emmie protested. 'To think of all you've done for them round here.'

'The Settlement has run out of funds,' Charles sighed. 'We have to beg, borrow or steal to keep the kitchen open.'

Later Flora confided in Emmie. 'We don't know how much longer we can survive living here. Charles's father cut him off financially some time ago. He's furious at his son's pacifism. He has a small stipend from the mission – and there's my work. But my patients can't afford to pay, so mostly they don't. Besides, more and more of my time is taken up with this court work.'

Emmie was taken aback by her candour. Flora saw her look. 'You need to know how it is.' She was matter-of-fact. 'We will do what we can, while we can. Nobody knows what tomorrow will bring.' She put an affectionate arm around Emmie. 'But we are more grateful than you can know to have your support. I knew from the moment I met you, Emmie, in that horrible slum, that you were special. Rab's told me how difficult it's been for you in the village recently. You're a brave young woman.'

'Not nearly as brave as Rab – or all of you here,' Emmie insisted.

'Well, I'm proud of you anyway,' Flora smiled. 'We'll all have to be courageous in the days ahead.'

Emmie spent a couple of days helping the doctor sort out the paperwork and compile notes for the forthcoming court cases, including Rab's. They learned that Reginald Hauxley was to be on the military tribunal. Charles was uneasy.

'Tactically, your best chance would be to use medical

evidence,' Flora advised. 'You could be exempted for your poor eyesight.'

Rab shook his head. 'We have to set a precedent for political conscience,' he said stubbornly. 'I won't fight in this war because I'm a socialist.'

Charles nodded in admiration. 'It's your decision. As long as you know we won't judge you if you change your mind.'

On the second evening that Emmie was there, a stranger turned up after dark. He ate with them, but said little. Emmie detected a foreign accent. Afterwards, he was given different clothes to wear – a sailor's jacket and cap. Then Philip took him away.

The following day, Rab suggested a walk up to Saltwell Park. He was restless; his tribunal appearance only two days away. The first buds were opening, but a cold wind whistled around them.

'Who was that man last night?' Emmie asked, as they reached the park.

'Don't know his real name,' Rab admitted, 'but he's a Russian Jew. The Runcies are helping him escape.'

'Is he in trouble?' Emmie was puzzled.

Rab glanced around, then steered her to an empty bench. 'Russia is an ally of Britain. The choice for Russians living here is join up and fight or be forcibly sent back to Tsarist Russia.' He kept his voice low. 'For a socialist and a Jew that means certain death.'

Emmie gulped. 'How do the Runcies get him away?'

Rab hesitated, then asked, 'You've heard of the Quakers' underground network for COs on the run?' Emmie nodded. Rab continued, 'The Runcies are part of it. They dress the men up as sailors and get them away on ships. The Russian will be working his passage to Sweden, most likely. Others go from Liverpool to America. That's the best bet. Plenty Quakers to take care of them over there – if they don't get blown up at sea,' he added grimly.

Emmie shuddered. 'The Runcies must be taking a great risk themselves. If they were caught . . . Mrs Runcie could never survive imprisonment.'

'They are remarkable people,' Rab agreed. 'For bourgeois liberals and believers,' he added with a wry grin.

Emmie snorted, 'You don't change, do you?'

'Neither do you,' Rab murmured, reaching for her hand. He rubbed his thumb across her fingers, touching her wedding ring. 'For all your chapelgoing, Mrs Curran, you're still a rebel underneath – like me.'

She pulled away self-consciously. He eyed her.

'Did something happen between you and Tom? He didn't hurt you, did he?'

Emmie flushed. 'He didn't mean to. He was very angry – about the leaflets.'

'I'm sorry. That was my fault you got involved.'

'No, it was my choice,' Emmie insisted. 'I should've seen how much it would matter to Tom. I can't blame him really.'

'You're very loyal,' Rab said.

She glanced at him, but saw no mockery in his face. Talk of Tom made her feel guilty and she stood up. They walked on. Emmie was aware that this might be the last time they could be alone together for some time – maybe for ever, if his appeal failed. Her heart began to hammer. If only she was free to tell him how deeply she felt for him – had always felt.

'Rab . . .' She stopped him suddenly, a hand on his arm.

He looked at her, smiling quizzically. Her heart squeezed. But the recent talk of her husband jabbed at her conscience. Tom had been wrong to hit her, but it was not enough grounds for her to betray him. She knew that whatever her husband thought of her, he still cared for Barny. For her son's sake, she must not weaken now.

'What is it, Emmie?' he murmured.

She glanced down, unable to meet his vivid gaze. 'If – if you lose your case – will you go on the run like the Russian?'

For a long time he said nothing. When she glanced up he was staring off into the distance, in the direction of Crawdene.

'Is that what you want me to do?' he asked, scrutinising her.

'Aye, if it would keep you safe,' Emmie gulped.

He touched her hair and she thought for a moment he would ruffle it. His smile was tender but brief.

'No,' he said quietly, 'I won't go on the run. I'll see this thing through, whatever the cost.'

Emmie looked away, her eyes stinging with sudden tears. How foolish to think Rab would act in self-interest. He had never shirked any ordeal in his life and she doubted he ever would.

They walked back to the docks with hardly another word. Flora came hurrying out to meet them, her face anxious.

'Bad news, I'm afraid,' she told them. 'The lists in today's paper. Captain Arthur Hauxley – he's missing.'

CHAPTER 21

The council chamber was busy all day, the corridors of the town hall thronged with those standing about waiting for their applications to be considered. All morning, the military service panel had heard cases in private from businessmen, public employees and solicitors asking for exemption on the grounds their business would be harmed. Four conscientious objectors were kept waiting until the late afternoon. The mayor was leading a panel of six men: the others being three councillors, a retired policeman and a representative from the military. Word came back that taking the place of the bereaved Hauxley was none other than Major Oliphant.

Emmie saw Charles blanch at this. He had sent messages of condolence to his sister at Ongarfield, but heard nothing. They all knew that Major James would be merciless in the wake of his son-in-law's probable death.

The gallery was crowded with supporters of the men. Charles got up to speak on behalf of a young postman.

'Laurie Bell has been a Sunday school teacher for five years. It is against all his Christian principles to kill his fellow men, whoever they are. He cannot, in all conscience, take part in any war.'

The major glared at Charles in disgust.

The mayor asked, 'Mr Bell, you're a postman taking wages from the public purse?'

The man nodded.

'So your conscience doesn't stop you taking the pay of the Government that's waging this war?' the mayor asked in contempt.

Charles interjected, 'Without his wages he would starve.'

Major Oliphant barked, 'If his conscience is so keen then he should starve rather than do this work.'

Charles faced his father. 'His older brother went down on HMS *Bayano*. His family depend on those wages too.'

'Then he should follow his older brother's example,' the major said waspishly, 'and take his place in the ranks.'

The panel conferred for barely a minute and refused the man exemption. Charles had a whispered conversation with Philip and withdrew. Philip supported the next applicant, but he too was turned down. The third, a Quaker, was refused total exemption but offered non-combatant duties.

As Rab took his turn, Charles came back in with a group of men. Emmie's heart leaped to see Jonas and some of his ILP friends. He nodded at her in encouragement. The chamber was full, the atmosphere suddenly charged.

Rab stood up and raised his bearded face to the tribunal. He would speak for himself.

'I'm a socialist and proud of it.'

There were cheers of support from around the chamber. The mayor barked for quiet. Rab carried on.

'I will have no part in a war that kills and maims my fellow comrades – men who are working for a better world for all humanity, no matter what their nationality. I belong to an international brotherhood and do not accept the boundaries that the imperialist rulers of Europe impose on us.'

'Hear, hear!' someone shouted.

'This war is being waged by militarists who are using it as an excuse to curb workers' rights – our hard-won rights. They seek to control us in the factories and the mines . . .'

There were louder cheers and clapping from all around the chamber.

'I'll not sit here and listen to this Red propaganda!' the major exploded.

The mayor raised his hand. 'Any more noise from the public, I'll clear the chamber. Get to the point, MacRae.'

'I refuse to take any part in this war, or help in any way towards its prosecution,' Rab said stoutly. 'I ask the tribunal for absolute exemption on grounds of conscience.'

A ripple of approval went through the crowd.

'Are you a Christian?' the retired policeman asked.

'No, I'm a socialist and atheist.'

'Then how can you claim conscientious objection?'

'On political not religious grounds,' Rab said calmly.

'Exemption's only allowed for strong religious or moral reasons,' his questioner pointed out.

'Socialist morals are the strongest kind,' Rab quipped. 'I'll recite you the Socialist Ten Commandments if you like.'

'He's wasting our time!' the major cried. 'This man's a born troublemaker – he's well known for his sedition.'

'Where were you born?' asked the mayor.

'County Durham.'

'So you are a native of England. Why won't you fight for England?'

'My country is the world,' Rab cried dramatically. Then with a twitch of a smile added, 'I just happen to be born in Gateshead.'

Laughter came from the back.

'Have you no loyalty to your country?' Major James snapped.

'My loyalty is to the international working class.' Rab was stubborn. 'To all those denied a proper life – those summoned to die in war for the very system of which they are the victims. So I'll not kill German workers.'

'But they're fighting England,' the retired inspector retorted. 'Fighting you.'

Rab raised a quizzical brow. 'Think you must be mistaken. I don't remember my name coming up in the German Reichstag.'

The major thumped the table. 'Your disloyalty is treasonable! A man who thinks so little of his country he puts the Hun first is beyond contempt.'

'The Ninth Commandment,' Rab recited. ' "Do not think that he who loves his own country must hate and despise other nations or wish for war. That is the remnant of barbarism." ' He glanced around him and caught Emmie's eye. 'I love the place where I live and the people I live among. No one has more passion for them than me.' Turning back to face the major, he declared, 'I will fight for these things, not with guns and bayonets, but with words and actions. I look for the day when we will all be free citizens of one country – world – living together as brothers and sisters in peace.' He smiled. 'That's the Socialist Tenth Commandment, by the way.'

People jumped up, cheering and clapping.

'Silence!' the mayor shouted. Conferring quickly with the others, he stood up. 'Mr MacRae, your claim is disallowed. You will report to barracks for duty as summoned. Clear the room.'

There was uproar among his supporters and shouts of, 'Shame!' Jonas and his friends burst into a rendition of 'The Red Flag'. They were jostled towards the door.

Rab raised his voice above the din. 'I do not recognise the right of this tribunal to judge my conscience or send me to war. Conscription's wrong!' he shouted. 'Introduce it, and a Kaiser or tsar is not far behind.'

'Get him out!' thundered the major.

Two policemen manhandled Rab out of the room, still protesting he would appeal. Major James leaned over as he passed and hissed, 'I'll make sure you're on a ship to France before any bloody appeal, you traitor!'

Emmie and her friends hurried out after Rab, euphoric at his stirring speech.

Jonas clapped his son on the back. 'I'm proud of you, laddie. Couldn't have put it any better. Keep your spirits up.'

But as they dispersed into the drabness of the March afternoon, their mood deflated. Rab had lost his case. An appeal would just be a delaying tactic, for tribunals were filled by men who supported the war.

Back at the Settlement, Flora rallied them. 'We'll appeal to the Central Tribunal in London. The NCF there can help put up a good case. This isn't over by any means.'

But Rab's military papers came the next day, ordering him to report to barracks in Newcastle.

'I see the hand of my father in this,' Charles said angrily. 'To come so quickly . . .'

Rab ignored the orders. As they waited tensely for him to be arrested, Emmie tried to change his mind.

'Let the Runcies get you away from here,' she pleaded. 'You can help fight this war from abroad. And it's one less man who they can force to do their wicked work.'

His smile was strained. 'They cannot force me to do anything.' He took her hand. 'Emmie, what you and the others do here is just as important. You can persuade the waverers to resist, encourage them to go to tribunal. You have no idea what a strength it was to me just to know you were sitting there in that courtroom, willing me on.'

'But it didn't do any good,' Emmie said in frustration.

'Aye, it did,' Rab insisted, gripping her hand. 'The memory will keep me strong when I'm gone from here.'

The next day, a sergeant came to arrest him for failing to appear at the barracks. It was early morning and he hardly had time to hug his friends goodbye. Rab was bundled into a truck and taken away.

Seeing how bereft Emmie was, Flora encouraged her to return to Crawdene and Barny.

'We'll send word if we hear anything. You should be with your family.'

'But you need help here,' Emmie protested half-heartedly.

'You can come back soon,' Flora suggested. 'Bring Barny too. We'll keep pressing for Rab's appeal.'

Emmie returned to Crawdene. When Barny rushed to the door at sight of her and threw himself into her arms, the soreness in Emmie's heart eased. She clutched the boy to her fiercely and covered him in kisses.

'By heck, I've missed you! I'm not letting you out me sight again,' she promised.

CHAPTER 22

Rab spent a night in a punishment cell, sleeping on a stone shelf, then was moved to a large cellar with other prisoners, all sharing a wooden stage as a bed. He recognised the young postman, Laurie Bell, from the tribunal, looking pale and frightened.

The others prisoners abused them. 'Another conchie. Bloody cowards!'

At night, they crowded around the two of them while one prisoner baited them.

'Make me sick, the pair of you. I'm not sharing a bed with scum like you.' He punched Laurie in the stomach.

Rab put himself between them. 'Leave the lad alone, he's doing you no harm.'

'No harm? It's filth like him would have us overrun by Germans,' the prisoner spat at him. 'Hope they shoot you bastards.'

The other men grew belligerent too, until the sergeant came in and ordered them all to lie down. They refused to let Rab and Laurie sleep on the communal mattress and they curled up as best they could on the cold stone floor.

Rab put an arm about the younger man and whispered, 'Courage, brother.'

In the morning, an officer marched in and ordered them to attention. They all jumped up, apart from Rab.

'Fall in, man, you're in the army now,' the officer barked.

Rab continued to sit on the floor. Laurie hovered beside him, wondering what to do. The other prisoners watched with interest.

'I'm sorry,' Rab said calmly, 'but I'm not ganin' to obey any military orders. I'm a conscientious objector.'

There was a stunned silence, then Laurie sat down beside him. 'Me neither,' he muttered.

The officer looked at them in dismay. After an embarrassed pause, he cleared his throat. 'It's back in the punishment cells for you – bread and water rations.' He turned and abruptly left.

One of the prisoners burst out laughing. 'By heck, did you see his face? Never seen anything like it.' He went over and offered Rab a swig of tea.

The tension dissolved and some of the men began to ask Rab about his opinions. Even the ringleader grudgingly admitted, 'Not such a yellow-belly after all. You'll be for it now, mind.'

In the middle of the discussion, the sergeant and a private returned and hauled Rab and Laurie off to the cells. After two days of refusing to put on uniform, undergo medicals or obey any orders, they were shoved into a van and taken to the railway station under armed guard.

'Where are we going?' Laurie asked nervously. He was paler than ever after two nights in the cold cell. He had kept Rab awake with singing hymns to lift his spirits.

No one would answer his question as they were locked into a goods van among crates of live chickens. After two hours on the jolting train, they were joined by others. Squeezed into the cramped carriage, they swapped stories. These other men were COs from the barracks at Richmond in Yorkshire. They were being taken south, but no one knew where.

The train journey seemed endless. Somewhere, after dark, they stopped and the chickens were unloaded. The men waited around on the chilly platform and then were transferred on to another train. Their guards ignored their attempts to chat. Eventually, the next day, tired and hungry, they disembarked at a busy station and were marched through the town. There were more than two dozen of them.

One man lifted his head and said, 'I can smell the sea.'

For the first time, Rab felt a real stab of unease. Major Oliphant's threat came back to him. *I'll make sure you're on a ship to France before any bloody appeal.*

But, he puzzled, why would they be rushing a group of untrained COs straight to the Western Front? They would be more hindrance than help. More likely they were on their way to some work camp.

They were taken to a makeshift barracks, once a school, and given a blanket each out of which to make a bed. They were largely left to fend for themselves. Over several days they were joined by a trickle of others until there were nearly forty in all. Rab recognised an older man, a miner from Chopwell who was in the ILP. He felt heartened just to hear the familiar accent.

'I've been talking to that young 'un.' The miner nodded at one of the guards. 'He let slip there's a ship waiting for us. But there's been an outbreak of measles among the crew. That's why we're not already on our way to France.'

'What they up to?' Rab asked.

The other man looked troubled. 'I think they want to make an example of us, that's what. If we disobey orders here in England, the worse they can do is chuck us in solitary. Over there, you get shot.'

Rab stared at him. But why was he so shocked? They were living under virtual military rule, every area of their lives ordered by the State and subject to draconian powers.

Rab answered with a grim smile, 'Well, we must have got them worried if they're ganin' to this much trouble to get rid of us, eh?'

'We need to get the word out,' his friend urged, 'before we sail.'

Charles and Flora first read the rumours in the *Manchester Guardian*. A group of COs were being sent hastily to the front by the War Office. The only explanation could be that they were to be court-martialled for refusing to carry out orders, and executed.

'Rab could be one of them,' Flora cried. 'We have no idea where they've taken him. No way of finding out!'

Charles said quietly, 'Maybe there is.'

He left for Blackton Heights that morning on Flora's bicycle. He had to dismount for the final mile, uphill to his old home, panting with the effort. The sight of thousands of daffodils bending in the breeze all the way up the drive gave him a surge of unexpected pleasure. He had forgotten the beauty of this place.

It was the cook who answered the door, flustered at the sight of him and the rusty bicycle.

'Half the staff have left, Master Charles. Major's out on business. Is it Ma'am you want to see? Miss Sophie's here too. Terrible about the captain.'

Charles nodded. 'I'll see myself up, Mrs Drake.'

Knocking on his mother's door, Charles let himself in quietly. His mother was sewing by the window, Sophie was jiggling a solid baby on her knee. The women were dressed in black.

They looked at him as if he were a ghost. His mother dropped her sewing.

'Charles, dearest . . .' She held out her arms.

Sophie clutched her infant, and eyed him coldly as he kissed their mother. She turned her cheek away when he tried to greet her too.

'And this is young Arthur?' Charles smiled. 'What a splendid boy.' He tickled the baby's chin. 'I'm so sorry about his father, Sophie,' he added sombrely. 'I pray for you and the boy daily.'

'I don't want your prayers, Charles,' she said bitterly, 'or your pity.' Their mother murmured an admonishment but Sophie ignored her. 'Why are you here? Begging on behalf of your precious conchies?'

Charles flinched. 'Just one, actually. Rab MacRae.'

He saw the colour rise in his sister's cheeks. 'Finally got the call-up, has he?'

'He may be one of several dozen being sent illegally to France,' Charles said. 'His appeal is still pending, yet the military have arrested him. I think Papa has something to do with it.'

Sophie jiggled her baby more vigorously. 'Good job too. Men like him should be made to do their bit for their country.'

'Not against their conscience,' Charles said quietly.

'Poppycock!' Sophie shouted. The baby began to cry.

Charles held out his arms. 'May I take him?' he smiled.

Sophie hesitated, then handed over the whimpering boy. Charles walked up and down, crooning and chatting to his nephew. Sophie watched them, realising with a pang that her brother was never likely to be a father.

'Why do you think Papa would know where Rab MacRac is?' she asked.

Charles stopped and looked at her. 'Because he was on Rab's

tribunal – made sure he was refused even non-combatant duties. Not that Rab would have accepted those either.'

'No,' Sophie agreed, allowing herself a rueful smile.

'Papa threatened Rab at the tribunal that he would get him to France before any appeal. I think his life is in great danger – and Papa is responsible. If we can at least find out where they are being held, we can stop them being shipped. Once they get to France, it may be out of anyone's hands.' He looked appealingly at his sister. 'You could ask for me. You're the only one he ever listens to.'

'Me!' Sophie cried. 'Why should I want to save that man?'

'For the sake of his family,' Charles urged. 'Remember how they once took you into their home – saved you from attack? They are good people – brave people. They've lost one son already. They don't deserve to lose another to this terrible war.'

Sophie's eyes flooded with tears. She marched over and seized baby Arthur from his arms. Without another word, she pushed past Charles and rushed from the room. He looked over at his mother in disappointment.

'Tell me about you and Flora,' she said softly. 'I so miss her visits.'

Charles smiled at her in gratitude and went over to sit beside her.

They talked for a long time, reminiscing as well as exchanging news. She pressed him to stay for lunch, but Charles refused.

'I don't want to upset Sophie more than I already have,' he said sadly.

'You haven't upset her,' his mother assured. 'She's punishing herself.'

'Why?' Charles was baffled.

'Because she never really loved Arthur, just married him on a wave of patriotic fervour,' his mother replied. 'She's balking at the thought of a year in mourning when she'd much rather be out doing something. But her lack of feeling makes her feel guilty too.'

'At least she has baby Arthur to occupy her,' Charles said.

His mother gave a dry laugh. 'Cook and the housemaid look after the boy more than Sophie. Your sister is not a natural mother, Charles. She was horrified when Arthur's nanny upped and left to join the VAD, but of course she couldn't say anything.

She wants the war to hurry up and end so she can throw herself into politics again.'

Charles laughed. 'Well, at least we're agreed on that.'

'Don't take her harsh words to heart,' his mother counselled. 'Your sister still admires you greatly.'

'Me?' Charles snorted.

'Yes, you. Admires the way you've just quietly got on with what you believe in, despite all the opposition from your father. I think she envies you your freedom, your love match to Flora.'

Charles smiled. 'For someone who shuts herself away from the world, Mama, you are an acute observer of human nature,' he marvelled. 'And probably the wisest person I know.'

'And you, my dear Charles,' she laughed, 'are by far the most charming of my family. Always were.'

They hugged in parting. As he made his way downstairs, he heard raised voices in the echoing hallway. He looked down from the gallery to see his father ordering Sophie back into the drawing room.

'I'll deal with this myself,' he barked. He was heading up the stairs as Charles hurried down the final flight. 'Don't know how you dare show your face round here! I'll not have you upsetting your sister and mother like this. Get out of this house!'

'I came for information, Papa,' Charles said calmly. 'I thought you could tell me—'

'I know why you've come!' the major thundered. 'If you think I'll help you find that treacherous MacRae, you're very much mistaken. I don't know where he is, but I do know he will get his comeuppance once and for all.'

'Comeuppance for what, Papa?' Charles said, stepping closer so they were on a level. 'For being anti-war or because he had the audacity to befriend the likes of Sophie and myself?'

'He's a dangerous man with dangerous ideas,' Major James snapped. 'He wants to turn the world on its head, as if common workers would have the first idea how to run things. MacRae would see us all ruined. And now he's a traitor. You heard him at the tribunal – he'd rather have the German proletariat overrun us. This war is as much about protecting society from anarchists like him as fighting the Boche.'

'His point exactly,' Charles answered. 'It's naked self-interest that is driving this war. You're doing very well out of this, aren't you? Pits going all hours, guaranteed prices from the Government. Not much incentive to stop it, is there?'

'How dare you?' the major gasped in fury. 'You're a disgrace – a traitor to your class. You've lived for too long among the scum of society. You're weak like your mother. That's why you're so easily taken in by ruthless men like MacRae. Well, I've seen to it that he does no more harm around here.'

'Haven't you punished him enough?' Charles tried one last plea. 'It wasn't his fault that Sophie fell in love with him.'

'In love?' his father cried in contempt. 'It was silly infatuation – you know how headstrong your sister can be. He took advantage of her. I should have got rid of him long ago.'

'As an objector, Rab will suffer enough wherever he is sent,' Charles reasoned. 'But to have him executed in cold blood for his beliefs – is that not against all we claim to stand for, as a Christian country? What about justice, forgiveness – and mercy?'

His father glared at him coldly. 'He's no Christian; he said so in public. Why should we show him Christian mercy?'

Charles looked at his father in despair. The gulf between them was so huge, he knew his arguing was pointless.

'You may get rid of Rab MacRae, Papa,' he said quietly, 'but you can't kill off his ideals. What Rab believes in so passionately will live on in others. And there will be others to take up his cross.'

His father's look was hard to fathom: loathing tinged with fear perhaps.

'If I catch you on my estate again, I'll have you arrested for trespass,' he spat. 'Get out!'

Charles walked away without another word. He mounted Flora's bicycle and pedalled off down the bumpy drive. Glancing round for one last look at his childhood home, he thought he saw Sophie's black-enshrouded figure watching him from the long drawing-room windows. He wondered how much she had heard of the argument. He waved in farewell. She raised a hand in reply, or maybe she was just touching her hair.

Charles rode away, thinking sadly of his mother, a free spirit trapped in this gilded cage of a mansion, wings broken long ago by tragedy and disappointment. He might never see her again, yet he knew wherever he went he took her blessing with him.

Back at the Settlement, Flora knew from his harrowed face that he had been unsuccessful.

'You mustn't blame yourself,' she consoled. 'And there's been a telegram from London. Our friends at headquarters are organising a deputation to the Prime Minister to hold him to his pledge that COs will not be shot.'

'Pray God it's not too late,' Charles said fervently. They held each other a moment.

'Rab's family?' Flora agonised. 'Should they be told?'

Charles nodded. 'Best to prepare them.'

'I'll send word to Emmie,' Flora said bleakly. 'She'll know how to tell them as kindly as possible.'

CHAPTER 23

Rab was still queasy from the rough crossing. From the hold of the ship they emerged, shackled and squinting into the daylight, and were marched in the rain over flat, muddy countryside to a holding camp. Men were being drilled on a makeshift parade ground in front of low-lying huts. The prisoners arrived, foot-sore and hungry, wrists chafing from the iron chains, but, after a meal of bread and tea, were made to march on.

Rab watched Laurie in concern. The young postman had not spoken since they left England. He had stopped singing hymns. His eyes were glazed in constant fear. Rab and Ernie Tait, the Chopwell miner, chivvied him to eat, but he no longer seemed able to swallow.

'Sip your tea, lad,' Rab encouraged. 'Got to keep your strength up.'

At a windswept railway station, they were herded into a cattle truck. After the prisoners had been crouching on their haunches for an hour in the gloom, the train pulled away sharply, throwing the men against each other. They travelled for what seemed like half the night, having to urinate in the corner, nauseated by the smell of vomit from the travel-sick, still chained together.

Rab was dozing on his feet, half resting on Tait, when they stopped and the side of the truck was pulled open. It was too dark to see where they were. Exhausted, they tramped behind each other, along a village street, then off down a track that ended in a farmhouse. They were ordered into a long building that stank of excrement and rotting straw, unshackled and locked in once more. They bedded down as best they could.

Rab was awoken by the shrill call of a cockerel. He became aware of horses whinnying and the constant noise of wheels trundling close by. As dawn seeped in at the dirty skylights, he could see the men were crammed into an old barn or stable. Laurie lay sleeping on a pile of filthy straw, his breathing ragged. Others coughed or moaned in their sleep, resting up against each other.

Ernie Tait nudged Rab and offered a puff from the stub of his cigarette. 'Last one,' he whispered. 'Blunts your hunger.'

Rab took it, his tongue stinging from the acrid tobacco. 'Where d'you think we are?'

Ernie shrugged. 'Towards the front, I'd say. Sounds busy.'

Soon after, the door was unbarred and two orderlies came in, carrying a milk churn and a sack, which they dumped down. The prisoners roused themselves at the sight. The door was locked again, leaving them in the dark.

'It's water,' one of them said in disappointment. 'How we supposed to drink it?'

Some pressed forward, tipping it to get at the water and quench their thirst. It splashed on to the foul straw. Others scrambled for the bread in the sack, fighting over the loaves.

Rab pushed forward in the half-dark. 'Haway, lads, we take it in turns. Line up for water. Every man gets a lid full. Ernie, you share out the bread. They may tret us like savages, but they'll not turn us into 'em.'

'Man's right,' someone said, shamefaced at his desperation. They queued up without protest.

Later in the day, the door opened again and a sergeant marched in, barking out names from a list for field punishment. Laurie was one of them. He looked at Rab in terror. Rab stepped forward.

'Where you taking them?' he demanded.

The sergeant shoved him back. 'Unless you're called, you stay here.'

A dozen men were led away under armed guard and the door locked behind them. The remaining prisoners waited all day for the others to return, or for more to be summoned out, speculating on the fate of their comrades. Outside there were shouts, men running, horses plodding, the occasional whistle.

Rab and Ernie encouraged the men to organise the crowded cell into some sort of order, piling straw to one side, away from the slop bucket which had to do for all thirty-seven. Then they sat and Rab encouraged them to talk about their experiences, the decisions that had led them to this point, to draw courage from each other.

Hours later, the orderlies came with more bread and water. Some time after that, the door opened again and their missing comrades were pushed through it. Even in the gloom, Rab could see that Laurie was in a terrible state. The young man staggered in and fell on to the squatting prisoners. He cried out in pain when Rab tried to lift him.

'Gave him a real going-over,' one of the others panted.

They moved aside, trying to give the returning COs room to catch their breath. They gradually told of their ordeal.

'Had us running round this field – hands on head – knee-deep in mud – weren't allowed to stop. Kicked and punched if you did. Laurie and the young lads were picked on the most. Fired shots over our heads to keep us moving.'

Rab propped Laurie up as best he could and dripped water on to his cracked lips. He hardly responded. Rab was filled with fury. He got up and went to the door, hammering on it hard.

'Guard!' he shouted. 'Open up. Lad needs a doctor.' When no one came, he thumped on it all the more, cursing them in frustration.

All through the night, Rab kept an eye on Laurie, trying to make him comfortable in the dismal cell. When morning came, he dipped his ration of bread in water and fed it to the youth. Laurie choked on the soft food and tried to turn away.

'You've got to eat,' Rab urged.

Laurie looked at him with hollow eyes as if he were a stranger.

Soon afterwards, the sergeant returned and called out a string of names. Rab and Ernie were among them. He ordered them out of the cell. They refused.

'Right, get 'em,' the sergeant shouted, and two soldiers hauled Rab to his feet. They dragged him out of the cell. He was almost blinded by the strong sunlight. Across the flattened ground in front, a sea of tents stretched away into the distance. He gulped in the fresh air and noticed the blossom on a tree close to the farmhouse. But the building was derelict, its windows gaping and roof gone. Then he was being shoved forward, his limbs stiff and aching from the hours of confinement.

They were marched at gunpoint to a rough parade ground that had once been a field. Large pools of stagnant water lay in the ruts. The sergeant ordered them to run around.

'Six times round, hands on heads!' he bellowed.

Some of the men began to jog, splashing through the puddles. Rab and Ernie stood their ground with a dozen others. The officer barked at them to move, then sent his men to force them. They were hit with rifle butts, punched and abused. Still, they refused to obey orders.

'Why you doing the bosses' dirty work?' Rab challenged the guards. 'We're your comrades, not the armchair patriots who sent you to war – the ones making millions out of this misery.'

'Shut up!' barked the sergeant, winding him with a punch.

The guards pushed them to the ground, kicked and stood on them, while the angry sergeant ordered them to crawl through the mud. Three men started to move, the others lay where they were.

The eleven resisters, Rab and Ernie among them, were dragged up and pushed at the end of rifles to follow the NCO. They were taken to a crumbling courtyard. A row of crudely fashioned crosses were spaced out in front of them. One by one the prisoners were tied up against a pole, their arms raised to shoulder height and strapped to the crossbars, their ankles bound at the bottom.

'You think you're Jesus bloody Christ,' the sergeant mocked, 'so let's see how much you like it now.'

He left them in the warming sun, crucified. It was not long before they were crying out for relief, arms numb. Rab felt sick with the pain in his shoulders, then faint from lack of breath. A private came round and splashed water to their lips. One man screamed out he would do anything they asked, just let him free. The sergeant told his men to cut him down and he was frog-marched away.

Rab heard Ernie trying to speak. 'Fourth Commandment – Honour – good – men,' he gasped, 'bow down – to none.' Rab felt a surge of courage at the familiar words. 'Five – do not hate,' Ernie groaned, 'but stand – up – for rights – and resist – oppression . . .'

Rab raised his head and strained to see his friend. He had fallen silent, exhausted by the effort.

'Sixth Commandment,' Rab panted. 'Do not be cowardly – love justice.'

The sky clouded over. Then a chill wind got up, it darkened suddenly and a heavy shower deluged them in seconds. The guards took cover. When it was over, they came back and cut down the remaining men. Two of them collapsed on the ground and had to be carried away. Rab only just managed to steady himself against the pole, his head swimming. More guards were called on to haul the men away.

Instead of being taken back to the communal cell, they were thrown into a tiny hut, shackled at the ankles and locked in the dark. Rab lay back on the hard earth, his limbs throbbing, ankles and wrists bleeding. They were too exhausted to talk. At some point they were brought water and bread. It was an effort to sit up and eat. The bread stuck in his parched throat like stone. As they lay trying to sleep on the hard ground without straw or mattress, Rab nearly wept at the injustice. Why were the soldiers being so vindictive? Why not just shoot them?

He fell asleep, hearing the whispered prayers of the man beside him. Some time in the night, he was woken by a distant boom. He jerked awake, thinking it was an explosion of gas down the pit and for a moment in the pitch-black had no idea where he was. After that, he could not sleep, plagued with thoughts of home and those he had left behind.

Ernie whispered his name. 'Rab, you awake?'

'Aye.'

'Courage, comrade,' the older man croaked.

'Why don't they just be done with it?' Rab whispered bleakly. 'Why torture us first?'

'They want to break us, lad. They'd rather we gave in than have to shoot us. Don't you see how that would look? Show us up for a bunch of cowards – shirkers – with no real conscience.'

Rab was sceptical. 'But surely they want to make an example of us – scare others off from doing the same?'

'Maybe that's what some in the War Office want,' Ernie grunted, 'but I think the military here think differently. What would you do if you had resisters on your hands – shoot them and make martyrs? That could lead to mutiny. Better to break their spirit and whip them into line.'

'Aye,' Rab murmured, 'I see your point. But with a war on, I'm surprised they're going to so much bother.'

'But that's the reason,' Ernie said eagerly. 'They've run out of men willing to die unthinkingly for their shabby war. Now they have to convince the conscripts. We're standing in the way of that.'

Rab felt a flare of hope. 'By heck, we've got them rattled. Few more like us and this war'll grind to a halt.'

'That's the spirit, lad,' Ernie said, gripping his arm in encouragement.

CHAPTER 24

In the morning, an officer appeared. He announced himself as their commanding officer and told them they were to be court-martialled for disobedience while undergoing field punishment. They were led to an outside trough, stripped, told to wash and issued with fresh army clothing. Then they were shackled and taken to one of the farm buildings. Inside a small room, bare but for a table and three chairs, a young officer greeted them nervously.

'I've been appointed to represent you at your Field General Court Martial,' he told them, going to the table and sitting down. 'The prisoner's friend. If you want one, that is. I need to take some statements from you – help with your defence.'

He opened an exercise book, pulled out a pencil and looked up expectantly.

'Our defence is we are conscientious objectors and should not be here,' Rab spoke up. 'My appeal is still pending. We've been kidnapped by the military.'

The young lieutenant looked at him in dismay.

'That won't help you here, I'm afraid. I need to say things about your good character – maybe some of you are pillars of your community?' He gave them a hopeful look.

Ernie snorted with laughter. 'Aye, Secretary of the Chopwell ILP.'

'ILP?' the officer queried.

'Independent Labour Party, lad.'

His face fell. 'You have to call me sir.'

'We stopped doing that when we left school,' Rab grunted.

The lieutenant ploughed on. 'You could say something like: you didn't realise it was so serious.'

No one said anything.

'Or you didn't know what you were doing,' the officer suggested. 'Promise you won't do it again.'

'And will the army promise not to beat us and crucify us again?' Rab asked quietly. 'We've been tret worse than any prisoners of war.'

'I don't know anything about that,' the soldier said, flushing. 'I'm trying to help you.'

'The best way you could help would be to join us,' Rab challenged. 'Lay down your arms.'

The lieutenant was appalled. 'You must be mad.'

Ernie said tiredly, 'Listen, lad, you're wasting your breath. We'll defend ourselves.'

The officer shook his head in disbelief. 'You don't seem to realise how serious this is. This comes from the top. You could be executed.'

'We know,' Ernie nodded.

The officer stood up abruptly and seized his book. 'Why are you doing this?' he asked in bafflement.

'To stop lads like you losing your lives,' Rab said simply. 'To stop all war.'

The lieutenant marched past them. He turned at the door. 'And I always thought conchies were a pack of cowards,' he murmured as he left.

They were taken back to the punishment cell. Soon after, they began to be called out, one by one. No one returned.

'What d'you think's happening?' Rab asked.

Ernie shrugged. 'Separating us to break our will, most likely.'

Rab's turn came. He was taken back to the stark farm room and told to stand in front of the table. Three officers sat behind it. One was the rank of major, one a captain and the third, glancing up sheepishly, was the young lieutenant who hours ago had been detailed to defend them. A large manual on military law lay open on the table.

The major started, 'I'm the president of this Field General Court Martial. Lieutenant Bowler will record the proceedings.'

Rab's name was read out along with the charge of

disobedience. The major asked him if he wished to speak.

Rab said, 'As a CO I don't acknowledge military authority, so your charge is meaningless.'

'Don't try to be clever,' the major snapped. 'We are close to the front line and can ill afford to spare time or men on the likes of you. That is why a Field General has been called. So if you have anything sensible to say, say it now.'

Rab was defiant. 'I've asked for exemption on moral and political grounds. My case has still to go to appeal. You have no right to try me. This is a mockery of justice.'

The major lost his temper. 'It's more justice than you degenerates deserve!'

The captain spoke up. 'Private MacRae, have you any mitigating circumstances? Perhaps you have lost a family member to the war and have acted out of grief, out of character.'

Rab reddened. 'Aye, I've lost a brother,' he admitted with difficulty. 'But that just makes me the more determined to oppose this war. I'll not have his death used as an excuse for further bloodshed and vengeance.'

The young lieutenant kept his head down, recording their words.

'Your so-called comrades don't feel as strongly,' the captain said with a pitying look. 'It's amazing how the shadow of execution concentrates the mind, makes men realise just how important life is – how important their families are, their country.'

Rab was contemptuous. 'I don't believe you.'

The captain gave him a rueful nod. 'You may be making a pointless sacrifice. But if you show a bit of contrition like the others,' he suggested, 'we could consider a lesser charge. I urge you to think again.'

Rab kept silent. He would not engage in their games. As Ernie had said, they were trying to break them, sow division among the objectors. The young lieutenant looked up at him expectantly. Rab shook his head.

The major said abruptly, 'Take him outside while we consider the verdict.'

Rab was outside a mere couple of minutes before he was summoned back inside.

'We have reached a unanimous decision,' the major said curtly. 'You are guilty as charged. The penalty for such a grave act is death by firing squad. Your papers will be sent to your commanding officer and to Brigade for comment, but as you have no record of past good service, this is a formality.' He looked at Rab with contempt. 'The final decision is taken by GHQ and the commander-in-chief, General Sir Douglas Haig.'

Rab felt numb at the stark words. He wanted to ask how long he had to live, but could not utter a sound. Moments later he was being marched from the room and stumbled out into the April sunshine. He was taken to a tiny holding cell in a crudely built line of huts and locked in alone.

There was a small barred window that looked out on the parade ground. If he pulled himself up on the bars he could glimpse the comings and goings of soldiers and supplies. But with hands shackled, he could only hold on for seconds and soon gave up trying. Rab knocked on the wall. There was an answering tap.

He shouted, 'It's Rab MacRae!'

'Ernie,' came back the muffled reply.

Someone on the other side knocked and shouted.

'Hoy!' cried the guard, ordering them to keep quiet.

But it was enough to fill Rab with renewed courage. He had comrades around him, despite what the captain had said. No matter what they did to them, they would stand firm together.

For the rest of the day, he sat in the patch of sunlight that moved around the cell, until it faded and the cold returned. His hearing became more acute as he strained to interpret the sounds from without. There seemed to be ceaseless motion, the clatter of boots, rumble of horse-drawn vehicles, shouted orders, clang of metal. In the lull between these harsh noises was the sudden trill of a bird or a snatch of song from a passing soldier. One of the guards kept whistling a tune that had been popular before the war, 'You Made Me Love You', and it reminded him of home.

Two days went by in this twilight world, where he saw no one to talk to but the guards who brought him food – a little thin soup with bread and strange-tasting coffee. One was surly and ignored his questions, but the whistler of tunes was more friendly. He was an apprentice baker from Middlesbrough who liked nothing better than a night at the music hall.

But Rab could only engage him in conversation for a few snatched moments. He had endless time to think and reflect. He wondered what was happening to the other men. Were some of them still being tortured? How many had given in and signed up to army rule? Had some already been shot? He pushed away such a grim thought. He would have heard the volley of a firing squad. Yet on one occasion, when the wind had been strong, he had heard the distant pounding of guns like far-off thunder.

At first Rab refused to dwell on his family and home. It was easier to think about his comrades and remind himself why he was there. But thoughts of home gradually took a hold. The whistling of the young guard set him humming tunes to himself. Suddenly an image was conjured up of Emmie at his kitchen table, head bent over her writing, stray curls of dark hair snaking down her cheek. He remembered her frowning in concentration; dark eyebrows, long lashes, full lips slightly parted.

Rab gasped at the bitter-sweet memory. He felt winded. Closing his eyes tight shut, he tried to remember more.

Barny has run outside to find Mannie in the workshop. Rab is supposed to be getting on with proofreading the *Messenger*, but all he can do is gaze at Emmie. His heart is full. He wants to reach out and touch her untidy dark hair, feel the softness of her skin. How long has he wanted to do this? He cannot remember when he first fell in love with Emmie. Perhaps he has always been in love with her, or perhaps he has only become fully aware of it now that it is too late.

Rab opened his eyes and stared at the brown-washed wall. Why had he never told Emmie how he felt? Was it because she was Curran's wife? But he thought nothing of conventional marriage; it was bourgeois, corrupting, where a woman was little more than the chattel of a man. Why had he never tried to tempt her away from Tom? He could see how unsuited they were, how the young Curran was gradually curbing her spirit, sapping her radicalism.

Yet Emmie had finally stood up to Tom's oppressive possessiveness. She had rebelled against the values of the Currans and protested against the war. How courageous she had been to defy them and how difficult it must be for her now, still living among them. Every day she must face censure and hostility, the pressure to give up and conform. Rab knew that his ordeal would soon be over, but hers stretched on for an eternity.

The next time the whistling guard came with food, Rab asked,

'Can you fetch me a pen and paper, marra? I want to write to me family before they come for me.'

The young baker looked nervous. 'Don't know about that. I'd have to ask—'

'Please?' Rab pleaded. 'Just the once.'

The guard shook his head in regret. 'I'd never get it past the censor.'

Rab was filled with frustration. He would never have the chance to say the things in his heart. But later, he thought better of the idea. What good would telling Emmie do now? Better that she'd never know.

On the third day of incarceration, Lieutenant Bowler came to prepare him.

'You'll be up in front of the whole company tomorrow,' he said. 'Your sentence will be read out – along with the other prisoners. You'll be allowed a wash and shave. Smarten yourself up.'

'So I don't look too degenerate?' Rab mocked gently.

'Would you like anything else?' Bowler asked, his look embarrassed. 'I can send the chaplain, if you'd like a chat.'

'Not much time to convert an atheist like me,' Rab teased. 'No, there's nothing I want.'

The next morning, just after sunrise, the guard came in and shaved him. Rab drank a cup of weak tea. Shortly afterwards, he heard the preparation outside. Barked commands were followed by the drumming of countless footsteps.

'Sorry,' the whistling guard apologised, 'I have to put these on you.'

Rab was put in leg irons and led outside. As he shuffled towards the makeshift parade ground, he was stunned at the sight of so many soldiers. There were hundreds of them, lined up on three sides of the muddy field, their ranks stretching into a blur. Moving awkwardly ahead were a dozen of his comrades. Behind him a voice cried, 'Rab!' He turned to see Ernie hobbling after him.

Rab grinned. 'Haway, you old gadgy, mustn't keep the colonel waiting.'

Rab slowed to let Ernie catch him up, despite the guard pushing him forward. Finally they arrived in the centre, huddled together like sheep, awed by the hush around them. It was humiliating, reminding Rab of a freak show at a travelling fair, all eyes trained on them in curiosity at their undignified shackled state. If only he had the courage to shout out to these men, what an opportunity it would be. But his throat was dry, his heart hammering. He glanced around his fellow prisoners and suddenly spotted Laurie.

The postman was ashen, his face strained but impassive. So they had not beaten him into submission. Rab was surprised. He caught the young man's look and smiled in encouragement. Laurie gave the slightest of nods back.

An officer marched forward and began to read out their names and numbers. Rab looked into the sky, watching clouds dance and swirl like a moving picture show. He breathed in the fresh air. It smelled of horse and hay, and new growth. A beautiful day.

'. . . whilst undergoing field punishment.'

Rab forced himself to concentrate on the loud, ponderous voice of the officer.

'The sentence of the court is death.' A long pause to let the gravity of their crime sink in. 'Confirmed by General Sir Douglas Haig.' A further pause. 'The condemned men will be taken out at dawn tomorrow and shot.'

The silence rang in Rab's head. He watched the proceedings as if they were happening to someone else. Laurie buckled at the knees and was prevented from falling by men on either side. Ernie swore under his breath. A flurry of cherry blossom appeared out of nowhere and scattered in the mud at their feet.

This was the last full day of life for these men pressed together beside him, their faces disbelieving, resigned, angry. Only when they were being ordered back to their cells did numbness lift and the pain of realisation grip Rab. This was his last day of morning sun, of blossom, of hope for the future. Tomorrow there might still be hope, but it would not be his. As he was led to the cell, he suddenly resisted. He stood rigid in the doorway, breathing in gulps of fresh air, frantically looking around, trying to memorise the sight of a tree, the clouds, a city of tents.

He was pushed into the darkened room, his feet unshackled. Then the door banged shut. He struggled to breathe, as if he already lay entombed. He tried to stem his rising panic, forced himself not to cry out. He lowered himself down, pressed against the wall and buried his head between his knees. He wept as silently as possible, ashamed of his tears.

Later, his whistling friend returned, and Rab was glad of the cell's gloom to hide his reddened eyes.

'Padre Hammond's here to see you,' he said cheerfully. 'I told him you wanted paper for a letter.'

The chaplain was tall and bald; he stooped to enter the room.

'Better off speaking to the Christian lads,' Rab told him when he tried to make conversation. 'Wasting your time on me.'

Still, the man stayed a while and Rab found himself telling him about Crawdene and the socialist Sunday school his father had started.

'We're not so very different, you and I,' the chaplain smiled.

Rab grunted. 'A vicar friend of mine runs a Settlement in Gateshead. He says Jesus Christ was the first socialist.'

'Could that be Charles Oliphant?' the chaplain exclaimed.

'Aye, it is. Do you know him?'

'I trained at St Chad's with him – good man. We lost touch. Is he still at the Settlement?'

Rab nodded. 'He's trying to keep it open – and help COs like me.'

'A pacifist then?' the chaplain asked in surprise. 'His father was an army man, I seem to remember.'

'They don't see eye to eye. Old man Oliphant would sell his granny into the army to keep this war going and his profits climbing.'

'This war is not about making money.' The chaplain sounded shocked. 'It's about doing the right thing – fighting for righteousness over evil.'

'War is the greatest evil,' Rab countered. 'How can you be a man of God and not preach peace?'

'I do preach peace,' Hammond said defensively.

'Give us peace, Lord, but not quite yet?' Rab mocked.

The chaplain laughed. '*Touché!*'

They talked about Charles, Rab's work, and the chaplain's days at Durham University. Soon they were discussing the poems of Matthew Arnold, the novels of Dickens and the politics of Keir Hardie.

The padre left him with a portable writing table, paper and pen, promising to deliver any letters he cared to write. Rab sat under the narrow window for a long time, contemplating the blank page on his knee. The afternoon light moved across the cell floor.

He wrote a letter to Charles and Flora, telling of his encounter with Padre Hammond. He told of his stout-hearted comrades, not wavering in the face of 'great trials', though he knew if he mentioned details they would be scored out. Then he wrote to his parents, a short affectionate letter, telling them to carry on the fight for socialism – and to give Peter his fountain pen.

Afterwards, he got up and paced the cell, restless and troubled. The light was fading from the window; his eyes were sore from straining in the dimness. Outside, someone went by singing 'The Homes They Leave Behind'. Rab stopped and strained to listen as the soldier's words faded and were gone.

He returned to the small writing desk, placed it on his knee and began to write his final letter.

CHAPTER 25

Emmie lived in a state of limbo in the rented flat in Berlin Terrace. In a fit of patriotism, Oliphant had renamed it Empire Terrace, but Emmie stubbornly refused to call her home by its new name. It was mid-April and the allotments were sprouting green; blossom from the trees around the chapel was scattered all over the village.

She had come to an uneasy truce with her in-laws, taking Barny to see them once a week and sharing the two letters she had received so far from Tom. They were short and factual, asking for news of Barny, telling her to take care of herself and the nipper. The first one came from a depot in Yorkshire, the second from France.

Emmie was shocked at how quickly he had been sent to the front. It all seemed so unreal, a bad dream from which she would wake soon. She shared her anxiety with the Currans, but what she could not share were her fears for Rab.

She had gone back to the Settlement a week after his arrest, but there was no news of his whereabouts.

'We're doing all we can, tell his parents,' Flora said, her face strained. 'MPs have been lobbied – Philip Snowden's going to raise the matter in the House. It's quite illegal what the military are doing.'

Flora promised to send word as soon as they knew where Rab was being held. A week ago, Flora had written a scrawled note of triumph. Asquith had issued a statement in the Commons, condemning the military authorities for defying pledges to

Parliament and ordering that conscientious objectors were not to be sent to France. The commander-in-chief was not to issue any death sentences without the consent of the Prime Minister.

Emmie hurried round to the MacRaes with the news. Helen gasped with relief, but Jonas was troubled.

'But we don't know where the lad is – so how do we know he hasn't already been sent – already executed?'

Emmie shuddered at the thought. She found it impossible to settle to anything, forcing herself for Barny's sake to do mundane chores and blot out fearful thoughts. Yet each day she awoke with a feeling of dread. She could just about pay the rent on the flat with Tom's army pay, but the prices of foodstuffs and clothing were soaring and she worried that she would have to give the flat up.

Daily she joined the queues outside the co-operative store or the butcher's, ignoring the sidelong looks and the whispered comments. Emmie knew what they said behind her back.

'Fancy her ganin' to help the conchies in Gateshead, with her man in the army.'

'I heard she had a fallin'-out with the Currans – that Louise won't give her the time o' day.'

'Strange lot, the MacRaes. Not surprising she's a bit wrong in the head, growing up with that lot.'

'Rab MacRae's been arrested, you kna.'

'Heard he was a German spy.'

'No, he's just a conchie.'

'Hung for taking part in the Irish rebellion, I'd heard.'

'She might be a spy, an' all.'

'Mind you, you've got to feel sorry for her, with her lad away to the war.'

Emmie carried on as if she did not hear their whisperings and wild gossip. There was so much rumour and misinformation flying about like the April wind that she was surprised she had not been ducked in the pit pond as a witch. Yet she knew most of these women, had sat and sewed clothes with many of them for two winters running, and she knew they were good at heart. They only repeated the propaganda in the censored press or the tale-telling of outsiders. No one in the village was openly hostile to her. It was only when she took Barny into Blackton to search for flour for bread or sugar to make rhubarb jam that she felt threatened.

Peter had his nose bloodied by a youth in Blackton when he discovered he was the brother of a conchie. The local vicar and many of the businessmen were staunchly pro-war. It was a village dominated by the Oliphants and Hauxleys. People would ask her if she was the woman who leafleted for the conchies and wasn't she the one who got her picture in the paper outside Rab MacRae's tribunal? With Barny at her side, Emmie thought better of arguing back and hurried on her way. Was it possible that this was the same town where they had rallied for peace less than two years ago? To Emmie it seemed a far-off age of innocence, when Louise had been her friend, dear Sam was still alive and Rab was preaching peace and Utopia.

Barny, a talkative, deep thinker at nearly four, was beginning to ask questions.

'Why are those women angry, Mammy?' he puzzled on their way back from Blackton on a day in late April. 'Will Daddy be back soon? Why is he fighting? Grandda says he's got to fight. Uncle Jonas says fighting's bad. Is Daddy being bad, Mammy?'

'No,' Emmie answered, 'he's not bad. But Uncle Jonas is right that we shouldn't fight.'

'Why is Daddy fighting?'

Emmie felt at a loss to explain. 'Because he thinks he's doing the right thing.'

She walked on briskly, Barny half running to keep up.

'Who are the Hun?' he asked suddenly.

'Don't call them that.' Emmie was sharp. She saw his startled look and slowed down. Putting a hand on his curly head of hair, she said more gently, 'It's a daft word they use for Germans. We're fighting a war against Germany – but lots of Germans are like us, ordinary people who don't wish us any harm. We should be trying to talk to them, not fight.'

Emmie smiled at his wondering face. Some people would accuse her of treason for the things she tried to teach her son. But she would not have him growing up a militarist like the Currans. Barny's generation would inherit a world at peace, the one that so eluded hers.

They walked on hand in hand. At the turnpike, they paused for breath and Emmie sat Barny on a stone wall to rest his small stout legs. He swung them out in front.

'Daddy fights you, doesn't he?' Barny startled her with his question.

'Why ever do you say that?' she asked, staring at him.

''Cos he hit you and you fell down,' Barny said solemnly.

Emmie gulped. She had hoped Barny had forgotten the incident. It was the first time he had ever mentioned it. She felt a wave of shame that her son should have witnessed such a thing.

'Daddy didn't think what he was doing,' she excused Tom, 'didn't mean to hurt Mammy. He was very sorry after.' She pulled the little boy close and kissed his head. 'He won't do it again.'

Together, they toiled up the steep hill into Crawdene. Helen was looking out for them at the end of China Street, beckoning them towards her. Emmie waved and shouted a greeting. Barny ran towards his favourite 'aunt'. But there was something about the distracted way Helen ruffled the boy's hair while regarding her. Helen's face was tight with strain.

'Come back to ours for a bit, pet,' she said, glancing away.

'What's happened?' Emmie asked in alarm.

But Helen would not say. Emmie followed her hurrying aunt along the street, heart thumping. When they got inside the cottage, she saw that Jonas was there in his dirty work clothes, gripping the mantelpiece as he stared into the smouldering fire. He turned. His harrowed expression made Emmie's legs buckle. She clung to Helen.

'Tell me what's happened? Is it Rab?'

Jonas just stared at her, his craggy, whiskered face as rigid as a death mask. Helen let out a half-sob.

'Letter came this morning,' she whispered.

'A telegram?' Emmie croaked.

Helen shook her head. 'Letter from Rab. Written on his last night . . .' Her voice faltered. 'There's one for you too. Sent it here . . .'

Jonas stirred. He picked a letter from the mantelpiece and handed it to her as if it scorched his fingers.

She could not take it – did not want to know – yet yearned to know.

'His last night?' she croaked. 'Then he's – dead?'

The question settled over them like fetid air. Jonas's broad shoulders heaved in a shrug or a wordless sob.

Helen shook her head. 'We don't know – all we have is this – no one's told us anything—' She broke off.

'Who's dead, Mammy?' Barny piped up.

His voice galvanised Helen.

'Haway, bonny lad,' she cajoled, 'let Mammy alone for a minute. We'll look for a bit bread and jam.' She nodded for Emmie to go. 'I'll bring him up-by in a little while.'

Emmie gulped at her stoicism. She snatched the letter from Jonas, unable to meet his pained eyes, and rushed from the cottage. Stumbling aimlessly along the street, she was overwhelmed by the need to get away. The enclosed streets pressed in around her, the watchful gaze of neighbours; the brooding, clanking pit, indifferent to their fate.

Stuffing the letter into her coat pocket, she turned and headed down the lane towards Oliphant's Wood, then skirted round the village and climbed the fell. Buffeted by the wind, she pressed on to Blackton Heights and Lonely Stones. Only then did she stop, heaving for breath, and crouch down in the heather. With her back pressed against a cold ancient standing stone, partially sheltered from the cutting wind, Emmie took out the letter and opened it with shaking hands.

My dearest Emmie,

This is the hardest letter I have ever had to write. General Haig has requested my presence before a firing squad tomorrow. I should be flattered that he thinks it as important to kill me as the enemy! I have written to Reverend Charles and Dr Flora – there's a canny padre here who knows the vicar. He won't convert me, but given a few more hours I may convert him to the cause of peace! I've written to Mam and Dad and Peter. It's easy to write to them because I can tell them what they already know, that I love and respect them and am grateful for teaching me the creed I have always lived by – love, peace and international brotherhood.

But you, sweet Emmie, live in ignorance of my feelings for you. For I have never spoken of the deep regard in which I hold you. I have watched you grow up, flower into a beautiful woman full of vitality and love for others. You have held your

225

counsel when I and others have said hurtful, hot-headed things, yet you have spoken out and acted bravely when it counted.

Proudly, I have watched you grow into a radical for the women's cause and for peace. You do not do so in any faddish way, to provoke and shock those around you, as the likes of Sophie O. do. Such people blow hot and cold like the seasons, but you carry on supporting the cause even when those around you turn on you and despise you.

I admire you for your loyalty – must confess to a touch of jealousy over your loyalty to Tom. What did he ever do to deserve it? That, I will never understand, Emmie.

But it is watching you with Barny that fills my heart to overflowing. You and the wee lad are like the best of companions, so happy in each other's company. You are the most loving of mothers. I picture you often, sitting in my kitchen, Barny on your knee as we discuss the newspaper. The looks that pass between you are pure delight. If there is a God, then it must in part be female, a mother, a cherisher of children.

Look how you have made me wax religious in my final hours! No doubt this will be chalked up as a victory to the padre. But, Emmie, it gives me comfort to know that, whatever happens in this war, you will have Barny to see you through it. One day, when he is older, tell him how fine a lad I think he is.

Emmie, forgive me for unburdening my thoughts to you so late in the day when there is nothing either of us can do about it. But I have to let you know how much I care for you, have always cared, ever since the day I brought you up from the town clinging to my back. Do you remember how we recited poetry? I found my soulmate that day, had I but known it.

I should have told you how much I loved you when I returned from Glasgow, heartsore, only to find my grief vanish in the face of your thirst for life, for love. You taught me how to feel true lasting love. I should have told you how much I loved you, when Curran started courting you, never thinking you would ever marry the lad. I should have told you how much I loved you when you helped me with the *Messenger*, leafleted around the village, risking the wrath of the Currans for your beliefs. I nearly told you how much I loved you that time in the park before my tribunal, but my courage failed.

Yet I do love you, Emmie, with all my being. I love you because you are strong and courageous and bonny and loving. I will always be grateful for the day I was sent to fetch you from Gateshead. I embrace you now, in my mind's eye, and wish above all else that I could embrace you in the flesh, even just the once. We will not meet in the next world, because I only believe in this one. But you will live on and struggle to bring about a better one, and that gives me courage to face tomorrow's dawn. You, dearest, will see the new dawn of socialism, for it *is* coming. It may be coloured crimson with the blood of the thousands who have died for it, but it *will* come. Our crimson dawn, Emmie.

Farewell.

Your loving comrade, Rab

Emmie sat, stunned, her cheeks stinging from tears dried by the cold wind. This was everything she had ever dreamed of hearing from Rab's lips. Why had he never told her? How had she never guessed his feelings, when her own were so strong? Yet she had never confessed her deep love for him and now she never could! She read the letter again, poring over each sentence, thrilling at the words, yet pained by them. They mirrored her passionate feelings for him; conjured up the moments of shared joy that she cherished too.

'Oh, Rab! My darlin', darlin' Rab!' she cried out.

How long had he really felt like this? Perhaps it was just the rantings of a condemned man, clutching out for comfort in his final hours. Yet Tom had guessed. What irony that her husband had been the one to recognise the love between her and Rab, when they had tried so hard to deny it.

Tom! Emmie's heart jerked with renewed guilt. Only now could she admit to herself that she had chosen the wrong man. She did not love Tom, though she had tried hard enough. For a time she thought she loved him, was flattered by his attention and possessiveness, wanted to grasp the love and security he offered, because she believed them impossible with Rab. What a fool she had been! She had nothing left in common with Tom – except Barny.

When she thought of her son and the things Rab had written about him, she wept anew. Barny was the most precious person in the world and Rab had acknowledged that. He was not jealous over her love for her son, as Tom was. For the first time she saw clearly how Tom craved love, demanded that she and Barny love him first and foremost. Tom was always anxious that Barny adore him, the way he never could his own father.

Yet, Emmie had to admit that if Tom was capable of loving anyone fully, it was their son. And for that reason she would stay with him. Even if Rab had lived and returned, she knew she was bonded to Tom for the sake of Barny.

Numbly, she folded the letter, tucked it safely away and stood up. The wind nearly knocked her sideways. It roared around her, snapping like a beast. The plantation below, which cosseted the Heights, sighed and moaned. She felt the first icy drops of a late spring hailstorm. The weather seemed to speak her desolation. Her Rab was gone. Somehow, she would have to carry on as he had willed her to do. Pulling up her coat collar around her frozen ears, she set off home.

CHAPTER 26

For two weeks the MacRaes mourned the death of their son. They were treated warily around the village. A few came to offer condolences and sit with them, many avoided them, as if their pacifism might contaminate. Emmie spent much of the day with Helen, hardly able to stomach the lecturing of the Currans.

'Bad blood will out,' Mrs Curran observed, with a timorous look at her husband.

Barnabas nodded. 'It's God's punishment for MacRae's atheist ways.'

She wanted to shout Rab's words at them, that God was like a mother, a cherisher of children, not a vengeful punisher of peacemakers. Their narrow-minded religion sickened her and she stopped taking Barny to chapel. She was tired of the minister exhorting them to bear the privations of war with a good grace and praise God for the valiant men fighting to free them from 'Junkerdom'.

She rounded on the Reverend Mr Attwater at the chapel door. 'And what are we reduced to here in England if not Junkerdom?' she challenged. 'A country where the military decide who lives and who dies; where workers cannot change jobs without permission of the bosses. Why aren't you preaching peace, Reverend, like it says in the Bible? Thou shalt not kill!'

She was filled with a new rage and took no heed of the Currans' outrage at her public rebuke. Being with the MacRaes was her only comfort. Jonas kept up their spirits with news gleaned from the ILP that they were not alone in their struggle. News leaked out of Germany that a large peace protest had taken place on May Day in Berlin with many arrested.

'See!' he declared. 'International socialism is not dead and buried. Our comrades are still out there and bearing the same burdens as we are.'

Then, one day at work, Jonas dropped the forge bellows and keeled over. He was taken by horse-drawn ambulance into Gateshead. Emmie walked to the hospital to glean news, leaving Barny with an anxious Helen. Jonas had suffered a stroke. He could not move his right arm and his speech was slurred.

'He may well recover,' said the distracted doctor. He was elderly, called out of retirement to help in the overcrowded hospital. 'Best to nurse him at home.'

Emmie decided to stay the night at the Settlement before returning with Jonas. She thought it strange the Oliphants had sent no message of condolence to the family; then it occurred to her in horror that they may not have heard of Rab's death. There were so many restrictions and delays, news may not have filtered through to her friends. There had still been no official word on Rab's execution or burial.

As she made her way to the Oliphants' flat, she found the once tranquil quad had been dug up and planted with vegetables.

'Emmie!' Charles cried, looking up from his desk. 'Dear girl. What a coincidence. Flora set off this afternoon for Crawdene with the news. But perhaps you've already heard.' He stopped, taking in her black armband. 'Emmie, what's happened? Who's died?'

She stared at him in confusion, touching the armband. 'Rab,' she whispered.

He frowned. Stepping towards her, he took her gently by the arm and steered her into a chair. 'Rab? You've been told he's dead?'

Emmie nodded, her eyes stinging with tears. 'We had letters from him – written on his last night before they – before he was – shot . . .'

'Oh, Emmie,' Charles said, his corn-blue eyes full of compassion, 'no one was shot. The Prime Minister intervened at the eleventh hour. We've been trying to find out for a fortnight where the COs have been taken. Yesterday we heard that some of the men returned from France are in prison near York.' He squeezed her hand. 'One of them is Rab.'

Emmie was stunned. She could not take it in. 'He – he's in prison?' she gasped. 'Not dead?'

'No, not dead,' Charles insisted. 'That's what Flora was coming to tell you – tell his parents that we finally had news of him. We had no idea you thought him dead. My poor girl. And Rab's parents – how appalling!'

'But they sent his letters,' Emmie said in confusion. 'Rab said he had written to you too.'

Charles shook his head. 'We never received it.'

Emmie gulped. 'He thought he was going to die.'

Charles nodded. 'Right up till the last minute Haig was determined to make an example of some of them. They must have gone through hell.'

Emmie began to shake with shock and relief. 'He's alive? Thank God, he's alive!'

Charles smiled and held out his arms. Emmie hugged him tightly, her spirits soaring at the sudden reversal of fortune. By some miracle Rab was still alive. He may be imprisoned, but he was living, breathing, existing somewhere in this world, not lost to them for ever. She burst into tears of joy.

Charles fetched her a handkerchief and a glass of water. When she could speak again, she told him of Jonas's stroke.

'Aunt Helen blames the shock of hearing about Rab,' Emmie said bitterly. 'He's always been such a strong man. And to think all that agony was for nothing . . .'

'I'll get Flora to go and see him as soon as she's back,' Charles promised. But Emmie could not wait to tell him. She went straight back to the hospital and insisted on being let in to see Jonas. Half laughing, half crying, she gave him the news of Rab's reprieve. His face twisted in a crooked smile, tears welling in his eyes. She gripped his hand as he tried to speak, but the words would not come.

'I know what you're trying to say,' Emmie assured him. 'It's grand news, isn't it? You get yourself better and don't worry about us – we'll manage fine. Take care, Uncle Jonas.' She kissed him tenderly.

Emmie stayed the night and was reunited with the Runcies

and Dr Flora. They talked of the huge workload of the Fellowship and plans for future resistance. Their pleasure in having Emmie with them once more was tempered by worry over Jonas.

'He must have a proper convalescence,' Flora was adamant, 'with exercise and a good diet. Perhaps he could go to the miners' hospital at Chester-le-Street. He'll have insurance through the Union, won't he?'

Emmie nodded.

'Then that's what we must arrange.'

They talked about Rab and the possibility of getting messages to him.

'From what we can gather,' Charles said, 'the COs have been given a year's imprisonment with hard labour.'

Emmie was shocked. 'Like a convict?'

Charles nodded. 'He's in for a very grim time.'

Jonas was moved to the miners' hospital. It was too distant for his family to visit easily, but Emmie knew the knowledge that Rab still lived would be the best tonic his father could have. She returned to Crawdene with mixed emotions: delight that Rab was alive, embarrassment at the letter she treasured and confusion about what she should make of it now. He had written it believing they would never meet again. He was free to say whatever he wanted, however fantastical. It was not written with the knowledge that he might one day return. Emmie had not told anyone of its contents, not even Helen, who must have wondered at her son's writing especially to Emmie.

She decided not to say anything, hiding the letter away under her clothes in the deep bottom drawer of the wardrobe. She would wait to see if he wrote again before she expressed her own feelings.

The weeks that followed were filled with helping Helen cope without Jonas's wages and being resourceful amid mounting prices and shortages. British Summer Time was introduced towards the end of May and Emmie took advantage of the longer evenings to forage in the woods with Barny and work in Jonas's allotment. She took over the digging and planting, while Barny helped Peter look after the hens and collect the eggs.

There were moments of deep contentment, sitting in the

evening sun, drinking elderflower cordial with Helen, listening to Peter playing his tin whistle to Barny as the boy laughed and ran around the small garden.

But such moments were fleeting. The net of conscription was being cast ever wider. That month, military service was extended to all men between eighteen and forty-one, including married ones. Helen shared her worry that Peter might yet be conscripted.

'All those that didn't pass their medicals last time have to be re-examined,' she fretted.

'But Peter's exempted 'cos of his job with Speed's,' Emmie pointed out. 'Besides, he'd never pass his medical or any tests. It'd be like sending a bairn to fight. Any doctor will see that. So stop your worryin'.'

The following month, Emmie got word from Flora that Charles had received call-up papers. She hurried to the Settlement to support her friends, taking Barny with her. Charles applied for absolute exemption on moral grounds, based on his Christian beliefs. The tribunal, on which Reginald Hauxley sat, refused. Two days later, before an appeals tribunal, the JP granted partial exemption and told him to report for non-combatant duties.

A furious Flora applied on his behalf to the Central Tribunal in London and the Pelham Committee that oversaw work schemes. Meanwhile, Charles failed to turn up at the recruiting office and was arrested. The local newspapers were full of his case, relishing the notoriety of a wayward son of the staunchly pro-war coal-owner.

All appeals for absolute exemption failed, but Charles agreed to non-combatant work that was not directly related to the war effort. He was sent to a prison camp in Wales and set to forestry work and quarrying. Flora was bereft at his going and threw herself relentlessly into her anti-conscription work and doctoring. The whole future of the Settlement was in doubt now that, without Charles, the mission had to close. The food kitchen struggled on, but they relied entirely on donations and the Runcies' dwindling pension. Seeing how Flora drove herself, Emmie spent two days a week at the Settlement, helping her deal with appeals and meetings, and keep in contact with the incarcerated men.

Wherever they could, they contacted local Fellowship members to visit COs in prison. If, as was usually the case, they were refused, bands of supporters would stand outside the prison walls and sing songs of encouragement.

Emmie organised one such group outside Newcastle prison when she discovered two COs had been moved there. While they sang 'The Red Flag' and assorted hymns, they flew a white kite over the prison walls, in the hopes that the men might see it or be told of it. Emmie imagined it was Rab inside and stood her ground when bystanders came to jostle and berate them.

But no word did come from Rab. Either it was too difficult for him to get a letter out, or he thought better of it. Perhaps he now regretted such a candid letter and was embarrassed to think of it. Finally she wrote to him, saying she was thankful he was alive and passing on news of the family. She alluded to Jonas's 'bad spell', but did not mention his long weeks in hospital or uncertain future at the pit. It was a chatty, neutral letter. At the end, she made reference to his letter from France.

. . . I understand it was written under great strain and you may now regret being so frank. Don't worry, I shan't repeat any of it, or mention it again. I know you wrote such things because you thought you were about to die. I was touched by your words, but as you say, I'm married to Tom. That's the choice I made, and for Barny's sake that's how it always must be.
Fond regards,
Emmie

With the summer came the grimmest of news from Flanders. The British had launched a huge offensive along the Somme in early July. At first, reports were vague. But as the month wore on, the toll of dead and wounded spoke of carnage on the front. Within a few short days, tens of thousands of men had died, whole battalions reduced to handfuls of survivors. The lists in the newspapers were endless; a day hardly went by without someone in the town or surrounding pit villages receiving a telegram of regret. People grew to dread the knock on the door.

Emmie waited anxiously for news of Tom. Was he in the midst of it? Had he been spared? She felt pity for Louise, when her former friend plucked up the courage to come round and ask her for news.

'Have you heard owt about our Tom?' she asked nervously. 'You will tell us the minute you hear from him, won't you?'

Emmie promised she would. She had not been to the Currans' since refusing to go to chapel and they no longer invited her round. Finally, in early August, she received a postcard from her husband. There'd been an outbreak of summer fever. He'd been in hospital during the Somme offensive and returned to find his company wiped out. He was being sent to a new battalion, in which most of the lads came from the West Country. They could not understand him and thought he was Scottish.

Emmie went round to the Currans at once with the news. Even the humourless Barnabas smiled in relief at the joke about being Scottish. Tom's mother pressed her to stay to tea, delighted with the news and to see her grandson again. After that, Emmie resumed her weekly visits, so that her mother-in-law could see Barny.

Increasingly, her time was spent at the Settlement. The casualties at the front mounted relentlessly, and the Settlement workers knew that the pressure would be all the greater to supply more men for the war machine. Restrictions on height and physical fitness were lowered, so desperate was the army for more recruits.

Whenever there were glimmers of hope in the press or from their friends, Flora and Emmie would share them with the Runcies at the end of the day. The *Herald* reported that peace meetings had been held in thirty-five German cities.

'And President Wilson is calling for a "league of nations" to keep peace in the world,' Flora read out to them one evening. ' "... to guarantee freedom of the seas, protect small nations and stop wars where there is violation of treaties",' she continued. 'At last, a politician with common sense and vision!'

'Not like that Lloyd George,' Philip grimaced, 'demanding Germany's complete downfall. And now he's Secretary for War.'

There was increasing unrest around the country, with strikes among engineers and in factories at working conditions. In late August, thousands of trade unionists converged on Hyde Park to protest against high food prices. By the early autumn, the price of bread had risen to tenpence a loaf.

Emmie and Helen were cheered by Jonas's return, but he was no longer strong enough to work in the pit forge. He was given a menial task on the bank, sorting stones from the coal among the boys and old men. His pay was reduced and his spirit seemed to wither with his fading physical strength. Helen and Emmie jollied him along as best they could, but it was only Barny who could bring a sparkle to his lacklustre eyes.

When Emmie had a spare moment, she would sit and read the newspaper to him while Barny sat at his feet, playing with the spinning top Jonas had once made him out of scraps from the forge.

By the end of the year, there was stalemate in the trenches. The country was battered by the loss of hundreds of thousands of men, and huge rises in the cost of living. To the dismay of Emmie and her friends, the bullish Lloyd George took over as Prime Minister, rejecting the peace overtures sent by President Wilson. There would be no stated peace terms, for Britain and her Allies were striving only for 'the knock-out blow' and Germany's total defeat.

With rising despair, Emmie stood outside the chapel that Christmas and handed out leaflets to the congregation.

'Join us in the demand for a negotiated peace,' she urged. 'Ask the ministers of religion why they are doing nothing.'

She did the same outside the parish church in Blackton. Some heckled and jostled her out of the way, but one man approached her and took the leaflet with interest. Emmie recognised him as a one-time member of the Clarion Club.

'It's Bill Osborne, isn't it?'

He nodded. 'I'd like to learn more about this,' he said eagerly. 'I've been called up and want to resist. Can you help me?'

Emmie told him to come down to the Settlement in Gateshead and they would help him present his application.

'We've helped plenty lads avoid this war,' Emmie assured him.

Bill took her aside. 'I don't just want me call-up put off a month or two,' he whispered. 'I want to go on the run. I heard women like you can help a man get away.' He looked at her expectantly.

Emmie felt uneasy. She did not want to talk about such things in public. Besides, she did not know this man well enough.

'I don't know anything about that,' Emmie told him. 'But I

suggest you come down to the Settlement and we'll see what we can do.'

'Aye, I'll do that,' he replied, touching his cap and quickly walking away.

CHAPTER 27

1917

Rab shivered in the bitter January cold of the exercise yard.

'Get moving,' the guard shouted at the prisoners. Rab shuffled around in heavy shoes with broken laces, feet like numb stumps, pulling his brown jacket tight around his shaking bony shoulders. His fourth prison in nearly nine months. He no longer cared where he was any more; each small cell, each grey yard was the same purgatory.

In York, his first prison, in the euphoria of still being alive, he had taken delight in fighting the system. The COs were segregated, forbidden to talk to anyone, ate alone in their cells and were punished for merely smiling at each other on their brief exercise outside.

Rab had communicated by tapping on the wall to his neighbour, Ernie Tait. Together, laboriously, they had worked out a code. He had stolen paper from the latrines and with a pencil stub begged from a sympathetic warder, had written messages to the other inmates to keep up their spirits. Another CO had been on slops duty and had taken the paper bulletins to distribute.

The COs went to chapel to see each other, and under cover of the hymn singing, sang messages about news they had gleaned from outside. This way Rab learned that the War Secretary, Kitchener, had died at sea, that married men were now conscripted and that there had been bread riots in Liverpool.

The warder who had given Rab the pencil was caught speaking to him, fined and moved to a distant wing. Shortly afterwards, Rab was sent to a different prison, split from his

238

comrade from Chopwell. Just before he went, a letter came from Emmie. His joy at reading her news was dashed at her lukewarm response to his declaration of love. She was embarrassed by it. He was a fool ever to have written it. He must put Emmie out of his mind if he was not to go mad.

At his new prison, Rab had refused to do hard labour – the stitching of sandbags – as it was directly helping the war effort. For two months he was confined to solitary, slept on a plank bed without mattress or pillow, was forbidden daily exercise and put on a restricted diet. All he could do was sleep and think, yet he was constantly tired and his mind tortured with thoughts of home and how they were coping.

He emerged weakened and depressed, to be transferred again, to a prison in East Anglia. Here he was given a slate and pencil to write with, but not allowed to send letters. He could read the Bible or improving tracts that the prison chaplain provided, but nothing from the prison library. Along with other convicts, he was given needle, string and black wax and put to stitching mailbags; eight stitches to the inch, ten feet to each bag, nine bags a day.

By the end of the first day, Rab's fingers were covered in black wax, blistered and bleeding. He had finished only three bags, two of which were rejected because of only five stitches to the inch. He was punished with half-rations.

The prison commandant liked to call him in for chats, challenging his beliefs.

'You're wasting your life away in here,' he told Rab, 'an educated man like you. And what for? You've made not the slightest bit of difference to the war effort. And what of your poor family? Don't you think it's unfair to put them through all this? You're safe in here from any backlash, but I bet they're facing hardship every day – extra hardship and vilification because of you. How are they surviving, do you know?'

Six months ago, Rab would have argued back, given as good as he got. His family supported him; COs were making a difference, he would not be tempted to give in. Instead he stayed mutely defiant and the commandant grew bored with baiting him. At the turn of the year, in deep snow and along treacherously icy roads, Rab was transported in a freezing prison van to yet another prison.

As he stamped around the frozen yard, chilled to the bone, eyes on the ground, someone coughed and bumped into him. He ignored it. On the second circle, it happened again. Rab glanced up in annoyance. A slight man with cropped hair stared at him with large hollowed eyes. He mouthed, 'Chin up, comrade,' and moved on.

Rab shuffled after him, in half recognition. As they circled a third time, he realised in astonishment who it was. As they passed the guard, he drew alongside and fell into step.

'Laurie Bell?' he whispered. The man gave a ghost of a nod. 'You bugger!' Rab exclaimed. The guard looked his way and he spluttered into a cough. With their backs to the guard, they slowed their pace long enough for another exchange. 'Thought you'd be dead by now,' Rab teased.

'You look like you are,' Laurie joked back. 'Prison not suiting you?'

Rab grinned. The cold on his teeth made him wince, but it felt good. He could not remember the last time he had smiled. They had no further opportunity to talk. Rab was returned to his brown-washed cell with its stinking jerry can in the corner and flea-bitten mattress. He paced around the cell, no longer listless, glancing at the barred window and the grey smudge of sky beyond. The window was too high up to see out of, and the view would be of blank stone wall, but it reminded him there was a world beyond. Under that same sky his family and friends carried on living.

The brief encounter with Laurie had jolted him back to life. He could not wait until tomorrow when he would see his comrade again, perhaps glean some news as to where he had been and what he knew of outside. Laurie, the timid, terrified postman! Rab had worried he would never survive two minutes in the penal system, yet here he was, giving him renewed hope. It was Laurie, not he, who was the strong one. Rab felt humbled and grateful.

A pale glimmer of light flared at the window for a moment: a ray of winter sun. Impossibly, a bird – a blackbird? – trilled out of view. It was over in a moment, but Rab felt his heart squeeze in pain at the unexpected beauty. Nature had ceased to matter to him these past months. He had grown used to a life without music or sunshine, just as he had grown used to going without tea, or sugar or tobacco. He thought he no longer missed them.

Crouching down on his hunkers, Rab bent his head. A sob rose up in his throat. They did matter, by God they did! Everything mattered. How he missed the world, missed walking the fell, arguing with his father, reading, music, his mother's touch – how he missed Emmie and Barny! Rab buried his head in his arms, not caring if they watched him through the peephole of his cell door. He gave in to tears. He cried for what he had lost and regained, cried because he could feel joy and pain once more.

CHAPTER 28

That winter was the coldest Emmie could remember. The flat never seemed to warm up, and she felt constantly hungry and tired. Barny had a permanent runny nose and chesty cough, no matter how many clothes she put on him. They went to bed wearing everything they had, piling Tom's old clothes on top of the covers, yet still she woke with a frozen nose and ice on the inside of the window.

She worried about Helen, who went down with influenza and took weeks to recover. For a while Emmie moved into China Street to nurse her and cook for Jonas and Peter, but Helen fretted that Barny or she would catch it too, and made them move back to Berlin Terrace.

Then March brought startling news. Jonas rushed in from work, brandishing the newspaper, his mouth pulled into a crooked smile.

"Ey done it!' he cried incoherently. 'Gone — bloody — Tsar!'

Emmie took the paper from him while Helen made him sit down before he had another seizure.

'Revolution in Russia,' Emmie gasped. 'They've got rid of the Tsar!'

'What — I — said!' Jonas laughed, catching Barny round the waist with his good arm and tickling him. The boy giggled and squealed to be free.

The mood in the village was jubilant for days. Socialist revolution had come to autocratic Russia without bloodshed. There was much talk about what it would mean. The Russians had declared the war over; they would no longer fight the Germans.

'This is the beginning of the end,' Emmie said gleefully to the MacRaes. 'With our biggest ally, Russia, out of the war, we have no reason to carry on.'

But despite the celebrations among trades unionists and Labour members, nothing changed. The Government was more bullish than ever. The Central Powers were now free to fight on one front – the Western one. Still, the MacRaes were buoyed by the news of change and determined to be optimistic.

Then came an unexpected blow. Peter was summoned by the recruiting office. Men under twenty-six were no longer allowed exemption on grounds of business or employment. Mr Speed was told to give up his delivery boy. The MacRaes appealed on medical grounds. After a cursory medical examination, Peter was reclassified as fit for active service.

'I'll be just like Sam,' Peter said proudly, pleased to be classed as a soldier and confused by his parents' opposition.

'The lad won't survive away from home.' Helen was distraught. 'He'll get picked on.'

Emmie hurried to Gateshead to help rally support for his appeal. At least they could try to get him exempted from front-line combat to serve on the home front.

Flora looked gaunt with strain. She had helped nurse Mabel through a bout of influenza, as well as carrying on Charles's work for the Fellowship. Philip was convinced they were under surveillance and was wary of taking in CO runaways at the Settlement.

Emmie thought of Rab's old room at Mannie's, or his workshop. They could be accessed from the woods without being overlooked by the street. She would ask Mannie whether he would take such a risk.

'It's possible I could find you somewhere in Crawdene,' Emmie told Philip, 'if it was just a holding place for a day or two.'

Philip put a hand on her shoulder. 'Dear Emmie, don't put yourself in danger. You have the boy to consider.'

'We all have someone to consider,' she answered stoutly. 'I'll do my part if I can.'

She thought of Rab and his comrades incarcerated in a distant prison. If she could save just one man from that fate she would do so willingly. None of them had heard from Rab for months.

All they knew was that he was being held in East Anglia and that there were restrictions on COs writing letters. But their own ones had gone unanswered and they did not know if any of the winter clothing and food they had scraped together to send had ever reached him. After nearly a year of hard labour, his state of health was a cause for worry.

Helping in the soup kitchen, Emmie found the miner Bill Osborne, who had approached her at Christmas. She had put him in touch with the Runcies.

'So you're still here?' she said in surprise.

'Got a medical exemption,' he smiled. 'Didn't have to join the "flying corps".' He winked at his mention of the Quaker underground network.

'That might not stop you being conscripted,' Emmie warned. 'Peter MacRae's being reclassified. It's a nonsense sending a lad like him to the front. He talks a good fight, but he couldn't harm a fly.'

'Aye,' Bill agreed, 'he's not quite twelve pence in the shilling, is he?'

'No,' Emmie sighed. 'He'd run a mile if he heard gunshot.'

Bill shook his head in disgust. 'Must make you really angry. If I was you, I'd get him away quick. Couldn't you hide him somewhere? You've got connections, haven't you?'

Emmie thought again of Mannie's. They could hide Peter and he would think it a big game. But for how long?

Emmie shrugged. 'Maybe . . . there is somewhere I have in mind.'

'Let me know if I can help,' Bill said earnestly.

'Thank you.' Emmie was grateful. 'The more of us at the appeal the better.'

The day of the appeal came, and Jonas and Helen brought Peter down from Crawdene. They hung around for hours, Peter soon tiring of standing in the corridor and wondering why they could not go home. Helen was close to tears when their turn was called.

As a JP, Reginald Hauxley sat in judgement, flanked by two other officials. He began by questioning Peter, his voice soft and considerate.

'You're a good worker, Mr MacRae,' he smiled. 'Your employer speaks highly of you.'

Peter looked behind him, thinking the man was talking to his father. Hauxley nodded at him. 'I'm referring to you, Peter. Mr Speed says you are very reliable.'

Peter grinned as realisation dawned. 'Never missed a day's work,' he said proudly.

'And you manage to remember the instructions he gives you?' Hauxley pressed. 'You can follow orders easily?'

'Aye,' Peter nodded vigorously.

'And you're good with horses, especially,' Hauxley smiled in encouragement.

'I feed and groom Lily and Farmer every day,' Peter answered. 'Lily's me favourite — known her since she was a foal on Mr Speed's holding. Farmer's a bit contrary — takes a bit of handling — but he's a grand—'

'Yes, quite so,' Hauxley interrupted him. 'Obviously very good with horses. How would you like to handle horses for the army, Peter?'

Flora sprang up. 'His parents are appealing the decision to send Peter MacRae into active service. He does not understand that looking after horses for the army will necessitate being at the front in a combatant role. Peter has no concept of what war is actually like. He has the mind of a child — the innocence of a child.'

Hauxley looked at her with ill-concealed contempt. 'Dr Jameson, no man knows what war is like until he experiences it at first hand. Peter appears to me a sensible and well-balanced young man. His medical report passes him as physically and mentally fit for active duty. His employer has released him for military service. What possible grounds are there for appeal?'

Flora gripped the chair in front of her. 'As I say, he has the mind of a child. Peter has no idea how far away France is. He thinks it is like going to Newcastle or Durham – somewhere just beyond his normal delivery round, beyond the bounds of his experience.' She turned and pointed to the MacRaes. 'His parents know him best. They know he will not last two minutes away from their care. He will be frightened and confused to be taken away from his home surroundings, and will therefore do more harm than good.'

Hauxley was dismissive. 'All new recruits have to experience such dislocation.' He turned to speak to the MacRaes directly. 'Peter will soon get used to it. And the army is caring of its young men. Rest assured, they will look after your son.' He gave a tight smile.

Jonas sprang up. 'As – they – looked after – yours?' he stuttered, forcing the words from his half-paralysed mouth.

Hauxley gave a look of loathing. 'I have no further questions.' He glanced at the rest of the panel. They nodded. 'We see no grounds for appeal. Peter MacRae will report to the recruiting officer as ordered. I'm sure this fine young man will do his patriotic duty proudly and be a source of pride to all those who love their country.'

Peter grinned. The room erupted in protest. Helen shook her fist at the panel.

'It's wicked what you're doing! He's just a bairn in a man's body. How can you think of sending him to fight? Murderers!'

Philip and Emmie closed in to protect her from the policemen moving towards her from the door.

'Leave her alone,' Emmie defied them. 'Can't you see she's upset?'

'Get her out of here now, or we'll arrest her,' one of them ordered.

Jonas took her by the arm, his face livid. 'Come, Helen.'

Peter watched them, his face crumpled in confusion. Emmie went to rescue him.

'Haway, Peter,' she murmured, slipping her arm through his.

'Have I done some'at wrong?' he asked.

'No, kidder, nothing wrong.' She squeezed his arm.

'Mam's cross at me,' he worried.

Emmie's eyes stung. 'Not at you, Peter. She's cross at the men up there – for sending you to war.'

'But I want to gan,' Peter said solemnly. 'If I'd been there to look after the horses, Sam wouldn't have fallen under that cart and been trampled. See?'

Emmie's heart squeezed at the sight of his eager face. She clutched him to her as they were hustled from the chamber. Outside Helen threw herself at her youngest son and wept openly. Peter grew agitated and Jonas stepped in to steer them away. Friends from the union were waiting to convey them back to the village.

Emmie had to return to the Settlement to collect Barny from Mrs Mousy's care. Bill walked back with her. He seemed as furious as she.

'A fool could see he's not fit for the army,' Bill raged. 'Shows how desperate they are. I think they're just being vindictive 'cos he's a MacRae. They're scared the likes of the MacRaes are about to start a revolution here. Bloody good idea too, if you ask me. Do you want to see revolution, Emmie?'

'Aye,' she said bitterly, 'if it would mean this war stops now, like they've done in Russia.'

He stopped her with a grip on her arm. 'Then do something,' he urged. 'Don't just let them get away with what they're doing. Strike a blow for Peter – for his parents – for all of us!'

Emmie felt filled with the same impotent rage.

Bill went on. 'Look at that!' He pointed to a row of recruitment posters on the wall beside them – old ones from last summer that still bore Kitchener's image. Bill began tearing at them, ripping them from the wall. Emmie looked around in alarm. If someone saw him he could be arrested. But he did not seem to care. Emmie turned to help him. She felt savage satisfaction in tearing the posters down. They hurried along the street, turning through a tunnel towards the docks. At the far end was a church hall, which was used as a temporary recruitment hall. Its notice board displayed a new poster, exhorting women to do their bit by going out to work. It showed smiling women loading gun shells in a factory.

Emmie grabbed it and tore it down, stamping it under her feet. Two people across the street stopped to stare. Bill took her by the arm and hurried her away.

'Good lass,' he crowed, as they slowed down two streets away. 'Now the next thing we have to do is get Peter away before the army gets its hands on him.'

When Emmie returned home, she found a note from Louise.

'Where are you? Come round as soon as you can.'

Her heart lurched in fright. Had they had bad news about Tom? She hurried over to the Currans' with Barny. From the end of the street she could pick out her in-laws' house; it was bedecked in red, white and blue bunting. A

Union flag hung from an upstairs window. Barny clapped his hands.

'Is Grandma having a party?' he cried.

They were met at the door by an excited Louise. 'Isn't it grand he's coming home?' she gabbled.

'Tom?' Emmie gasped.

'Aye, of course Tom! Letter came two days ago. Didn't you get one?'

Emmie hesitated. She had not had a letter from Tom in over two months. Perhaps they had gone astray. She had not dwelled on why Tom should still write to his parents but not to her. 'I – I've been down Gateshead. Peter MacRae's appeal.'

'Oh, Emmie,' Louise said impatiently, 'you'll have to stop all that now Tom's got leave.'

'How long for?' Emmie asked, heart hammering.

'Two weeks,' Louise said in excitement. She picked up Barny and swung him round. 'Your daddy's coming home, just think of it! What a change he'll see in you.'

Barny's face lit up. 'Daddy's coming! Can we have a party, Mammy?' He struggled out of his aunt's hold and flung himself at Emmie.

'Course we can,' Emmie grinned.

Mrs Curran appeared and put out her arms to receive Barny. He ran to her.

'We'll have a great big party,' his grandmother promised. 'It's already planned. We'll have it here, of course. Nothing but the best for your daddy. Mammy's been far too busy to see to things.' She gave her daughter-in-law a reproachful look.

Emmie ignored the slight. 'When does he get here?' she asked.

'Day after tomorrow,' Mrs Curran announced, 'at Central Station in Newcastle.'

'Thank you,' Emmie smiled. 'Me and Barny will gan to meet him.'

'Oh, we're all going.' Mrs Curran smiled. 'Reverend Mr Attwater has offered to take us down in his trap. He's organising a special service of thanksgiving on Sunday for Tom's safe return. You'll come, won't you?'

Her mother-in-law's look was nervous, as if she were afraid Emmie would spoil it all in some way.

Emmie swallowed. 'Course I'll come.' She held out her arms to

Barny and the boy came running. She hugged him to her. 'Barny can't wait to see his daddy again.'

CHAPTER 29

Emmie spent the following day making the house as welcoming as possible. She spring-cleaned the kitchen and bedroom, and took Barny to the woods to pick daffodils for the table. She scoured the village for currants, begged some flour from Helen and made Tom's favourite griddle scones.

Helen was putting a brave face on Peter's going. She would not hear of Emmie's idea of hiding him.

'I'll not see him get into any more trouble than he has to,' she said with resignation. 'He's not like Rab – our Peter would never survive a spell in prison.'

Emmie put out a hand and squeezed hers. 'Rab'll be out in a month or so,' she encouraged.

Helen's eyes filled with tears. 'Aye, just as one comes back, I lose the other.' She turned away and briskly set about measuring the flour Emmie wanted. She would talk no more about it, stoic as ever.

Barnabas took a half-day off work for the triumphant trip into Newcastle to collect his brave son. Emmie sat with Barny on her knee, joggled in the back of the trap with the Curran women, while Barnabas sat up front with Mr Attwater. The last time Emmie had spoken to the minister was at Christmas, to berate him for doing nothing to help bring about peace. He was coolly polite to her and once again Emmie wished she had been allowed to go alone to meet her husband.

It was over a year since she had waved him away down the back lane, his tender words of contrition lingering after his going. Despite his illness at the time of the Somme offensive, Emmie knew Tom must have seen gruelling front-line action. Last summer and autumn, some of the bloodiest and most costly battles of the whole war had taken place, judging by the casualty lists.

However mixed her feelings were for Tom, Emmie was determined to make his leave as happy as possible. She and Barny would give him all the attention he needed; their home would be a haven from the barbarity of the trenches.

At the station, it was noisy and chaotic. Trains drew in late and overcrowded. The men ushered the women and Barny into the ladies' waiting room and told them to be patient. They would be summoned when there was any news. Emmie sat in frustration, trying to keep a bored and hungry Barny occupied and quiet. They played I spy umpteen times and sang all the nursery rhymes they knew. They went to the toilet more times than was necessary.

Finally, Emmie lost patience and went out to look for the men. She spotted them coming towards her, waving.

'London train's pulling in now,' Barnabas called. 'Go and fetch the others.'

But Emmie was not going to be ordered around any more. She pulled Barny by the hand.

'Haway, let's find Daddy,' she grinned. 'Grandda can fetch them.' They ran past an open-mouthed Barnabas, laughing.

The train sighed to a halt and doors banged open. Soldiers threw out kitbags and milled on to the platform. Emmie held up Barny so he could see. Scores of passengers hurried towards the barriers and waiting loved ones. The Currans caught up with them and craned for a sight of their son. Away down the far end, Emmie thought she saw Tom. He seemed to be having difficulty with his kitbag. Another soldier came to help him. The platform was almost clear before the Tom-like figure wended his way to the barrier. Emmie decided it was not him. His hair was close-cropped; he looked too full in the face. He walked differently, staggered almost.

But he was grinning at them. Louise shouted out, 'Tom! Over here!'

Emmie's stomach twisted. Something was not quite right. Even before he got through the barrier with the help of his friend, Emmie realised what it was. Tom was drunk. His eyes were unfocused, his grin inane. As his companion pushed him through the barrier, Tom clapped him on the back.

'Danny, this is me family,' he cried. 'Look, there's me little lad! Come here, Barny. Come meet friend – Danny. Everyone meet Danny.' He started to giggle. 'Me best mate.'

Tom lurched at Emmie and Barny. 'Me darlin' missus, gi' us a kiss.' He planted a slobbery kiss on her lips. He reeked of alcohol. Emmie recoiled. Barny drew away, burying his head in Emmie's shoulder.

'Come on, little nipper.' Tom laughed loudly. 'Gi' yer da a cuddle.'

Barny refused to look at him, alarmed by the booming voice, the smell he did not recognise. Emmie could feel him shaking.

'Give him a minute, Tom,' she murmured.

Tom frowned in annoyance.

'Give him here, woman,' he ordered, trying to prise Barny from her arms. Barny clung on like a limpet.

Grandma Curran encouraged, 'Go on, pet, give your father a hug.'

Emmie kissed the boy and whispered, 'Do it for Mammy.'

Barny looked round, his eyes fearful, but loosened his hold. At once Tom grabbed his son to him.

'See, Danny!' he crowed. 'Little smasher, eh?' He gave Barny a wet, noisy kiss on the cheek. 'Look at you – twice size,' he slurred.

'Ugh, Daddy, you smell nasty!' Barny complained.

Danny laughed. 'We've been telling him that for months.'

The Currans hovered around their son, patting him and pretending nothing was wrong.

Louise began to gabble nervously. 'We've got a party arranged for you – there's that many folk want to see you, our Tom. By, it's grand to see you – and looking so well. Isn't he looking well, Mam?'

Mrs Curran nodded agreement. Barnabas took control.

'I'll take his bag, thank you, Danny. Come along, let's get Tom home.'

Mr Attwater offered Tom's companion a lift.

'No, ta,' he laughed. 'Ganin' to quench me thirst on the way home.' He punched Tom playfully on the shoulder. 'Meet up later, eh? Like I said, Blacksmith's Arms on Croft Street.'

Tom nodded, glancing defiantly at his family. 'Aye, later, Danny lad.'

With his friend gone, Tom's bravado faltered. His eyes were suddenly bleary, his head sagged. Barny twisted and whinged in his arms.

'Want Mammy,' the boy whined.

Tom gave Emmie a resentful look and thrust the boy back at her. 'Have him, then.' He swung an arm around his sister instead. She staggered at the sudden weight. Tom laughed as Barnabas steadied them. 'Haway then, little sister, tell me all the gossip.'

The rest trooped out of the station behind Tom and Louise. Emmie caught the look of dismay that passed between Tom's parents. She was surprised Barnabas had not taken his son to task for being so openly drunk and in front of the minister. But nothing was said. All of them except Barny were pretending that Tom was the same. They climbed into the trap and squeezed up next to each other. Maybe it was high spirits and too much time on the slow journey north with Danny that was to blame.

Before they were out of Newcastle, Tom was asleep on Louise's shoulder, snoring softly. Emmie gazed at him. He looked peaceful and younger again, the redness in his eyes hidden, the tightness around his mouth eased. No one spoke as they jostled home. Just before they arrived in the village, Mrs Curran leaned forward and put a hand on Barny's knee.

'Isn't it grand to have your daddy back, pet?'

Barny did not answer. He continued to watch his sleeping father with the caution of a hare to a hunting dog. Emmie felt his small hands tighten on hers.

'Course it is,' Emmie answered for him.

The trap had hardly pulled to a stop at the end of Denmark Street when Barny was scrabbling over the side. Half the street had come out to greet Tom. One of the neighbours lifted Barny down and the boy disappeared into the sea of legs and skirts.

Tom woke with a start at the noise of cheering, his eyes and mouth wide with alarm. When he realised where he was, he relaxed and grinned. His father and the minister helped him down, Barnabas waving people aside.

'The lad's very tired – needs to rest before doing anything,' he decreed. 'Make way, make way.'

The neighbours fell back, with only the occasional whispered comment about the state Tom appeared to be in. But they were forgiving. He was back from war and a son of Barnabas Curran could be excused much. Who were they to begrudge the lad a little tipple on his first day of leave?

Emmie followed the small procession, peering out for Barny. She wished she had insisted to the minister that he drop them off at Berlin Terrace. Instinctively, she felt that these first few hours would be important to how the rest of Tom's leave went. They needed time together, just the three of them, in their own home, getting to know each other again. But the Currans were not going to allow it.

It was then that Emmie wondered what Louise and her parents might have written to Tom in their letters over the past months. Had they told him disapprovingly of her work for the Fellowship and the tribunals, of the petitions and leafleting outside chapels and churches? How much of her anti-war work did he know about? As they guided a weary Tom through the door, Emmie wondered if that was why Tom had stopped writing to her.

Her husband was put to bed in Louise's room and left to sleep. Emmie went out and found Barny playing in the street with the other children. The game was English vs Germans. Some of the older boys were arguing as to which side Barny should be allowed to join.

'His da's a hero,' one said; 'he's on our side.'

'Na, we're not havin' him,' argued another, 'his mam's a Hun-lover.'

'Aye, German spy!'

'Traitor!' One of them pushed Barny aside. As the boy fell back, Emmie rushed forward.

'What d'you think you're doing, picking on a bairn half your size?' she demanded, hauling Barny to his feet.

'Sorry,' one of them muttered. The others stared at her sullenly.

'You don't know what you're saying,' Emmie said more gently. 'You shouldn't call people names. How can a lad of barely five years old be a traitor, eh? And I'm not a spy – unless you call interfering in your game spying.' She smiled at them. 'It's just some of us in this village believe that war is a bad thing – and it's the likes of you and Barny that suffer the most. There's not enough food any more, is there? And I bet you all know someone who's gone to war and not come back.'

The children were nodding at her now.

'It's not fair on you bairns,' Emmie went on. 'That's why lots of us think it's time the fightin' stopped. We're not traitors – we love our country and our people – and we want to make it better for all of us, not just the few rich ones. So,' she brightened, gazing round, 'can Barny join in? Doesn't matter which side he's on, does it? You're all friends when it comes down to it.'

'He can be on my side,' Jacky, one of the biggest boys, said at once. 'Haway, Barny, over here. Have to run fast, mind.'

Barny grinned and nodded, running over to join him.

Emmie wandered back to the Currans' to see if she could help prepare the tea.

Later, Barny came running in the house, crying.

'Did you fall over, pet?' his grandma exclaimed over his bleeding knees.

'P-pushed me!' he sobbed.

'Who did?' Louise demanded, as the women crowded about him. 'I'll box their ears.'

'Jacky's m-mam.'

'His mam?' Emmie said in disbelief. She sat the boy on her knee while Mrs Curran fetched water to bathe his scrapes.

'Tell us what happened, Barny,' Louise encouraged.

The boy gave a juddering sigh. 'We was playing English and Germans. I was on the English. We got the Germans and put them in Jacky's coal shed – and Jacky makes them come out one by one. And we have broomsticks and Jacky says shoot.' Barny stopped, craning round to look at his mother.

'Go on,' she said gently.

Barny said, 'I drop the broomstick 'cos I don't want to play any more. And Jacky says I'm a yella conchie and his mam comes out and says I can't play with him 'cos . . .' he gulped.

''Cos what?' Emmie asked, fearing the answer.

''Cos you're me mam,' Barny mumbled.

Emmie went cold. She had been at school with Jacky's mam. They had sewn together at the Guild. Now, because of this war, this ordinary, sensible woman was teaching hatred and intolerance to her son. It was spreading among the children like a poison.

Louise gave Emmie a resentful look. 'See what you're doing?' she accused. 'They're pickin' on the bairn 'cos of your meddling.'

'You've got to stop,' Mrs Curran said fearfully.

Emmie would not be cowed. She cuddled Barny. 'Jacky's mam was wrong to say and do what she did,' she told her son firmly. 'And you were right to put down your broomstick if you wanted to.'

'No he wasn't!'

They all jumped in shock. Tom filled the doorway, his face creased and haggard.

'You should've got yer stick and gone bang, bang, bang!' he cried, lunging at them with a pretend rifle. He laughed at their gasps of horror. Barny burst into tears again.

'Tom!' Emmie admonished.

'Haway, nipper,' he commanded, 'come to yer da.'

Barny clung to Emmie, wide-eyed in alarm.

'He's had a scrape,' Emmie explained.

Tom regarded them with bloodshot eyes. 'Don't be so soft. Come on, Barny.' He held out his arms impatiently.

'Go to Dadda,' Emmie coaxed. 'He's waited a long time for a cuddle.'

Barny slipped off her knee but went no further. Tom lurched forward and scooped him up, pressing him tightly to him.

'Still your dadda's little soldier, eh?' he said, scraping his bristles against his son's soft cheek. Barny squealed and pushed away. Tom laughed harder. 'I see I'll have to toughen you up, little nipper. Been with lasses too long. Mammy's boy, are you?'

Barny put a hand to Tom's chin and shoved it away from his. 'You're scrapy like a matchbox.'

They all burst out laughing at once. 'Still bright as a button,' Tom said in delight. 'Got yer mam's looks and yer da's brains.'

He pretended to drop Barny. The boy gasped in shock, then Tom gripped him tight, laughing. He did it again, but Barny struggled to be let free. He twisted round and gave Emmie a pleading look. She stood up.

'Why don't you have a wash before tea?' she suggested. 'Barny could help you fill the basin. He loves playing with water.'

He gave her a dismissive look. 'I'll not have my son learnin' women's work. Our Louise can fill the tub.' He held on to Barny. 'Haway, nipper, we'll gan and play dominoes in the parlour with Grandda till me bath's ready. Get away from all these lasses.'

He lurched out of the kitchen, Barny clutched in his arms. The small boy looked unhappily over his shoulder at his mother. She nodded at him in encouragement. If only they could get home and be alone, she wished fervently. Tom was just showing off in front of his mother and sister.

She helped Louise fill the tub with hot water and set up a screen of towels over the clothes horse, then called Tom in.

'I'll gan round to Berlin Terrace and fetch clean clothes,' she said quickly.

'Empire Terrace,' Mrs Curran corrected.

Emmie ignored her and went. She took her time walking down the bank, breathing in the faint smell of new growth through the reek of coal fires. She loved the moment when spring took a grip on the fell, sprinkling the ditches with primroses. Back at the house, she banked up the fire and put a china 'pig' in the bed to warm the chilly sheets. Tonight Tom would lie beside her for the first time in over a year and Barny would have to stay in his own truckle bed. Emmie felt a surge of nervousness. She had grown used to life without Tom. Swiftly, she looked out a clean shirt, underdrawers and trousers, and returned to the Currans'.

Tom's mother had done her best to put on a special tea of boiled ham and vegetables, ginger steamed pudding and custard, tea and fruit cake. Emmie had contributed cabbage and potatoes from the MacRaes' allotment. The cake she knew was saved from Christmas, the tea and ginger must have cost a fortune. All foreign foodstuffs were many times the pre-war price. Emmie now drank tea made from herbs that she could grow.

Tom ate quickly as if time were short. He glanced up awkwardly from time to time.

'What you all staring at?' he asked defensively. 'Got gravy on me chin or some'at?'

'Just so happy to have you home, lad,' his mother reassured.

No one else ate half as much; they were no longer used to such big meals.

'We'll take a walk up to the Temperance Club afterwards,' Barnabas decreed.

Emmie's heart sank. She glanced at Tom and for a moment thought he would protest. He shrugged.

'If you want,' he said, his mouth full.

Barnabas nodded and began to list all the other events he had planned while his son was home.

'There's the party for the neighbours on Saturday, thanksgiving service Sunday, talk at the club Wednesday – thought you'd want to say a few words about your experiences – and the Attwaters want us round for tea on Friday—'

Tom banged down his teacup with a clatter. 'No! This is my leave, not yours. I'll decide what I do.' He glared at his father. 'And I'm not givin' any damn talk to the club – or anyone else!'

They stared at him in astonishment. For once, Barnabas was lost for words.

Tom stood up. 'Haway, Emmie, we're ganin' home,' he ordered.

Emmie glanced at the others. 'Thanks for a grand tea, Mrs Curran,' she said, feeling sorry for her crestfallen mother-in-law.

'Aye, Mam,' Tom muttered, as he pulled on his jacket and picked up his kitbag.

They trooped out, the Currans following them to the door in silence. Barny attempted to kiss them goodbye, but Tom yanked him by the hand.

'Don't be so soft,' he snapped. 'It's not like you're never ganin' to see them again.'

They set off without a word, Barny clamped to Tom's free hand, running to keep up with his urgent pace.

'Slow down, Tom,' Emmie said. 'You'll trip him up.' Tom ignored her and quickened his step. 'Let me carry him,' she offered, seeing the panic on Barny's face.

'Got legs, hasn't he?' Tom muttered. 'Walk'll do him good – he's skinny as a runt.'

'He walks plenty,' Emmie replied. 'We gan all over. But he's skinny 'cos we don't have as much food these days. That meal your mam put on was special – we don't normally see half that amount on our plates.'

He bristled. 'You get me pay. You say I don't earn enough?'

'I'm not saying that,' Emmie replied. 'I mean it doesn't go half as far as it did a year ago – even six months ago. If it wasn't for the MacRaes' allotment—'

He turned on her, pulling Barny to a stop. 'Aye, I wondered how long it would take before their name came up,' he snarled. 'From what I hear you're practically living round there. Why do I bother paying for a place to keep you in, eh?'

Emmie flinched under his hostile stare. 'The only time I've been there for more than a night was when Aunt Helen had the flu,' she answered in a hushed voice, trying not to attract attention in the street. 'I love our flat. Come on, let's get Barny to bed.'

But Tom did not want to be mollified.

'And what's all this about you helpin' at tribunals? You tryin' to shame me on purpose?' he cried.

'Let's talk about this at home,' Emmie cajoled.

'We'll talk about it now,' he shouted. Children playing in the twilight stopped to stare. A couple of men standing on the corner smoking turned to watch. 'You've been helpin' the conchies, handing out them bloody leaflets again, takin' my son down to that Settlement, haven't you?'

Emmie faced him. 'Aye, I have.'

'I'll not have him mixin' with them yellow-bellies,' Tom thundered.

'Those "yellow-bellies" are some of the bravest people I know,' Emmie argued back, 'and they're the only people attempting to keep you alive by bringing this war to an end.'

They stood glaring at each other.

Suddenly Barny piped up. 'No more shouting. I want to gan home.'

Tom looked down at him angrily and Emmie thought he would shout at the child too. Suddenly, the fight went out of him. He sighed and hunched his shoulders. Without another word, he stomped off down the street, Barny in tow and Emmie following.

Once at the house, Tom appeared to calm down. Emmie quickly got Barny ready for bed. When they came back into the kitchen, Barny in his nightclothes, Tom was swigging from a whisky bottle. He must have brought it in his kitbag.

'Give Dadda a kiss,' Emmie said, hiding her dismay, 'and maybe he'll tell you a bedtime story.'

'No stories,' Tom said firmly. But he put down the bottle and held out his arms. Barny hesitated then went across and craned up to kiss his father. Emmie felt a wave of relief. Tom was so volatile that any slight from Barny might trigger off another rant. Tom patted his son's head and sent him off.

'Keep to your own bed, mind,' he warned. 'No comin' in Mammy and Dadda's bed the night.'

Emmie's insides lurched. They would have to wait until Barny fell asleep before going to bed. She pulled on another cardigan and sat by the banked-up fire. Tom carried on drinking from the bottle.

'Get the fire blazing,' he chivvied.

'We have to be careful with coal,' Emmie said quietly. 'We don't get it free any more.'

'My fault again,' Tom said with a sneer.

'People help us out,' Emmie murmured.

'Bloody MacRaes, no doubt.'

Emmie looked at him. 'I told you about Jonas having a stroke, remember. They have little to spare. And now Peter's been called up—'

'Peter?' Tom spluttered.

Emmie nodded. 'Tried to appeal, but Hauxley and his cronies decreed he must go.'

'By, they must be desperate if they're takin' that dafty.'

She watched him drink. He was sunk in thought. Eventually he shook his head. 'They shouldn't have picked him. He'll be scared out his wits – what's left of them.' He sounded quite sober, sorrowful even.

Gently, Emmie asked, 'Tell me what it's been like for you, Tom. I've wondered so much, but you tell so little in your letters. I know it's out of kindness—'

'Kindness?' He spat out the word. 'I don't write 'cos there's nowt to write about.' His look was savage. 'Just one day like the next, tryin' to stay alive, tryin' to kill a few more bastard Germans.'

Emmie tensed. He seemed full of a cold anger. Fruitless to argue with him – they stood on either side of a gaping chasm of belief. She tried to change tack.

'What would you like to do tomorrow? We could take Barny up the fell.'

'I want to sleep,' Tom said impatiently.

'Afterwards then,' Emmie encouraged. 'Barny would like—'

'Shut up about bloody Barny,' he shouted. She stared, open-mouthed. He went on aggressively, 'Why's everyone tellin' me what to do? I'll decide, all right? And I'm not ganin' to any teetotal bloody party. If they want to see me they can come here. I want a bit peace and quiet in me own home. Is that too much to ask?'

'No,' Emmie answered quietly, 'that's what I want an' all.'

'Champion!' he shouted and took a swig. The bottle was almost empty.

'Let's gan to bed, Tom,' Emmie suggested.

He looked wary. 'You go, I'll come in a minute.'

For the first time she wondered if he might be as nervous as she was. Emmie went out to the water closet in the back yard. The stars were bright in the sky as she crossed back again. A good omen. She lay in bed waiting for Tom to join her.

Just as she was drifting off to sleep, he stumbled in, groping around in the dark. He climbed in still half dressed and lay there breathing heavily. She could tell from his breath that he was facing her. Emmie reached out an arm and placed it on his shoulder. He shifted towards her, kissing her roughly with whisky-laden breath.

Tom groped at her clothing, pulled back her hair. She tried to slow him down, stroking his head, covering his face in soft kisses. But he fastened his mouth back on hers and leaned his weight on to her. Their lovemaking was quick, mechanical, joyless. He did not even bother to undress. He seemed impatient, full of anger, as if it were a punishment for her, an ordeal for him.

Without even a word of good night, Tom rolled over and fell asleep. Emmie lay, fighting back tears, aching physically, her mind numb. There was no trace of the old Tom, no hint of the tenderness of which he had once been capable. This man was an angry, cold-hearted, embittered drunk. He repelled and frightened her. She wished she could go to Barny and hold him for comfort, but she dared not move for fear of waking Tom.

As the night wore on and sleep eluded her, Emmie listened to the ragged breathing and moaning beside her. From time to time, Tom cried out incoherently and once he sat bolt upright and stared rigidly ahead of him. His face was a mask of terror.

'Tom?' Emmie whispered in alarm. 'What is it?'

But he did not see or hear her; he was still fast asleep. She put a hand to his forehead. He was drenched in sweat.

'Lie down,' she coaxed. He groaned, then lay back, curling into a tight ball.

She wondered what nightmare haunted his sleep and felt a stirring of pity. The strain of trench warfare must be intolerable.

His mind was fragile, his nerves shattered. Emmie determined once more to try to make Tom's leave as peaceful and happy as possible. They would put the bad start behind them.

CHAPTER 30

For the first two days, Tom did little more than sleep, eat and smoke cigarettes by the fire. He was edgy and moody, starting at the sound of footsteps in the yard or when the coal sparked and spat on to the hearth.

'Shurrup!' he would bark at Barny if he talked too loud, dropped a spoon or scraped a chair. 'Can't you keep the lad quiet?'

Tom refused to go round to his parents' house or to see anyone.

'Tell them I'm sleepin',' he muttered, retreating into the bedroom when someone knocked at the door.

Emmie felt awkward turning people away and making up excuses. She knew the Currans did not believe her and blamed her for keeping Tom to herself.

'We've done all that baking!' Mrs Curran railed, when Emmie relayed the message that Tom could not face the party. 'What will we tell the neighbours?'

'Tell them he's had a year in the trenches,' she replied with spirit, 'and wants a few days' peace.'

On the day of the party, he paced around the kitchen like a caged animal, yet snapped at Emmie for suggesting he should get some fresh air and walk down to the shops with her.

'Where've you been?' he asked suspiciously on her return. 'You've been out hours.'

'Queuing, what else?' Emmie sighed, dumping her meagre shopping on the table. 'I'm ganin' down the allotment this afternoon. Why don't you come and lend a hand? It would do you good—'

'Stop tellin' what's good for me all the time, woman!' he cried.

Emmie held her temper. 'Well, you could take Barny out instead.'

The boy glanced up anxiously from the hearth where he had settled to draw a picture for Peter on a piece of cardboard. Tom regarded him with vacant eyes as if he had forgotten he was there.

'Aye,' he muttered, 'maybes I will.'

Emmie was heartened by this small show of interest. She brought out oatcakes and fish paste as a change from bread and dripping, and a bowl of stewed rhubarb sweetened with honey she had bartered for eggs. They ate in silence, Barny's usual stream of chatter stemmed by fear. This man opposite, who claimed to be his dadda, was always shouting and he did not like talking or singing at mealtimes. Barny hoped he was going to go soon and his real dadda would come instead.

Emmie got Barny into his coat and cap, as the wind was still chill, and told him to do what his father said. She spent the afternoon working hard in the garden, planting seeds garnered the previous season, chatting to Peter. He would be gone in a few days.

'I'm ganin' to camp,' he told her excitedly.

Emmie stopped and leaned on the spade, pushing dark ringlets out of her eyes.

'Peter,' she said gently, 'it won't be like a holiday with the Clarion Club. You do know that, don't you? You'll be gone a lot longer and your mam won't be able to visit.'

Peter looked at her solemnly and nodded. She shaded her eyes in the spring sunshine and held his look.

'I love being here in this garden,' she mused. 'Do you, Peter?' He nodded. She stepped closer. 'If ever you get sad or lonely or a bit frightened – and every soldier does; it's not a sign of weakness – I want you to think of this place,' she said softly. 'You can close your eyes and think of this garden, the chickens running among the beanstalks and your dad's chrysanthemums. The sound of the pit and the clatter of Lily's hoofs up the lane. The smell of the coal fires and the henhouse – the smell of the earth. Do it now, Peter.'

She watched him as he closed his eyes.

'Can you see it, Peter, smell it?'

'Aye,' he nodded, then opened his eyes. 'But I'm still here.'

Emmie smiled. 'It was just a practice.'

He gave her a quizzical grin.

'It just means wherever you are — however far from home — you can take a little bit of it with you in your head,' she explained. 'And no one can ever take that away from you.'

He gave her a bashful look. 'Wish I could take you an' all, Emmie. I never feel frightened when I'm with you. But the trouble is the army would never have you — you being a lass and not likin' fightin' and that.'

She laughed. 'You're right there, bonny lad.'

He carried back the onions and carrots they had dug to the MacRaes, and Emmie took a handful to put in a broth. She promised to bring Barny round to see Peter before he left and hurried away before they could question her too closely about Tom.

She found Barny squatting by the hearth, still in his coat and cap. The fire was nearly out.

'What you doing? Where's your da?' she asked, getting him out of his coat. Barny said nothing. 'Oh, lad, you've wet your breeks.'

His small face crumpled. 'Said I had to stay here and not m-move,' Barny gasped, on the verge of tears.

'It's all right,' she assured quickly, 'nowt to get upset about.'

She changed him into dry clothes. There was no sign of Tom anywhere.

'Can you remember what Dadda said — where he was ganin'?' she asked again.

'Thirsty,' Barny mumbled. ' "Dadda get drink. Barny stay here and not move." That's what Dadda said.'

Emmie's heart sank. Tom had gone out drinking. He could be anywhere. She set about scrubbing the vegetables and making the broth. Evening came, but Tom did not return. She fed Barny, then suggested they go for a walk before bedtime. They skirted the village, Emmie scanning the streets for sign of her husband. She could not go into any of the pubs or clubs, and she knew her search for him was fruitless. A small part of her still hoped he was out walking somewhere, not drinking himself senseless. All she could do was return home and wait.

They were both asleep when Tom came crashing in the bedroom. He swore at them and fell on to the bed. Emmie got up, trying to hush him while removing his boots. He ranted, foul-mouthed, but none of it made much sense. In a few minutes he had fallen into a drugged sleep.

She bent over Barny and stroked his head.

'Why does Dadda shout?' he asked.

'I don't know,' she answered forlornly, 'but he's asleep now.'

'Mammy? Is it 'cos of the war?'

Emmie swallowed hard. 'Maybe. Sleep now, pet lamb.'

Sunday morning came and Emmie made a decision. She shook Tom awake and thrust a cup of tea at him.

'It's an hour till chapel,' she said briskly. 'Your parents expect you. If you do nowt else this week you can manage that to keep them happy. I'll not be blamed for you not ganin'.'

He squinted at her through bloodshot eyes and groaned. 'Leave us alone.'

'No, I won't.' Emmie steeled herself. 'There's a basin of water on the washstand and I'm frying bacon for breakfast. Up you get.'

He sank back, groaning and cursing her. She pulled the covers off him and left the room. Tensely, she made the breakfast, forcing herself to chat to Barny while wondering what Tom would do. A short while later, she heard a splashing of water and a long-drawn-out groan. He emerged half dressed, scowling and creased-faced, and stomped out to the water closet.

He ate in ill-tempered silence while Emmie dressed Barny in his best breeches and pulled on her threadbare white blouse. Together the three of them set out for the chapel, questions about the previous night unanswered. The Currans' relief at seeing them was transparent. Barnabas led them into the family pew, proud of his uniformed son.

Emmie's mind wandered as the minister poured praise on the men serving their country, and Tom in particular, and they sang 'Onward, Christian soldiers', and 'Fight the good fight'.

She allowed herself to think of Rab and wondered if he would be free in another month. But free for how long? He was still conscripted. The military would come looking for him again, sooner rather than later. This time the Fellowship must persuade him to escape, go overseas if necessary. If Tom could be so

266

changed by a year in the army, what toll would a year of hard labour and solitary have taken on Rab?

After the service the family stood about talking outside, while well-wishers shook Tom's hand and slapped him on the back. Emmie noticed how the Attwaters ignored her, as if she were not worthy to be Tom's wife. Others too were wary and avoided conversation. Instead, they fussed over Barny and told Tom how like him he was growing. Tom nodded and smiled, exchanging banalities, yet his face was tense, his hands clenching and unclenching. Before they left the chapel grounds, Tom had been pressed to half a dozen tea invitations.

They retreated to the Currans' for Sunday lunch and Tom wolfed down the food before collapsing in a chair in the parlour and sleeping it off. They stayed for tea, wading through food that should have been eaten at the cancelled party, and Mrs Curran sent them home with more. When Emmie suggested they call in on the MacRaes and give them some scones, Tom lost his temper in an instant.

'We're not feedin' them bloody heathen anarchists!' he cried.

'We can't eat all this before it gans stale,' she protested. 'And Peter leaves the day after the morra.'

'Then we'll feed it to the bloody pigs!' Tom snarled and, seizing the basket of food from Emmie, began hurling scones over the fence into a neighbouring allotment. Emmie was speechless with annoyance. She took Barny by the hand and hurried on without another word.

When Tom caught them up at home, he was still spoiling for an argument.

He rounded on her. 'I hear you've been helping conchies escape. I've been defendin' me country – me family – and all the time you've been hidin' yellow-bellies. Where do you hide them, Emmie? In the coalhouse? Under me bloody bed?'

'Don't talk daft,' she replied. 'I've hid no one. Who's told you such tales?'

'That's what they're sayin' round Blackton,' he said angrily, grabbing her by the arm.

'So that's where you've been drinkin',' she said impatiently, 'and listening to bar-room tittle-tattle when you should've been looking after our son.'

'I'm not a nursemaid!' he bawled.

'No, you're a father.' She glared. 'Not that you've paid your son more than two minutes' attention since you came back.'

'Shurrup.' He struck her hard with the back of his hand.

Emmie grabbed at the table to stop herself falling. She tasted the sweet bitterness of blood on her lip. She faced him, her eyes defiant. Barny ran to her and flung his arms about her legs, staring in mute terror at his father. Tom looked at them in fury.

'That's right, turn the lad against me,' he accused. 'He hates me and it's all your fault! Well, the pair of you can gan to hell!'

Tom shoved the table at them, threw a chair out of his way and stormed out of the door. He banged it angrily behind him. Emmie listened to his footsteps march away down the lane, clutching Barny to her. When she could hear them no longer, she let go a long breath.

'Oh, dear God,' she whispered, 'where is this going to end?'

Tom went missing. The next day, Emmie went round to the Currans' looking for him, but he had not gone there. They searched around the village and went over to Blackton, but no one had seen him. After two days, the police were called in and the scandal of his argument with Emmie and disappearance was fanned like fire around the village. Sergeant Graham came to interview her, asking strange questions about her political friends.

'What's this got to do with Tom?' Emmie demanded in confusion. But he would not say.

It was the day Peter left. She rushed round to wave him off, steeling herself against the disapproving glances and whispered comments of her neighbours. Even Mrs Haile from upstairs, a long-time friend, would not speak to her. Barny gave Peter his indecipherable drawing of a horse and Peter gave him his spare tin whistle in return. Emmie hugged him goodbye and he wept like a baby, until Mr Speed chivvied him into the van for the journey to the station.

'I'll come round when I get back,' Helen promised, with an encouraging smile.

After fruitless searches up on the fell, Emmie kept to the house with Barny, as the gossip about her grew.

Louise relayed the wilder accusations.

'They say you're in with dangerous revolutionaries,' she said suspiciously. 'Some say you're carrying on with a conchie – that Tom's found out. You're not, are you?' Louise blushed as she asked.

Emmie laughed in shock. 'Course I'm not. We had a row over Barny, like I said,' she repeated wearily. 'Tom hit me and walked out.'

'You must have really got him angry for Tom to do that,' Louise accused hotly. 'If he's gone and done some'at to himself, I'll never forgive you!'

That was what plagued Emmie's mind too – the thought that Tom might take his own life. He was so unstable, he was capable of anything.

Helen and Jonas were Emmie's strongest support.

'Come and stay with us till you hear some'at,' Helen pleaded.

But Emmie refused. If Tom returned and found her gone to the MacRaes it might tip him into madness for good.

Five days after his disappearance, Tom rolled up in the village on a passing farm wagon with his drinking friend Danny. He staggered home, stinking and dishevelled, demanding food for himself and his friend. Emmie's wave of relief on seeing him alive turned quickly to fury.

'We've been out of our minds with worry, Tom!' She took him to task. 'How dare you gan off like that without a word? The things they've said about me this past week don't bear repeating. And all the time you were boozin' in Newcastle!'

Tom laughed as if it was all a big joke. 'Told you she was fiery, Danny lad.' He nudged his mate. 'Sit yourself down and wor lass'll fetch you a plate of some'at tasty.'

'Fetch you some'at tasty?' Emmie railed. 'You'll gan to Sergeant Graham and tell him you're alive, else you'll get nowt.'

But Tom ignored her and the men settled by the fire to play cards, filling the room with smoke from their cigarettes. Emmie was furious. She was about to storm off to the Currans with the news, when she realised Barny had fled the house. Gnawing panic gripped her. She pulled off her apron and went to look for him. Halfway down the street, she saw him running towards her with PC Collier.

'Lad tells me his da's returned,' Johnny grinned.

Emmie stared at Barny in astonishment. 'He did?'

'Aye, and he's brought a friend called Danny, so I hear.'

Emmie ruffled her son's hair. 'By, you're a clever lad.'

Johnny agreed. 'Not much gets past this young 'un. I'll just come and see for myself, then I'll leave you to it.'

The young policeman took a quick statement from Tom. He was vague about his movements, but the Blacksmith's Arms in Newcastle seemed to have been his home all week. Emmie had no idea where he had got the money to drink, but no doubt the sight of his uniform provoked people into buying him liquor.

That night, Danny slept on their sofa and Tom made love to her with the same aggressive indifference as the first night. She was nauseous at the smell of his grubbiness and stale breath, glad only at the brevity of the sex.

Danny stayed on for several days, an amiable but selfish guest who did not lift a finger to help or offer a penny towards his keep. Tom treated her with contempt, Danny with benign indifference.

Louise visited, but Tom's parents stayed away. By all accounts they were scandalised by his behaviour and refused to see him until he sobered up.

'They blame you, Emmie,' Louise told her.

'They would,' Emmie sighed impatiently.

'Well, Tom would never have tret us like this unless you'd pushed him to it with all your politics.'

Emmie had had enough. 'There was a time when you and Sam used to think the way I did,' she reminded her. 'When standing up for what you believed counted for some'at round here. Now all you seem to care about is keepin' up appearances. Your parents won't even come round to see Tom, they're so frightened of losing their precious dignity. If they cared about their son at all – or you your brother – you'd be fetching in the doctor and asking why he's acting like a monster!'

Louise went puce with indignation. 'Don't you lecture me about me own flesh and blood.'

Tom swayed to the yard door. 'Hoy, what's all the shoutin' for?'

Louise snapped, 'Ask her – she's the cause of all the trouble.' She turned on her heels and stalked out of the yard.

Tom and Emmie stared at each other hopelessly.

'Tom,' she hesitated, 'I've been thinking. Maybe you should gan and talk to the doctor.'

'Doctor?' he snorted. 'What for? I'm fit as a lop.'

'Night-times,' she struggled for words, 'you're gettin' nightmares – you shout out in your sleep – not gettin' proper rest. I know there's some'at on your mind—'

'Bloody rubbish!' Tom growled. 'I'll not have any quack tellin' me I'm a loony.'

'They won't, Tom,' Emmie tried to reason, 'but they might have medicine—'

'Shurrup and fetch us a some'at to eat, woman,' he demanded, and retreated indoors.

Tom's leave drew to an end. He treated home like a barracks, eating, sleeping and whiling away the dead time, waiting with Danny for the pubs to open. He pawned bits of china and linen to fund their drinking.

'You can fetch it back with next month's wages,' he told Emmie when she complained.

Two days before he was due to leave, she faced up to them.

'Danny, it's time you left. Tom needs to see his family before he gans away. No doubt you need to see yours,' she added pointedly. He had talked of a wife and three children. She pitied them more than herself.

Emmie ignored Tom's protests and made up a picnic for Danny. 'Here, this is the last you'll get from me. It's a forty-minute walk down the bank to Gateshead to the nearest tram stand. Ta-ra, Danny.'

The man left meekly, seeing his scrounging days had run out.

'See you in a couple of days, Tom lad,' he grinned and left.

Emmie set about cleaning up the mess of cigarette butts and empty bottles, washing the blankets that Danny had used on the sofa and hanging them out in the April breeze.

'Tonight,' she told Tom, 'you'll gan and make your peace with your family. Tomorrow's for us and Barny. We'll take him up on the fell for a picnic, eh?'

Tom nodded in resignation.

Emmie did not go with him to see the Currans. She was still smarting from the way they had colluded in the rumour-mongering and blamed her for Tom's bad behaviour. But she let Tom take Barny. They returned, chatting together as they crossed the yard, and Emmie prayed the worst of his stormy moods were over.

That night in bed, Tom did not roll over and shut her out after making love.

'Emmie,' he whispered, 'I don't want to gan back.'

She put out a hand and touched his face. 'Tell me,' she answered.

For a long moment there was silence, then his voice came low and rasping.

'There was this raid . . . bloody shambles . . . didn't see the Germans till they were flying in over the top. Some lads –' he hesitated – 'well, it was too much and they ran off.' He took a deep breath. 'Top brass came down hard – make an example of 'em, they said. Two dozen got death sentences.'

'Two dozen!' Emmie gasped.

'Aye, but most got off with prison – commanding officers spoke up for 'em.'

'Most?' Emmie queried.

Tom's voice was husky. 'Three didn't. One was a lad named Curly – been in since 1915 – came from Sunderland way. Used to volunteer for night skirmishes – nowt he wouldn't do. Except that day . . . ran off screaming like a bairn. That put the wind up us more than the Germans. If Curly could lose it . . .' Tom's voice trailed off.

'Oh, Tom,' Emmie murmured, putting an arm about him, 'that's terrible. You never said you'd lost a marra.'

Tom stiffened. 'He wasn't a marra. Just knew of him – him being one of the old-timers.'

'But still . . .'

'That's not the worst of it,' Tom said harshly. 'I'm not bloody soft – lads die around us all the time. And he was a deserter, so they had to do some'at.'

'Then what, Tom?' Emmie asked quietly.

She heard him gulping, struggling with the words. 'It wouldn't happen normally – but it was up the front line and things were a mess – they had to act quick. So they got the firing squad from our unit – we got Curly.'

Emmie froze in horror. 'Not you, Tom?'

'Aye, me!' he croaked. 'We had to line up – twelve of us; six standin', six kneelin'. And Curly's sittin' on this chair, blindfolded with a scrap of paper pinned on him. And we had to turn about and some of our rifles were unloaded – then they mixed them up and gave them back to us . . . I tell you, me legs were like water. And we fired at that bit o' paper.' Tom shuddered. 'But he was still kickin',' he moaned.

'No, Tom!' Emmie cried.

'Doctor said he wasn't dead. So this officer – the marshal – he goes up and fires right into Curly's head!' He sobbed loudly.

Emmie grabbed him to her. 'Oh, my poor, poor man!' She stroked his head and tried to soothe his juddering, weeping body. 'It wasn't your fault. You should never have been made to do such a thing – it's barbaric.'

He curled up in her hold like a small boy desperate to be comforted.

'No one should have to go through what you went through,' she said bitterly. 'Killin' our own men just to terrorise others into carryin' on this terrible slaughter. When will they stop?'

Tom's sobbing lessened. They lay together, numbed by the outpouring.

Emmie whispered, 'I don't want you to go back, Tom. You don't have to. The doctor could sign you off with shell shock – get you to a hospital for a bit. You need a proper rest – let your mind heal.'

'I'm not a bloody basket case,' he bristled, suddenly tense. 'And I'll not hide behind any doctors. I'm not a shirker like your precious conchies.'

'They're not shirkers,' Emmie protested wearily. 'Rab was sentenced to death as well, you know – was saved from the firing squad at the last hour. But he was prepared to die for the cause. Thousands of men like him are resisting. You could too.'

'Me? Never!' Tom said savagely, pulling away from her. 'They should've shot the bastard.'

'You don't mean that,' Emmie said in dismay.

'Aye, I do. Curly was worth ten o' his kind.' Tom was suddenly suspicious. 'Where is he now? Have you got him in hidin'? You have, haven't you? He's the bloody conchie they say you're having a fling with.' He grabbed her shoulders and shook her. 'Always knew Rab MacRae was after you. Just waited till me back was turned—'

'Stop it, Tom!' Emmie protested, frightened at his sudden volatility. 'Rab's in gaol and I'm not having any fling.'

'I don't believe you,' he cried.

'Why not?'

''Cos there's this lad ganin' round Blackton spoutin' off that he knows things about you – that you trick lads into being conchies and promise to get them away to Ireland or some'at. Lure them in.'

'Who said?' Emmie's heart banged in fear.

'Some lad called Osborne. Said he knew you well – one of MacRae's bloody socialists. Nearly knocked his block off. But there's no smoke without fire.'

'My God,' Emmie whispered. 'Bill Osborne?'

'That's the name,' Tom said harshly.

Why was Bill Osborne spreading vicious tales about her?

Tom shook her again. 'It's true, isn't it? You bitch, it's true! Rab's your fancy man? How many others have there been, eh?'

'None!' Emmie was indignant.

'You're lying,' he shouted. 'You're a lying whore!'

He pushed her back and banged her head on the iron bedstead. Emmie cried out.

Barny woke up with a start. 'Mammy? Mammy! Where are you?'

'It's all right, pet—'

'Shurrup!' Tom bawled, striking her. 'Don't speak to him. Whores don't speak to my son.'

Barny started to wail and cry out for his mother. Tom grabbed Emmie by the hair and dragged her off the bed. She tried to fight him off, but he punched her in the breast, sending pain shooting through her. Then he winded her in the stomach.

The next moment, he was shoving her into the kitchen. Lurid orange light flickered across the hearth, like tongues licking the dark. Tom threw her on the floor. She panted for breath, trying to raise herself up. For a few seconds she could not see him, then he was lunging out of the shadows, wielding his thick army belt.

The first blow whipped around her ear and neck. Emmie screamed and threw her arms up in protection. The second blow caught her across the chest. She crumpled on the floor, burying her head in her arms. He whipped her again and again, across her back, her arms, her legs, her feet. He raged like a madman, foul-mouthed and screaming. Emmie thought he would kill her, yet all she could think about was Barny. Where was her son? She hoped he was cowering in bed and not witnessing the attack. If he should step in Tom's way . . .

Emmie gritted her teeth and took the rain of blows. He would not kill her. She would live through this. She would survive this for Barny's sake. For Barny . . .

The frenzy came to an end, Tom's energy spent. He stood over her, panting and sobbing. Emmie lay slumped on the floor, not moving.

CHAPTER 31

The dawn light crept in at the window. Emmie lay on the cold linoleum. She must still be alive because when she opened her eyes she could see the outline of the fender. The fire was out. She tried to move, but pain surged through her. If she lay quite still, it was almost bearable. She closed her eyes again.

Later, when she awoke, Emmie felt a presence nearby. She attempted to look round, but her neck, head and shoulders were rigid. Panic registered. Tom was waiting to deal out a further beating.

'Who's there?' she whispered.

A hand rested on her back, making her wince and cry out.

'Mammy?' Barny said in concern. 'Get up now, Mammy. Time to get up.'

'Barny?' she croaked. 'I can't . . .'

A worried face peered over her, upside down. 'Dadda's gone.'

Emmie let out a small whimper. 'Thank God.' Relief spread through her, immediately followed by fear that he would soon come back. 'Gone where? To Grandma's?'

'Not Grandma's,' Barny said. 'He went down the hill, not up the hill.'

'Did he take his bag?' Emmie asked.

'Aye,' Barny nodded.

'D–did he say anything?'

Barny thought for a minute. 'He said you were a horse.'

'A horse?' Emmie said faintly.

'Like he was shouting in the night, Mammy,' Barny said, frowning.

Shame flooded her as she realised Tom must have said whore. Her son had heard and seen everything. She made a huge effort to stir from the floor. Her whole body pulsated in pain.

'Need to get to bed,' she gasped. 'Just lie down for a minute.'

She struggled on to her hands and knees and crawled towards the bedroom. Barny followed her, not sure if it was a game. He watched her haul herself on to the bed and crawl under the covers. Emmie sank back, exhausted from the effort. Closing her eyes, she fell asleep again.

Barny woke her. 'Mammy, I'm hungry.'

Emmie felt light-headed, wondering where she was. It must be the afternoon. She could not move, did not want to move, never wanted to move again. She was pinned down with pain and the burning shame of what Tom had done to her. Her husband had whipped her like a dog – no, more savagely than any man whips a dog. And he had done it sober. This was not the drunken Tom who had made their life a misery these past two weeks. This was a new Tom who had sunk to an even lower level of brutality. Never again would she trust him. She wanted him nowhere near her – or her son.

'Mammy, I want to eat,' Barny whined.

Emmie closed her eyes. 'Find yourself a bit bread and cheese in the pantry,' she whispered. 'Water in the jug. Pour it carefully.'

Barny gave up badgering her and climbed off the bed. Emmie fell asleep once more.

She woke and dozed and woke and slept. She was aware of Barny climbing in with her and then it was dark and she slept again.

Banging on the back door woke her. She froze. It was morning once more.

Louise's voice called, 'Where are you all? Tom, you'll be late for the train. Minister's waiting.'

Emmie lay huddled under the blankets. Did her bruising show?

'Barny, where's your mam and dad?' Louise questioned.

'Mammy's in bed,' Barny said solemnly. 'Dadda's gone.'

Louise came barging into the bedroom. 'What's ganin' on? Emmie, are you sick?'

'Aye,' Emmie mumbled, pulling the blankets up higher. 'Just a bit. It'll pass.'

'Where's our Tom?'

'Left,' Emmie managed to speak. Her lips and mouth were dry as sand. 'Yesterday.'

'Whatever for?' Louise demanded. 'You didn't row again, did you?' When Emmie said nothing, she gave a sigh of impatience. 'Fancy spoiling his going away,' she accused. 'Bet you're not sick at all – just ashamed that he's left you early. That's it, isn't it?' Emmie kept silent. 'Well, you've spoiled it for everyone else an' all! Now we'll never have the chance to say goodbye.' She glared down at her sister-in-law. 'You don't deserve our Tom. You've changed. You're hard and selfish. Not the lass I used to call me friend. I don't know you any more, Emmie.'

She spun round and stalked out of the house. Emmie squeezed her eyes shut against hot tears. Perhaps she was all those hateful things Louise said she was. She had failed as a wife. Somehow she must be to blame for what had happened. She was hateful. It was her fault that she had married Tom, knowing that she could never love him enough. She had spent too much time and energy on other things, neglecting him. Once he had told her she would make a good pitman's wife, but she had not. She had always wanted more from life and yet she had achieved nothing.

Emmie lay racked with sobs, tortured and desolate. The bedroom door swung open again. She heard the rattle of cup on plate.

'Here you are, Mammy,' Barny announced. He plonked a plate on to the bed. It held cold fried potatoes from two days ago and a half-spilled cup of water. 'Drink it,' he commanded.

Emmie gazed at him. He peered back at her. 'Drink it all up.'

Emmie leaned up with difficulty and reached for the water. She splashed it on her lips. It tasted like nectar. She gulped it down.

'Ta, Barny,' she whispered. 'Can I have some more, pet?'

He nodded, took the cup and refilled it. She was amazed and grateful.

'Shall I gan and fetch Grandma?' Barny asked.

Emmie felt panic choke her at once. 'No!' she gasped.

'But you're sick, Mammy.'

'No, pet, just very tired. I need to rest in bed, that's all.' She looked at him wearily. She wanted to reassure him she was all right, but hadn't the strength. Barney was a good little lad, who could get himself a drink and play quietly alone until she felt able to get up. The Currans must not know what had happened; she was in no state to bear their condemnation.

'Can you be a very good lad and let Mammy sleep? I'll get up later and make us some dinner. But you mustn't fetch anyone. Mammy can't see anyone.' Emmie lay back, utterly spent from the effort of talking and drinking the water.

Soon she fell asleep again. She dreamed vividly of running away, of Tom chasing and catching her, but then turning into someone else who sat her down and gave her tea. She dreamed of the Lonely Stones and waiting for something or someone who never came. Then she was being chased again.

Emmie woke in the half-dark. Barny was lying on his own bed, fully clothed, asleep. She had no idea what day it was, let alone the hour. She wished she could live for ever in this twilight world where she did not have to move or think. But of course, she could not stay like this. For Barny's sake she had to go on living. One day she would have to face the world again. The thought appalled her.

Cautiously, she groped for the side of the bed and got to her feet. She swayed dizzily. Aching and stiff, she shuffled to the door, steadying herself on the washstand and doorframe. Bit by bit, Emmie edged her way across the kitchen and out into the yard. Cold air hit her, sharp and fresh. She almost fainted. Forcing herself to cross the yard to the closet, she locked herself inside. No one had seen her. She was safe.

Emmie hobbled back to the house, fearful of a neighbour accosting her from a window or a child running into her yard as a dare. She imagined how they gossiped about Tom leaving early, under a cloud, and how she was to blame. The only people who would not judge her were the MacRaes. Emmie let out a sob. How she longed to be with them; for Jonas to talk courage into her, to have Helen's arms around her.

But then the humiliation of Tom's beating engulfed her anew. They must never know. They had already lost so much. It would break them. They might feel guilty at not being there to protect her. Or worse still, they might wonder if she had brought it on herself. Better to keep the assault unknown. She would get through this alone. Except she was not alone. She went and stood over Barny and stifled her weeping. Poor bairn! What future did he have with her?

Emmie struggled with her darkest feelings. He would be better off without her. His father would not be violent if she was not there. She would never have to face Tom or his family or the neighbours again. She would go to the kitchen drawer and take out the sharp paring knife . . .

Barny stirred and whimpered in his sleep. Without thinking, she bent down and caressed his forehead, smoothing back the wayward curls. He was too hot in his jersey. She slipped it over his head without waking him. Emmie buried her face in its warm smell. How could she possibly think of leaving him! She went back to bed, clutching the jumper, and fell into a deep dreamless sleep.

The next day, Emmie forced herself to get up. Wincing with the pain in her limbs and back, she refilled the coal-hod and coaxed the fire back into life. Barny watched and fetched kindling from the coal shed. When it was going, she fried up some stale bread with the last remaining egg and they shared it between them. The kettle boiled and she brewed a pot of tea.

'Can we gan to the woods the day, Mammy?' Barny asked eagerly.

Emmie's heart began to pound. They would have to walk past the Attwaters' manse or go round by Siam Street, which backed on to the Currans'.

'Not today, pet,' she said hastily. 'It's ganin' to rain.'

'Can we see Auntie Helen?' he pleaded.

She shook her head. 'She'll be busy.'

Barny scowled. 'I want to gan to Auntie Helen's! You promised, Mammy.'

'Tomorrow maybe,' she sighed.

'No! I want to gan the day. Please, please!'

'Oh, stop shoutin',' Emmie snapped, pressing her hands to her pounding head.

Barny gave a reproachful look. 'You and Dadda shout.'

Emmie burst into tears. Barny stared in horror. He rushed to her and threw himself in her lap.

'Don't cry, Mammy,' he sobbed, 'please don't cry.'

Emmie tried to stop but could not. She no longer seemed in

control of anything. It terrified her. Eventually she managed to prise the unhappy boy from her lap.

'You gan and play in the yard,' she told him. 'We'll gan out later.'

He went and she sat and stared at the dirty plates. She did not have the energy to move them. Later she heard him playing in the lane with some of the other children. The discordant notes of his tin whistle pierced the air. To her relief he seemed to forget about going out later in the day. Emmie boiled up some beetroot and baked two potatoes in the oven for their tea. They went to bed early.

The following day, Emmie determined to go to the shops. She was out of provisions. She buttoned up her coat and pulled down her hat, forcing herself to look in the mirror. An ugly red weal snaked across her left cheek and on to her neck. A purple bruise stained her left temple and brow-bone, standing out against the deathly pallor of her skin. She pulled her hat further down over her eyes and tied a scarf around her neck.

Turning to take Barny by the hand, she was suddenly overwhelmed by panic. She stood rigid in front of the door, unable to move, her heart hammering, palms sweating. Emmie dropped Barny's hand.

'You'll have – to – gan to the – shops for Mammy,' she panted.

She took a deep breath and repeated the things they needed from the store: dripping, candles, matches, suet, ham knuckle and flour. She wrote them down on a scrap of brown paper, wrapped it around some money she had hidden from Tom in the pantry and placed it carefully in the boy's pocket.

'Give this to the shopkeeper, no one else. Ta, pet.' She kissed him, gave him the string bag and propelled him out of the door.

Barny seemed excited by the mission and half skipped, half ran out of the yard. Emmie sat tensely in the kitchen. What a coward she was! He would lose the order. He could not carry such a load all the way home.

Half an hour later, Barny clattered in the back door, the string bag hoisted over his narrow shoulder like a sack of coal, and dumped it at her feet. He grinned up at her in triumph.

'Clever lad,' she whispered tearfully. 'You're Mammy's clever lad.'

The next day she sent him out again to collect some eggs from the allotment. He had done so with Peter many times and she knew her son could manage the task. Emmie was kneeling painfully, sweeping the hearth, when he returned. In alarm she heard him chattering to someone as they crossed the yard. There was no time to flee into the bedroom. She watched the door in fright.

'Emmie! The bairn tells me you're sick.' Helen bustled into the room. 'You should've sent him to fetch me. We've brought some carrots and greens, as well as the eggs.'

Helen stopped and peered, adjusting to the gloom after the brightness of outside. 'Emmie?' She stepped closer. 'Let me take a look at you.'

Emmie turned her face away. Helen bent over her.

'Look at me, lass,' she cajoled, gripping her shoulder. Emmie winced at the pain. Helen lifted her hand quickly and pushed back Emmie's hair. Even in the shadows she could see the bruises on her face and whip marks across her neck. 'Oh, Emmie! Me darlin' lamb. Did Tom do this?'

Emmie hung her head, too ashamed to admit it even to Helen. Helen kneeled down beside her and gently enfolded her. 'Does it hurt all over?' she whispered.

Emmie swallowed down a sob.

'Dear God, what possessed him?' Helen said, dumbfounded.

'He hates me,' Emmie whispered. 'C-called me a wh—' She could not bring herself to utter the word, it was so shaming. 'They all think I'm a—'

'No,' Helen stopped her. 'Don't listen to what people say. You're a good lass, a brave lass – there's none better.' She held and rocked her gently as Emmie succumbed to tears. 'Tom was wicked to do this. If he was here I'd give him a piece of my mind, by heck I would!'

Barny piped up. 'Will you make Mammy better, Auntie Helen?'

She turned and pulled the boy into her embrace. 'Course I will, pet lamb. You were a brave boy to come and tell me.' She said to Emmie, 'I should've come to check on you sooner. We had no idea – folk tell us nothing these days – I'm sorry.'

They clung to each other.

'I'm that ashamed,' Emmie confided, 'I can't face anyone.'

'You don't have to,' Helen comforted. 'You'll come and live with us till you get your strength back. No argument.'

Helen moved briskly around the house, packing clothes into a canvas bag and gathering food into a pan. She damped down the fire and helped Emmie into her coat.

'Put this shawl over you,' she suggested. 'Barny, take your mam's hand.'

They shut the door behind them and walked together down the lane. Emmie stared at her feet and did not meet the look of anyone. Somehow, she managed to get to China Street without fainting with fright.

In the privacy of the cottage, Helen peeled off Emmie's blouse and skirt and studied her wounds. She clucked in sympathy, angrily berating the absent Tom. They boiled up hot water and filled the tub. Gently Helen washed her, patted her dry and dressed her as if she were a child. Emmie nearly wept at such tenderness.

When Jonas returned from work, he grew agitated at the news of Emmie's treatment. He spluttered, his speech still slurred from his stroke.

'Go round – old man Curran's – have it out. That laddie – learned brutality from that p-pious bastard.'

'Jonas!' Helen admonished. 'Watch your tongue in front of the bairn. And you'll do no such thing. Emmie wants no more trouble from those people. They've washed their hands of her and we don't want them round here causing her bother, do you hear?'

Jonas blustered in frustration, cursing all Currans as capitalist warmongers. The next day he came back in a filthy temper. The proud Scot had been unable to prevent himself upbraiding Curran for his family's ill treatment of Emmie. They had nearly come to blows in the pit yard. Dissention was growing among the pitmen, a staunch core protecting Jonas from the vilification of the others. Day by day, unrest stirred in the village, quarrels breaking out between neighbours, overwrought with shortages and the constant worry about a war that appeared to be without end.

Cocooned from the tensions beyond, Emmie gradually unburdened herself. She spoke of Tom's disastrous leave, his drinking and violence, disappearance and reappearance with Danny. She told of his falling-out with his parents, his increasing paranoia about her involvement with COs and his confession about being in a firing squad that brought on his final brutal assault. The MacRaes' patient understanding helped Emmie to feel less guilty.

'You're not to blame for any of it,' Helen insisted.

'C-course not,' Jonas agreed. 'World's gone mad – young Curran's taken it out on y-you.'

'He even thought I was having an affair with Rab,' Emmie admitted awkwardly. 'That's what seemed to spark off the beatin'.'

Helen and Jonas looked at each other for a long moment.

'And you're not?' Helen asked quietly.

Emmie reddened. 'No, course not. Why do you think that?'

Helen smiled sadly. 'Because it's obvious to everyone but you how much our son cares for you. In that letter from France, he told us. Said we had to look after you and Barny as much as we possibly could.'

Jonas grunted. 'Would think he was your m-man the way he telt us.'

Emmie looked away. 'But, he's not.'

She thought of Rab's letter to her and knew she should have destroyed it long ago. If Tom ever found it, she knew he would kill her – or kill Rab. She was a fool to have left it lying in a drawer where it could so easily be discovered.

The next time Helen took Barny out to the shops, Emmie steeled herself to go back to her house and root out the letter. People stopped and stared at her as she walked down the lane on to the main street and turned up towards Berlin Terrace. They looked hostile. She was sure someone spat as she passed. Emmie forced herself on. She was imagining it.

She was weak, unused to the exercise, and took an age to walk the short distance. She became aware of people behind. A group of boys began to follow. Someone threw a stone at her back.

'Traitor! Traitor!' they chanted.

Emmie's heart banged in fright. She quickened her pace. Another stone flew past. Emmie spun round dizzily and confronted them. There were six or seven young boys, some adults standing further off.

'You should be at school,' she challenged. 'Get yourselves off there now.'

They stared back, then one shouted out, 'And you should be in prison, missus!'

Emmie went puce. She turned and hurried into Berlin

284

Terrace. They pursued her, laughing and shouting, goading each other on. She would go and find Johnny Collier to sort out these truants. Emmie almost ran the last yards to her house, fumbling with the latch and slamming the door closed behind her. Surely they would not dare break into her home?

Breathless, she leaned against the door until her racing heart calmed down. The house was chilly and damp without a fire. She went into the bedroom and pulled out the deep drawer of the wardrobe. Feeling under the linen, wrapped in Barny's baby shawl was the letter. Emmie put it to her lips and stood up.

She let out a scream. Two faces were pressed against the window staring in at her: a boy and a young man. Emmie rushed forward and pulled down the blind.

'She's in here!' someone shouted. She could hear footsteps. They were crossing her yard! The back door rattled.

Emmie froze. They could not break in, it was bolted. Suddenly she was unsure if the front door had been locked before Helen led her away. She dashed out of the bedroom and into the tiny porch. Cobwebs hung at the door from lack of use. The large key was in the lock. She turned it quickly; it had been open. 'Mean as a key,' Jonas always said. Now she needed keys to protect her from her own people.

Emmie returned shakily to the kitchen. She drew down the blind above the dresser and retreated to sit in the semi-dark by the ash-laden hearth. They would soon tire of their game and go away. She would just have to wait. But the noises outside did not diminish – if anything it sounded as if more people were gathering in her yard, older voices calling to each other.

Emmie sat there over an hour and still her persecutors did not go away. She clutched Rab's letter, read it over and over to give her courage. She would give the world to have him with her now, facing whatever it was gathering outside her door. Suddenly she was filled with anger at her situation. Why should she have to cower in her own home like a prisoner? She had done nothing wrong. She would face them and be done with it.

Emmie struck a match and put it to the edge of Rab's letter. She knew the words by heart. No one else would ever read their tender, intimate confessions. She could protect him from that at least. She watched it burn to ash in the grate. Then she went to the back door and unbolted it. Pulling it half open, she stopped in shock.

The yard was full of people, men and women as well as the boys. A cry went up like the baying of dogs.

'There she is! Get her!' They surged forward. Emmie tried to slam the door shut. A man stuck his boot in the crack. She kicked his shin in panic. He moved, she heaved on the door and threw the bolt across.

Emmie panted in fear. Who were they? They shouted and hammered on the door, calling for her to come out and face them.

'We don't want traitors round here!' cried a man's voice. The crowd chorused in agreement.

There was something familiar about the voice but Emmie was too panicked to work out what. She stood back from the door and crouched behind a chair. Surely someone would come and rescue her soon. Helen would wonder where she was. Thank goodness she had not brought Barny here.

All at once, there was a terrifying smashing of glass and a brick came hurtling through the kitchen window. It landed inches from Emmie, glass splintering across the linoleum. She screamed in fright.

'Come out, Hun-lover!' a man bawled.

'Out, out, out!' the others chanted.

Emmie crawled under the table. How had it come to this? All her ideals, her hopes for peace in ruins. How had she ended up in this joyless place, cowering like a mouse under a kitchen table with her neighbours screaming for her death? Clamping her jaw together, she would not give them the satisfaction of hearing her cry.

It seemed an eternity that she waited for them to break in and lynch her. Then she became aware of other shouts, imperious orders.

'Stand back, get back now! Let us deal with this. Should be ashamed of yourselves! *Back*, I said.'

There was a hammering on the back door. Emmie held her breath.

'Mrs Curran? Let us in, Mrs Curran. It's the police.'

Emmie's heart leaped. They had come to save her. Halfway out from under the table, she stopped. What if it was a trick?

'Who are you?' she shouted back.

'Sergeant Graham, ma'am. Open up. You'll not be harmed.'

She heard him ordering his men to clear the yard, chivvying the crowd back. It was Graham's voice. She crept to the back door and opened it. Standing in the afternoon drizzle, she saw Johnny Collier by the door.

'Oh, thank the Lord,' she gasped. 'I thought I was . . .' She caught the tense look on his face.

'You've got to come with us, Emmie,' he said quickly. 'I'll not let them harm you.'

Sergeant Graham rushed up. 'Emmie Curran,' he barked, 'I'm arresting you under the Defence of the Realm Act. You'll come with me, please. Don't make a fuss and there'll be no more trouble.'

Emmie stared at them. 'Arrested for what?' she asked, even as they bundled her out of the door and across the yard.

'For behaviour likely to harm the war effort and detrimental to the morale of the people,' he gabbled. 'Hurry up, I can't guarantee your safety if you don't come now.'

Emmie was hustled down the back lane by half a dozen policemen, the crowd jeering as she went.

'Good riddance!' they cried. 'String her up!'

'Who are they?' Emmie gasped, as Johnny pulled her along.

'Crowd from Blackton,' he answered. 'Keep moving, lass.'

At the end of the lane, they bundled her towards a horse-drawn police van. She resisted.

'Where you taking me?' she asked in alarm.

'It's not safe for you here,' Graham said curtly.

'Gateshead,' Johnny murmured.

Emmie was choked by panic. 'But I have to see me bairn – they don't know what's happening – Helen and Jonas—'

But they heaved her into the back.

'Please!' she begged. 'Just let me say goodbye—'

As the door slammed shut, Johnny shouted, 'I'll tell them, lass, I promise.'

Emmie strained to see out of the high-barred window, as the van shook and joggled down the street. She glimpsed only rain-spattered roofs, then she was jolted to the floor. She could hear people running alongside, bawling insults and banging on the sides of the van.

Emmie clung on, as they lurched downhill. All she could think of was Barny and how he would be wondering where she was. Would her son ever forgive her for disappearing out of his life without a word of explanation or farewell?

CHAPTER 32

Emmie spent a sleepless night in the police cell, lying on wooden slats for a bed, her mind tortured with thoughts of her abandoned son. The only comfort was thinking that Helen and Jonas would take care of him. God forbid the Currans should try to claim guardianship of Barny. As light stole into the dismal cell, she forced herself to be optimistic. Perhaps nothing would come of the charges and she would be home in a day or two. She was still unsure what evidence they had against her.

They came for her later that day. Emmie was taken before three magistrates, one of whom she recognised from Peter's tribunal. She was charged with tearing down recruitment posters.

The police called their witness. Emmie was dumbstruck as Bill Osborne stepped forward. He recounted the incident of the posters with a sorrowful face.

'I tried to stop her, but she was like a mad woman – real anger and hatred as she ripped them off the wall.'

Emmie stared, open-mouthed. Bill had goaded her on, knowing how upset she was about the failure to get Peter exempted.

'Was this out of character?' a magistrate asked.

Bill shook his head. ''Fraid not. She'd come under the influence of a group of revolutionaries in Crawdene – the MacRaes – and then got in with pacifists at the Settlement in Gateshead. She's a member of the NCF – leaflets for them. Mrs Curran's part of a dangerous network intent on undermining the war effort and the stability of this country. That's why I had to come forward and report her to the police.'

Emmie went cold at his words. Osborne was a government informer. Not only was she in trouble but all her friends were at risk. She tried to think how much he had learned about their work. Names and addresses of resisters, anti-conscription meetings and leaflets, the Quakers' underground network of men on the run? But perhaps they had stopped using the Settlement as a hideaway by the time he came? In her panic, Emmie could not remember. But either way, she had put her friends in danger by introducing him to the Settlement. What would happen to the Runcies and Dr Flora?

Osborne left, glancing at her with a glint of satisfaction. The magistrates began to question Emmie about her work at the No Conscription Fellowship. Emmie rallied her thoughts.

'There's nothing illegal in that,' she defended. 'The men have a right to appeal on religious or moral grounds – we make sure they have their fair say.'

'But you go further,' one of them accused. 'You actively seek to persuade men not to enlist.'

Emmie looked at him in silence. Let them prove it.

'You befriended Osborne,' he went on. 'You even offered to get him out of the country.'

'I did no such thing,' she retorted.

'So you admit to knowing the man?' the magistrate said quickly.

Emmie's stomach clenched. 'He's a local man, used to be in the Clarion Club.'

'You are well known around Crawdene and Blackton for your extreme views,' he said with a hard look. 'You have been cautioned for handing out unpatriotic leaflets before – and yesterday you caused a near riot in your village.'

'They were not my neighbours,' Emmie replied hotly, 'they were folk from Blackton, no doubt stirred up by your spy Osborne. There are plenty in Crawdene think the way I do – that the war should be stopped.'

'The old bruises on your face and neck suggest otherwise, Mrs Curran,' he said waspishly.

Emmie reddened.

'Is it not true that your own family believe you are a traitor, that you and your degenerate friends wish to bring about the ruin of this country?' he accused.

Emmie was defiant. 'The betterment of this country.'

The youngest of the magistrates intervened. 'Let us stick to the facts. We have not been presented with hard evidence of secret networks and conspiracies – that is mere hearsay. But the posters – are you willing to admit to defacing government property?'

After a moment's hesitation, Emmie nodded.

They found her guilty of unpatriotic behaviour and therefore in breach of the Government's emergency powers. She was sentenced to six weeks' imprisonment with hard labour in Durham Prison.

'Think yourself lucky you are not charged with anything graver,' the chairman said curtly.

Stunned, Emmie was led away. How could she warn her friends about Osborne? How could she let the MacRaes know what had happened to her? How would she survive six weeks away from her beloved son?

Locked into a tiny cell within the prison van, in which she hardly had room to sit, she was taken to Durham. She had passed the bleak, smoke-blackened prison walls at every Miners' Gala day, pitying the incarcerated so close to the beauty of the riverbanks and gaiety of the gala.

There was no glimpse of Durham as she was bundled from the prison yard through heavy metal gates. As they clanged behind her, she heard the cathedral bells tolling across the river, as if mourning the taking of her freedom.

Emmie was stripped, plunged in a tepid bath and given prison clothes and a yellow disc with a cell number. She was to be kept separate from the other women and given a restricted A diet for a week for the gravity of her crime. Along spidery gangways and up metal staircases, her escort led her to a cell at the end of the high corridor. The silent warder pushed her in and slammed the door shut. Emmie listened to the rattle of keys and the sound of the spy hole cover being lifted then dropped. A sinister eye was painted on her side of the door, a Cyclops that watched her wherever she stood.

She looked around the spartan cell; three paces one way, two the other. It smelled of urine, contained no bed, just a wooden board with a blanket, a stool and a chamber pot. The window was

291

too high up to look through even when she stood on the stool. But she could hear the cathedral bells striking the quarter-hour and that gave her comfort, as if a friend kept watch through the dark hours.

Emmie awoke, cold and stiff, to the sound of keys scraping in the lock. The warder brought in a breakfast of bread and cold weak tea.

'What's your name?' Emmie asked.

The lean-faced woman gave no answer and locked her in once more. An hour later, a different warder came to fetch her.

'You're on mailbags. You're to sit away from the others and not say a word. If we catch you talking, you're in solitary for a week.'

'What's this then,' Emmie quipped, 'the Waldorf?'

'I said no talking,' the woman barked.

Emmie was led down three floors and into a gaslit room where women sewed around a long table. They stopped to stare.

'Carry on,' the warder ordered, 'and no one's to talk to prisoner D359.' She pointed Emmie to a stool in the corner and commanded one of the other prisoners to show her what to do.

'Can I speak to her then?' the young woman asked nervously.

'Just about the sewing,' the warder warned.

Under her breath, between instructions, the prisoner asked, 'What you done – murder or some'at?'

Emmie shook her head. 'Ripped up a recruitment poster,' she whispered.

The woman looked at her in disbelief. She carried on showing her how to stitch with the huge skewer-sized needle.

'If you do it like this, you can get three stitches to one pull,' she murmured. 'You one of them anarchists?'

'No – pacifist,' Emmie said, her head down. 'And you?'

'Thievin',' the woman answered. 'I've eight brothers and sisters to support.'

Emmie wanted to ask her more, but feared getting her into trouble.

By dinner time, her back was aching and fingers numb. As she went to put her things on the table, one of the prisoners stabbed her hand with a needle.

'Bloody traitor,' she hissed.

Emmie gasped at the sharp pain.

'What's wrong?' the warder asked suspiciously.

Emmie clutched her hand. 'Nothing. Just caught me hand on the needle.' She looked at her attacker, who glanced away.

She was taken back to her cell and locked in for the rest of the day. The mute warder came in with greasy suet pudding and treacle. Emmie forced down the indigestible food. She sat on the stool, her body aching from the old bruising, her hand throbbing from the rusty needle. She got up and walked to the window, back to the door, to all four corners, then repeated the exercise in reverse. It must be raining outside, for the odd droplet spat on to her cell floor from the narrow barred window.

Emmie gave up pacing and sat down. She already felt tired and hungry again. The empty hours dragged on until a supper of Bovril and bread. She lay down on the wooden board. The gaslight hissed out, though it was still daylight outside at the high window. Emmie wrapped herself in the blanket and tried to sleep, but thoughts of Barny plagued her. Was Helen putting him to bed at that moment? Was Jonas telling him a story? She pictured him settling down on the truckle bed she had once used as a child, the firelight illuminating his pensive face, asking when she would be back. Emmie cried herself to sleep.

The next day followed in the same monotonous pattern. On the third day, the anger that had been simmering inside boiled over.

'When can I gan outside for exercise?' she demanded. 'I'm a political prisoner. I shouldn't be shut away like a convict. I want me own clothes back. I want to see the governor. Are you listening to me?'

The warder retreated as if she had not spoken. In frustration, Emmie picked up the tin of skilly and hurled it at the closing door.

'And I'll not eat any more of this filth,' she cried. 'I wouldn't feed it to a pig!'

The disc in the painted eye slid open as if blinking away the gruel that ran down the door.

'I know you're spying on me,' Emmie raged. 'I want to see the prison boss.' She hammered on the door. 'I'll not stop till you fetch 'em.'

She beat her fists on the door until she was exhausted. Emmie wedged herself into the corner adjacent to the door, so that the eye could not see her. She sat shaking, hugging her knees. The walls pressed in on her. She began to feel pangs of hunger and regretted her rashness.

At tea time, she did not acknowledge the sullen warder who pushed in the tray of bread and cocoa. Emmie forced herself to ignore the food, though her mouth watered at the smell of the hot drink. She watched them take it away again. The lamp hissed out. Somewhere far down the corridor she heard wailing. It went on half the night, jarring her frayed nerves.

The next day, she refused to eat and refused to do hard labour. She was taken away to a dark basement cell and put on bread and water rations as punishment. Here, there was no daylight and she could not hear the bells chiming. The food was pushed in through a hatch in the bottom of the door, so she did not even see her gaoler. There was nothing in the cell but a Bible and a slops bucket. She curled up on the stone floor and used the Bible as a pillow.

Emmie's resolve collapsed. She ate the bread, making each crumb last as long as possible, holding it in her mouth until it melted. She drank the water. Her days and nights merged into each other, marked only by the arrival of the punishment rations, a wooden board at night time and the gaslamp being turned off for endless hours. Emmie would move only to eat, then lie down again. She put herself into a comotose state, like a hibernating animal, trying to preserve her dwindling strength.

After a while she hardly knew where she was. One minute she was shivering with cold, the next burning like a fire. She had strange, vivid dreams of her home being burned down by an angry mob and not being able to save Barny. She awoke screaming in terror to find herself in a pit of darkness, her nostrils filled with the smell of her own fear.

Six days later, she was half carried back to her original cell. A warder she had not seen before gave her a pitying look and slipped her an extra blanket.

'It's not right what they're doing to you,' she whispered. 'I've a brother in the navy and every day I pray it'll be the last of this terrible war.'

Emmie was too weak to speak more than a whisper of thanks. But the woman's kindness soothed her and kindled a small flame of hope inside. She was put to scrubbing out cells and put on a B diet, which allowed some meat and watery vegetables. Emmie gave up trying to win political status. She was halfway through her sentence and all she cared about was being freed and getting back to Barny.

At night, she was kept awake by a wheezy cough she had developed in solitary. Not since her childhood sickness had she felt so weak. She lay for long hours, thinking about her son and how she would provide for him when she was out. She no longer wanted to take Tom's army pay — it was blood money and she would not be kept by a man who could beat his wife so cruelly. She would stay with the MacRaes. But what if that should bring them strife from the wider community? It might be putting them and Jonas's job in jeopardy. Goodness knows how far Osborne's poisonous rumours would have spread. She would have to leave Crawdene — go to the Settlement. But what if the Runcies and Dr Flora were no longer there?

Exhausted though she was, Emmie could not sleep with such anxious thoughts racing through her head. It was then that she allowed herself to think of Rab. What date was it? Mid-May? He would be about to be released. If only she was there to see him, to have a few brief days together before the military rearrested him. She would tell him how much she loved him, had always loved him. She soothed herself to sleep imagining she was wrapped in Rab's strong, loving arms.

One day, towards the end of her sentence, while scrubbing a metal gantry, Emmie fainted. She was taken back to her cell and visited by the prison doctor. She lay weak and light-headed while he gave her a cursory investigation.

'You have a chest infection,' he said. 'Nothing much you can do about that in here. I see you have an extra blanket already.' He gave a disapproving glance. 'I'll recommend your rations are supplemented with cod liver oil.'

That night she was feverish, crying out and babbling in her sleep, awaking to find her blankets soaked. She struggled to do her morning's hard labour and collapsed again. The sympathetic warder helped her back to her cell, but no sooner had she lain down, than Emmie began to haemorrhage. The terrified woman ran for help.

Semi-conscious, Emmie was stretchered to the hospital wing, which was full from an outbreak of summer fever. She was taken to the insane ward where there were bars instead of doors.

295

Emmie was aware of screaming and high-pitched laughter. She thought she had been put in a cage. She lay bleeding on a bare mattress while a half-bald woman stared at her through the bars. They were coming for her, Osborne and the magistrate and Major Oliphant. They were preparing the gallows for her now; she could hear the hammering of the joiners, the chattering of the expectant crowd. Their faces loomed at her from the ceiling, laughed at her through the bars . . . Emmie passed out.

When she woke, it was dark. Restless noise ebbed and flowed around her. Someone was singing and crying softly at the same time. She tried to move, but her body felt as heavy as iron. A damp cloth had been placed on her forehead. She slept again. In her fretful dreams, someone hovered over her, wiping her face and body. Sometimes it was like ice melting, at others like scalding water trickling down her body. She cried out and tried to push them away, but was never strong enough. Emmie knew she was trapped for ever in a world of ceaseless torture, pitiful noise and frightening faces. She would never be rescued because no one knew where she was. Or perhaps she was already dead and this was Hell . . .

The next thing she was aware of was an orderly standing over her, shaking her awake.

'Doctor's here to see you,' the woman said briskly.

Emmie's eyes hurt as she tried to focus. She was in a barred cell, but lying on a bed with a mattress, in between sheets. Her head rested on a pillow. It felt so good she did not want to lift it.

'How are you feeling?' the doctor asked awkwardly.

Emmie puzzled. 'Where am I?'

'In the prison hospital. You've had a fever.' He hesitated. 'And you've suffered a miscarriage.'

Emmie stared at him. What was he talking about?

'You've lost a lot of blood,' he went on, more matter-of-fact. 'You won't have to return to hard labour. I've recommended that you stay here until you're well enough to be released.'

He turned to go. Emmie struggled to raise her head.

'Miscarriage?' she whispered.

He looked at her and nodded. 'The early stages – but you were pregnant. Did you not know?'

Emmie gulped and shook her head.

'I'm sorry,' he said quietly, and left.

Emmie could no longer take refuge in strange delusions. Her body felt as fragile as dead leaves, but her mind was clear. She was pregnant – *had* been pregnant. Tom's terrible visit had borne one delicate flower – a second baby. Imprisonment and hard labour had crushed it. Tom, if he cared at all, would blame her. If not for her reckless actions, she would never have been sent to prison. Guilty thoughts whirled around her head. Did she mourn this baby's loss? How could she when she did not even know of its existence? Yet she felt empty, desolate, cheated. A brother or sister for Barny, gone.

How had she not guessed? Thinking back, she had not had a period for over two months, but she had vaguely put it down to bad diet and the strain of prison duties. In truth, she had not thought much about it at all. All her energy had been put into staying alive, lasting her sentence without losing her mind.

Perhaps it was the one thing that might have brought her and Tom back together, bound them in an uneasy truce. A baby. The symbol of a new start, a new life. Now the chance was gone. It would be best if Tom never knew.

After two days, Emmie was able to stand and move around the cell. She stood at the open bars and tried to talk to the staring woman opposite with the bald patches. She had observed her pulling out clumps of hair and weaving the strands around her fingers. She talked to herself while she picked out the hairs on her arms, berating herself in a language Emmie did not recognise.

'You have bonny hair,' Emmie smiled. 'Why do you pull it out?'

The woman stared at her suspiciously, coming to her cell door and gripping the bars. She babbled in her own language.

'I'm sorry, I don't understand.' Emmie shrugged helplessly. 'Why don't you plait it? You'd suit that.' Emmie took a coil of her own lank hair and demonstrated.

The woman stopped her frantic pulling. For a fleeting moment, Emmie saw understanding flicker in her dark eyes as the woman half smiled. Then she was babbling and sobbing again. Emmie gave up.

The next day, Emmie was transferred to the main hospital wing. It was three days till her release and she was permitted to write a letter home. She composed a brief note to the MacRaes, saying she would make her own way back to Crawdene to collect Barny. She had been allowed no correspondence during the six weeks and had no idea what had been happening in the outside world.

As she sat on the edge of the bed, finishing the letter, one of the orderlies came in with her dinner. Emmie could see from the grey of her dress that she was an inmate. Emmie barely glanced up as the woman put down the tin of watery potato stew.

'Ta,' Emmie said. The woman did not hurry away as they usually did.

'Want me to take that for you?' she asked.

Emmie looked closer. There was something familiar about the voice, the shape of the face under the voluminous cap. She looked into the woman's bold dark eyes. It couldn't be? The woman's broad mouth pulled into a wry grin.

'Nelly?' Emmie gasped. 'It's never you?'

Nell gave a snort. 'And who would have thought the saintly Emmie would've ended up in the nick too?'

'Never saintly,' Emmie laughed.

'No,' Nell agreed, 'you were always more trouble than you let on.'

Emmie gazed at her long-lost sister. She ought to feel angry. The last time they had met, Nell had tried her best to break up her marriage and disappeared with her and Tom's precious savings. Nell had used them all: Dr Flora, Charles, Tom, herself – even the Reverend Mr Attwater. That was the way her sister was. Yet, after all that had happened, Nell's faults seemed almost harmless. From the day their father had died, Nell had determined to look after herself.

'Still, you'll be out shortly,' Nell said brusquely. 'Not going on any more peace marches, I don't suppose?'

'Don't suppose anything,' Emmie said stoutly.

'Must be daft,' Nell retorted. 'Why do you bother? You could've died, from what I hear.'

'I do it because I have to,' Emmie said simply. 'For me, there's no other way to live.'

Nell shook her head in incomprehension. 'What about Tom and Barny?'

'I hope Barny's still there when I get out,' Emmie said quietly.

'But not Tom?' Nell questioned. Emmie said nothing. Nell asked, 'He gave you them marks on your shoulders, didn't he?'

Emmie looked at her startled. 'What marks?'

'I've seen them, Emmie, when I washed you down,' Nell said impatiently. 'Don't pretend to me. You've got scars from a beating.'

Emmie looked into Nell's eyes and nodded. She shuffled over so Nell could sit beside her. 'Was it you bathing me face when I had the fever?' she asked.

Nell sat down. 'Yes. Someone had to do it. I worked out early on, you get clean sheets and better food if you work in the hospital. It was just chance I looked after you – gave me quite a shock, I can tell you.'

Emmie was not convinced by her sister's offhandedness. She covered her hand with hers.

'Ta, Nelly,' she smiled. 'I think you saved me.'

Nell withdrew her hand quickly. 'No, you saved yourself. You're a tough 'un underneath that butter-wouldn't-melt look of yours.'

Emmie laughed softly. They looked at each other for a long moment.

'Look at the pair of us,' Nell sighed. 'Father would spin in his grave.'

'What happened to you?' Emmie asked.

Nell fiddled with a loose thread on her sleeve. 'Went back to Jackman. Things were fine and dandy till he got called up. Tried to get out of it by poisoning his skin with lead, but they saw through it.' Nell hesitated. 'The thing was, me and Jackman, we never got wed. So I couldn't claim his wages. Sent the military round snooping – said I wasn't a deserving wife – meaning they thought I was a whore.' She gave Emmie a defensive look. 'Well, what else could I do without job nor money? So I did what they thought I did anyway. Caught me down the quayside, with a sub-lieutenant. He got told to scarper, I got prison,' she said with a bitter laugh. 'Suppose that shocks you?'

'No,' Emmie replied, 'nothing about this war shocks me any more. They should've paid you Jackman's wages. You're not to blame.'

Nell suddenly smiled. 'Thanks, Emmie.'

They reached towards each other and briefly hugged. It felt so good to be touched that Emmie would have hung on, but Nell pulled away. She stood up.

'Gives us the letter and I'll see it goes in today's post,' she offered.

Emmie put the wafer-thin paper into the envelope and sealed it. She wrote on the MacRaes' address. Nell glanced at it, but made no comment. She shoved it in her apron and left.

Afterwards, Emmie wondered if her sister would post it. She still did not trust Nell. She decided it did not matter. Soon she would be free and would make her own way home, even if she had to walk the whole way. She hardly saw her sister again, just once in the distance, to nod to each other. Emmie chided herself for not finding out how long Nell had left inside or where she would go on release. Nell seemed content to bide her time here rather than be left to fend for herself on the streets. All Emmie knew was that her sister was better at surviving than most.

The day of her release came. Emmie was stripped of her hospital clothes and given back her own. Even in the short period of imprisonment, she had lost so much weight that her skirt hung loose about her hips. They gave her a piece of string to secure it round her waist. She was escorted along the labyrinth of prison corridors, doors unlocking before her, then clanging shut behind. She shuddered at the sound of keys rattling and scraping in the locks as she was marched towards the main gates.

'There's someone here to collect you,' the warder said casually, as they crossed the final high-walled courtyard.

Emmie's heart leaped. 'Who?' she asked.

'Doctor someone,' the woman answered, unconcerned.

Emmie's weak legs began to shake. 'Dr Jameson?'

But the woman was talking to the guard, who unbolted a low door cut into the massive iron gates. Then they were pushing Emmie through into the summer sunshine. She blinked, half blinded by dazzling light and the vivid green of a line of trees. The sudden colour made her dizzy. She groped at the wall to steady herself. The next moment, Flora Jameson was rushing towards her, arms outspread, and catching her in a tight embrace.

'Dearest Emmie!' she cried.

Emmie clung on, too overcome to laugh or cry. 'You're safe,' she croaked. 'Thank God.'

'Course I am,' Flora replied.

'How did you know . . . ?' Emmie said faintly.

'MacRaes sent me after they got your letter,' Flora explained. 'I've borrowed the Runcies' trap.'

'Then they're all right too?' Emmie whispered in relief. 'And Barny?'

Flora nodded and glanced around. 'Let's not talk here. Come along, I'll tell you as we drive.'

She helped Emmie over to the horse and trap and pulled her into the seat beside her. As they jogged out of Durham City, Flora told her how the Settlement had been closed down and all their records seized after Osborne's allegations. A widowed Quaker landowner had offered refuge to the Runcies in a tied cottage.

'That's where we're going now,' Flora said. 'We thought it wasn't safe for you to return to Crawdene – not at the moment. This place is quite remote.'

'B–but Barny?' Emmie stammered. 'I must see him.'

Flora gave her a reassuring look. 'Dear girl, of course you will see him. He's waiting at The Grove for you.'

Emmie's spirits soared. Tears of relief welled in her eyes. 'Thank you,' she sobbed.

'My poor child,' Flora said in sympathy, 'you've been through such a lot. You look so thin and pale – and you've been ill with fever too. I don't suppose they gave you any of our letters?'

Emmie shook her head. 'How did you know I'd been ill?'

'Your note,' Flora said. 'One of the warders scribbled on the bottom.'

Emmie caught her breath. 'Oh, Nelly! That must have been Nell. She was in there with me – on the hospital ward.'

This time it was Flora who gasped in shock. Emmie told her all she knew of her sister. Flora was visibly upset by the sudden news.

'Perhaps we could help her when she gets out?' Emmie suggested.

Flora gave a long sigh. 'Perhaps. But, Emmie, I'm leaving the area.'

'Leaving?' Emmie repeated.

'I'm going to Wales to be near Charles. I hope to be able to visit him at the camp – he's allowed one visit every month. His morale is low, I can tell from his letters. I intend to stay there until he's released.'

'But you'll come back when it's all over?' Emmie pleaded. 'Open the Settlement again?'

Flora smiled wistfully. 'We can but hope.'

After a pause, Emmie forced herself to ask, 'And Rab? Did he come home?'

Flora looked ahead as she spoke. 'Briefly.'

Emmie's heart twisted. 'They've arrested him again?'

'No,' Flora said, giving her a quick flash of a smile, 'he's gone into hiding.'

Emmie's hands flew to her mouth, stifling a cry of joy. Her vision blurred with tears. 'That's grand,' she whispered. She waited for Flora to say more, but she did not. Perhaps she did not know where he was or did not want to put him in danger by telling even his closest friends.

They both fell silent as they drove upriver, leaving behind the most westerly pit villages and heading into wooded slopes on the fringes of Weardale. Emmie dozed to the rhythm of the carriage, unable to keep awake, even with the thought of seeing her son again so soon.

She was woken by Cobbles, the pony, slowing to a walking pace. They were passing through a set of rusty iron gates, half off their hinges. All around them was a canopy of high trees rustling in the June breeze, a cool green haven. Bluebells covered the ground on either side of the mossy track. Emmie's eyes smarted, her senses overwhelmed by the colours and smells of the woods. She gazed around in wonder. The trees thinned out on to open hillside, with a squat Georgian house sheltering beneath in the distance. It reminded her of the fell above Crawdene.

'The Grove,' Flora announced. 'The cottages are down by the river.'

In front spread rough pasture, running down to a narrow fast-flowing river. There appeared to be no sign of habitation, just sheep grazing. But as they dipped down along the stony track, they suddenly came across a row of low wooden cottages tucked in under the bank. Narrow cultivated gardens ran down to the river edge.

Playing outside one, surrounded by ducks, was a small, dark-haired boy. Emmie's breath caught in her throat. At the same time, the boy saw the carriage appear and he began to run, the ducks chasing after him. Emmie almost fell from the trap in her haste to reach her son. She was shaking and crying as she stumbled forward, blinded by tears of joy.

'Mammy!' Barny shouted in delight. 'Mammy!'

Moment later, he was jumping into her arms, amid a cacophony of ducks. Emmie fell to her knees, hugging him fiercely and squeezing her eyes shut.

'My darlin', darlin' lad!' she sobbed and laughed in the same breath. 'I've missed you so much.'

The ducks scattered as a shadow fell over them. Wiping away tears, Emmie looked up. Squinting, she saw a man smiling over them.

'Welcome home, Emmie,' he said warmly.

It was Rab.

CHAPTER 33

For a long moment, Emmie stared up at Rab. He was thinner, gaunt around the eyes, his chin clean-shaven to reveal hollowed cheeks. But his smile was broad and his blue eyes shone with warmth. Emmie clutched Barny, unable to stand.

'Oh, Rab,' she whispered. 'Have I died and gone to Heaven?'

He laughed softly. 'This is as near as it gets, lass.'

Barny struggled out of her hold, eager to show her the cottage and the ducks. He gabbled about the number of ducklings.

'We feed them every day, don't we, Rab? And Mr Runcie helps us get them in the shed at night 'cos the fox will come and gobble them all up.'

'Haway, Barny,' Rab grinned, 'let's get your mam indoors. She's had a long journey and she's tired.' Rab leaned down and reached for Emmie. 'Put your arms round me neck.'

Emmie did so, but as he pulled her up she gasped in pain. Her whole body felt tender to the touch. Rab's face creased in concern.

'Oh, Emmie, what have they done to you?' he said angrily.

She crumpled at his words. 'Hold me,' she croaked. 'Please hold me.'

Gently, Rab gathered her into his arms and she dissolved into tears. Behind them, Flora called to Barny to help her with Cobbles, and the boy ran to her.

'Rab,' Emmie sobbed, 'I've dreamed of this so many times. In prison – it kept me from madness. The thought of seeing Barny again – and you . . .'

Rab kissed her tenderly on her forehead. 'It was the same for me. I'm going to care for you now,' he promised.

Lifting her up, he carried her down the bank. She weighed nothing in his arms. Emmie studied his face, hungering for every detail, joyful to be in his arms at last, even though it hurt her physically. She did not want to know how little time they might have, or think of the future. All she wanted was for that moment to go on for ever; Rab holding her in the June sunshine, the air so clear she could hear the sheep grazing, and Barny's high-pitched chatter as he helped tether Cobbles.

Rab took her into the first of the cottages. Up close, the buildings appeared dilapidated, patched together with bits of boarding, chicken wire, railway sleepers and carriage windows. Inside, the cottage looked less like an allotment shed. It was sparsely furnished, with a bed, small table, two stools and an armchair. But there were mats on the floor and red gingham curtains and a stove that gave out the sweet, aromatic scent of burning wood.

As Rab laid her on the bed, she noticed a tea chest of clothes – hers and Barny's. Another one was upturned by the bed. On it was a candle and the poetry book Rab had given her so long ago. He pulled the rough woollen cover around her.

'I'll make you some tea,' he offered.

But Emmie held on to his hand. 'Sit with me first.'

He smiled and sat down, cradling her hand in his.

'Tell me about this place,' Emmie murmured.

'It was built by pitmen – evicted in the strike of 1910. Mr Calvert, who owns this land, let the families come here. They would've starved otherwise. Huts have been empty till the Runcies came.'

'Who else is here?' Emmie asked.

'Apart from the Runcies, just me and Laurie Bell in the house next door. We were in prison together.'

'The postman?'

Rab nodded. 'He's in bad health. Told him to gan for a medical – the army would exempt him now. But he's that pig-headed. Said if they won't give him absolute exemption for being a CO then they can go to the devil.'

'Sounds like someone else I know.' Emmie gave him a wry look. 'This Mr Calvert is taking a great risk having you here, isn't he?'

'Aye,' Rab agreed, 'these Quakers are grand people. If the military come for us, Laurie and me will say we've just arrived – squatted without the owner's knowledge. Calvert doesn't even know our names, so he has nothing to hide if questioned.'

'Still, it's dangerous,' Emmie worried. She put his hand to her lips and kissed it. 'I don't blame you not wanting to gan back to gaol. Six weeks was an eternity. Don't know how you managed a year – not the way they tret the likes of us.'

Rab moved closer, smoothing back her limp hair. 'Emmie! I'm not frightened of going back – though there were times I nearly gave up. I've gone on the run so I can be near you. I needed to find out how you felt – after I wrote that letter. I know you said you'd chosen Tom, but I know what he did to you, Emmie. You don't have to stay with him. I can't offer you a soldier's pay or even a proper roof over our heads, but I can love you more than he ever will.' He looked at her with fierce eyes. 'I love you more than any other man ever could. But it's a dangerous future I'm offering, Emmie, for you and the lad. I'll not blame you if you turn it down. I just want to know if my love is returned.'

Emmie's tears spilled down her pale cheeks, her eyes huge and dark-ringed.

'I've always loved you,' she whispered. 'How did you never see it, you foolish man?' She gave a choking laugh. 'I'm not afraid of danger, nor do I care about the future.' She reached out and touched his face. 'If we only have a month together – a week, a day – it will be worth it. Whatever happens, I will always love you, Rab, *always*.'

He gave a small, exultant cry and pulled her into his arms. Tenderly he kissed her lips for the first time.

At that moment, Barny ran in. 'Mammy, don't gan to bed. Come and see the ducks. Aunt Flora's coming in the boat. You come too, Mammy.'

Reluctantly, Rab and Emmie pulled apart. 'Your mam needs to rest,' Rab told him firmly. Barny's face fell. 'I'll take you out in the boat,' Rab promised. The boy brightened at once.

'You sleep, Mammy,' he ordered. 'I'll fetch a fish for tea.'

Emmie smiled at them both. 'That's grand, bonny lad.'

She watched them go, then sank back into the bed. It smelled of camphor and traces of Barny. Emmie closed her eyes, feeling at peace for the first time in months. The last thing she heard was the splash of ducks on water and her son's laughter, before she fell into exhausted sleep.

It took a week before Emmie was back on her feet. Flora stayed to help nurse her back to health, sharing the bed with her while Barny slept in a box bed that Rab had made him. Laurie helped cook, Philip and Rab worked the allotment gardens, Barny fed Cobbles and fished, Mabel mended clothes and instructed Laurie in the making of cordials and pickling onions. Little by little, Emmie was able to help the small band of comrades.

After ten days, Flora took her farewell. Philip decreed he would be the only one to take her down the valley to the nearest station, to prevent attention being drawn to strangers. Barny protested at being left out of the trip and cried when the doctor hugged him goodbye.

'You'll be twice the size when I see you again,' she joked. 'I'll bring your Uncle Charles to visit and you can teach him how to use that fish trap.'

Emmie hugged her tightly. 'Thank you for everything you've done for us,' she gulped. 'We owe you so much.'

'You owe me nothing.' Flora smiled in affection. 'You and Barny have given me more pleasure than you will ever know – Charles too.'

'Give him our love,' Emmie said tearfully. 'Tell him we'll all meet again in peacetime.'

'In peacetime,' Flora echoed.

They waved her away until the carriage disappeared into the trees. Rab gave Barny a ride back on his shoulders. The rest of the day, Emmie worked in the garden, chatting to Laurie as he shelled peas while Rab took Barny off to the woods to snare rabbits.

Philip came back with flour and oats and a precious bag of sugar he had bartered with his wife's cordial. That evening they cooked on an open fire by the riverbank and sat around in the long evening twilight, discussing the news from the newspaper Philip had brought. There was an upsurge of fighting on the front at a place called Passchendaele, food riots in Germany, a resumption of war by the new Russian parliament against the wishes of Lenin's Bolsheviks. They talked late into the night, Barny falling asleep in Emmie's lap.

Rab lifted the boy for her and carried him to his box bed, tucked in behind the stove. Barny hardly stirred.

'So full of fresh air,' Emmie mused. 'It's a little bit of paradise for him.'

'And me,' Rab said in a low voice. In the glow of a midsummer night, Emmie could see his searching look. She held it a moment, then looked away. Rab turned. 'Good night, lass,' he murmured, and left.

Emmie's heart raced. Had he wanted to stay the night, now that Flora was gone? Part of her yearned to lie with him, yet she was wary. The thought of her miscarried baby still plagued her. She was not ready for intimacy, but did not know how to tell Rab. She went to bed alone, lying long into the night, listening to the bark of a fox in the nearby woods.

July came and a group of gypsies appeared in the woods with brightly painted wagons. At first, Emmie and her friends were cautious of the newcomers. They did not want word spreading around the area of the nature of their community. But it was not long before Barny had made friends with a boy called Ned and brought him back for tea.

Gradually they got to know Ned's family. The Kennedys were tinkers from south-west Scotland, who relied on agricultural work. They moved about, picking up casual work as well as news. A socialist convention in Leeds had demanded negotiated peace, but their proposed mass meetings had been banned. There was a rash of strikes from the Mersey to the Clyde over long working hours and rising prices.

'There's talk of industrial conscription,' Ned's older brother said. 'Fit lads that are in essential jobs are being pressured into wearing badges to say they're able-bodied.'

Rab was indignant. 'Aye, and you know what that means? Next thing is they'll be bringing in the old men and the unskilled to take their place.'

Ned's father, David, nodded. 'And packing them off to the front.'

'It's a wonder there hasn't been revolution.' Rab threw up his hands in despair.

'Folk are too ground down with surviving,' David grunted.

'Dead or in prison,' Laurie added bitterly.

'Not all.' Ned's mother, Lily, spoke up. She told how she had been approached in Liverpool by some women factory workers. 'Wanted me to join a peace crusade,' she said, wide-eyed. 'Said it was time working-class lassies got together and did something before we were left with a country of widows and orphans.'

Emmie looked at Rab in encouragement. Later, as they stood watching the boys throwing pebbles into the chuckling river, she said, 'I think the tide might be turning in our favour. People can only take so much.'

They walked arm in arm along the riverbank as the sun set. Flies danced above the water. Rab pulled her down on to a sandy bank.

'Emmie,' he said, looking at her intently, 'you know I want to lie with you.'

Her heart jerked.

Rab went on, 'I don't hold with marriage promises, only the ones made between lovers. A lass should be free to love who she wants, not be tied like a serf to a husband.' He stroked her cheek. 'But you, Emmie, I'm not sure what you want. Do you still feel tied to Tom by your vows? I know you're more religious . . .'

'No,' Emmie said, 'I believe in a loving God, not one who condones wife beating. I feel nothing for Tom – and I would risk my soul to lie with you, Rab.'

'But something is holding you back?' he challenged her.

Emmie let go a heavy sigh and told him about miscarrying in the prison.

'I'm frightened of intimacy – the risk of losing a babe again,' she confided.

Rab gripped her to him. 'My poor Emmie,' he groaned.

They held each other for a long time. In the still evening, they could hear Barny chattering with Ned about fish and desert islands. Emmie broke their silence.

'Has Barny ever talked about Tom to you?'

'No,' Rab answered.

'Me neither,' Emmie said, thoughtful. 'Tom frightens him.'

'And you?' Rab questioned.

Emmie looked at him. 'What frightens me is the thought of having to gan back to Tom for Barny's sake.'

'You don't have to,' Rab insisted.

'But what if he tried to take Barny from me?' Emmie

agonised. 'As his father, he's Barny's guardian. I have no rights – especially if we . . .'

Rab looked at her in bewilderment. 'Are you telling me, if Tom survives the war, you're prepared to go back to him?'

Emmie looked at his overwrought expression and hated herself for the pain she caused him. 'If it's the only way I'll keep Barny with me, then yes, I'll gan back to Tom.'

Rab turned from her in frustration. 'My God!'

Emmie quickly gripped his face between her hands.

'Look at me,' she urged. 'I love you, Rab, and I'll lie with you tonight. But you must know that this time together might be our only time. If Tom won't let me and Barny go when this war is over, then I'll stay with Tom till Barny's old enough to choose for himself.' She searched his handsome face for understanding. 'Just so you know – so there's no misunderstanding or bitterness later.'

Rab's expression was grim in the evening light. She thought she had hurt him too much and wished she had never mentioned Tom. He intruded into their haven like a storm cloud.

'I don't understand,' Rab said at last, 'but I'll accept what little piece of heaven you'll give me, Emmie.' He leaned forward and kissed her.

In relief, Emmie's arms went round his neck. She kissed him back with urgency. When they broke away, Rab smiled. 'Haway, lass, it's time for bed.'

They stood up and hurried back to the cottage, arms linked around each other.

CHAPTER 34

As high summer arrived, Emmie and Rab became lovers. They lived each day as if it might be their last, working side by side in the garden, sharing their meals, talking, reading to each other and playing with Barny. At night, when the light was too dim for reading or mending, they would go gladly to bed and make love. Emmie was never happier than falling asleep cradled in Rab's arms, the warmth of his breath on her hair.

Daily, they expected the police to find their hideout or a military vehicle to trundle up the track with arrest warrants for Rab and Laurie. But no one came. Each day that ended peacefully in their cottage was a precious gift.

September and the harvest came; the Kennedys, their best source of news, moved on. Occasionally, a letter would be left by the widower Calvert for the Runcies under a milk churn at the top of the bank. This was how news came from Flora and the MacRaes, addressed to the Runcies and their 'family'. Flora's letter told them little, save that she was working in a hospital and saw Charles once a month.

'She must be frightened of its being opened and read,' Emmie commented. 'Your mam tells us more.'

From Helen's childish handwriting they learned that Peter was handling horses for the medical corps and that Jonas was working in the forge again because of a shortage of skilled blacksmiths. He was excited at the Labour Party's break with the National Government, but furious at the refusal to let them attend the Socialist Peace Conference in Stockholm.

'What Peace Conference?' Rab demanded eagerly.

Emmie shrugged helplessly. They were cut adrift from the world. She shared his frustration, yet feared the invasion of the outside into their Utopia. They were living as they had always dreamed the world should be, everyone equal and at peace.

'Perhaps Philip could go up to the big house and ask what they know,' she suggested.

Their friend came back with the news of great unrest over shortages and a women's peace crusade that was sweeping the large cities of the north. Labour leader, Henderson, a traitor in many socialist eyes for condoning the war, had resigned from the Government.

That night Rab turned restlessly in bed. Neither of them could sleep.

'Let's go for a walk,' Emmie whispered.

Outside, the river moved like molten silver under a full moon as they followed its course.

'We should be out there helping,' Rab said in frustration.

'I know,' Emmie agreed, 'but it's too dangerous. As soon as you show your face, they'll have you back in prison.'

'Maybe that's where I should be,' Rab said grimly. 'How can we change the world hiding here?'

Emmie took his arm. 'We've already changed it. Look at the way we live!'

Rab sighed with impatience. 'But it's not enough!'

'It is for me,' Emmie said with passion.

'We need to change things for the millions who are suffering the effects of this war,' Rab insisted.

'And how does ganin' back to prison serve any purpose?' Emmie demanded. 'I need you, Rab. Barny needs you!'

Rab stared at her in the moonlight. 'Good God, Emmie, have we grown that selfish?'

'Why is it selfish to want you to live?' Emmie cried. 'Didn't you say that year in prison nearly finished you? Next time it could be for longer. COs have died from hard labour, you know.'

'Of course I know – and I'm prepared for that,' Rab said stubbornly.

'Well, I'm not,' Emmie retorted. Rab pulled away from her.

Emmie felt herself growing tearful and a familiar queasiness gripped inside. 'Please, Rab, you've done your bit – done more than most. There are others to take up the cause – thousands of others, by the sound of it.'

Rab was uncompromising. 'We're burying our heads in the sand. We can't stay here while others are risking their lives for us – at least I can't.'

'And if it means ganin' back to prison?' Emmie challenged.

Rab held her look. 'Then I'll do it.'

Emmie swallowed her panic. 'Well, I can't.'

Rab sighed. 'I don't expect you to. You've got Barny to take care of—'

'It's not just Barny,' Emmie interrupted. 'I can't gan back there again, because I won't risk losing another bairn.'

Rab looked nonplussed. 'What d'you mean?'

'I mean,' Emmie whispered, 'I'm carrying our bairn.'

Rab stared at her, dumbfounded. She began to tremble. 'That's why I don't want all this to end. I'm ganin' to have your baby, Rab.'

'Oh, Emmie!' Rab gasped, and reached out for her.

Their arms went about each other in a fierce hug. After that, they retreated to the warmth of their bed and Rab kissed her tenderly.

'I'll stay till they come for me, if that's what you want,' he promised.

After that, they never mentioned his going away, though Emmie felt it lay between them like a bruise. She worried that Rab resented her for keeping him there with the excuse of the baby. Perhaps she had been unfair mentioning it when she had? She too felt guilty at their relative safety. What would Flora have done in her situation? She thought fondly of her friend and mentor, and wished she was there to confide in. Mabel was so frail and forgetful that Emmie could not talk to her about such things.

Rab and Emmie continued to make love as the nights grew chilly, but he was cautious in the way he touched her as if fearing to harm their unborn child.

Rab was digging up turnips with Barny the day Philip appeared with a letter. Emmie took it. Helen's writing was scrawled across the page. Her heart thumped in shock as she read its contents. Her breath caught in her throat. She rushed out to find Rab.

313

'What is it?' he asked in alarm, seeing her ashen look.

Emmie held out the letter. 'I'm sorry,' she said, tears flooding her eyes. 'It's your da . . .'

Rab dropped his spade and took the letter, his eyes pained as he read of Jonas's death. He had collapsed again at the forge, but this time there had been no recovery. The funeral was in a week's time, to allow Peter to return on compassionate leave.

Emmie went to Rab and hugged him in sorrow. She felt a huge sob rise up inside him as he buried his face in her hair. Barny watched them in bafflement.

'Is Rab crying, Mammy?' he asked. 'Why's Rab crying?'

'Uncle Jonas has died, pet,' she explained.

The next moment, Barny was throwing himself at them and all three were in tears. Emmie thought, with a squeeze of her heart, how much the kind, passionate Jonas had been a father to her. He had battled all his life on behalf of others and he had given her a home more loving than any other she could have wished for. How poor Helen would miss him! Thinking of her aunt all alone and grieving, Emmie knew that they had to go. Even though it would mean certain arrest for Rab. The military would be waiting for just such an occasion to flush Rab out of hiding. And they would punish him severely.

When Rab looked up, he said, 'You know what I have to do, don't you?'

Emmie looked at him through her tears and nodded. 'We'll all gan.'

Rab frowned. 'No, Emmie—'

'I'm not lettin' you go on your own,' she insisted. 'Helen needs us.'

Rab clasped her to him. 'I love you, Emmie,' he rasped, 'more than my life.'

On their final night at the cottage, Emmie and Rab sat up late by the warm stove, talking quietly, reminding each other of special moments from their summer together.

'I've never been happier than with you and Barny,' Rab reflected. 'Thank you, Emmie.'

She gripped his hands. 'There'll be other times to come,' she insisted, 'even better times – when the war's over, when the baby's born—' Emmie stopped, choked. She saw the sadness in his handsome eyes and knew he doubted such a time would come.

They went to bed and lay awake in each other's arms, everything said, dreading the morning light. When it came, Emmie got up and woke Barny, dressed him in his best breeches, which were now too short, and watched him eat the porridge she could not swallow. He was excited about the trip to Crawdene and seeing his beloved Auntie Helen and Peter again.

Philip drove them to the station and gave them money for the train journey to Gateshead. They arrived back in Crawdene an hour before the funeral service. To Emmie's surprise, people came up to them in the street and shook Rab by the hand.

'Brave lad,' one man said.

'Good on yer,' said another. 'Sorry about your father.'

Their glances towards Emmie were more cautious. Most made a fuss of Barny instead.

The three hurried to China Street. Helen nearly fainted at the sight of them stepping through her door. She cried out their names and ran to embrace them.

Emmie burst into tears as Helen hugged her.

'You look well,' Helen cried. 'The bairn's grown – oh, Rab, you shouldn't have come!'

He held his mother. 'I had to see the old man on his way,' he smiled.

Peter, who had arrived home the previous day, was already showing Barny the body laid out in the open coffin on the table. Emmie went to hold the boy's hand.

'Is he sleeping?' Barny asked. Despite Emmie's telling him, he was finding death a difficult idea to grasp.

'He's dead,' Peter answered. 'He won't wake up.'

Barny looked round at his mother in concern. She nodded.

'He's gone to be with Uncle Sam in Heaven.'

'No, he hasn't,' Peter contradicted. 'Me da didn't want to gan to Heaven. Didn't believe in it. He said Heaven should be here on earth, didn't he, Rab? He was always saying that.'

Emmie and Rab exchanged looks. 'Aye, Peter lad,' he smiled, 'he was always saying that.'

'That's as maybe,' Helen snorted, 'but he's gettin' a proper burial and if he doesn't like it, he can come back and haunt me.'

Barny turned away, his curiosity dispelled, and demanded Peter play him a tune on his tin whistle. The others fell to talking about the funeral arrangements and Helen told them of the tea the

315

Clarion Club were laying on in the Co-operative Hall afterwards. They had a short time to tell her about their life at The Grove, but they had decided to say nothing about the baby in case word got back to the Currans. Emmie dreaded coming across them.

Rab was more concerned with what Helen would do. Now Jonas was dead, she no longer had the right to live in the cottage.

'Why don't you go back with Emmie and Barny?' he urged.

Helen looked torn. 'I can't,' she said in a hushed voice, glancing at Peter. 'I need to be here in the village for when the lad gets leave or comes home for good. If he came back and couldn't find me, he'd gan to pieces.' Her face was creased in sorrow. 'He's taken it bad about his da – doesn't show it, but I can tell. He thought the world of his da.'

'We all did,' Rab said softly, his eyes full.

There was no more time to talk, as neighbours filed in to help carry out the coffin. Rab and Peter took their turn carrying their father's body, struggling up the hill to the windswept graveyard. Helen had arranged for a retired minister from Ongarfield, vociferous in support of peace, to take the service. Emmie was astounded at the number of villagers who turned out to follow the coffin and pay their respects: men from the lodge, workmates, fellow socialists, rival gardeners in the annual flower festival, friends from the Clarion Club. There were a smattering in uniform, like Peter. Others, from the Clarion Club, were dressed in mauve or grey rather than the black of religious mourning. People divided by the war, but united in their admiration for Jonas.

They stood in untidy rows, huddled against the biting wind and a sudden October squall as the minister intoned over the open grave and Rab helped lower his father's coffin into the dark earth. Emmie's heart ached for him, as he stood with head bowed, his lean face harrowed. He had sparred often with his rumbustious father; they were too alike not to clash. But they had loved each other with a fierce loyalty that no amount of disagreement could break.

Suddenly Rab turned to the crowd of mourners, his dark hair whipped by the wind, and raised his voice.

'My father spent every day of his life trying to make this a fairer world,' he bellowed. 'Justice for all, was his motto. No more

316

poverty; no more war. These were the ideals he worked for. And why should we not have them?' Rab demanded, stabbing a finger at the air.

People were looking around, wondering what others made of his intervention. For the first time, Emmie caught sight of Barnabas Curran, his face stony in disapproval. Her heart lurched.

Rab had his eyes fixed on something in the distance behind the crowd. He went on. 'My father did not live to see his fairer world. His dying means my mother will be thrown out on the street, for she no longer has a husband or son working for Oliphant, so she cannot remain in one of his cottages. Never mind that she spent the best years of her life keeping her family healthy and fed for the pit. No, she is no longer needed, so out she goes. Where is the justice in that?'

There were murmurings in the crowd, but whether of agreement or dissent, Emmie was not sure. She glanced at Helen's anxious face, but his mother did not stop Rab.

'My father dies leaving one son in uniform and one son with a criminal record for refusing to put on that uniform. He loved both sons equally, but he hated this war over trade and territory that divides brother from brother, comrade from comrade, German from Briton,' Rab's voice boomed out. 'The best way we can honour the memory of my father is to embrace our fellow comrades, not kill them. Stop the slaughter!' Rab cried. 'In the name of Jonas MacRae, stop the war!'

Some people called out in agreement. There was a ripple of applause amid the stirring of unease. The old minister stepped forward and put a warning hand on Rab's arm. He nodded and, moving away from the grave, kissed his mother. Emmie stared at him, baffled. He turned and caught her look. Rab's eyes shone with passion. He smiled, his look tender yet full of regret. He mouthed goodbye.

Then he was striding off, casing his way through the crowd. As Emmie watched him, she suddenly saw what he must have seen all along. A group of policemen was toiling uphill into the wind, hats clutched under their arms. Sergeant Graham led them. Emmie's heart thumped in fright. But Rab strode quickly towards them, not wanting a scene in the graveyard. She watched them take him by the arms and march him away. Emmie stumbled over to Helen and they gripped each other in support.

Rab did not look back. Helen groaned as if she would faint. Quickly, Mannie stepped out of the crowd and took Helen's other arm.

'Haway, lass, keep your head up,' he encouraged, 'for Rab's sake – for Jonas's sake.'

Somehow, they managed to steer Helen from the bleak, treeless graveyard and down the hill. Only in the main street did Emmie look around for Peter and Barny. She caught sight of Peter, but there was no sign of her son.

'Where's Barny?' Emmie called to him in alarm.

'With his grandda,' Peter answered, pointing back up the hill.

Emmie looked round. Barnabas was leaning down talking to Barny, a hand on his shoulder. She rushed back to fetch him.

'Barny, come to Mammy,' she beckoned.

Her father-in-law glowered at her. Emmie's heart thudded. What had Barny been saying? She nodded at Barnabas. He straightened up, a hand still grasping his grandson.

'You'll be stopping in the village now that MacRae's been arrested?' It sounded more like an order than a question.

Emmie flushed. 'I'll stop as long as Aunt Helen needs me and no longer.'

He stepped towards her, still gripping Barny's jacket. 'You belong here – you're Tom's wife, not that traitor's,' he hissed. 'And this is my grandson. You have a home in Empire Terrace and a duty to your husband to be there when he returns. Or have you lost all sense of decency, living among scum like MacRae?'

Emmie glared at him. 'If that's how you feel, then why show your face at a MacRae funeral?'

Barnabas snapped, 'Jonas was a member of the lodge – I had to show my respects.'

'You hypocrite,' Emmie said with scorn. 'Jonas despised you as an armchair patriot. He blamed you for turning Tom into a violent wife-beater – a Bible in one hand and a belt in the other. He pitied you your joyless life.' She added with quiet insistence, 'I will live where I please – and how I please. Let go of my son, Mr Curran.'

His look was thunderous, but he dropped his hold on Barny. The boy ran to Emmie and grabbed her hand. Emmie turned and hurried away, her heart pounding, half expecting her father-in-law to run after her and grab Barny back.

'What did you say to Grandda?' Emmie asked anxiously.

Barny's look was fearful. His chin trembled. 'I told him about the fishin'. Was that wrong, Mammy?'

Emmie's heart squeezed. 'No, pet,' she reassured quickly, 'you've done nothing wrong.'

'Can we gan back to The Grove?' Barny asked tearfully. 'I want to go back with Rab. Is that where he's gone, Mammy?'

Emmie nearly wept. She pulled him along. 'We'll gan back there soon,' she promised. 'But Auntie Helen needs us now.'

CHAPTER 35

Helen was given a week to get out of the colliery cottage. Mannie came to her rescue by offering the room that Rab had occupied.

'It's not much,' the old man said apologetically, 'but it's a roof over your head till Peter comes home. You can store your furniture in the outhouse.'

Helen swallowed her pride and accepted gratefully. Only with Emmie did she let her bitterness show.

'A lifetime of hard work I've put into this house,' she said bleakly, 'and now I'm packin' me bags like a tinker.' She folded clothes of Jonas's that would do for Peter. 'Rab was right – we should have got out of here years ago and rented somewhere.'

Emmie tried to comfort her. 'When the war's over, and Rab and Peter are back, we can start again somewhere else.'

'We?' Helen asked sharply. 'What about you and Tom?'

Emmie flushed. 'I don't want to go back to him,' she said, glancing away.

Emmie helped Helen dismantle her home. They sold most of the furniture to the incoming tenants, pawned Jonas's suit, the set of crockery, spare linen and pictures. What was left of her possessions were transported round to Mannie's in three wheelbarrow loads.

Emmie felt a pang of yearning for Rab as they settled Helen into his old room. Mannie had got the fire going. Rab's tartan blanket was still on the bed and a pile of musty pamphlets and old *Blackton Messengers* lay on the dresser. Barny ran around looking for the dominoes he used to play with.

'Where's Rab?' he asked. 'Will he be coming back soon?'

The women exchanged sorrowful glances.

'Not for a while, pet lamb,' Helen answered.

That night they all bedded down in the small room. Emmie and Helen talked quietly while Barny slept.

'I'll get Mr Calvert to find out where Rab's been taken,' Emmie whispered. 'He has links with the NCF.'

'Will you manage without him at The Grove?' Helen worried.

'Of course,' Emmie assured. 'There's another CO – and the Runcies. We grow our own food and Barny's a canny fisherman these days. I want to gan back as soon as possible – don't want to be beholden to Tom or have to live in Berlin Terrace. If there's anything you want from there, just take it.'

Helen regarded her sadly. 'You're not coming back, are you? Not ever.'

'That depends on Tom,' Emmie murmured.

'And Rab?' Helen asked.

Emmie unburdened herself at last. 'We love each other and want to stay together. I'm expecting Rab's child.'

Helen gasped. 'Oh, Emmie! Does Rab know?'

'Aye, he does.'

Helen let go a deep sigh. 'Tom will never forgive you, lass, or the Currans. Oh, I fear for you.'

'I'm not afraid of the Currans,' Emmie replied. 'All I fear is that Tom might try to take Barny from me. That's why I've told Rab I'll gan back to Tom if it's the only way of keeping the lad.'

'And the babe?' Helen questioned.

'I could pass it off as Tom's if I have to,' Emmie said with resignation. 'I was carrying his bairn, till I miscarried in prison,' she said bleakly.

Helen reached across and stroked her head. 'Oh, Emmie, I'm that sorry. What terrible times these are.'

Emmie dissolved into tears at her tenderness. 'It's me that's sorry – sorry for bringing shame on you. I've brought you nowt but trouble and I can't see an end to it.'

Helen hushed her. 'Your Uncle Jonas and me – we've always been proud of you – ever since the day you came. I don't give two pins for what other folk think – if I did, I'd have worried mesel' into an early grave long ago.' She brushed the tears from Emmie's face. 'I'm glad about the baby – glad for you and Rab. I can see how happy you make each other. You'll find a way of being together. Like you said – when the war's over we can all start again.'

Word soon spread where the widowed Helen had gone. Some looked askance at her for taking a room in Mannie's house, gossiping about them.

'More than just a family friend, I'd say.'

'Did you see the way he held on to her at the funeral – and Jonas not cold in his grave?'

'There's no smoke without fire.'

Others were more sympathetic and brought round bits of food. Helen let it be known that she was willing to do mending for a few pennies, but she was not known for her sewing skills and only bachelor pitmen came with odd jobs, more out of pity than necessity.

One Saturday in late October, Louise Curran appeared at Helen's door.

'I'm sorry about Mr MacRae,' she said stiffly. 'How are you, Emmie?'

Emmie stared at her one-time friend. Had Louise been one of those who had hounded her from the village? Had she been glad to see her go to prison as punishment for disloyalty to Tom? She quelled her feelings of resentment. At least she had the courage to seek her out now.

Louise clasped her hands. 'I was wanting – wondering – if I could see Barny?'

Reluctantly, Emmie nodded and opened the door wider. The boy was standing on a chair helping Helen stir a pan of soup. He looked round when his mother called.

'Auntie Louise is here to see you.'

Barny stayed where he was, spoon in hand.

'Hello, Barny,' Louise smiled, and held out her arms. He hesitated, then climbed off the chair and went to greet her. 'I've missed you. So have Grandma and Grandda.' She cuddled him. 'Would you like to see them? Grandma's made a cake with raisins – bet you haven't had that since we last saw you.'

'Louise,' Emmie warned, 'don't go bribing the lad.'

'Please, Emmie,' Louise appealed, 'can I just take him round for an hour or so? Mam's that eager to see him.'

Emmie weakened at Louise's pleading. She looked at her son. 'Barny, do you want to visit Grandma?'

The boy looked between them and nodded.

'See!' Louise said in triumph. 'I knew he would. It's not fair to keep him away from his family.'

As soon as she had agreed to it, Emmie regretted doing so. There was no knowing what Barny might say about Rab or their life at The Grove.

She could settle to nothing all afternoon. As the day faded and Louise did not return with her son, Emmie's concern grew.

'Go and fetch him,' Helen advised, unnerved by Emmie's fretting.

Emmie hurried round, not even bothering to pull on her coat. When Louise answered the door, she pushed past her.

'You said an hour. Where is he? Barny!'

She barged into the Currans' parlour. Barny was sitting at the table puzzling over a jigsaw with his grandparents. A half-eaten cake and plate of scones stood on a silver stand, making her mouth water. Barny looked up, startled at her sudden appearance.

'It's time to come home, pet,' she ordered, holding out a hand. 'Thank Grandma for having you.'

Barnabas stood up. 'Our grandson would like to stay the night. Mrs Curran's made up his bed. Louise can bring him back after chapel and dinner tomorrow.'

'No,' Emmie said in panic. 'Thank you, but no.'

'Barny's religious education has been badly neglected,' he said sternly. 'We have a duty to Tom to make sure his son's being properly looked after. Sounds to me as if the lad's been allowed to run wild as a savage in this place you've been hiding him.'

Emmie faced her father-in-law. 'Barny's never been so happy or healthy, so you've no need to worry. Louise said nothing about having him for the night. Barny's a comfort to Aunt Helen and that's my first concern. He can come to you another night.'

She stepped forward and put a hand on Barny's arm. The boy looked stubborn.

'I want to stay, Mammy,' he declared. 'Grandma's got bread-and-butter pudding.'

'Another time,' Emmie said, hauling him from the chair. He whined in protest.

'Leave the boy be,' Mrs Curran said querulously.

'What harm is it if we have him here the night?' Louise demanded. 'At least he'll get a decent meal for once. You can see his ribs he's that skinny.'

Emmie felt resentment engulf her. The Currans were still comfortably off, despite the privations of war. Barnabas was making good money from all the extra work, Louise had her job at the shop, Mrs Curran did not have to see her life's possessions pawned off in an afternoon like Helen had. And now they were attempting to take over her son, winning him with rich food and treats that she could not afford to give. She knew it would not stop until they had complete control over Barny, just as they had always strived to dominate Tom.

Emmie grabbed her recalcitrant son and shoved him towards the door, not bothering to argue further. She just wanted to be out of that claustrophobic house, stuffed with furniture and self-importance. With Barny howling and the Currans remonstrating behind, Emmie fled down the passageway and out into the darkness. She did not stop till they were safely back in India Street, pushing Barny into the cramped room.

The boy flung himself on the floor, kicking and screaming until he was quite exhausted.

Emmie sank into a chair, her nerves in tatters. Helen did not have to ask. As she comforted Barny with a drink and cajoling words, she eyed Emmie.

'You have to go,' she urged. 'Don't worry about me. You need to get the bairn away from here – away from those people.' She dropped her voice. 'I never had the chance to tell you, but when you were in Durham Gaol they were always round at our door demanding to see the bairn. Said he was their responsibility – that you weren't fit to keep him. Barnabas said some terrible things that I'll not repeat. Jonas stood up to him, of course. But now he's not here to protect you—' Helen broke off.

Emmie reached out and touched her in comfort. 'Thank you for keeping Barny safe – you and Uncle Jonas. I'll never be able to repay you for all you've done for me.'

Helen smiled sadly. 'You don't have to. Just see this war out – for Rab's sake. That's all the payment I want.'

Emmie nodded, too overcome for words.

Helen added, 'You mustn't come back – not till this is all over.'

The women hugged each other in regret.

CHAPTER 36

1918

As the war entered its fifth year, rationing was introduced to alleviate high prices and creeping starvation. Long-suffering Mabel caught pneumonia and, having not the strength to fight it, died all too suddenly. Laurie, housebound with a bad chest, was as bereft as Philip, and Emmie found herself in charge of the monthly trip to town to pick up supplies. She worried for the baby, which stirred in her womb, though she was so thin it hardly showed under her coat. But it concerned her more to think of them running out of food, should snow come in February and cut them off.

She took Barny to help with old Cobbles and they struggled through the swollen river and over icy tracks. It took all day to go the few miles into Standale and back. But shopkeepers took pity on the chattering pale-faced boy and were generous with the measures of tea, lard and bacon. Emmie and Barny returned, frozen and worn out, to the communal fire that they kept going in the Runcies' cottage. Emmie clasped a copy of the *Herald*.

'This'll cheer you – general strikes in Prague and Budapest,' she told the men eagerly. 'The workers have had enough – they're striking for peace. Rumour is the famine on the Continent's much worse than here. And listen to this: martial law has been declared in Berlin after strikes by the socialist Spartacists.'

Emmie placed another log on the fire and poured Barny a cup of hot tea with numb, shaking hands. 'Here you are, bonny lad. Barny was that helpful with Cobbles – right little coachman. You've taught him well, Philip.'

Philip smiled absent-mindedly.

'And here's something to celebrate – House of Lords have passed the bill giving women over thirty the vote. Wouldn't Mabel have cheered?' Emmie said, eyes shining.

Philip looked up as if hearing her for the first time. 'She would indeed,' he nodded, turning from her and blowing hard into his handkerchief.

Emmie was determined to keep their small commune going. Laurie was too frail to face another prison term and Philip's cheerful optimism had withered with his wife's death. Without her care, he would give up too. At Christmas, the elderly Mr Calvert had shut up The Grove and gone to London to stay with relations where he felt he could better lobby the Government. He had left them with a plentiful supply of wood and assured them they would have no trouble with the local authorities, but Emmie felt the more vulnerable without his protection.

So Emmie kept to herself her worries over Rab. The last she heard had been two months ago, a message through Mr Calvert that he was in prison in Liverpool. He was facing a harsh five-year sentence of hard labour. Emmie did not like to dwell on what that was doing to him physically, let alone to his mental state. She knew how much harder it must be for Rab to return to prison, knowing the deprivations he would face. She speculated as to why no letters came from him. Was he in solitary for refusing to do prison work, or was he anxious to keep attention away from The Grove and his comrade Laurie? Emmie did not allow herself to entertain the thought that he might be ill or even dead. If that were the case, Helen would surely have got news to her. So she preferred no news to bad news, almost dreading that there might be a message for her under the milk churn on the track to The Grove.

As the spring came and her pregnancy approached full term, Emmie fretted over how she would manage. She had made enquiries about midwives in Standale and had the name of one who was prepared to travel up to The Grove if fetched in the trap. Yet she did not like the idea of strangers coming and prying around the encampment. They might gossip about the young man with the persistent cough, of whom there was no record.

Then, one day in early April, Barny came scampering into the cottage, holding up a dead rabbit.

'Ned's back,' he cried. 'His da gave me this. Come and see, Mam.'

Emmie toiled up the bank after him, breathless but overjoyed to see the spiral of smoke from the Kennedys' camp in the woods. Lily came out to greet her, noticing her pregnancy at once.

'Emmie! When's it due? Is Rab pleased?' She saw the look of warning on Emmie's face. 'Sit down and tell me everything,' her friend said, waving the boys away to play.

Two days later, Emmie went into labour as she was digging up beetroot. She sent Barny for Lily, who came at once.

'I've delivered babies all over the place,' Lily reassured, boiling up water and helping Emmie into the cold, damp bed. 'This is a palace compared to some.'

The labour was quick, and the baby small as it slithered into the world, but Emmie used up the last of her energy to bring it out. She lay, utterly exhausted, as the infant gave a querulous wail.

'A bonny baby girl,' Lily cried, thrusting her into Emmie's arms. 'What will you call her?'

Emmie gazed at the tiny, wizened creature with a shock of dark hair. 'Mary,' she whispered, 'after me mother. And Helen after Rab's.' She kissed her daughter's soft head.

'Mary Helen,' Lily repeated, 'that's a grand name for the wee lassie.'

She bundled the baby up in a warm blanket and left them both to sleep. Emmie closed her eyes, thankful her labour was safely over. Somehow she must get word to Rab about his new daughter. She knew that whatever state he was in, the news would give him the determination to carry on.

Rab had to be helped from the punishment cell. Light stabbed his eyes. He could not speak, his throat raw from the tube they had forced down it days ago. A year in prison and he was to be allowed to speak on exercise for forty minutes a day. Except he was now too weak for exercise and no longer had the power of speech. The warders dragged him back to his cell and locked him in.

He tried to remember the turning point, the moment he had broken. For months he had held out, refusing to stitch mailbags, going on hunger strike to protest at the treatment of prisoners. It was no longer just the COs who concerned him, but the others, brutalised and degraded by prison conditions. They were locked up like animals in cages, sent mad by staring at blank walls for endless hours, months, years. He saw it corrupting the young warders, hardening them. He saw how ill the prison chaplain became after a death sentence was carried out.

Rab's mind was blank of much that had happened this past year, but he remembered the execution. He had passed the condemned man in the corridor, chained to a warder. Rab did not know his crime. Their eyes had met and they had nodded. Rab was haunted by the thought he was one of the last people the man had seen, yet he had been allowed to say nothing.

The three days the prisoner had been on his landing, the inmates had been restless and the warders short-tempered. On the man's last night, they heard him screaming out for the doctor or the governor to release him. Rab buried his head under his blanket, trying to block out the howling, but could not. He had flashes of panic as he remembered his own time in a condemned cell in France, as the dawn came up on what he thought was his last day. The fear was indescribable; it tore at his guts.

He wanted to rush and bang on his cell door to demand the man's release, but knew it would end in a flogging or solitary. Rab had gritted his teeth and clamped his hands together to stop himself acting. The chaplain had been called and eventually calmed the man down.

The next morning, no one had been allowed out of their cells as the prisoner was led out to the gallows. Rab heard the door being unlocked, the sound of footsteps ringing along the landing, the hushed silence. No noise was made until, shortly afterwards, the tolling of the prison bell announced that the man was hanged. Someone at the end of the corridor began to cry.

At chapel the following Sunday, the chaplain had been absent. He reappeared a week later, looking gaunt and ill, and gave them a sermon about Jesus promising heaven to the murderer on the cross. Two weeks later, he had been replaced. Rab had gone on hunger strike.

But it was not the execution that had been the final straw. It was a dandelion. All summer he had thought of Emmie, knowing that their baby would have been born. But he had heard nothing. Was it a girl or a boy? Had something gone wrong? Had the baby died? Had Emmie died? Perhaps Tom had been invalided out of the army and she had gone back to him. Endlessly, he tortured himself with such thoughts. The only letter he had received recently was from his mother, but that was before his latest spell in solitary and it had told him nothing of Emmie or Barny.

Rab's barrel-ceilinged punishment cell was mostly below ground level, but the top of his narrow window gave a glimpse of the floor of the exercise yard. Every day he feasted his eyes on the tramping feet of the prisoners and tried to make out their conversation. One day, he had noticed a green stalk of a dandelion growing out of a crack beside his window. Its vivid colour made his eyes water to see such beauty spring from the drab uniform grey.

Each day, he pulled himself up so that he could gaze on the green blade and watch in expectation as the tight head began to flower. He thirsted for the bright yellow head to shine into his cell like the sun. But before that could happen, a gardening party came round the yard and pulled the weed up by its roots.

Rab sank on to his cell floor and wept. He wept at the destruction of beauty and because he knew that the summer was over and it would not grow again. Somewhere out in the world were Emmie, Barny, and their baby, a symbol of beauty clinging on to life. Now he had to face yet another winter without them and did not know how he would get through it. The dandelion was too fragile to survive; perhaps they all were.

Yet as he wept and railed at the injustice, Rab knew above anything else that he wanted to survive. He wanted to live to see Emmie again, to see green fields and dandelions, to fish with Barny, to hold his baby. Desire for life surged through his broken body, even as it collapsed under the strain of malnutrition and incarceration.

He gave up his hunger strike and submitted to prison regulations. After a further week in solitary, he was back on the old landing. Fellow COs banged their cell doors to welcome him back, some shouting out to him in defiance of the warders. Yet Rab hung his head in shame, knowing he had reached the end of his endurance.

The weeks that followed were full of rumours about the war ending. Central Europe was collapsing in disarray, German sailors were mutinying, Bavaria was in revolt. The other inmates

330

discussed the news every day as they tramped around the yard in the autumn rain, but Rab did not join in. He felt detached from it all, as if they discussed another world to which he no longer belonged. He hardly noticed the sleet down the back of his neck or remembered the names of those who stamped past him in an attempt to keep warm. He did not have the energy to keep up and they had grown used to him not speaking.

One November day, a fellow CO clapped him on the back.

'They're going to sign,' he grinned. 'Bloody war's nearly over. Sooner or later, they'll have to let us go.'

Rab looked at him, nonplussed. He struggled to speak. 'Sign w-what?' he whispered.

'The Armistice, matey,' his companion cried.

The next day, as Rab sat in his cell, conjuring pictures out of the familiar cracks in the whitewash, there was a sudden blare of hooters beyond the prison walls. He jumped, startled at the noise. From the cells around him, prisoners began to bang on their tin plates, shouting and hollering. Over the din came the peal of the chapel bell.

For a stunned moment, Rab thought it was the beginnings of a prison riot. Then he remembered what the man in the yard had told him. This must be the end of the war. He tried to get to his feet, but his knees would not hold him. It was the moment for which he had waited so long, battled so hard. Now it was here, he felt numb and empty. What had it all been for? Sam and his father were dead. Gentle Peter was a soldier, his widowed mother eked out a pittance in a village that no longer respected her. He was a pathetic, broken man, no use to anyone.

Rab reached under his blanket and pulled out the shard of slate he kept hidden. He had picked it up once in the yard. Over the weeks he had sharpened it on his cell wall. He pressed it to his wrist in despair. Rab pierced his shrunken skin with the slate and watched in detachment as a bead of blood oozed out. It had all been quite pointless. For all their bravery and sacrifice, they had not been able to stop the war. For over four years it had reaped its bloody harvest until the strongest aggressor had won. How long before the next? How long before Barny and his generation were being conscripted?

The sudden image of Barny's grinning, trusting face came unbidden into his mind, as vivid as if he had seen the boy yesterday. Rab felt winded. Barny, the lad he had loved as fiercely as if he had been his own.

And Emmie. What had happened to his beloved Emmie? Rab's heart squeezed. She had been exiled from her home, cast out by her husband and family, criminalised by the war. But had she survived? Did she wait for him? All at once, he realised he *had* to know.

Rab dropped the slate, a sob rising deep inside. It shook him to his core.

As the cacophony of celebration carried on along the landing, no one heard the racking sobs of the silent, brooding man who had once been known as Radical Rab.

CHAPTER 37

1919

Emmie and her friends at The Grove lived in a strange limbo. The war was over, but the hardship and rationing appeared worse than ever. Emmie waited tensely for word of Tom's return or Rab's release. Surely the authorities would not make him complete his five-year sentence now that everything had changed? The thought was unbearable. Helen had written once since the end of the war; she did not expect Peter home till the spring and had heard nothing of Rab. Philip was attempting to find out Rab's whereabouts through Mr Calvert, who remained in London. She had lost touch with Flora and wondered if their letters had been intercepted.

Still, she managed to keep their household going, cheered by Barny's companionship and Mary's easy-going nature. Her baby was small but growing and nearly able to walk, giggling at the funny faces Barny pulled to entertain her as she tried to follow him around. Mary was dressed in cut-down clothes given by the Kennedys before they left in the autumn. Her eyes were the same piercing blue as Rab's, bringing Emmie joy and pain whenever she gazed into their intensity.

Laurie left for Gateshead, full of hope he would be re-employed as a postman, but was back in a week.

'They won't take conchies,' he reported bitterly, 'and the town's not safe. There's soldiers out on the streets 'cos of the strikers.'

'Strikers?' Emmie queried.

'Aye,' Laurie nodded, wide-eyed, 'dockers, pitmen, railways –

all demanding shorter working hours and jobs for the demobbed.'

'Finally we're standing up for ourselves,' Emmie said eagerly.

Laurie shook his head. 'They're clamping down hard. Talk of rations being cut until strikes are called off.'

Emmie was outraged. 'Land fit for heroes, is it? That's what they promised.'

Laurie was cynical. 'They just said that to get re-elected. Nothing's changed for the working class.'

'And your family?' Emmie asked in concern. 'Did you find them?'

Laurie looked away. 'No,' he said quietly. 'Street was bombed two years ago, everyone's gone. Lad who runs the corner shop thinks they moved across the river, but he wasn't sure. I don't know where to start looking for them.'

Barny, who had been listening by the fireside, went over and climbed on Laurie's knee.

'You can be in our family if you like, Uncle Laurie.'

Emmie saw Laurie's chin tremble. 'Aye, course you can,' she smiled. 'We'll take care of each other like we always have.'

As the winter waned, Emmie wondered why she heard nothing from Tom. He must be home by now. Had he washed his hands of her for good? Or was he ill? Influenza had been raging through crowded towns and villages for months and she was thankful her children remained isolated and healthy. At times the waiting was unbearable and she contemplated going to Crawdene to confront him and beg for her release. But the thought of seeing Tom again filled her with dread. Better to stay out of the way and hope he no longer wanted her as his wife.

Such hope was dashed by the arrival of a letter in late March from Barnabas. Her stomach turned to think he had found out where she was, but then Barny had told his grandfather about The Grove and Barnabas would have made it his business to discover their hideaway. The letter was abrupt and to the point. Tom was home and needing his wife and family. She should thank the Lord that he was safe. It was a disgrace that she stayed away instead of giving him a hero's welcome. If she did not return, they would send the police to fetch her.

In consternation, Emmie confided in Laurie and Philip.

'I can't go back,' she agonised, 'not without knowing what's happened to Rab. But what if they send the police?'

Laurie was doubtful. 'They're just trying to frighten you. The police aren't going to chase round the county for a disgruntled husband.'

'And it's not Tom that's asking for you to go back,' Philip pointed out. 'Perhaps it's just his parents who feel so strongly. They have their pride – their reputation in the village.'

Emmie took heart from this suggestion. She still did not know how Tom felt. He would have to come and fetch her himself if that's what he wanted.

Philip encouraged her to stand firm. 'I'll write again to Mr Calvert and see if he can do anything to lobby for Rab's early release.'

Emmie carried on as before, yet with the daily fear that the Currans might appear to bully her back to Crawdene.

A month later, Philip came hobbling down the track with a letter from Mr Calvert. He handed it straight to Emmie, his elderly face full of anticipation. She tore it open and read.

'Rab's being released,' she gasped. 'Next week – on the first. That's May Day!'

'From Liverpool?' Philip asked.

Emmie read on. 'No, he's in London,' she said in dismay. 'No wonder he's never replied to my letters. Mr Calvert is offering to meet him and put him on a train north.'

'That's splendid,' Philip cried.

'I'll write straight away accepting,' Emmie said. 'Ask him to telegraph with the time of his train.' She hugged the baby and rushed down to the river to tell Barny. 'Rab's coming home,' she cried.

The boy whooped in excitement. Emmie felt light-headed with relief that the waiting would soon be over.

Spring was coming at last to the fell and she tackled the garden with renewed vigour. Laurie and Philip helped as much as they could, though both were frailer than ever. They had insisted on giving Barny and Emmie, who was breast-feeding, the main share of rations all the past year. Now Mary was beginning to take puréed vegetables that Laurie prepared for her. The kind man would occupy the baby while Emmie worked. The lethargy and breathlessness that had slowed her down these past months was lifting with the thought of Rab's imminent arrival. She sent a letter to Helen to relay the happy news.

On the day of Rab's release, Emmie got up early, unable to sleep. While walking down to the river, she heard a commotion of birds in the woods. She looked up to see rooks scattering into open sky and wondered what had disturbed them. Her heart leaped. Perhaps the Kennedys were returning early. How pleased they would be to hear of Rab's release. What a special day this was. But the birds settled and silence descended again. Glancing up during the day from weeding, Emmie did not see any telltale sign of smoke to show the camp was once again inhabited, nor did Ned rush down to seek out Barny.

Yet, that day and the next, she could not shake off the feeling that a presence was there, that she was being watched. With Mr Calvert away for so long, there had been poachers and scavengers over the months and it was possible other travellers or out-of-work drifters might have chanced upon the sheltered spot. She felt more vulnerable than ever before and longed for the day Rab would be back to help her shoulder the burden.

Though there was no sign of anyone camping in the woods, Emmie told Barny to stay closer to the cottages, for he was apt to wander upriver to make dens or observe the wildlife. Some day soon, she would have to think about sending him to school, perhaps down in Standale with Ned when he returned in the early summer.

Two days later, the telegram arrived with the news that Rab's train would reach Durham at two thirty on Monday the fifth. 'Needs plenty rest,' it ended. Emmie had a pang of alarm at the state Rab would be in. The journey might exhaust him further. She abandoned plans to take Barny to meet him.

'He might need to rest for a night before coming on here,' she explained.

Barny howled in disappointment, demanding to come too.

'I need you to be a big lad and help Laurie with the fire and looking after Mary,' Emmie cajoled. 'I'll be back as quick as can be.'

Barny continued to protest. 'I want to see Rab! Want to see the train. It's not fair!'

Emmie was about to give in when Laurie intervened.

'Haway, Barny, we'll go trapping in the woods, catch

336

something for tea. Show Rab you're a proper huntsman, eh? Just you and me. He'll be that proud of you. And it's better than travelling all day – as soon as you're there you'll be turning round and coming back again.'

Barny was mollified. Yet he showed his annoyance with Emmie by refusing to kiss her goodbye or help Philip with Cobbles when he took her down to the station. Emmie cuddled Mary and handed her over to Laurie. She waved, but Barny turned his back and ran off down to the river. Emmie felt a stab of guilt for leaving him.

'Don't worry,' Philip comforted, 'things will be easier once Rab's back with us. You're not the only one who's missed him.'

Emmie smiled and slipped her arm through his. Her old friend had lost everything, yet had managed to rekindle his optimism. Now they could all look to building a new life with Rab and the children. Perhaps they could persuade Helen and Peter to join them.

Emmie's excitement grew as the train trundled down the valley to Durham. She arrived in the city with half an hour to spare. Wandering out into the town, she experienced a wave of nostalgia for the days before the war when she had marched through these streets at the galas and for women's emancipation, planning for a glorious future. Yet, at twenty-six she was still disenfranchised, and Rab and Laurie were denied a vote for five years because of their opposition to the war. As she hurried back into the station, Emmie was filled with a new restlessness. She had been in isolation for too long, just trying to stay alive. She should be doing more to help bring about a new society. Revolution was sweeping Europe and workers all over the country were agitating for better conditions. She and Rab must be a part of it.

Standing at the barrier, she watched the London train pull in. Doors clattered open and porters rushed forward to lift down luggage. Passengers swarmed up the platform and passed through the gate. She saw a thin elderly man being helped down from a carriage, clutching a cap and carrying a small cardboard case. As he turned, she caught the familiar outline of nose and chin. Her heart thumped in shock. It was Rab, grey-faced and head shaven. His ill-fitting suit hung loose around his shrunken frame. He looked twice his age.

Emmie gulped down her horror and waved. He came slowly, almost shuffling, his look anxious as he scanned the crowd at the barrier. When he came through the gate, they stood staring for a long moment, too emotional for words. Then Emmie put out her arms. Rab held on to the case as she hugged him, his body stiff and lifeless.

'Rab,' she whispered his name, pained at the lack of recognition in his sunken eyes, 'it's Emmie.'

'Emmie?'

'Aye, it's me,' she answered, tears brimming. She touched his face gently. He flinched.

'Emmie,' he repeated the name like a talisman, 'Emmie.'

She slipped an arm through his. 'Haway, let's go for a cup of tea.'

She led him out of the station, hoping the sight of familiar streets would jolt his memory. But he became breathless quickly and she steered him into the nearest café, ordering tea and toast with precious money saved for an emergency. As they waited for their snack, Emmie took his bony hands in hers and caressed them. She spoke softly of the commune, of his old friends, of Barny and saw a flicker of interest cross his gaunt face.

He struggled to speak, but she could not make out his words.

'Did you get any of my letters?' Emmie asked.

He looked at her blankly as if he could not remember.

'Did Mr Calvert tell you anything?' she asked. Again he looked uncomprehending.

She squeezed his hands. 'You have a daughter, Mary Helen. A bonny daughter, with dark hair like Barny's, but your blue eyes.'

For the first time, Rab's eyes focused properly and Emmie knew he understood.

'M–Mary,' he whispered. His cracked, colourless lips curved into a half-smile.

'Aye, Mary,' Emmie smiled back. 'She had her first birthday last month. And she's already walking. Babbles away in her own language. I can't wait for you to see her.'

'Me an' all,' Rab said hoarsely.

Emmie gulped in relief. Already she was seeing flashes of the old Rab under the guise of this confused, frail man. She abandoned any idea of staying longer in Durham. Rab needed to get home where she could nurse him and the liveliness of the children could lift his battered spirits. She watched him let his tea grow cold before he drank it. The toast he hardly touched, so she ate it hungrily.

Slowly they made their way back to the station and on to a train for Standale, choosing an empty carriage. Emmie talked to him all the way about what she knew of his mother and Peter, of Mabel dying and Laurie returning to them. She avoided mention of Tom or Barnabas Cullen's threatening letter. Rab seemed too fragile to take in that much so soon. Instead she talked of Barny and his firm friendship with Ned, and how the Kennedys would be returning any day.

'The lad was that cross at not coming to see you,' Emmie said, 'but I thought it might be too much for you all at once.' She eyed him cautiously.

Rab took her hand and studied it, as if it was something exotic. She saw the effort it took for him to speak.

'I – love you,' he rasped.

Emmie's heart soared. She leaned over and kissed him in the empty carriage.

'I love you too,' she whispered tearfully.

At Standale there was no way of alerting Mr Runcie to their return. A strong westerly wind had got up and Emmie feared Rab was too frail for the uphill walk to The Grove. But he brushed aside her concerns and took the path out of the village. He laboured up the steep fell, his breathing ragged, and Emmie made him stop to rest at frequent intervals and drink the water she had brought. The sun had dipped behind the hills by the time they reached the wooded overgrown drive.

Rab galvanised himself for one last effort, forcing himself on, driven by the thought of seeing Barny and his new daughter. They emerged from the woods on to the grassy bank above the cottages. Emmie listened out for the sound of her children's voices, but all was quiet.

'Laurie must have them in bed already,' she grinned.

Rab did not move. He stood staring at the familiar scene of river, corrugated roofs and narrow gardens. With alarm, Emmie saw tears streaming down his face as he choked back a sob.

She took his hand. 'Don't upset yourself.'

He shook his head. 'This place,' he wheezed, 'I saw it in my dreams. The colours – it's almost too much. I haven't seen grass –

seems like a lifetime.' He stopped, exhausted by trying to explain.

Emmie leaned up and kissed his sunken cheek. 'I understand,' she smiled. Slipping an arm through his, she led him down the bank towards their home.

Quietly, she entered the cottage, not wanting to wake the children if they were already asleep. All was quiet. She put down Rab's case. Peering into the gloom, she could not make out a shape in Barny's bed. She glanced at the big bed, but he had not crawled in there either. Puzzled, Emmie went to look in the cot. It was empty. She felt the first stirrings of unease.

She turned to Rab. 'They must be in the other cottage – maybe Mary wouldn't settle.'

Emmie went quickly, not waiting for Rab to follow. She called out to her friends.

'Hello! We're back!'

The door to the Runcies' opened and Philip stared out in alarm.

'It's all right,' Emmie reassured, 'it's only me. Look, Rab's here!'

'My dear boy.' Mr Runcie came forward, seized his hand in a firm shake and clapped him on the shoulder. 'Come away, come away.'

He seemed agitated, glancing around nervously.

'The bairns are with you?' Emmie queried.

Philip avoided her look. 'Please come inside.'

Emmie rushed in ahead of the others. The room was lit by the rush lamps that the Kennedys had taught them to make. Laurie was sitting in a chair by the fire. He stood up the moment he saw her, his arm in a sling. Even in the dim light she could see the cuts and bruising around his left eye.

'What's happened?' she gasped. 'Where are the bairns?'

Laurie gulped. 'He came to fetch them. I tried to stop him, but he was too strong. Knocked me down. I didn't—'

'Who?' Emmie demanded, yet the dread inside told her who.

'Tom Curran,' Laurie said, almost in tears. 'I'm sorry, Emmie, I'm so sorry.'

She swung round and faced Philip. 'Barny? The baby?'

'He took them both,' the old man said. 'I couldn't stop him – he attacked Laurie.'

Emmie pressed her hands to her head, crying out in horror. 'No! It can't be true. My babies. Please, no!'

'When did it happen?' Rab asked hoarsely.

'Just after Emmie left,' Philip replied.

'It's like he was watching,' Laurie said, 'waiting for the right moment.'

'The coward!' Emmie cried. 'Why didn't he face me?'

'Wanted to know where you'd gone,' Laurie said unhappily. 'I didn't want to tell him.'

'He knows about Rab getting out?' Emmie demanded.

Laurie nodded.

Philip explained, 'He forced Laurie to tell – he had a gun, Emmie. He was so angry I feared he would use it.'

Emmie was shaking violently. Rab reached out to hold her.

'I'll go after him, bring them back,' he panted.

She pushed him off. 'Don't be daft – you can hardly stand. Tom would kill you.'

Shock was followed as quickly by a sudden rage. How dare he take her children? Tom did not love them – Mary was not even his. Madness and spite were all that drove him. Well, nothing would stop her getting her children back.

'I'm the one that's ganin' after him,' she declared savagely.

CHAPTER 38

The nearer Emmie drew to Crawdene, the greater she dreaded it. Only the thought of seeing her children again spurred her on up the bank. She had been travelling since early light, walking into Standale to save their ancient pony, leaving Rab sleeping an exhausted sleep. She had left before he woke, not wanting to risk another confrontation.

'You'll not go on your own to face that man,' he had fretted, both knowing that she would.

He was too ill, Philip too frail and Laurie too injured. Besides, she wanted her friends to stay and tend to Rab.

'I want you to get well again,' Emmie had countered. 'I need you to be strong, Rab, not dead,' she had added bluntly.

He had faced her bleakly. 'Are you coming back, Emmie?'

'Course I am. Why shouldn't I?'

'You once said you'd go back to Tom if it meant keeping Barny,' he reminded her.

She had turned away. 'It won't come to that,' she answered brusquely. 'I'm bringing the bairns home, not stopping in Crawdene.'

Now, as she trudged up the steep bank, fixing her sight on the familiar skyline of pithead and hunched terraces, her heart banged in fear at the ordeal ahead. Emmie decided suddenly to go to Mannie's and seek out Helen. She would ask Rab's mother to go with her so she did not have to face the Currans alone.

Emmie tried to ignore the looks of astonishment and curiosity from passers-by as she hurried up the main street. One or two raised a hand in half greeting, then stopped self-consciously. Others were openly hostile.

'Fancy her showing her face round here,' one woman declared to her companion, not attempting to lower her voice.

'Aye, the cheek of it,' the other agreed.

Emmie ploughed on, red-faced. At the turning to India Street, a man blocked her way. She recognised him as a workmate of Tom's, a chapel member.

'Let you out of prison, have they?' he sneered. 'Too soon, if you ask me.'

Emmie tried to pass. He stepped in front of her again.

'Crawling back, are you? I doubt Tom'll have you. Soiled goods, from what I hear. MacRae's fancy woman.'

'Let me past,' Emmie demanded.

'You're a disgrace to this village,' he said, spitting at her feet as he walked away.

Emmie hurried on, gulping down her panic. For the first time she felt fear for her own safety. She could only guess at the rumours that must be flying around the village about her and Rab. They were already vilified by many for being pacifists, criminals who had been imprisoned. But that was nothing to the censure they would face for being adulterous, no matter that her husband was violent and abusive.

She rushed into Mannie's yard. The brick paving was cracked and choked with weeds, the outhouse that had once been Rab's printing works was half fallen in. The back door was bleached in the sun, its dark red paint peeled away. An air of neglect hung over the ramshackle house. Emmie knocked and opened the door. Inside, Helen's room was half bare of furniture, the table and chairs gone, but the floor was scrubbed clean and a jam jar of bluebells adorned the work bench under the window. Emmie nearly burst into tears to see them, a sign that Helen's spirit was not broken.

She went outside and knocked at Mannie's door. When she was on the point of giving up, the door opened and the old man hobbled out. His puzzled look cleared as recognition dawned. They clasped each other in delight.

'By, lass, it's good to see you,' he croaked. 'Helen's been that worried about you. The things we've heard . . . Some say you're back in prison, others that you're on the street.'

'But I wrote and told her all was well — that Rab was gettin' out,' Emmie protested.

'Rab's free?' Mannie cried. 'We didn't get any letter.'

Emmie quickly explained why she had come. 'Tom's stolen my bairns,' she said bitterly. 'I want Helen to come with me to get them back.'

Mannie's face clouded. 'She works at the manse — cleaning for the Attwaters. Takes Peter with her — his nerves are bad since he came home last month. Mr Speed wouldn't take him back.' He gave her a sorrowful look. 'Emmie, don't get your hopes up. The Currans aren't going to hand over the children just 'cos you ask them. And you being with Rab — well, people round here don't approve.'

He glanced away, embarrassed. 'It's not been easy for Helen — you've caused a bit of a scandal, if truth be told. She's lucky to get the Attwater job — minister's more forgiving than most of his congregation.'

Emmie bristled. 'It's nothing to do with Helen. People shouldn't hold it against her.'

'Aye, but they do,' Mannie said, his look awkward.

Emmie saw that her presence was making him uneasy, for all that he was pleased to see her. She would have to face the Currans alone.

'Tell Helen and Peter I called,' she said, turning away, her heart sore.

'Aye, lass, take care of yourself,' Mannie called after her. 'And all the very best to Rab!'

She felt a wave of loneliness as she left India Street. How she had wanted to feel Helen's comforting arms about her, as protective and loving as when she was a child. But what Rab and she had done had made Helen an outcast in her own village. She felt ashamed, despite her love for Rab. But more, she felt mounting fear that her mission to reclaim her children was hopeless.

Emmie forced herself to carry on round to Berlin Terrace. Only the thought of seeing Barny and Mary gave her the courage to knock at her old door. There was no reply. She tried to open it, but the door was locked. Peering through the dirty window, she saw her old kitchen was in shadow, no fire burning in the grate. It looked unlived in. As she contemplated going round to the front of the house to try the other door, a woman appeared at the upstairs window.

'What you want?' she called. Emmie did not recognise her.

'Where's Tom Curran?' Emmie demanded.

'At his mam's,' the woman answered. 'No one's lived there since his missus ran off with a conchie.' Then she slammed down the window before Emmie could ask any more questions.

With mounting dread, Emmie made her way up the village to Denmark Street. She wondered if she was imagining the gathering of lads on the street corner, the muttering of women at their doors as she passed. Was word spreading that quickly that the notorious Emmie Curran was back?

Her heart was pounding so fast as she approached the Currans' she could hardly breathe. But perhaps she would be lucky. Barnabas would be at work and maybe Tom would be too. She had no idea if he was back working at the pit. She would appeal to Louise and her mother to let the children go.

Emmie rapped on the door with the gleaming knocker. After a long moment of waiting, Louise answered. They stood staring at each other.

'What you here for?' her sister-in-law asked in hostility.

'You know what.' Emmie kept calm.

'Tom doesn't want to see you.'

'That suits me,' Emmie replied. 'It's me bairns I want to see.'

'You can't,' Louise said dismissively. 'Our Tom won't allow it.'

'Let me in, Louise, please,' Emmie said urgently. When Louise hesitated, Emmie pushed past her.

'Mam! Tom!' Louise shouted in panic. 'Emmie's here. I couldn't stop her.'

Emmie burst into the parlour, searching for her children. 'Barny?' she called out. The room was empty. She rushed into the kitchen, Louise trying to grab her by the arm.

Mrs Curran rose startled from her chair, her mending falling to the floor.

'Emmie . . .'

'Where are they?' Emmie demanded. 'I want to see my children.'

'Hush, you'll wake them,' Mrs Curran said in a fluster. 'They're having a nap.'

Emmie turned to rush from the room and make for the stairs.

But just as she reached the door, a tousled-haired figure loomed over her. Tom pushed her back in the kitchen, his face creased from sleep, his look belligerent.

'Wondered how long it would take you to come,' he sneered. 'On your own, are you? Lover boy too scared to face me, eh?'

His face was fuller, a boozer's face with a purplish nose, his once handsome eyes bleary and faded. Like Rab he had aged, but not with malnutrition and hard labour. He looked as physically strong as ever, but his face was scored with bitterness and disappointment.

'Tom, let me see the bairns,' she pleaded.

He opened wide his arms. 'No kiss hello for your husband first?' he mocked. 'Show a bit respect, eh?'

'For a man who beats his wife?' Emmie said in disdain.

'Don't speak to our Tom like that.' Louise was indignant.

'But it's true, isn't it, Tom?' Emmie challenged.

'You got above yourself,' Tom snapped. 'But that's all in the past. I'm willing to forgive you – seeing as you've come back like a dutiful missus.'

'You're never going to take her back, are you?' Louise cried in dismay. 'She's shamed us all.'

'I'll do what I want!' Tom shouted suddenly.

'Tom, dear—' his mother began.

'I haven't come back,' Emmie interrupted. 'I've just come for my children.' She appealed to Tom. 'They need their mam, surely you see that? They're too young to be without me. If you love Barny you'll let him come to me.'

For a moment she thought he was wavering, then the hard look returned. 'You're not fit to be their mam,' he hissed. 'I've seen the way you live – like savages in that dirty little cottage – and with those men. Do you whore for them an' all, Emmie, or just for MacRae?'

Emmie flinched at his invective. 'Stop it, Tom.'

'I'm taking care of the bairns now. They don't want to see you and I don't want you coming anywhere near them again. Not unless you repent of your sins and come back to me like an obedient wife should,' he challenged.

Emmie stared at him in horror. In that moment she knew she could never go back to him under any conditions. She despised the person he had become. She would wither under his harsh rule. And with a wave of despair, she realised that she could not subject her children to such a loveless home. Emmie remembered suddenly how terrified Barny had been at the violence in Berlin Terrace. Barny and Mary must not be brought up in such a climate of fear.

'I'll never come back to you, Tom,' Emmie declared.

Just at that instant, a muffled wail came from the room above. Emmie's heart jerked.

'Mary!' she cried. 'Let me go to her.'

'No.' Tom gave her a savage look of triumph. 'You take one step and I'll take me belt to yer.'

'Please, Tom.' Emmie was on the verge of tears as her baby's crying grew more insistent. 'She needs her mam – I'm still feedin' her myself.'

Louise said, 'She's taken fine to the bottle.'

Emmie ignored her. 'Let me take the baby,' she begged, 'please, Tom.'

But Tom's expression did not alter.

'How come you never bothered to tell Tom he had a lass?' Louise needled. 'Didn't bother to tell any of us.'

Mary was bawling now. Emmie turned to her mother-in-law in distress. 'Please go to her,' she pleaded. 'She needs a cuddle.'

Mrs Curran looked anxious but said, 'She's fed and changed; there's nothing she needs. Best let her cry. Too much fussing spoils a child. And I'll not have a grandbairn of mine brought up spoiled.'

Emmie's nerves snapped. 'She's not your grandbairn!'

They all stared at her. Tom prodded her with a finger. 'Meaning?' he glowered.

Emmie faced up to him. 'Meaning Mary is Rab's daughter, not yours.'

Louise and her mother gasped in shock. Tom glared at her in disbelief. In an instant he raised his hand and struck her across the face.

'Whore!' he bellowed.

Emmie staggered then righted herself. She dug her nails in her palms to stop herself crying.

'So you'll let me take her?' she demanded. 'You can't want Rab's bairn, can you?'

'Get out!' Tom roared, seizing her by the arm and dragging her forward. 'Get out of this house and never come back!'

He yanked her into the corridor. Emmie cried out at the pain as he wrenched her arm. Suddenly there was a noise on the stair behind.

'Mammy?'

She swivelled to see Barny at the top of the stair in his underclothes.

'Barny!' she yelled.

'Mammy!' her son cried. 'Don't go, Mammy!'

'Get back upstairs,' Tom shouted, 'or I'll skin yer backside.'

Emmie struggled to throw Tom off as the boy screamed for her not to leave him. But Tom was too strong and in a moment was throwing her out of the door and down the steps. He slammed the door in her face and bolted it shut. Emmie hammered on it.

'Give me back my bairns!' she screamed.

A crowd of onlookers began to gather in the street, but Emmie did not care. She banged her fists and bawled like a madwoman, but to no avail. Inside she could hear Barny crying and Tom shouting, but no one came to let her in again.

People began to call at her to keep the noise down, to go away. Someone threatened to fetch the police. But Emmie clung to the doorstep, unable to leave, quite hysterical. Finally someone pushed their way through the baiting crowd.

'Out the way – let me pass!'

Suddenly Helen was reaching out and snatching her with protective arms.

'Emmie! Come away, pet.'

Emmie grabbed on to Rab's mother, babbling incoherently about her children.

'There's nothing you can do about it now,' Helen said firmly. 'Don't let Barny hear you – you'll just upset him more. Come with me, pet.'

Emmie responded to Helen's calm voice, allowing herself to be led away. They were jostled as Helen hurried her down the street, people calling out their disapproval.

Back at Mannie's, Helen made her drink tea and calm down. Peter eyed her nervously from the doorway. The sight of Rab's brother made Emmie more composed.

'Peter,' she said, holding out her hands to him, 'it's grand to see you.'

But he stayed where he was, silent and watching.

'Doesn't speak much,' Helen said quietly, 'doesn't play his tin whistle – doesn't do much of anything, poor lad.'

Peter slipped away. Emmie and Helen looked at each other, quite at a loss.

'I'd hoped to take you and Peter back with me,' Emmie whispered, 'as well as the bairns.'

Helen sighed. 'At least here I have a job of sorts. And maybe one day, Peter's nerves will get better and he can work again.'

'What should I do, Auntie Helen?' Emmie asked forlornly. 'I can't bear the thought of leaving and not being near the bairns. If I stayed here with you a bit, I'd have the chance of seeing them, wouldn't I?'

Helen gave her a pitying look. 'Currans will never let you near them, you know that. And feelings are running too high in the village – best to stay away.' She took Emmie's empty cup. 'You and Rab – you've still got each other. He needs you now more than ever. Do you still want him?'

Emmie held her look and nodded.

'Then go back to him. Get your strength back, the pair of you,' Helen encouraged. 'Maybe Tom will get tired of the bairns and hand them back.' She put a hand on Emmie's head and stroked back her hair as if she were a young girl again.

'I'll keep an eye out for Barny and Mary,' she promised. 'And Mrs Curran and Louise are not bad people – they won't neglect your bairns.'

That night, Emmie shared the bed with Helen. Emmie had suggested to Peter that she take him back to The Grove for a visit, thinking the place would do him good.

'You could help with Cobbles, Mr Runcie's old pony – and it would lift Rab's spirits to see you.'

But Peter had shaken his head and turned his back on her. Emmie had hidden her disappointment; somehow this silent rejection by the once-affectionate Peter hurt her more than Tom's cruel words.

The next morning, the women rose early, breakfasted and prepared for Emmie's journey. Helen packed her a hard-boiled egg, bread and a bottle of cold tea. They hugged each other tight.

349

'Look after that son of mine,' Helen smiled tearfully, 'and I'll look out for yours.'

Emmie nodded, too choked to speak. She left the village with a heavy heart and the intolerable thought of her children waking at the Currans' without her. At the road junction with Blackton, she stopped and glanced back for a final view of Crawdene.

The pit was wreathed in smoke from dozens of coal fires; Oliphant's Wood shimmered with the fresh green of early summer. Perhaps Louise would take Barny there later in the day. Envy gnawed inside and the view blurred in sudden tears. Far away, the school bell beckoned the children to lessons. Emmie wiped her tears impatiently. She would not be beaten by this attempt to reclaim her children. As long as she lived, she would go on fighting for the right to see them, the right to bring them up.

As her vision cleared, she saw two figures hurrying down the dirt road towards her. They were shouting something. Was it at her? Emmie turned away, not wanting to be confronted by more hostile villagers. Then she heard her name clearly.

'Emmie! Wait!'

Turning back, she recognised the familiar figures. Helen and Peter. She began to walk towards them, quickening her pace.

Reaching her, Helen panted, 'The lad wants to come with you after all.'

Emmie looked at Peter in surprise. He nodded and gave a half-smile directly at her. It was his first sign of friendliness, a glimmer of the old Peter.

'That's grand!' Emmie exclaimed.

Helen nodded at her in encouragement. 'Aye, it is.' She kissed her son's cheek swiftly. 'You do as Emmie says and be a help to her,' she ordered. 'And here,' she pressed his tin whistle into his jacket pocket, 'you might want this.'

The women smiled at each other in understanding. Peter would be a comfort to Emmie and Rab, and in return they would try to heal his wounded mind.

Emmie set off, her sore heart eased a fraction by Peter's mute companionship.

CHAPTER 39

1920

Peter's short stay drifted into the following year. Gradually, he regained confidence in handling horses, helping the Kennedys with theirs when they returned to the woods. Eventually he spent all day with the tinkers and they accepted him as one of their own, taking him off to local fairs and to help them picking in the fields when the harvest came. It gave Emmie bitter-sweet pleasure to see Peter's friendship develop with Ned, how they splashed in the river and explored together the way that Barny had done.

To see Peter flourish once more was her one consolation. As soon as she had returned to The Grove, word had come that Tom wanted a divorce, citing her adultery with Rab. Knowing how appalled the Currans would be at the scandal, Emmie realised just how much Tom must hate her to go through with it. But Tom knew how to hurt her most. Emmie cared little for the public humiliation, but the repercussions for the children were devastating. The courts upheld Tom's right to take both her children from her for good, convinced by his insistence that Mary was his too.

It was like bereavement, yet worse. She could never see them again, yet they carried on living beyond her reach. Did they think of her? Did Mary even remember her now? What were they told – that she was dead, or that her sinfulness meant they must never come into contact? Daily, she tortured herself with thoughts of them. Helen's infrequent notes told her little, save that her children were still alive and healthy. Rab's mother was not allowed to visit them either.

It poisoned Emmie's relationship with Rab, each riddled with guilt at what had happened. The divorce proceedings had come at a time when Rab needed her most, when she was still nursing him back to health. Should she have left him and fought harder for Barny and Mary? But the courts frightened Emmie. All she knew was that the law gave her no rights over her precious children. The only way she could have kept them would have been to beg Tom to take her back and submit to his rule. Perhaps that was what he really wanted, but Emmie knew she could not do it – not even for her children. It was this realisation that crippled her with guilt. Unable to admit this to anyone, least of all Rab, Emmie found herself incapable of loving him.

Rab recovered some of his old strength, but his spirit was blighted. He blamed himself for Emmie's grief, yet he resented her in some obscure way for not taking care of his daughter. If only she had stayed with the children and not come to meet him. But he knew this was destructive thinking. Tom would have taken them anyway, and maybe harmed Emmie, for she would have struggled like a vixen to keep them.

Yet sometimes Rab caught Emmie looking at him and he knew by her bleak expression that she regretted choosing him. It turned his heart cold. Without Emmie he was nothing, would not be living if she had not nurtured him back to life after his long imprisonment. But he could not tell her this, for they no longer spoke their feelings, fearful of spilling into angry recriminations. So Rab kept himself busy in the garden and spent time with the men. He and Emmie lived under the same roof, shared the same bed, but were like strangers to each other.

After the divorce, Emmie could hardly bear to be touched by Rab. She was consumed by guilt at abandoning her children. The haven at The Grove was turning into a bucolic prison from which there seemed no escape. She yearned once more to be campaigning for women's rights, among like-minded women. Yet Rab seemed to have lost his old passion for justice and social revolution. All that interested him was gardening and sharing cigarettes with Laurie.

Then in the autumn, things came to a head. Philip received a solicitor's letter informing him that Mr Calvert, their benefactor, had died. As he was childless, his estate passed to a distant cousin, who wished it to be sold. They all knew that sooner or later they would have to leave. One chilly October evening, they sat around the fire talking about what to do. The Kennedys were preparing to leave, uncertain as to whether they could use the woods again the following spring.

'I want to gan with them,' Peter declared.

The others exchanged looks.

'But your mam, Peter,' Emmie began, 'she'll want you home, won't she?'

'I'm happy with the horses,' Peter said stubbornly. 'Ned said I could gan when they do.'

'It's up to the Kennedys,' Rab shrugged. 'I don't see why he can't.'

'But what if he changes his mind?' Emmie worried. 'He won't know how to find us.'

'I'll find me way to Crawdene,' Peter answered. 'Mam'll tell me where you are.'

Emmie felt panic rise. She did not want Peter to go; he was someone for her to look after, a buffer between her and Rab.

'We'll have to ask your mam first,' she cautioned.

'He's a grown man,' Rab said in irritation.

Emmie glared at him. 'Aye, but he still needs someone to look out for him.'

'The Kennedys will look out for me,' Peter answered simply. 'Don't you worry, Emmie.'

Emmie bit her tongue and the others continued to discuss the future. Laurie suggested they might be able to find a smallholding down the valley and grow enough food to have a surplus to sell. They could hire themselves out at harvest. Emmie remained silent, until Philip asked for her opinion.

'I want to gan back to the town,' Emmie announced abruptly. 'We're not country people and I'm tired of living hand to mouth like this.' They stared at her in surprise. She tried to explain her restlessness. 'We're radicals – we should be doing more. I used to think this place was the Utopia we were looking for, but it's not. It was just a temporary refuge from the war. We should be getting stuck into our old campaigns,' she said with an impatient wave of the hand. 'Lasses my age still don't have the vote. Pitmen are having their wages cut. Schoolboys are being made to drill like soldiers ready for the next war. And what are we doing about it? Nowt!'

She swept them with a challenging look. 'Well, you can carry on playing at being peasants, but I'm ganin' back to Tyneside.'

That night as she lay sleepless, Rab asked, 'Do you want me to come with you, Emmie, or not?'

'Make up your own mind,' she said impatiently. 'You've always said we can come and go as we please. Free love – isn't that what you call it? Don't feel tied to me.'

'Is that how you feel – tied down?' Rab asked, his voice hardening. ''Cos it was never meant to be like that.'

'No, it was meant to be me and you and the bairns,' Emmie said, trembling, 'but that's never going to happen. There's nothing for me here any more. I hate this place without Barny and Mary – every day it reminds me of them. It's like having me heart ripped out!'

Rab sat up in agitation; she could sense him staring at her in the dark.

'And what about us, Emmie?' he demanded.

'I don't know,' she cried. 'As long as there was hope of gettin' the bairns back this is where I wanted to be – all of us together. But now there's no point in being here – we're just hiding away from the world outside. And if I can't be a mam to Barny and Mary, then I want to be of use in some other way. Why don't you feel like that, Rab? The man I fell in love with was going to change the world – our socialist Utopia – you lived and breathed it. Remember, Rab? What happened to all that?'

Rab struggled to speak. 'They beat us, Emmie. The militarists, the capitalists – they won. I gave every ounce of myself to the cause, but they bled me dry. I don't have the fight in me for any more. I just want to live in peace and quiet. Can't you understand that?'

Emmie felt bitter disappointment. 'No, I can't. We've all suffered, Rab. But striving for a better world is still the only thing that really matters. Jonas and Helen taught me that.' She added bleakly, 'A lad called Radical Rab taught me that.'

After a long silence, he said quietly, 'I'm sorry, Emmie. I'm going to stay here till I'm thrown off.'

Emmie's insides twisted. 'Why?'

''Cos it's the one place I've been really happy,' he whispered. 'Thinking of it kept me from going mad in prison.'

Emmie's eyes stung with tears. 'It was thinking of people – not places – that kept me sane,' she answered, turning away from him. Neither of them spoke again.

Peter left with the Kennedys the following week. By the end of the month, Emmie had packed up her few possessions. She and Philip were returning to Gateshead. A contact in the Women's International League was offering temporary rooms in her house for a month. Laurie was staying with Rab until the estate was sold.

On a raw November day, they all journeyed in the trap to Standale station. Emmie felt numb with failure. All her passion for Rab, her striving for a better life, had come to nothing. She was a divorced woman with a bundle of clothes to her name. Two locks of dark curly hair pressed inside a book of poems was all she had to remind her she was a mother and had once had a life full of joy and richness of spirit.

Everyone was subdued. Rab hardly looked at her as she climbed down from the cart and he handed over her bag. He sat holding the reins, his jaw tense, eyes empty of expression. Emmie felt a sudden urge to kiss his bearded face. All at once, she longed for him to put his arms about her. Why were they parting like strangers? Did they mean so very little to each other now? They had suffered so much together. If only he was coming with her, perhaps they could rekindle what they had lost. But he had made it plain he did not want to be with her and was no longer interested in their old radicalism.

She gulped, her mouth dry. 'Goodbye, Rab.'

He flicked her a look. Were his eyes bright with tears? She could not tell under the shadow of his cap.

'Bye, Emmie. Take care,' he murmured.

Philip returned from buying their tickets. He reached up and shook Rab by the hand. They nodded to each other. He clasped Laurie to him, then took Emmie by the arm and led her gently away. 'The train's in.'

Emmie did not look back, for fear of weeping openly. She stared out of the carriage window, watching the stone cottages of Standale disappear in a belch of smoke. With a huge effort, she concentrated on tomorrow. She would throw herself into real work once more and drive herself so hard, it would stifle the sadness that threatened to overwhelm her.

Rab handed the reins over to Laurie and said he would walk

back. Climbing above the village he peered for a final view of the train as it snaked its way down the valley. He thought his heart would burst with grief. How had he let Emmie go without even a proper goodbye? He had fought the impulse to grab her to him and embrace her in front of the others. Even at the last minute, if she had asked him to, he would have jumped on the train and gone with her. But she had not.

Emmie had been eager to get away. She no longer loved him and he could hardly blame her. For the rest of his life he would live with the guilt that her children had been stolen from her, because she had dared to love him.

On the empty fell, Rab cried out to the skylarks.

'Please forgive me, Emmie! I love you. I'll always love you!'

CHAPTER 40

1921

Early the following year, Emmie secured a clerical position at the offices of the ILP across the river in Elswick and Philip helped out occasionally with printing jobs. They earned enough between them to rent an upstairs flat in Sutton Street. Relentlessly Emmie drove herself, working long hours to fill the gaping emptiness she felt inside. She avoided other people's children and the agony of not seeing her own was often intolerable. Many's the time she set out for Crawdene, deluding herself that a glimpse of Barny and Mary would ease her pain. But she knew that it would be far worse to see them and not to hold them, than not see them at all. Tortured by such realisation, she stayed away.

It was in Sutton Street that Emmie and Philip learned of the new clinic and mission recently opened in Lemington, the next-door neighbourhood.

'They say it was started by conscientious objectors,' Philip told Emmie. 'But folk who are hungry and sick don't trouble over such matters.'

The next Sunday, Emmie and Philip attended the mission service out of curiosity. The service was under way by the time they got there. They peered in disbelief at the Anglican priest.

'It's Charles!' Philip cried aloud. 'Charles Oliphant!' Emmie gasped in delight too.

A woman at the front turned around to stare. Her grey-red hair framed a familiar face. It was Dr Flora.

'Emmie!' she exclaimed, and ignoring the shooshings of those

357

about her, rushed to greet her old friends. They sat together till the close of the service, Emmie and Flora arm in arm.

Afterwards, Flora and Charles took them to their small terraced house. Over lunch, they each told of all that had happened in the intervening years. Charles had been moved from the camp in Wales to one in Devon, then to East Anglia. Flora had wanted to keep in touch, but feared drawing the authorities' attention to the hideout at The Grove so had not written. They had tried to make a new life in East Anglia after the war, but both had been drawn back to Tyneside. The Gateshead Settlement had been sold and demolished for housing, so they had started the Lemington mission.

'Charles's dear mother left him a legacy in her will,' Flora explained, 'despite his father trying to withhold it. Sophie won him round. We used the money to come back here and start again. We tried to find you, but heard The Grove had been sold and everyone gone.'

Charles talked with enthusiasm about their new work. 'The clinic is often overwhelmed. Flora could do with more help. It benefits women and children the most. Would you be interested, Emmie?'

'Perhaps,' Emmie considered.

They did not press her, knowing how talk of other people's children must pain her.

When they made to leave, Flora took her aside.

'And Rab – do you hear from him at all?'

Emmie shook her head. 'I hoped he might come back when The Grove was sold. His mother knows where I am, but he hasn't been back to Crawdene either, as far as I know.'

'I'm so sorry, Emmie.' Flora hugged her.

It was the beginning of Emmie's revival of spirits to be reunited with her old friends. They had been through so much together that the bonds between them were stronger than most. They spent many evenings that summer walking in Elswick park discussing the issues of the day, or around Emmie's kitchen table over late suppers. As well as her office job, Emmie braced herself to help out at the clinic at weekends. In time, to her surprise, she found working with the sickly children eased her own loss. She began to campaign for better child and health care.

Flora and Charles persuaded her to stand in the local council elections as an ILP candidate and helped her campaign. To Emmie's amazement she was almost elected, only narrowly beaten by the Liberal who had served the ward for eight years.

That autumn, Emmie and Flora joined the League of Nations Union and helped in the early planning of a peace conference to be held the following year.

'It's concentrating on the suffering of women and children caused by war,' Emmie told Philip, who was now housebound by arthritis. 'You can help proofread this.' She handed him a typeset copy of a pamphlet called 'No More War'.

Emmie filled up every minute of every day and worked late into the evenings. She gave herself no time to dwell on her lost children or think about Rab. Most of the time she managed to smother any thoughts of them, as if they belonged to another life that was dead and gone. Only at night, in dreams, did they appear to her vivid and alive. She held them and kissed them, then woke bereft as they vanished. Sometimes her children were disappearing on trains and she was running to catch up with them but never did. Other times they stood at the bottom of her bed, silent and solemn, and asked her who she was. When she dreamed of Rab, he was always young, fit and laughing, with no gaunt looks or mental scars.

Emmie would cry in desolation after such dreams, but to the outside world she never showed a trace of the loss she carried inside.

In the spring of 1922, Emmie took leave from work and travelled with Flora down to London for the peace conference. At one of the fringe meetings, Emmie spoke. She appealed directly to women.

'We need to organise for peace, the way the militarists organise for war. It takes years. We must start now. We have to teach our children that there is no such thing as a war to end all wars. War always leads to more war – more killing, more widows, more orphans. They make our children honour Empire Day at school. Why don't we have a Peace Day? The warmongers have money and power and centuries of tradition behind them. What do we women have against all that? I'll tell you what! We have our bodies, our minds, our courage, our nurturing spirit. We are life-givers, not life-takers. We demand peace. We demand, no more war!'

Afterwards, a balding man came up to her and shook her by the hand.

'Ernie Tait. Well spoken, lass,' he smiled. 'I've heard you before – in Newcastle. Recognised the name. A lad I was in prison with used to talk of you.'

'Oh?' Emmie laughed. 'That's a strange recommendation.'

'We were COs together in the war,' he explained. 'I'm from Chopwell, so we palled up, him being a County Durham lad an' all.'

Emmie's heart missed a beat. 'Who was that?'

'Rab MacRae. Canny lad. You used to run a radical newspaper with him, didn't you? He told me all about it. Glad to see you're still involved in politics. Too many dropped out after the war – gone back to their own lives till it all happens again. But like you said, you have to plan for peace.'

Emmie nodded, flustered by the sudden mention of Rab. 'I'm afraid Rab lost the stomach for it too. Prison crushed his spirit.'

Ernie gave her a quizzical look. 'Radical Rab? Didn't look very crushed the last time I saw him.'

Emmie gave a start. 'You've seen Rab – recently?'

Ernie nodded.

'When? Where?'

'He's living in Chopwell – lot of radical lads like him round our way. Rab's trying to start a Communist Party branch. Went to Moscow last year,' he chuckled. 'He's blacklisted at the pit, mind.'

'How's he making a living?' Emmie asked, her heart thumping at the revelation.

'Doing a bit teaching. Lives like a gypsy in this old railway carriage in Chopwell Woods. Shall I tell him you were asking after him?'

Emmie swallowed, her mouth dry. 'Aye, tell him,' she murmured.

'Keep up the good work,' he nodded, and left her staring after him.

Flora found her sitting, shaking from the news.

'What on earth's the matter? You look pale as a ghost.'

'Rab's in Chopwell,' Emmie gasped. 'He's been in the area all this time, yet none of us knew – not even his mam. He's walking distance from Crawdene.'

'Will you go and see him?' Flora asked gently.

Emmie shook her head. 'He must want to be left alone – or he would have come to find me. Do you think Helen does know, but hasn't told me?'

'It's possible,' Flora sighed, 'if Rab asked her not to.'

Emmie swallowed the tears in her throat. 'He's joined the CP. At least he's found the fire in his belly again.'

'Dear Rab!' Flora exclaimed. She shook Emmie's shoulder gently. 'Go and see him. What's the harm in it?'

All the journey home, Emmie wrestled with the idea. She longed to see Rab again, yet feared his rejection. Why had he never tried to contact her? He must know where she was and what she was doing, for his friend Ernie Tait did. It must be because he did not want to. Rab had put that part of his life in the past, just as she was trying to do. If she turned up out of the blue, it might unleash painful memories that he preferred to keep deeply buried. She understood that. It was the same for her.

By the time they reached Newcastle, Emmie had decided against contacting Rab. Yet the encounter with Ernie Tait had been deeply unsettling. She made her way home, still dwelling on it, unable to push it from her mind. She would discuss it with Philip and see what he thought.

The old man greeted her in agitation.

'We have a visitor,' he gabbled. 'She's in your room. Came yesterday looking for you – insisted on coming back today. I'm sorry, Emmie, but it must be important and she wouldn't tell me.'

'Who is it?' Emmie asked in irritation, feeling exhausted.

'Young Mrs MacRae,' Mr Runcie said with an anxious look, 'Tom's sister.'

Emmie's insides lurched. Without taking off her hat or coat, she marched into the back room to confront Louise.

'Why are you—'

'Oh, Emmie!' Louise sprang from the bed, cutting off her indignant question. 'I had to come. I didn't know what else to do. It's terrible what's happening.'

'Calm down,' Emmie cried. 'What's terrible? Has something happened to one of the children?' Her breath stopped in her throat.

Louise stared in fear, a hand over her trembling lips.

'Tell me!' Emmie commanded. Louise dissolved into tears.

Emmie steered her back to the bed. 'Please, try and say what you came to say,' she pleaded more gently.

Louise took a deep gulp. 'It's Tom – he's not right in the head. We've been looking after the bairns – honest we have, Emmie – I've tret them like me own.'

Emmie felt a stab of jealousy, but said nothing, nodding for her to go on.

'But then that woman came back,' Louise said with distaste, 'and now he won't let us see Barny or Mary. Says he's ganin' to marry her and give them a proper mam. But she doesn't care two pins for the bairns – just wants Tom's wages and a roof over her head. Common as muck. And they drink like fish. I go round and she won't let me in. She comes into the shop drunk and orders me around—'

'*Who*, Louise?' Emmie demanded in agitation. 'Who is she?'

Louise's look was distraught. 'Nell – your sister.'

Emmie felt her legs turn to water. She groped for the bed and sat down.

'Nelly's got my bairns?' Emmie whispered in disbelief.

Louise nodded. 'She's turned Tom against his own family. Me father tried to reason with him – went round to fetch the children for chapel – but Tom attacked him – broke his jaw.' Louise began to sob. 'Tom's always out drinking since he took up with Nell – neglects the bairns. The truanting officer's been round twice for Barny – and there's never any washing hanging out. They live in a pigsty.'

Emmie felt leaden. 'And what do you expect me to do about it?' she asked bitterly. 'You've kept me away from me own son and daughter for three years, remember?'

'I know,' Louise said in distress, 'and I'm sorry, Emmie, truly I am. It was wrong of us – I see that now. I was that jealous of you having bairns – I wanted a bit of what you had. I've always wanted what you've had,' Louise confessed, 'ever since we were lasses. You seemed that happy with the MacRaes – always having a laugh.'

'Oh, Louise!' Emmie said in despair. Her deep resentment of her former friend turned to pity at her pathetic, tear-swollen face. How sad to think Louise had harboured such childish envy all these years.

Louise sniffed. 'Will you talk to Tom? You're the only one he's ever listened to. He might come to his senses. You could tell Nell to go.'

'Tom stopped listening to me years ago,' Emmie said, 'and Nell will do exactly the opposite of anything I suggest.'

'Then take the bairns!' Louise urged. 'Something has to be done.'

Emmie stood up. 'Aye, something does.' She touched Louise's shoulder and summoned up forgiving words. 'You were right to come – it must have taken all your courage.'

She took her sister-in-law through to the kitchen and made her eat before she left. It was mid-afternoon when Louise set off for the station.

'Will you come back with me now?' Louise asked.

Emmie shook her head. 'I have something I must do first.'

She went to seek out Flora, explaining everything and asking her to look in on Philip that night.

'Let Charles go with you,' Flora urged.

But Emmie refused, assuring her friend she would be careful. Then she set out for Chopwell.

CHAPTER 41

The sky was darkening and a squall hit as she entered the shelter of newly budding trees. A grocery van – a converted army ambulance – had given her a lift as far as the village, the driver pointing her east to the wagon way that cut through Chopwell Woods.

'Will you be all right?' he asked her anxiously.

Emmie nodded. 'I'm visiting an old comrade.'

'Rab MacRae?' he questioned.

'Aye.'

When she tried to pay for her lift, he waved her away. 'A friend of MacRae's is a friend of mine – he taught me mam to read.'

In the gloom, she almost missed the green-painted carriage nestling under a large oak and half covered in briars. It was the smell of wood smoke that drew her to the hidden dwelling. She had a sudden vivid memory of the cottage at The Grove – the smell of the wood stove, Barny and Rab fixing a fishing line in the doorway to catch the last of the light.

'Anybody there?' Emmie called out. She knocked. All was silent. She hesitated then opened the door and called again. Still there was no answer. Emmie went in.

It was surprisingly roomy: a stove, a bed, a table with a lamp unlit, a solitary chair and a wall of shelves full of books and cooking pots. With a pang, Emmie saw a volume of poetry on a pile of sheet music by the bed. A world of words and music set in a forest – Rab's world. Feeling like an intruder, she turned to leave when she heard a twig snapping under a boot outside.

Moments later, Rab was ducking through the door. He gasped in surprise at the shadowy figure.

'Who— Emmie, is that you?'

'Aye, it is,' she gulped. 'I'm sorry, the door was open . . .'

They stared at each other, completely lost for words. Rab moved first. He pulled out matches and crossed to the table, carefully lighting the lamp. Its weak blue flame shed a ghostly light.

'Sit down, please.' He indicated the bed. 'Don't have a comfy chair, sorry.'

Emmie perched on the edge, watching him pour them stewed tea from a pot on the stove. He handed her a tin mug. Her hands were shaking as she took it. She had planned to tell him straight away about the children, beg his help in freeing them; now she did not know how to begin. He would think she was just using him, and perhaps she was. She had not worked out what she would do beyond the rescue.

She sipped at the strong tea. Rab turned up the lamp until it glowed a warm yellow, chasing back the shadows. He had lost his gaunt, haunted look. His beard was fuller, his broad shoulders filling his jacket once more. The sudden swell of emotion Emmie felt for him was so strong, she had to look away. Glancing at the floor, she saw a pile of newspapers and leaflets. It was just like his room in India Street. He followed her look.

'There are some of yours in there,' he grunted.

'Mine?' Emmie queried.

'Campaign leaflets – from when you stood for the council. And articles you wrote before the peace conference. You're doing well, Emmie.'

She flushed in amazement. He had followed her at a distance, not forgotten her.

'And you've joined the Communists. I met Ernie Tait at the conference.'

'So that's how you found me,' Rab said, scrutinising her over the rim of his mug.

'You didn't want to be found, did you?' Emmie questioned.

Rab put down his mug. 'You were getting on with your life, Emmie, just like you said you would. I didn't want to stop any of that.'

'But to be living here all this time and not even let me

know . . . I didn't even know if you were still alive!' she accused.

He shifted uneasily. 'For a time I hardly was,' he murmured, 'after you went away. I nearly gave up, Emmie. Then Laurie got sick of me — said he was joining the CP and I could go with him or stay and rot in self-pity.' Rab gave a sudden snort of laughter. 'We ended up on this trip to Moscow, the pair of us. Worked on a collective farm for a month. Laurie met this lass on the way back — he's still in Berlin, as far as I know.'

'Why did you come back?' Emmie asked. 'No lass for you?'

He leaned towards her, his gaze steady. 'There's never been any lass but you, Emmie.'

She felt her heart twist. Trembling, she stood up and put her mug on the table.

'Then why did you never come and find me?' she challenged.

''Cos you stopped loving me,' he said simply, 'and I couldn't blame you. I didn't love the man I'd become either — couldn't see beyond my own troubles. Not like you, Emmie. You take on everyone's burdens. I had to learn how to care again — love again.'

Emmie swallowed. 'So that's why you came here — to be on your own — sort yourself out?'

'Partly,' Rab admitted. 'But also to be near you.'

'I don't understand,' Emmie puzzled.

Rab's voice was low and intense. 'I couldn't be with you but, being here, I could be near your bairns — my bairn. I'd been the cause of your separation, but at least I could keep an eye on them for you. I take an evening class once a week in Crawdene — I watch Barny come out of school and he waves to me.'

Emmie was stunned. 'You've seen Barny!'

'Aye, and the wee lass. As bonny as you, is our Mary. I spoke to her once when she was blackberry picking.'

Emmie cried out, 'Oh, Rab!' She stumbled towards him, holding out her arms.

Catching her, he pulled her to him. They clung on tight, Emmie sobbing into his shoulder.

'Our daughter, our bonny lass,' she wept. 'That's why I came. Louise told me Tom's out of control. She fears for the children. Nell's got them. Did you know about Nell?'

'Aye,' Rab admitted.

Emmie pulled away. 'Since when?'

Rab held on to her. 'Your sister came back last year. I told

Mam to say nothing to you. She wasn't happy keeping you in the dark, but I knew how upsetting it would be – and you could do nothing about it. But recently it's been getting worse. I confronted Nell – offered her money if she'd tret them right. She just laughed in my face – said they were Tom's problem not hers.' His grip tightened as he grew agitated in the retelling. 'I went to Sergeant Graham, but he told me to stay away, said it was up to Tom how he brings up his own.'

Emmie groaned. 'Rab, help me save them!'

He hugged her again and kissed her hair. 'I'll do anything you ask me, Emmie.'

Tearfully, Emmie reached up and kissed him.

'I need you more than ever,' she whispered tenderly. 'I've never stopped loving you, *never*. Please believe me.'

Rab gave an exultant cry and kissed her back. His embrace was passionate and tender and full of longing. He was light-headed at having found her again.

Finally, Emmie pulled away. 'Tonight, Rab – we must go tonight. I can't wait any longer.'

By the time they walked into Crawdene it was completely dark. The black, rain-laden sky was moonless. They made straight away to Berlin Terrace. Emmie walked into her own home by the back door and was immediately hit by the smell: dampness, rotting food, urine. The kitchen was cold, the fire out, the only light coming from a candle on the table. It spluttered in the sudden draught, nearly out.

Rab took another from the mantelpiece and lit it. The house sounded deserted.

'Tom?' Emmie called boldly. 'Nell?'

Rab held up the candle, illuminating the unwashed crockery piled on the table, the clothes strewn over chairs, the hearth covered in ash and cigarette ends, the empty bottles.

'The bedroom,' Emmie urged, pushing Rab gently towards the closed door.

It was locked. Rab noticed a bolt high up and pulled it back. It had never been there in Emmie's time. They pushed open the door. The room smelled musty with a strong waft of stale urine. Rab knocked into a chamber pot that was brimming with unemptied slops. Emmie gagged as she groped towards the large iron bedstead. The bed was unmade and empty. Peering into the dark, she saw there was no truckle bed that used to stand under the window.

'There's no one here,' Emmie hissed.

Just then, they heard a small cough. Emmie crouched down and felt under the bed. She touched something warm and heard a gasp of fright.

'Barny?' she whispered. She leaned further into the dark and grasped hold of a blanket, a warm shape beneath it. Someone whimpered in fear.

'Rab, shine the candle down here,' she said quickly.

As the light flickered under the bed, Emmie saw a pale face with large, staring dark eyes.

'Barny!' she cried. 'Pet lamb – it's Mammy!' She reached in and pulled at the rigid boy.

He was shaking, gazing at her in suspicion, too terrified to speak. Emmie gathered him to her. He was long and skinny like a rabbit, his dark hair shorn close to his skull. 'Barny, oh, Barny, don't be afraid. Mammy's got you, pet.'

'Mammy?' he puzzled.

'Aye, it's your mam,' Rab smiled, gently rubbing the boy's head. 'You're safe now.'

In relief, Barny wriggled out of his blanket and wrapped his arms around his mother's neck. He burst into tears. Emmie held him and rocked him in her arms, choking back the sobs in her own throat. To hold her son again gave her unimaginable joy.

'You're all right, bonny lad,' she crooned. 'Everything's ganin' to be all right from now on.'

'Barny, where's your sister?' Rab asked more urgently.

'Over there,' he croaked, 'in the bottom drawer.'

Rab scrambled across the floor. Peering into the deep drawer of the wardrobe, he saw Mary lying in a nest of blankets, thumb in mouth, sound asleep. Gently he reached in and lifted her out. She started awake, her blue eyes widening in panic. The small girl let out a howl.

Rab hushed her in reassurance. 'I won't harm you – I'm your daddy.'

Cradling her on his shoulder, he left the candle on the floor. Emmie helped Barny to his feet. She stretched out to touch Mary.

'My little lamb,' she said tearfully. 'You won't remember me, but I'm your mam.'

Mary gazed at her with uncomprehending eyes. Her chin trembled again, but the sight of Barny clutching the stranger seemed to calm her.

'We're taking you to safety,' Emmie promised.

Barny piped up. 'Are we ganin' to live with Uncle Laurie again and fish in the river?'

Emmie and Rab exchanged looks.

'No,' Emmie said, 'but Mr Runcie's still with us.'

Rab added, 'And I'll take you fishing in a different river – or maybes right down by the sea.'

Emmie took Barny's cold hand and felt a small answering squeeze that made her heart soar.

'Come on, Emmie,' Rab urged. 'Let's get out of here.'

Emmie searched around quickly for clothes but could find none.

'Just wrap them in blankets,' Rab suggested.

As they made for the door, they heard shouts across the yard. Emmie froze. Barny began to whimper again, clinging on to his mother.

'Th-that's me da,' he said in a small voice. 'He's been drinkin'.'

Nell's voice laughed harshly as she shouted back. Tom banged into something and cursed loudly.

'Out the front door,' Emmie ordered.

They ran from the room and down the narrow corridor. Emmie seized the handle. The door was firmly bolted, no key in the lock. The back door banged open, blowing out the guttering candle. They could hear Nell laughing and Tom fumbling about and knocking into furniture as he tried to light a lamp.

'Try the bedroom window,' Emmie whispered.

She followed Rab back, but as they passed the open door to the kitchen, the lamplight flared and Nell spotted them. She screamed. Mary wailed in fright. Rab turned to Emmie with a warm look of encouragement.

'Follow me,' he murmured and walked straight into the kitchen.

When Tom saw them, he swayed in astonishment.

'What the hell—'

'Emmie!' Nell cried in disbelief.

Tom stared at her, open-mouthed, then focused on Rab. 'What you doin' here, MacRae? Put her down! She's my lass.'

Rab held on to the crying Mary. 'You're not fit to be anyone's father,' he said with contempt. 'I've not seen animals tret worse. Mary's mine and Emmie's – and we're taking her and Barny with us.'

'Like hell you are!' Tom snarled. 'Mary's good as mine. She makes up for the bairn Emmie lost in prison – that bairn would've lived if you hadn't got my missus mixed up in bloody conchie business!'

Emmie gasped, looking accusingly at Nell. 'How dare you tell him!'

Nell's look was defensive. 'What did it matter? Made Tom feel better about keeping the lass. And don't blame me for finding a bit comfort where I can – you've always had it easier than me, always,' she slurred with drunken self-pity. 'Anyhow, your marriage was over – you'd got Rab. Isn't that what you always wanted?'

'I want my children,' Emmie replied. 'You've no right to keep them.'

'But *I* have,' Tom growled, shoving away a chair and lurching towards her.

Quickly thrusting Mary into Emmie's arms, Rab barred Tom's way. Tom took a wild swing at him, which Rab dodged easily.

'Come on, nancy boy pacifist,' Tom goaded. 'Fight me for 'em like a man.' He lunged at Rab again, who blocked his fist and pushed him back. Tom fell into a chair.

'Haway, Emmie,' Rab said, turning quickly and steering Barny to the back door.

Emmie hurried into the yard and was halfway across, carrying Mary, when Tom bawled behind them.

'Stop, you're not ganin' anywhere!'

Suddenly there was an ear-splitting crack. Emmie swung round to see Tom waving a gun at them. Her heart pounded in shock. The smell of gunshot filled the sharp air. Nell screamed. Rab was clutching his shoulder, his face set in a startled grimace.

'Rab!' Emmie cried in horror.

'Oh my God, Tom!' Nell whimpered in disbelief. 'You've shot him.'

'Go with the bairns,' Rab panted, leaning against the yard wall.

'No, she's mine,' Tom thundered, staggering across the yard, aiming the pistol at Rab's head. 'You'll not take her, MacRae.'

'No, Tom!' Emmie cried.

'Put the gun down, Tom, for God's sake,' Nell bawled.

Barny clung to Emmie. Mary wailed loudly. Beyond there was noise in the back lane, running and shouting. Rab was hunched against the wall, Tom standing over him.

'I'll finish off the job the army should've done years ago,' he raged. 'Put you out yer misery, yer yellow-bellied bastard! If it wasn't for you, Emmie would still be with me. You took what was mine, now I'm takin' it back.'

'She's − not − yours for the taking,' Rab answered breathlessly. 'Emmie's a woman − not a possession.' He winced at the red-hot pain searing his shoulder.

'Well, you'll not have her,' Tom said in fury, thrusting the gun at him and cocking it.

Rab looked back in defiance. 'You think you can take my freedom that easily?' he grimaced. 'I've − had − what no other man has had − real freedom with Emmie − freedom of mind − and − spirit . . . no one . . . can take . . . that away . . .' Rab closed his eyes as the pain engulfed him.

Emmie clutched at the children, hiding Barny's face from the terrible scene.

'Please, Tom, no!' she begged. 'Killin' him won't change anything. Let him live and be a father to Mary. That's all I ask, Tom.'

Tom swung round to face her, his features contorted in hatred. He stared at her blindly, then something in his expression changed.

'I want you back, Emmie,' he cried. 'That's all I want − for things to be like they always were − you and me and Barny. It wasn't meant to be like this.'

She gazed at him in disbelief. His angry face crumpled in despair.

'I need you, Emmie . . .' A noise rose up in his throat like the cry of a wounded animal.

Emmie held his look. 'Let us go, Tom,' she pleaded softly. 'Please let us go.'

Suddenly, behind her came a shrill whistle and the stamp of running boots. The commotion in the back lane erupted into the yard. Johnny Collier and another policeman pushed their way past Emmie.

'Tom!' Collier shouted. 'Give me that.' He stretched out his hand for the gun.

Tom seemed on the point of handing it over, then hesitated.

'Goodbye, Emmie,' he whispered. Then in one swift move, he pressed the pistol to his temple and pulled the trigger.

CHAPTER 42

Tom's suicide and the attempted murder of Rab were headline news the following few days, but Emmie did not read them. She stayed at the hospital, keeping vigil by Rab, while Flora and Helen looked after her children. The bullet was removed, but Rab developed a high fever and his life hung on a thread.

When she was allowed in to see him, Emmie stroked his head, talking to him quietly about the old days at China Street with his family, of India Street and the *Blackton Messenger*, of The Grove and their short months of happiness together. She sang to him and read poetry.

'Don't you dare die on me!' she railed at him one afternoon, despairing of his pulling through.

Charles came to sit and pray with him, even though they knew Rab would not want it. But Emmie would do anything to keep Rab alive.

The next day, as she paced the hospital grounds, waiting to see him, Nell appeared.

'I'm not stopping,' she said defensively, before Emmie could speak. 'Just came to say goodbye. I'll not be bothering you again – I'm off for good this time. There's nothing to keep me here.'

They stared at each other. Emmie's disgust at the way her sister had treated the children gave way to pity. Nell looked so forlorn despite her defiant words.

'How's Rab?' Nell asked more gently.

Emmie gulped. 'Fighting for his life.'

Unexpectedly, Nell dashed forward and hugged her. 'I hope he pulls through. I know how you care for him.' Nell kissed her forehead like she was a child. 'I don't know what it's like to love a man,' Nell murmured. 'Apart from Da.'

Emmie clung to her sister, swallowing tears. Then just as swiftly, Nell pulled away and turned to go.

'Stay, Nelly.' Emmie reached out. 'I can't bear to think of you with no place to live. Flora would help—'

'No,' Nell cut her off. 'I've caused you all enough bother. Anyway, I'm off down Leeds to look for Jackman. Don't worry about me.'

Briskly, Nell walked away with a tap of high heels, turning once to wave, then was gone.

Trembling, Emmie sat down on a bench and tried to calm herself. For a long time, she thought back to their childhood days and her tempestuous relationship with Nell. With regret she had to admit it had never recovered from their abrupt separation and their mother's momentous decision to send her to the MacRaes. Dear beloved Helen and Jonas.

All at once she was filled with a sudden strong presence of Jonas. Emmie's heart stopped. She could almost hear the old man talking of Rab. His loud laughter rang in her ears. *No one makes me as angry as that lad – and no one makes me more proud!*

Emmie had an overwhelming feeling that something had happened. Jonas had appeared to her. He was calling Rab home. In panic, she fled back to the hospital. It was not yet visiting time, but she barged past the matron on to the ward.

'Rab!' she gasped in horror. His bed was empty, stripped back. Tears of despair stung her eyes. Her beloved Rab was gone.

'Look here!' the matron called, bustling after her. 'What do you think you're doing?'

'Where have you taken his body?' Emmie cried.

'Body?' Matron repeated. 'Mr MacRae's taking a bath. Now will you please—'

'Emmie?'

Emmie spun round at the familiar voice. Rab was being wheeled into the room in a bath chair.

'Rab!' she sobbed, and flew to greet him. She crumpled at his feet, crying and laughing in relief. 'I thought you were . . .'

The matron followed, tutting in disapproval. 'What a fuss!'

Rab laid a tender hand on Emmie's head and ruffled her hair. She clung to him, choked with emotion.

'She causes a stir wherever she goes, Matron,' Rab joked weakly.

'That I can believe,' Matron snorted, and left them alone.

Emmie looked up into Rab's loving eyes, full of their old vitality.

'I had a premonition,' she whispered. 'Jonas came to me – it was like he was calling you back – said he was proud of you. I thought it must mean the end.'

Rab smiled. 'I never did do what the old man told me.' He stroked her face. 'Maybes he's giving us his blessing. Not the end, Emmie, but a new beginning – for us and the bairns, eh?'

She seized his hand in exultation and kissed it.

'Aye, Rab,' she smiled, her heart brimming with love, 'nothing can stop it now – our crimson dawn.'